JACKSON PLACE

Cover illustration by Robin Rogers Cloud

Lyrics from "Jack Straw" by Robert Hunter are used by permission of Ice Nine Publishing Co.

Other permissions pending.

ISBN: 1499530838
ISBN 13: 9781499530834
Library of Congress Control Number: 2014909321
CreateSpace Independent Publishing Platform
North Charleston, South Carolina

JACKSON PLACE

A NOVEL

John H. Taylor

By the same author

Patterns of Abuse, a novel (Wynwood Press, 1988)

For Kathy

PART ONE

August to October 1974

Just Watch

People sometimes tried to sneak into the White House. Tonight, Emily was sneaking out.

As she opened the door of the northwest gate, the one closest to the West Wing, she smiled guiltily at Carl, the handsome uniformed Secret Service agent who always flirted with her. She only had trouble with high heels when she was nervous, and she had never been more nervous in her life. Stepping over the threshold of the little guardhouse, she tripped and almost fell flat on her face.

"Are you okay, Miss Weissman?" he said, jumping to his feet and peering over the reception desk. As she recovered her balance, he looked at her calves and ankles with an expression of deep concern.

"Eyes front, officer," she said, smoothing her pleated skirt down the front of her thighs. Carl studied this maneuver as well. "I'm just going out for a second. Be right back." She opened the door facing Pennsylvania Ave.

He called after her. "Strange night to go out," he said.

"Strange night, period," she said, waving so Carl could see she had her wallet and ID. The door clicked shut behind her. The sidewalk was crowded with protestors and tourists, who were all dappled with long summer sunset shadows. The mood was momentous and festive at the same time. She felt dozens of eyes glance at her for a minute. Nobody recognized the short redhead in the navy blue dress.

She smiled to herself. Maybe they wondered if she was the secret love child of the president and his notorious redheaded secretary, Rose Mary Woods.

Then she realized that in two and a half hours, they would know exactly who she was.

It was 7 p.m. on Thursday, August 8, 1974, the day the White House had reliably informed its press corps and the world that President Richard Nixon would announce his resignation.

She turned east, crossed 15th St., walked half a block south, and entered the Old Ebbitt Grill, inhaling air conditioning and the smells of cigar smoke and frying cheeseburgers. She walked quickly along the bar, hoping she didn't run into anyone from the office. A flight of stairs at the back led down to the rest rooms and a small row of phone booths.

She entered one of the booths, closed the folding door, and took a deep breath. Then she dialed home, reversing the charges. Her father answered, which he only did when he was expecting a call or was worried about something. Otherwise it would ring until Elijah came back or her mother finally picked up. He told the operator he would pay for the call.

"I'm sorry I didn't call for your anniversary on Tuesday," she said.

"Your mother was a little disappointed," he said in his kind voice. Emily could picture him in his plaid sweater and corduroy slacks as he sat at the kitchen table with the *Detroit News*. Her mother was probably still at the sink, washing the dinner dishes. "I told her you were busy, getting ready for tonight."

She closed her eyes. Busy didn't quite capture it. She had been conspiring fiendishly to shatter her colleagues' lives and plunge the nation into chaos. She wondered if her parents would ever speak to her again. She said, "Did you guys have fun? I hope you took mom out."

"Top of the Pontch, after work," he said proudly. They couldn't quite afford it, but Emily's mother loved the view of the Detroit River from the restaurant in the Pontchartrain Hotel.

"Well done, dad," she said. When he didn't respond right away, she said, "I wish I could tell you more about what I've been up to."

They had gotten used to Emily not being able to talk about work. "We trust you," he said. "At least it will be over soon." Sidney and

4

Marian Weissman had despised Richard Nixon for their entire adult lives. They'd voted for John F. Kennedy in 1960, Hubert Humphrey in 1968, and George McGovern in 1972. In 1969, they'd even gone to a demonstration against the Vietnam war at Wayne State University, during the October Moratorium. She had been in college in Ann Arbor and had called her father and asked if the Revolution offered a senior citizen discount.

She'd always been more conservative than her parents. They had raised her with a heart for justice and those in need. She'd just drifted toward the political center. They'd finally come to terms with it. But they couldn't hide their disappointment when she told them she was going to work in the Nixon White House at the beginning of the Watergate summer of 1974.

Emily heard Marian say something. Her father said, "Your mother asked about Irwin. When does he plan to take the bar? You still seeing him?"

Sitting in the darkness, twirling the phone cord with her free hand, she smiled. Sidney's Irish Catholic bride had become a card-carrying Jewish mother, always wondering about her boyfriends and their professional prospects. Her last year of law school in Cambridge was a breeze. Irwin Fried had been a pleasant distraction. But he was too serious and not sexy, and he didn't like the Rolling Stones or baseball. "Tell mom sorry," she said.

"I didn't like him, either," he said. "So we'll see you soon? I assume you'll get some time off."

Emily said, "Dad, I need you and mom to watch tonight."

"Like we'd miss it? Your mother and I have been waiting to see Nixon get what he deserves ever since Alger Hiss."

Emily and her father had been having this argument since she was in high school. Hiss was a New Deal-era diplomat whom a friend, Whittaker Chambers, had accused of being a Soviet spy. As a young congressman from California, Nixon had ridden the case to political superstardom. "Nixon was right," she said. "Hiss was guilty. Besides, you were grateful for Vietnam. Remember we said a prayer for the president because of the draft, because Bennie didn't have to go." Benjamin was her little brother, now in his last year of college.

"He should've ended it four years ago," he said.

She pressed. "He ended it."

He relented. "Blessings on him for that. Blessings on you, too. You'll come see us soon?"

"Please, dad. Just watch."

2

Skip, Bill, and Big Dick

Rear Admiral Skip Wiggins and Captain Bill Sanchez were getting ready to celebrate, too. While Emily was talking to her dad, they were eating steaks and French fries in the underground mall in Crystal City, Virginia. In about half an hour, they'd take their beers to the lounge and find comfortable chairs close to the TV so they could savor every succulent bite of Nixon's shit sandwich.

They worked two and a half miles away, at the Pentagon. It was a big night back at the office. The secretary of defense, Jim Schlesinger, had everyone on high alert. But Skip and Bill were off duty tonight and wearing civvies. Even when they were on duty, they were barely there. They were both shuffling paper while they prepared for early retirement. Wiggins was associate director of naval nuclear propulsion. Sanchez worked in the manpower and personnel office. Since they hadn't seen one another much since being so ignominiously reassigned in 1972, they'd decided to stage their very own reunion, just the three of them – Skip and Bill, who were childhood friends from Brownsville, Texas, and their limp-wristed, commie-loving pussy of a commander-in-chief.

They'd spent dinner reminiscing about the good old days, when they'd spied on the White House for the Joint Chiefs of Staff. Wiggins, the top national security aide to the chairman, Thomas Moorer, had managed to get buddy Bill installed as his deputy. A Navy yeoman assigned to the National Security Council, Charles Radford, stole thousands of top-secret documents from White House desks and burn bags and passed them along to Wiggins and Sanchez.

"Charlie almost got busted that one time," Wiggins said, "cleaning out Kissinger's briefcase while he was in the crapper on the aircraft, on the way to East Bumfuck with Milhous." He took a big gulp of his beer. "The Secret Service sitting right around the corner would've been all over him like a cheap suit if Henry had come back any sooner. But Charlie had 'em Xeroxed and back in Kissinger's bag in something like three minutes. Craziest goddamn thing you ever saw."

"Good thing Henry wasn't just taking a leak."

"That time, we got the memcons from his Beijing advance trip in '71 plus his talking points for the Vietnam peace talks in Paris. I passed it all right up the line to Moorer."

Wiggins shook his head and smiled at his beer, remembering his halcyon days and the vital work they'd done, protecting the United States from Nixon's reckless policies. As a congressman, senator, and vice president, he'd brilliantly impersonated an anti-communist. Hell, he'd gotten his start by exposing Alger Hiss. But in the White House, he'd fallen under his adviser Kissinger's spell. Before long, he'd hopped onto Air Force One and kissed every red ass from Beijing to Bucharest.

Moorer had authorized the move against the White House once the contours of Nixon's foreign policy became clear – arms control treaties and cultural exchanges with the Soviet Union, bringing the troops home from Vietnam, and even peace overtures to Mao and the chicoms. Three generations of soldiers, sailors, airmen, and Marines trained to kill communists, for this?

"We might still be in business if somebody hadn't leaked the memo about the Paks," Bill said. Nixon and his henchmen got suspicious after a columnist learned that Nixon and Kissinger favored Pakistan over India when they went to war in December 1971. They'd traced the leak back to the Pentagon.

"The one thing the Nixon plumbers got right, and we got screwed," Wiggins said. He saw the waitress walking by and waggled his empty glass at her without looking up. Six months later, the plumbers broke into the Watergate, and everybody knew how that turned out.

When Nixon's sleuths interrogated Radford, he cried like a girl and fingered Wiggins and Sanchez. "If Nixon had any balls, he'd have fired Moorer and had us court-martialed," the admiral said, pushing his plate away and draping his arms over the back of the booth. "But he was afraid to take on the military."

Sanchez studied his friend's angry, pale face. Wiggins had put on twenty pounds since the reassignment. His wife used to have four stars glittering in her eyes and the big house and other trappings of a fleet command in her sights. When she realized her husband's involvement in the Radford scandal meant there'd be no more promotions, she left him.

In fairness to Mrs. Wiggins, life with the admiral couldn't have been easy. It was all black and white with him, always had been, even back in school. Sanchez wasn't sure that Nixon was quite as bad as the cabal around Moorer had made out. He'd bombed the bejesus out of North Vietnam on a couple of occasions in 1972. Sanchez didn't think talking to Moscow was the worst idea in the world, either. It was a credible alternative to his wife and kids being turned into water vapor during the exchange of three thousand megatons of nuclear explosives as the result of a misunderstanding between the White House and the Kremlin over some event in Vietnam, Berlin, or East Bumfuck.

Sanchez said, "One of the White House guys said during my deposition that they considered our project to be the first stage of a military coup."

Wiggins didn't answer for a moment. He looked at his friend and leaned forward. "He was right," he said quietly. "That's what I've been trying to tell you all these years, Billy boy. Look what's happening before our very eyes."

Bill grinned and said, "Like you'd know the inside story of Watergate based on your intimate knowledge of reactor output and fuel consumption."

The admiral shrugged and looked at his watch. "Believe what you want to believe," he said. He grabbed his beer and began to slide out of the booth. "Let's burn rubber. Five minutes till the axe comes down on the big Dick."

3

Another Historic First

Gordon Partington III, Richard Nixon's speechwriter, entered the impossibly tense room and recoiled first from the cold and then the smell of someone's gaudy perfume laced with the television technicians' sweat. He threaded his way among colleagues and sloppily dressed, indifferent-looking strangers. Finding an empty spot between the fireplace and a sconce, he settled in to watch the annihilation of all that he loved.

Like a pastor before services, Gordie had washed his face and hands and combed his thick blond hair before coming in. Though he'd been awake for two days, his pinstriped gray suit was rumpled but serviceable, the jacket neatly buttoned.

His wash-and-wear, blue and white-striped button-down shirts and paisley ties had once set him apart from Bob Haldeman's fraternity boys, over-groomed southern Californians in starched white dress shirts and rep stripes. What do you get if you drive a red convertible slowly through the University of Los Angeles campus? A diploma, or so went the old gag. If the car had a Nixon bumper sticker, you also got an office in the West Wing. Gordie went to Andover and Princeton and could sometimes see both sides of a question, so the frat boys never trusted him. But they were all gone now, dressing for meetings with their criminal defense attorneys instead of staff meetings at the White House.

Much as Gordie loved this room, tonight it was the last place in the world he wanted to be. He considered it to be sacred space, consecrated to the New England-bred principles of good government he cherished – the imperfectability of man, taking care of those who really needed it, and otherwise leaving him alone. For most of the last five and a half years, they'd been high priests of enlightened pragmatism and great-power drama. Gordie and Nixon's other writers had stood there proudly when their announcements about great issues of war and peace, all the administration's coveted "historic firsts," had been broadcast to tens of millions.

But Oval Office speeches required turning half the Oval Office into back stage. Gordie had always been put off when he saw the black rubber cables snaking along the blue and gold carpet, lighting fixtures that looked like silver umbrellas mounted on music stands, and interlopers laughing at their inside jokes. His bushy eyebrows gathered into an expression of puritanical revulsion. The situation stank, and so did they.

Peering around the cameras, he saw the woman who went with the perfume in a halo of light around the president's desk. She had curly blonde hair held back by a ponytail and wore cowboy boots and jeans stretched across what seemed to Gordie to be a comically inflated bottom.

He glared at her from the shadows. She was dabbing around the old man's widow's peak. He held his big head still. His lips twitched in acknowledgement of the reassurances that Gordie thought she must have been whispering to him. As the makeup was applied, he was trying to keep his small, darting eyes closed, but sometimes, when his eyelids fluttered, Gordie could see him fix curiously on the woman. He wasn't around people such as her very often. Even tonight, he was probably trying to see down her blouse. One of the few secrets the Nixon White House had managed to keep was that he had a wandering eye, especially when the woman was smart and pretty.

Gordie was only interested in her work. Stroke by stroke, she erased some of the outward signs of weariness and worry. She stepped back and nodded encouragingly. Before she turned away, she reached across his chest and patted his hands, which he had set on the desk in front of him, his delicate fingers entwined on top of a manila folder, which contained history's first presidential resignation address, his and Gordie's last collaboration.

Nixon's face looked calm and, thanks to the woman's efforts, a lot healthier than the last time Gordie had seen him. He smiled grimly in the dark. At least he'd leave a decent corpse. If it were really going to come to that, he could have been laid out in the Oval Office for a day or two, since either Nixon or Al Haig, his chief of staff, had ordered the air conditioning as low as it would go in August.

Still standing against the wall opposite Nixon's desk, Partington sniffed the air again. The cold stench of failure. But still the frisson of power. Gordie could think of no earthy reason why it should feel different around powerful people. But while Nixon was disgraced and broken, it was still there, like a force field, as though the effect of everything he'd done, every life enhanced or destroyed, would stick to him forever.

And what about what Nixon could still do, even in these last few hours? What if Vietnam flared up, or the Russians started something? Gordie imagined an aide rushing in and whispering in Nixon's ear, telling him of yet another crisis demanding his attention. Nixon had always made a fetish out of crisis. He could turn ordering breakfast into an existential struggle, a clash of civilizations. *I know they like eating bagels and crepes at Princeton, Gordie, but it's just not for me.* His greatest crisis was giving up power before his time. It had never been done before, not once. So while by all accounts the Nixon presidency was in its dying moments, the night was young.

"May we have a level, please, Mr. President?" someone said.

"A *what?*" Nixon barked the question. He knew what an audio level test was but wanted them to think he didn't, since no serious person would, and certainly no person occupied with ending wars and undertaking great initiatives. Before the technician could answer, he continued wearily, "Oh, yes, of course. One two three four five six seven. Is that good enough? Do you need more?"

"That's fine, sir. Thank you."

Nixon, who usually regretted being rude, tried to compensate. "I could do it again," he said. "I understand it's important. We all have to do our jobs. I could've done mine better."

"Thank you, sir," the man said. "We have it." Gordie thought the man had spoken gently enough. Still, the speechwriter was always imagining dialog for other people. The technician might have added a little something. *I'm sure this is hard for you, sir; I'm sorry.* But what does he care? Maybe he hates him, like everyone else in the media. Maybe he had someone die in Vietnam.

Nixon also could have said something gracious to the stranger. *I never know what to do or say when I'm anxious and self-conscious, which is the case pretty much all the time, so I take it out on people such as you, my political enemies, and peasants in small Southeast Asian countries.*

Gordie shifted his weight from one foot to the other and steeled his weary, wandering mind. That wasn't fair, and he knew it. If there was one thing Nixon had agonized about for his whole first term, trying desperately to do the right thing, it was that bastard of a war. Anyway they'd spent far too much time trying to repackage America's misanthropic geopolitical genius. As Nixon was fond of saying when shredding Partington's more Whitmanesque exercises, sappy wasn't his style. Tonight of all nights, let Nixon be Nixon.

Haig had told Gordie to start writing over a week ago, after the Supreme Court ruled that Nixon would have to give investigators more of the tapes he'd secretly made of conversations with his aides. Gordie hated the idea. He thought they should keep fighting. But the public's furious reaction to the tape transcripts the White House released last Monday afternoon convinced even him that Nixon would have to go.

All week he sent drafts over to the West Wing, and Nixon would send them back, crisscrossed in blue fountain pen ink. On Wednesday, Barry Goldwater led a solemn delegation of Senate and House leaders, all Republicans, to tell Nixon he was going to be impeached by the House and that he had 15 votes at most in the Senate. He'd need 34 senators to avoid being convicted. Nixon knew it already. The visit of erstwhile congressional allies was a set piece in his ritualized emasculation, like King Arthur being stabbed in the crotch with his own sword.

They'd still been working last night, Gordie in his office taking notes on his IBM Selectric, Nixon calling from his bedroom on the second floor or his hideaway office in the Old Executive Office Building. He'd been reflective, self-pitying, maudlin. Resigned. He had Gordie add a paragraph on his initiatives with China and Russia. He raged half-heartedly against his tormenters. He apologized for letting everyone down. Once Gordie thought he was crying. Nixon would mutter "thank you" or "fine" and hang up without waiting for a response, and Gordie and his secretary would get to work on another draft. She typed it ten times in five days.

On Thursday, Nixon gave it to his secretary, Rose Woods, who typed it once more in capital letters using a large-font ball so he wouldn't have to wear his reading glasses. Nixon had always refused to use a TelePrompTer. He thought it looked more authentic to read from a written text, glancing up and down and turning the pages.

Woods's typescript was the one in the folder on his desk. Before a broadcast, he would underline words for stress, maybe add a sentence or two. Sometimes he'd warn the speechwriters about a drop-in, but it usually caught them by surprise. They were his reminders that it was not theirs but his.

"Twenty seconds, sir," said the technician. Gordie heard the door open and close and saw that Haig had slipped in. They nodded to one another. It was just as Gordie looked back at the desk that Nixon turned to his left, opened the top drawer, and removed another folder.

"I don't suppose you have any idea what that's all about," Partington said to Haig in a hissing whisper.

"My purview of operational responsibility did not include preparation of tonight's address," Haig said. "So you tell me."

Silent monitors facing the back of the room showed the live feed for the three networks – an exterior shot of the White House, then the presidential seal.

"Maybe he decided to use an earlier draft," Gordie said. "Or maybe Rose's copy was mysteriously erased by a sinister force."

Haig watched Nixon as he put the first folder in the drawer and opened the second. When Haig had said last December that "some sinister force" may have erased eighteen and a half minutes of one of the tapes that Congress had subpoenaed, Partington and everyone else knew he meant Nixon. "Up yours, Gordon," Haig whispered.

"Five seconds," said the technician, who counted four with his fingers and then pointed to the president of the United States.

14

When Nixon began to speak, Gordie's eyes grew wide. He'd memorized the text. This wasn't it. Nixon was doing a drop-in? *Now?* Was he actually winging his goddamned resignation speech? Haig grasped at his arm. He brushed Haig's hand away and strained to hear.

Nixon's voice wasn't amplified, and the sound on the monitors was turned off. Then he raised his voice and stared into the camera. The two men got every word. "As president, my principal responsibility is to ensure that our carefully balanced system of constitutional government is not shortchanged," he said, his eyes steely and narrow, "for the sake of what is convenient for any one individual, even if he is the president."

Four or five more aides came in, including Emily, the new girl in the counsel's office, the one just down from Harvard at the beginning of the summer. Partington didn't think she'd ever even met Nixon or been in the Oval Office before. She was holding yet another manila folder. Scared as he was, his rectitude was offended again. She was too new, too junior to be here.

Most of the staffers knew something was going terribly wrong and looked suspiciously at Partington and Haig, who were just standing there staring at the president, who was now nearly two minutes along without having read a single word he was supposed to have read.

Emily, a small, pretty woman with shoulder-length red hair, was fixed on the president. "Therefore," he said, looking calmly at the camera, though it appeared his hands were shaking a little, "regardless of demands to the contrary by my critics and many well-intentioned people around the country who are understandably weary of Watergate, I shall not resign the office of president of the United States. Effective immediately, Vice President Ford will assume the duties of acting president under the provisions of Section 3 of the 25th Amendment to the United States Constitution, which govern a president's temporary incapacity to fulfill his office."

Haig swore to himself and stormed out. Gordie watched the thick molded door ooze shut and thought he might throw up. Was he witnessing a coup? Would tanks be circling the White House? And where the hell had Haig gone?

The president continued. "This will enable my advisors and me," he said, "to mount the defense before the United States Senate to which, in the event of my impeachment by the House of Representatives, the president is entitled and which our Constitution wisely provides. All the work of the presidency and oversight of the executive branch will be carried out by our able and experienced acting president."

Three or four people arrived and inched along the wall shoulder to shoulder, including Jim St. Clair, Nixon's lawyer, and Len Garment, the White House counsel. They were glaring at Gordie, too. He shrugged and shook his head. Garment nodded with a limp smile. He and Gordie had been friends for years and recently partners in formulating the administration's Indian affairs policy. They knew that Nixon had gone off the reservation before, although never like this.

St. Clair didn't know his client as well as the other two men did. He spoke, and they answered, in whispers, since Nixon was still talking. "You must've known, Gordon. Len. For Christ's sake."

"I didn't," Partington said. "I've just spent three days locked in my office writing another speech. Where the hell's Haig?"

St. Clair said, "He just came to get Len and me."

"Where's he now?" Gordie said. He wasn't the only one in the White House who worried about Haig's four-star authoritarian streak. His Pentagon buddies had been busted a few months before for spying on the White House because they thought Nixon was soft on Moscow and Beijing. He'd been for resignation before the rest of the staff. Gordie wondered if Haig was on the phone with Jim Schlesinger or maybe the Joint Chiefs at the Pentagon, telling them not to worry, he had our lunatic president under control.

"Haig said he was calling Ford," Garment said.

"Did he know?" Gordie said.

"Haig?" St. Clair said.

"He meant did Ford know," Garment said.

Partington said, "I definitely meant Haig, but now that you mention it, what's the story on Jerry? I can't imagine that he acquiesced in this. Section 3 is for sick presidents, not scandals." He almost never raised his voice, but panic and exhaustion had gotten the better of him. Almost yelling, he said, "Does anybody have the slightest idea what 'acting president' actually means in this hellish nightmare of a situation?"

"I do," a woman said in a girlishly high voice. "It's not especially complicated."

The three men turned toward Nixon, whom they'd momentarily forgotten. The speech was over. Emily, the new girl, was standing at his right side, fixing them with a determined if somewhat petulant expression. In the bright TV lights, they saw that she had green eyes and freckles. The president was also watching them thoughtfully. Looking down, she opened the manila folder she'd been holding and laid it in front of Nixon. They could see it contained two sheets of paper, each bearing a few lines of typescript. Nixon took a pen out of his suit coat pocket, scanned the top page briefly, signed his name to both, and slammed the folder shut.

He pushed his chair back. Everyone in the room – technicians, aides, and attorneys – stood stunned and silent. No one had thought to turn the room lights back on, so he still looked like an actor on a stage. In his growly baritone, he said to them all and to none, "Someone please tell Mrs. Nixon that we're moving to Jackson Place tonight." Then he and Emily followed his Secret Service agents out of the room.

Garment looked at Partington and St. Clair. His usually bemused face was twisted in astonishment and shame. Emily Weissman was a 25-year-old kid with skinny legs, about six minutes out of law school, who worked on his own staff. He hadn't talked to her for a total of more than 15 minutes. He was pretty sure she was supposed to be working on the 1974 presidential pardon list.

St. Clair was seething. He said to Garment, "What the hell's going on in your shop? Is she sleeping with him?"

"I didn't think she was quite his type," Gordie said with a desperate smile. "She sure fucked us."

4

Split Executive

Two hours later, Emily sat in front of Garment's desk in the White House counsel's office, across Executive Way from the White House in the Old Executive Office Building. With her navy blue jumper, she wore a white blouse with a crocheted collar buttoned at the neck and blue pumps, her stocking legs crossed at the knees. Partington was at her left and Ron Ziegler, the White House press secretary, at her right. The men had taken off their jackets and draped them over the backs of their chairs. The stewards had brought coffee for the men, tea for Emily. Ziegler was drinking scotch.

For a moment, they just listened to the ticking of a 150-year-old wall clock that Grace Garment had found at an antique store on the lower East Side. Garment, Partington, and Ziegler couldn't think of anything more to say. Bob Haldeman, Nixon's ex-chief of staff, liked to say that you can't put the toothpaste back in the tube. Because of Emily, Nixon was still the president, and Jerry Ford, his handpicked vice president, was now acting president. Though stunned by what had happened, they were beginning to turn their attention to tomorrow.

The office furniture was heavy, dark, and vaguely colonial. John Dean, Garment's predecessor, had displayed a Rand McNally map cabinet behind his desk. After Nixon fired Dean and made Garment his counsel in the spring of 1973, Len had put up a huge black and white portrait of Duke Ellington, his shiny hair combed close to the scalp, smiling through a cloud of cigarette smoke. Garment and Ziegler were smoking, too. During the pause in the conversation, Garment was staring a hole through a photocopy of one of the pieces of paper Nixon had signed after his speech. It read:

To the President Pro Tempore, United States Senate

Due to the distractions of the Watergate matter, specifically impeachment proceedings in the House of Representatives, I am unable to satisfactorily discharge the powers and duties of the Office of President of the United States.

Richard Nixon, President of the United States of America

Garment, his rubbery face pulled out as long as it would go, also fingered a photocopy with the same message as addressed to the speaker of the House. Section 3 of the 25th Amendment required the president to communicate simultaneously, or nearly so, with both houses of Congress. In the first ten minutes of the meeting, before the four had even sat down, as they shouted at one another and interrupted each other by shouting louder, they'd decided to have the letters delivered by military couriers, themselves escorted by uniformed Secret Service agents, to the Washington, D.C. homes of Jim Eastland, the Senate's president pro tempore, and Speaker Tip O'Neill. Each courier obtained the recipient's signature and noted the time. The moment both letters had been delivered, it was understood that Gerald Ford had become acting president – understood, that is, by the three shell-shocked men in Garment's office, as advised by Emily, who at the moment was the nation's most influential constitutional scholar.

They would learn later that Eastman had accepted and signed for the letter without a word except "thank you." O'Neill had invited the courier in for a drink so he could ask what the hell was going on at the White House. The courier, an Army colonel, had thanked O'Neill and declined.

After their decision about the letters, Ziegler had left to brief the press. He'd returned 22 minutes later bathed in sweat, lit a cigarette, and asked if Garment had anything to drink. Len opened a desk drawer and brought out a bottle of Johnny Walker Blue Label and poured some in a teacup and handed it across.

Ziegler, who was only 35, was thin, handsome, and haunted. His dark, slicked-back hair had gotten longer in recent weeks and

John H. Taylor

now touched the top of his collar in the back, where it curled up. People outside the White House didn't like him, but most inside it did. During press briefings he hid his friendliness and dark sarcasm. Before Watergate, he hadn't been in Nixon's inner circle, but for a year or more, since the staff had imploded, he'd been serving as confidante and confessor. Nixon's agony had weighed on him. He had been drinking and smoking too much.

On Emily's other side, Partington had his right elbow resting on the arm of his chair and his chin on his hand. His head bobbed up and down as he spoke wearily. "It should have said 'owing to'."

Emily said, "That's exactly what I wrote. He insisted on 'due to'. He said he thought 'owing to' sounded…" She paused, looking uncertainly at Gordie.

"Effete?" he said. "Sissy? Liberal? Homosexual?" Emily nodded. He smiled thinly.

"And what's with that 'satisfactorily'?" Ziegler said. "That's not in the fucking Constitution."

Garment said, "Your interns look that up for you in the back of the World Almanac?"

Emily said, "The president added 'satisfactorily' to the clause because this isn't a medical incapacity, like Eisenhower's stroke or heart attack. He's substantially incapacitated by a time-consuming partisan political—"

Garment interrupted her. "Nobody believes Watergate has anything to do with politics or national security. They think their president's a crook."

"It's political because they're all politicians," she said.

Still propped on his arm, Gordie said, "If you're writing for the president, you also have a constitutional duty not to split the infinitive."

"Nor to split the executive," Garment said. "We've got one president across the street in Jackson Place and another one— Say, where is the temporarily most powerful man in the world?"

"Al Haig says he's staying at their house in Alexandria for the time being," Ziegler said.

"So why did the old man move out?" Gordie said.

20

"To make a point," Emily said. "He's relinquished presidential power and its principal symbol."

"What's Jerry going to do?" Gordie said.

"Al's not sure," Ziegler said. "He'll want to make a point, too. Not seizing power too boldly and so on. He wasn't going to move in for a week or so, anyway, to give Tricia and Julie a chance to get the family quarters cleared out. I'm not sure about that part now, since the Nixons at least theoretically intend to triumph over their persecutors and return home. Do you move their stuff out or not? Maybe there's a fold-out couch up there someplace for Jerry and Betty."

"Shouldn't Ford be here in the White House now, you know, meeting with somebody or something? Haig, us, whoever?" Garment said.

"Oh, I agree," said Partington. "Having Ford sneak over here at midnight is bound to reassure an anxious public and wary press corps."

Ziegler emitted a long, keening sigh. The reporters had been screaming questions as he'd entered into the briefing room. "The old man was supposed to resign, and they knew it," Ziegler said, slumped low in his chair, sipping his scotch, and dangling his right foot atop his left knee. "They say we cheated, lied, stole, and covered up again. They're speculating about a coup, about Nixon being mentally imbalanced, about his staff being incompetent—"

Garment, squinting thirstily through cigarette smoke at Ziegler's drink, said, "Hard to argue with that."

Ziegler continued, "Did we trick Ford? Was Ford in on it from the beginning? Somebody even asked if we did it this way because we found out at the last minute that Ford's dirty." He cocked his head at Emily. "And watch your back going home, gorgeous, because you're the only person in the country who's less popular than Nixon."

"Ron," Garment said quietly, warning him to be civil to Emily and, in absentia, the president.

Ziegler sighed and rubbed his eyes with the heels of his hands and said, "Can we go over it again?"

As students of the art of wielding delegated power, the men were still hungry for Emily's every word. They still couldn't quite believe that she had managed to defy the whole apparatus of the executive branch as well as the expectations of elite opinion, which in the last few days had coalesced around the view that Nixon's abdication was necessary and inevitable. They were also grappling with their own mixed feelings. Until a couple of hours ago, they'd been anticipating that their waking nightmares would at least be over by the weekend. Now who could say when they would end?

Haig had put the machine in motion the instant Nixon said he'd quit. Military and congressional leaders had been notified. The State Department cabled U.S. diplomatic missions and told them to prepare to offer reassurances of American constancy to their worried host governments. Henry Kissinger, the secretary of state, phoned trusted journalists and promised that foreign policy would remain in strong, sure hands, namely his. Photographers memorialized the weeping Nixon family's awkward group hug in the solarium in the White House family quarters. Ziegler's staff photocopied Nixon's speech for the media. At Andrews AFB, Air Force One was fueled and provisioned for the flight to El Toro in Orange County.

But as one of Nixon's other writers, Ray Price, had once put it, Nixon had decided, undecided, and redecided. As it turned out, it wasn't up to the White House or Cabinet or a legion of executive functionaries or congressional leaders or the whole mighty host of armies and navies or all the angels in heaven. With his slashing two-word signature, Nixon rewrote history.

Seconding Ziegler, Garment said, "Do tell us again, Miss Weissman, the fable of the wise rabbi of Harvard Square."

"Wait till Haldeman finds out a big liberal Jew talked the old man out of resigning," Ziegler said.

"Two Jews," said Emily. Garment smiled at her. In spite of it all, he couldn't help growing fonder of Emily Weissman.

Her father, they had learned, was a hospital handyman in Detroit, her mother a sales clerk. She went to Cass Tech High School before getting scholarships to the University of Michigan and Harvard Law School. While in Cambridge she'd attended a conservative synagogue, Temple Beth Shalom. When she graduated, and the rabbi heard she was going to work in the White House, he'd invited her to his office. "He told me to tell Nixon that whatever he did, and whatever he'd done wrong, he couldn't resign," she said. "'The Congress can't quit, the Supreme Court can't quit, and the president can't quit'."

"Judges and senators quit," Ziegler said.

"Rabbi Roth said the president was different. Elected and yet sovereign, head of government and also chief of state, with a semi-mystical relationship with the American people and history. He said the president's only recourse was to let the system work. And then there was his accountability shtick. He said impeachment and a Senate trial amounted to a political atonement ritual. Innocent or guilty, the president has a moral obligation to himself and the world to go through the fire." Emily didn't know this, but the night before his speech, Nixon had found a letter on his pillow from his younger daughter, Julie Eisenhower, urging him not to resign, beseeching him to "go through the fire just a little bit longer."

"And you told him all this," Ziegler said to Emily. "The president. The very first time you met him."

"When Len arranged for me to go in for a meet-and-greet in June, right before his Mideast trip," she said. "He laughed and said he'd take it up with Dr. Kissinger and with Prime Minster Meir when they got to Tel Aviv. We took a picture in front of the Elvis flags, and I left. It was a three-minute meeting."

"You'd think when he was consulting the four or five Jews he trusted, he'd have included you, Len," Ziegler said mildly.

Garment's cigarette was only half burned, but he ground it into the ash try and lit another. Ziegler wasn't the first to tease him about being one of Nixon's domesticated Jews. They all had to deal with his anti-Semitism. He thought Jews were liberals who put Israel first. He had even ordered the frat boys to count the number of people working at the Bureau of Labor Statistics who had Jewish names. He was convinced they were cooking unemployment numbers to make him look bad.

It was worse when Haldeman was still around. The ex-chief of staff was such a breezy bigot that whenever they were together, the insecure

Nixon overcompensated. Garment and Kissinger both dreaded the day all the tapes came out. They knew they'd sound like toadies for failing to repudiate Nixon's slurs. Saying yes in the Oval Office came easy even when the heart screamed no.

An eternal Nixon contradiction was that while he abhorred his purportedly left-wing Jewish countrymen, he revered most of the Israeli leaders he'd known – David Ben-Gurion, Yitzhak Rabin, and especially Golda, a homely socialist from Milwaukee. During the Yom Kippur war last year, he sent her 23,000 tons of tanks, artillery, and other equipment over the objections of almost everyone in the administration, including the chairman of the Joint Chiefs, who claimed that Israel was getting the equipment because Jews controlled the banks.

So the Jew-hater saved Israel, and tonight, another pint-sized Midwestern Jew had saved Nixon, if only for a few months, until the Senate voted to convict him, which everyone was sure it would. No, Garment couldn't help growing fonder of Emily Weissman. "But the photo op wasn't all," he said.

"We met again on Monday evening, in the family quarters."

"Without anyone else knowing, it appears," Ziegler said.

"I assume the switchboard knew. He called me in my office and said he had been thinking about our conversation in June," she said. "He said to take the elevator. The agents were expecting me." The Nixons greeted her on the second floor. Pat looked tired. Her eyes were red. She seemed to Emily to be too thin. Nixon introduced them and said that he and Emily were going to talk about the day's tape transcript release, just checking one of the legal nuances, nothing important. The first lady had looked surprised and given Emily a long, appraising look, but after a moment she left them alone.

He showed her to the Lincoln Sitting Room, right across from the elevator and stairs, and closed the door. It had once been a telegraph room, installed near the end of the Civil War so Lincoln wouldn't have to walk to the War Department to talk to his generals. Nixon had taken it over as a study. He liked to work in small spaces. In the corner was a comfortable brown easy chair and ottoman, a gift from Pat when they'd moved to New York in 1963 after he lost his race for California governor. He spent long hours with his feet up, chewing on the temples of his reading glasses and making notes on a legal pad.

He was famous for building fires in the middle of summer, but as Emily sat down in an antique chair opposite Nixon, she saw that the fireplace was cold.

She had grown up in a small apartment in Highland Park, a suburb of Detroit where almost everyone seemed to work at the Ford plant or Chrysler headquarters. Her father's hospital job and her mother's selling cosmetics at Hudson's meant that Emily, Bennie, and their parents had enough to get by but almost nothing for vacations, college, or home improvement. The fireplace in the living room hadn't worked since she was a little girl. It was a simple problem. The lever that opened the flue and let the smoke out had broken off. The building manager said the repair was the Weissmans' responsibility, but Sidney never got around to it.

Those long-ago fires, and the sweet smoke smell that had clung to the air, had made her happy. She thought briefly about sad, dark fireplaces as the president sank into his easy chair. Then the hard grey eyes of the world's most powerful man reclaimed her attention. *The frisson of power.* Nixon looked tired, which she'd expected, but he seemed prepossessed, which she had not. In her stomach and trembling sinuses, she suddenly felt the moment's enormity. A billion people would be curious about this meeting. Apparently only two knew it was occurring and why.

Emily had always dreamed of doing big things. But her teenaged fantasies of greatness hadn't always run to the world historical. While her parents worked and her brother did his homework, she spent her afternoons after school with her headphones on, imaging she was the Seekers' Judith Durham performing in the lunch room in junior high, introducing her friends to songs she'd written such as "Georgy Girl" and "A World Of Our Own." Janis Joplin's first album came out when she was in high school, catapulting Emily to superstardom belting out "Ball and Chain," a furious, thundering blues, in amphitheaters and arenas.

When she wanted to be prettier, she was Judy Collins, Joan Baez, or Diana Ross. She decided later that she had just wanted people to pay more attention to her. Now she had Richard Nixon's full attention; and for a moment, she'd been afraid to open her mouth.

Ziegler said, "Saving it for your memoirs?"

Emily did feel a little possessive about her experience. She also wondered about the propriety of offering too many details, especially to Ziegler, who might have been tempted to use them to win back the White House press corps. "Are you really entitled to a word-for-word report, Mr. Ziegler? Do you think that's what he wants?"

"Give us the gist," Garment said.

"Okay," Emily said, with a sarcastic lilt that Garment, at least, was beginning to find charming. "Let's start with this. What you gentleman need to understand is that he still doesn't think he did anything wrong, at least nothing impeachable."

Garment frowned and looked at his lap. If that was Nixon's game, it wasn't going to wash. On Monday afternoon, the White House had released the transcript of a conversation that had been recorded by Nixon's secret system on June 23, 1972. Haldeman told him that the FBI's investigation of the June 17 Watergate burglary was going "in some directions we don't want it to go." He said that ex-counsel John Dean and John Mitchell, the former attorney general who was running Nixon's campaign committee, had suggested having the CIA tell the FBI to scale back its investigation. Nixon agreed.

The tape proved that he and his top aides had organized the Watergate cover-up from the beginning. On the evening news, anchors and correspondents called it the smoking gun. Scores of congressmen and senators demanded his resignation.

As the firestorm raged into Monday evening, Partington worked on Nixon's speech, Haig put the machinery in motion, Pat Nixon wept in her bedroom, and Nixon asked Emily to tell him again what the rabbi had said. "The president told me he'd considered the acting president route a few weeks ago. A couple of members of Congress suggested it," she said. "He said he had thought it a rather fatuous idea, as he put it."

Partington, who had been silent for some time, smiled to himself. "Fatuous nonsense" was Nixon's favorite phrase. He had crossed it out of a dozen of Nixon's own drafts of speeches and messages.

Garment said, "Did it occur to you to recommend that he include in this pivotal conversation some of us who've been living and suffering through this for a year and a half?"

Emily paused. She still didn't know quite what to make of these men. She had never spoken to Ziegler or Partington before tonight. She'd shared most people's opinions of the unsmiling press secretary and his relentless stonewalling.

Around the office Garment had been a remote, vaguely paternal presence. In the crisis atmosphere that had prevailed throughout her weeks in the White House, there weren't any staff meetings. So she went about her business, reading letters requesting presidential pardons. Most that reached her desk were from civil rights and antiwar activists convicted of minor crimes during demonstrations and white-collar criminals who gave a lot of money to Nixon and other Republicans.

Most of Garment's phone calls, which Emily could hear through his open office door, were about Watergate. He'd wrap up by saying "Is it too late to burn the tapes?" and laughing grimly. He was famous for advising Nixon not to do so the year before.

It was invigorating to have been in conversation with such powerful men over the last four days, beginning with the most powerful of all, and to have held her own. The White House was a man's world – the top officials, Secret Service agents, blank-faced Marine guards. But the masculinity seemed more nuanced on the inside – Nixon's insecurity, Garment's fatherly mien, Ziegler's angry vulnerability, Partington's quiet wit. With it all dissolving around them, she was certainly not encountering Nixon and his men at their most confident and masterful. Still, it had reminded her more than she would have expected of lively conversations with her fellow law students about politics or cases they were studying, when 90% of winning was a confident command of the facts.

It was also like talking to her father, who hadn't gone to college but had read widely and started speaking to her as a adult when she was about twelve. Sidney wasn't around much because of his long hours, but when he was home, he was always attentive. They sometimes read the same books so they could talk about them over dinner. He loved Hemingway and J. D. Salinger, which she didn't always understand, though she loved that he seemed to think otherwise.

Her favorite times with her father had been at Briggs Stadium. Her mother worked weekends, so usually it was just Emily and Bennie on Saturday or Sunday afternoons. Her very first game was on a week-night. She was about six; her brother was still a baby and stayed home with Marian. She remembered walking with her father along a dark-ened passage toward that light-soaked space – the long white lines, the emerald grass, the clay-red diamond after it had been raked and hosed down, just before determined figures in brilliant white would surge from the home dugout, scattering the dirt with their cleats.

"I understand you're from Detroit," Nixon had said Monday eve-ning. "That's going to be a goddamned mess. I'm afraid it's a lost cause. Too bad. The blacks deserve better. But they aren't up to run-ning it."

"Yes, sir."

"Do you follow the Lions? The Tigers? I probably shouldn't put a woman on the spot."

"Baseball especially. My dad and I even got to see one of the World Series games in '68. A friend from his work gave us his tickets."

"What does he do?"

"He fixes x-ray equipment at Harper Hospital, Mr. President."

The son of a grocer, Nixon perked up at this reference to Emily's working class background. He said, "Would that have been game three, four, or five?"

Emily, who had prepared for a different line of inquiry, had to struggle for a moment to remember. "I know it was the only home game we won. We took three out of four in St. Louis."

"I'm aware of that," Nixon said. "You were there for Game five. Lolich versus Gibson."

"No, sir," she said. He stared at her. "I'm so sorry, sir, but I don't think Mickey Lolich and Bob Gibson met until the seventh game. In ours Lolich pitched for Detroit, but Joe Hoerner started for St. Louis and got the loss."

Nixon looked away. "Of course I couldn't see much of that series on TV," he said, "with the campaign and so on and so forth." He glanced back, tugging playfully at his lower lip with the end of his glasses. "You were too young to vote in 1968."

Emily smiled. "I'm the daughter of two union members from Detroit, Mr. President, so I can't hold out much hope that I would have voted for you instead of Vice President Humphrey. But I did vote for you last time."

"Why is that? It wasn't necessary."

"You suspended the draft lottery the year my brother would have been eligible. Thank you, sir. We all thank you. When you ended conscription last year, we said a prayer for you at Shabbat."

He looked embarrassed. "Well," he said, readjusting his position in his chair, putting on his glasses and picking up his legal pad.

Garment had wondered why Emily didn't think to invite Nixon's more experienced hands to the Monday evening meeting. "It wasn't my meeting, obviously," she said. "I guess he wanted a fresh perspective, or maybe a more innocent one, from somebody who hadn't gone through all this with him. Didn't you assume it was over? Did any of you recommend he stay and fight?"

"He told me it was all over on April 30 last year, the day he fired Haldeman," Ziegler said. That had been when he realized that he'd lost the leverage he'd need to wrench aid for South Vietnam out of a Watergate-fixated Congress. Ziegler had been one of the last to acquiesce in the push for resignation, having urged Nixon to fight through to a Senate trial, but he gave up, too, after the June 23 tape came out.

Emily said that Nixon had asked her to write 1,500 words "just in case" and to tell no one what she was doing. Garment remembered seeing her office door closed all day Tuesday, but since he'd been thoroughly occupied with the buildup to history's first presidential resignation, he had spared her no further thought. Emily and Nixon had quietly sent drafts back and forth through the Secret Service.

"Who put your draft in his desk drawer?" Ziegler asked.

"An agent," she said. "I gave it to him at about six-thirty. He hid it before the TV crew arrived. The president told me to come in with the letters after he started. If he was reading Mr. Partington's speech, I should shred the letters and get our speech back and shred it, too. If he was reading our speech, then—" She caught herself and shot an embarrassed glance at Gordie, whose expression was blank.

Then Garment's door flew open, and Al Haig, the White House chief of staff, strode in. He was stocky and broad-shouldered and shorter than he appeared on television. In contrast to his three rumpled male colleagues, he looked fresh and strong. He wore a crisp white dress shirt and regimental tie with his dark pinstriped suit.

Emily stood to offer her chair. Haig didn't sit down or look at her. The other three didn't seem especially impressed by him. "What's up, Al?" Garment said.

"I have just been on the telephone for two hours with the president, the vice president, by which I of course mean to refer to the acting president, and the secretary of state," he said.

"How gracious of Henry to cede so much of your valuable time to his subordinates," Ziegler said.

Haig didn't reply; and now he looked at Emily, stone-faced. "I should probably leave you gentleman alone," she said. No one disagreed.

Gordie stood. "I'll walk you to your car," he said.

Haig said, "You'll be back right away, I trust."

"I will not," Partington said, touching Emily in the small of her back and guiding her toward the door.

"I beg your pardon?" Haig said, glaring.

"You'll have my resignation letter in the morning, general. Good night. God bless you all, and God bless all our assorted presidents." He smiled sadly, and they were gone.

Haig finally sat down. He looked inquiringly at Garment, who said, "Gordie wrote the speech, he was standing there, and nobody told him."

Ziegler gestured at Garment with his empty teacup. While Garment was opening his desk drawer and bringing out the scotch, Ziegler said, "Sometimes the old man doesn't have a clue."

5

She Got His Nose

In mid-summer, the southern air settled over Washington like a great soggy tent, fetid and close. But an especially brutal heat wave had broken earlier in the week, so Friday, August 9, 1974 was clearer and cooler than usual. Except for the constitutional crisis, it was a pretty morning. Coffee perked and bacon sizzled, the papers arrived on driveways, walkers and joggers dotted Rock Creek Park, and the Smithsonian was packed with tourists.

Some of Washington's seasonal visitors acted as though the circus had come to town for their personal entertainment. On their way from Ford's Theater to the Kennedy graves at Arlington, sightseeing buses clogged Pennsylvania Ave., lingering in front of the White House longer than usual. Scores clogged the sidewalk in the sunshine on the mansion's southern perimeter, poking their long lenses and Instamatics through the iron fence bars, hoping to see the Fords. Democracy hung by a thread, some asserted, but framed like a needlepoint portrait against billowing clouds and the brilliant blue sky, the White House looked as though it would stand forever.

Hundreds more had crowded into Lafayette Square, which occupied the north side of Pennsylvania Ave., right across from the White House. The Nixons were staying in a narrow townhouse at 716 Jackson Place that the government had bought in the 1950s. At the beginning of his presidency, Nixon had set it aside for former presidents when they visited Washington. By choosing it over Blair House, famous for housing the Trumans while the mansion was being renovated, Nixon had probably been taunting those who didn't think he could possibly become a former president quickly enough.

Reporters and photographers mingled with the sightseers and with protesters, who taunted Nixon back. One held a sign reading, in homage to the Dionne Warwick hit of a few years before, "Do You Know The Way To San Clemente?" Two more had climbed onto the base of the statue of a horse-borne Andrew Jackson at the center of the square and unfurled a crudely painted banner that said "Fuck Nixon And The Amendment He Rode In On."

Wearing a pale blue Lacoste shirt and tucking his hands into the front of his jeans, Gordie Partington spent the morning circulating in the crowd on both sides of Pennsylvania Ave. After last night's events and this morning's papers, which were every bit as bad as Ziegler had predicted, Gordie had felt discouraged enough that he wanted to inhale the carnival atmosphere as an antidote to the prevailing apocalypticism.

The Washington *Post*'s eight-column headline read, "Defying Congress And His Own Advisors, Nixon Refuses To Resign." Alongside its main story, which dwelled on Gordie's humiliation, the *New York Times* had a news analysis titled "Experts Dispute Nixon's Claim Of Presidential Disability." The *Times*' lead editorial posed this question: "Who Controls the Military?" As Ziegler had warned them last night, no one thought much of Emily Weissman. She'd been seen with the House and Senate letters and had left the Oval Office trailing Nixon. It didn't take reporters long to figure out that she'd written the renegade speech. At his press briefing the night before, Ziegler had confirmed that she was a recently arrived member of Garment's staff and put special stress on his assurances to the caustic and deeply skeptical reporters that Nixon's senior staff had been unaware that she was even talking with the president, much less advising him not to resign. The *Post* ran her unflattering high school yearbook photo.

Most observers assumed that Nixon had hatched the idea and used the naïve young woman as a cat's paw. A distinguished *Times* columnist, Tom Wicker, wrote, "After all, this is a president who knew he couldn't get his veteran advisers to do his bidding when it came to launching dirty tricks, punishing reporters with FBI investigations, and using the IRS to harass his political enemies. For those dirty jobs, he turned to the young, foolish, and amorally ambitious. It is to this ignominious niche that history is likely to relegate Miss Weissman."

While Gordie wouldn't have been quite that harsh, he did feel betrayed by Nixon's recklessness. They'd all given him their best and sometimes, on his orders, their worst. Last night, he hadn't been thinking about any of them. It appeared he'd only been thinking about himself.

Wandering through Lafayette Square, Gordie stopped a few steps away from a man and woman in their fifties who were peering at the Nixons' quarters. They were standing up against the stanchions the Metropolitan Police has erected to keep people off the sidewalk. "I'm worried about Pat," Gordie heard the woman say in what sounded like a southern Indiana drawl. "Do you think she's in there?"

"Where else would she be?" the man said.

Reacting to a tremor of excitement in the crowd, the couple and Partington peered north toward H St. and saw a carefully dressed young couple walking toward them hand in hand. Recognizing them quickly, the reporters began to shout questions. While the woman, a blonde with shoulder-length hair and a wedding cake smile, stared straight ahead, her pale patrician husband, who walked as awkwardly as his father-in-law, couldn't keep his eyes off the long row of cameras.

As if buoyed by the cheers, jeers, and questions, the woman drifted up the half-flight of stairs to the front door of the townhouse. The man looked over his shoulder, paused, and let go of his wife's hand. With an ingratiating smile, he raised his own, palm out, and twisted it slowly back and forth like a sovereign greeting his subjects.

"Oh my goodness," the older woman said. "Tricia Nixon got his nose."

"Whose?" her husband said.

"Her father's. They hid it in *Life* magazine or airbrushed it or something. You remember the Rose Garden wedding."

"What's his name again?" her husband said.

"Edward."

"She always looked like hard work and low pay to me," he said, looking around at the crowd. "And I'll bet Edward didn't bargain on this."

Gordie Partington smiled grimly. None of them had. He turned away and went home.

6

Do You Agree?

Garment had told Emily Weissman that since she'd had a busy night, she didn't have to be at work until 6:30 a.m. on Friday, when she'd be expected to recommend whether as acting president Gerald R. Ford should take the oath of office as the Constitution seemed to prescribe.

"That was an easy one," she said in her high, lilting voice. She was using the same chair in front of Garment's desk, breathing his cigarette smoke while they drank their coffee. She'd gotten a couple of hours' sleep and looked fresh and alert. He had, too, but did not.

He looked her over surreptitiously. Grey skirt, sheer stockings, her legs crossed, a brilliant beam of sunlight through his office window glancing off the muscle that ran along her left calve. A hint of perfume.

His wife Grace's insistently ticking wall clock helped refocus his attention. "Well?" he barked.

"Absolutely, positively not," she said.

"Even though the Constitution – the actual main part of the Constitution, before you even get to the new stuff – says that you have to take the oath of office before you execute the office?"

"That just applies to the president."

Garment took a long draw on his cigarette, exhaled, and squinted at Emily through the smoke. "But isn't Ford going to execute the office as though he were president?" he said.

"Yes, but under the provisions of the 25th Amendment, whereby he became acting president the instant Congress was notified."

John H. Taylor

"And under the 20th Amendment," Garment said, "the president instantly becomes the president at noon on January the 20th."

"According to the Constitution he still has to take the oath before he begins doing the job, which is why they time the oath as close as possible to noon eastern time."

Garment leaned back in his chair and crossed his legs. "So what if war breaks out during the inauguration ceremony," he said, "noon comes, he hasn't been sworn in yet, and there's no time because he has to begin giving nuclear launch orders?"

Emily grinned and said, "That sounds like the George Carlin routine about Irish kids trying to trap the priest with impossible scenarios. 'So, uh, faddah, if God is all-powerful, can he create a rock too heavy for him to lift?'"

"Don't use a fake New York accent when arguing with a New Yorker. Answer the question."

"The president probably has to take the oath before incinerating Moscow."

"Probably?" Garment said with a sarcastic sneer.

"Wouldn't you feel just a little better about it if he had? But let's leave your Talmudic hypothetical about the mystical true source of the president's authority to the rabbis. The acting president without question doesn't get sworn in. Number one, the 25th Amendment doesn't provide for it. Instead, it makes absolutely clear that the powers of the office transfer to him upon congressional notification. Number two, we can't swear Ford in as president because Nixon's still president, which is exactly why the amendment doesn't call for the oath."

"And you know this because?"

"I wrote a paper about it in college."

"Really?"

Emily smiled and said, "So far as you know, yes."

Garment smiled back. "So why don't we swear him in as acting president?" he said.

"So now you want to add 'acting' to the constitutional oath? Weren't you the one who was upset that we added 'satisfactorily' to the letter?"

"That was Ziegler. But I didn't like it, either."

36

"Besides, Ford has already been sworn in as vice president."

"Johnson had already been sworn in as vice president, but he took the oath after Kennedy was killed. Did he have to?"

"Not technically," Emily said, "because he had became president automatically under the provisions of the 25th Amendment, and as a matter of fact, he began giving orders immediately."

"Oh, really? Such as?"

"Such as 'This plane doesn't leave Dallas without Kennedy's body aboard' and 'As president, I order you to administer the oath of office'. In that case the preponderance of the oath's effect was symbolic, reassuring the American people that someone was in charge after a devastating trauma."

"Watergate is also a devastating trauma."

"The president's still alive, Len."

"Don't get me started. So let me make sure I understand. If you become acting president under the 25th Amendment, you're not sworn in, but if you become president under the 25th Amendment, you are."

"Exactly."

Garment took another long draw on his cigarette. "Agreeing with you makes me feel really strange inside," he said. "I'll tell Haig. But what if Ford wants to take the oath anyway?"

"I think he'll be relieved he doesn't have to. He's going to come in here walking a line between exerting too much authority and not enough. He's a good politician. He'll understand that it's an overreach to take the oath as president when the president is sitting a hundred yards away."

"Like Vice President Nixon refusing to sit in the top chair in the Cabinet room after Eisenhower's heart attack."

She dangled her foot at him, leaned back in her chair, and smiled. "Ironically enough," she said in her cute little voice. *Jesus*, Len thought. And Grace's wall clock kept ticking.

Emily was right about Ford. He arrived from his Alexandria townhouse at 7:40 a.m., greeted the household staff, poured himself a cup of coffee, and went to the Oval Office for a national security briefing from Henry Kissinger and his aides from the State Department and

National Security Council. He never took the oath of office. Instead, he executed the office of president, and began to rebuild trust between the White House and its press corps, by appointing his friend Gerald terHorst as press secretary. A former Marine, terHorst had been in Washington as a reporter and bureau chief since 1958. If reporters were going to trust anyone, it was someone such as he, who'd been covering the story himself until a few days before.

TerHorst spent most of his first morning in the press room trying to set boundaries. Why did Nixon do it? *Ask Nixon.* What did Ford think of it? *Ask Ford.* When can we ask him? *Why does it even matter what he thinks?* When can we ask him? *Let me know as soon you guys run out of news, and I'll see what I can do to get him to talk to you.* When will the House of Representatives take up impeachment? *Ask the House.* Had Ford expected Nixon to resign? *Yes.* Asked six times in different ways: Did Nixon inform or even hint to Ford that he'd decided not to? *No, no, no, no, no, no.* Did Ford know or had he or any of his aides ever spoken to Emily Weissman? *Hell no.* So what could Jerry terHorst talk about? *As soon as you're interested again, inflation, arms control, energy policy, Vietnam, Cambodia, China, and the Soviet Union.*

The first of two awkward grey areas for the new regime was the Watergate special prosecutor. Since he and his staff now worked for Ford, terHorst couldn't very well say the acting president was staying out of Watergate. He could only pledge, promise, and swear on a stack of his Grand Rapids grandmother's Bibles that the White House wouldn't impede the criminal investigations and prosecutions being carried on alongside the House's impeachment process. TerHorst's credibility on this question was sound, since authentic abhorrence of Richard Nixon seemed to ooze from terHorst and almost everyone else who'd arrived at the White House with the acting president.

Alexander M. Haig, now working as Ford's chief of staff, was a grey area of epic, indeed planetary proportions. Nixon loyalists distrusted him for his early advocacy of resignation and his ties to the Pentagon and intelligence agencies. The press thought he looked too slick, like a character in "Seven Days In May," a movie from the 1960s about a military coup, and suspected him of abetting Nixon's cover-ups. Ford's people didn't trust him because he'd been lobbying for a pardon for Nixon after his resignation and because Nixon hadn't actually gotten around to resigning. They wanted him replaced with someone who had closer ties to Ford. But the acting president, while eager to demonstrate his autonomy, didn't think a staff housecleaning was appropriate when Nixon was still president. For the time being Haig, would stay.

Ford spent a half-hour early Friday afternoon deliberating with aides about how to staff Nixon. Most saw no justification for giving the shifty bastard the use of anyone on the public's payroll besides Secret Service agents and his valet. Nixon had already sent word that he expected to be billed for his meals. Jim St. Clair, his personal attorney, who would be in charge of his defense in the Senate, was paid out of Nixon's pocket. Thanks to a quick opinion memo from the attorney general's office, everyone understood clearly that the White House counsel now represented the institutional interests of the acting president, not Nixon.

Garment himself blunted terHorst's proposal that Emily Weissman be either fired or sent across Pennsylvania Ave., if she wished, to join her creature in exile. Garment argued successfully that she hadn't done anything wrong, and besides, he still needed her.

Finally, Ford said Nixon could have Ziegler. His job title, "White House liaison to Mr. Nixon," also took a half-hour. Its thrust was that Ford would have someone keeping an eye on Nixon, whereas there was considerable worry that it would go the other way around.

"Do we really trust Ron Ziegler?" terHorst asked Ford.

Puffing his pipe, the acting president said, "As a matter of fact, I believe I do."

So on Friday afternoon Ziegler ran the Lafayette Square media gauntlet and mounted the stairs to Jackson Place. He found Nixon in a bare little room on the third floor with a desk and his easy chair and ottoman, which had just arrived from the White House. In blue slacks and a tweed sport coat with a tie and red sweater vest, Nixon was as informal as he ever got in a business meeting. He had his stocking feet up, balancing his legal pad on his lap and tugging at his lower lip with his reading glasses.

"St. Clair says the House will vote to impeach by mid-September," Nixon said. "The Senate gets it in early December. They want it done by Christmas. That's actually helpful. It'll be even worse for us by January."

"There'll be fewer Republicans in the Senate next year," Ziegler said.

Nixon grimaced. He and Watergate were why the GOP would get wiped out in the November elections. "How's poor Jerry?" he said. "Bumbling around, I suppose, trying to find Latvia on the map. Probably driving Henry up the wall already."

"Henry hasn't called you?" Ziegler was surprised.

Nixon shook his head and said, "Why do you suppose he hasn't?"

Once again, Ziegler felt the gravitational lure of Nixon's curiosities and compulsions. Nixon was already trying to recalibrate their relationship. Ziegler had started as press secretary and become confidante. Now Nixon needed an agent. Ziegler could guess how the next four months would play out. Since he'll only want to talk to Kissinger and Haig about foreign policy, it was going to be a problem if they were keeping their distance. Nixon wouldn't want to talk with Ziegler about the nuances of his legal defense, either, because he wasn't a lawyer.

Instead, he'd suck him dry of every drop of information about what was going on at the White House. He'd deploy him on secret reconnaissance missions. He'd have him call people to plant ideas or get their reaction to something that had happened. He'd use him to run interference with his wife and daughters. And they'd sit here for hours every day as Nixon, who would have almost nothing else to do, conducted his endless Socratic dialogues, obsessively seeking agreement and affirmation. *Don't you think? Do you agree?*

Ziegler closed his eyes and took a deep breath. His value to Nixon over the last year, as Watergate metastasized, had been at its greatest when he pushed back against his most preposterous statements. In the chaotic days after Haldeman's resignation, for instance, Ziegler sat stoically during one of Nixon's tirades about everyone in Washington being out to get him. *Don't you think? Do you agree?*

Finally, he'd said, "Mr. President, my view is that it is not a correct assumption to assume that all of the Congress and all of the press have the objective of destroying the president."

Nixon had stared at him for a moment. Finally, he had said softly, "I didn't mean all. No."

So sitting in the house at Jackson Place, Ziegler said, "I have some guidance for you from the acting president. Actually, from Al Haig on behalf of the acting president."

Nixon struggled to sit up straighter in the big, soft chair. "Some guidance, you say? You have some *guidance*?" He slapped his reading glasses against his legal pad and shifted his weight again. He fumbled with the pad and glasses as though he'd lost control of his hands, and his voice shook with rage. "By all means given me the guidance of the former House minority leader," he said, "the mediocrity I put in the vice presidency and the goddamned Oval Office. I'm hanging on Jerry Ford's every one- and two-syllable word."

Ziegler pressed on. "The principal concern is unity."

"Whose unity?"

"Ours and Ford. Yours and Ford. The feeling is that this is a constitutionally delicate moment, executive authority is in an ambiguous situation, and there needs to be some symbolic indication that you both understand and acknowledge this and are on the same page. Some gesture of– "

"—Unity. Fine, fine. What do they want us to do, go to the beach and hold hands?"

"No, sir. We're— You're— Mr. President, they want you to go to church."

"I beg your pardon?" Nixon said, now sounding more alarmed that angry. "No, I won't. The son-of-a-bitching National Cathedral, for Christ's sake? No, sir. So that I can sit there while some sanctimonious cocksucker preaches at me about reconciliation and peace and justice and all that crap? Never. It's not going to happen, Ron."

Ziegler took a deep breath, stared at Nixon, and said, "Actually, sir, you didn't ask anyone's opinion when you did this, and I don't believe they're asking your opinion now."

Nixon was silent. His eyes blazed. But Ziegler held his ground. Nixon had been known to freeze out aides who stood up to him, but Ziegler knew that at this point, he was the only aide Nixon was going to get. Still, he quickly offered what he hoped would be the good news. "We're not going to National Cathedral. We're going to St. John's tonight, for evening prayer."

"What in the name of God's hind tit is evening prayer?"

"For one thing, there's no sermon. It's twenty minutes tops."

Nixon looked interested but skeptical. "How the hell do you have a church service without a sermon?"

"They just do. It's Episcopalian."

"I know it's Episcopalian. And it's Ford's church, of course."

Ziegler said, "Nancy's and mine, too."

Nixon closed his eyes for a moment. "So they're not going to say anything whatsoever about the situation."

"Just a prayer." Nixon looked worried again. Ziegler reached into his briefcase for a sheet of paper. "I have it here. Do you want me to read it?" Nixon nodded, chewing hard on his glasses. "They're just going to add Ford to the usual prayer they say every night. *Almighty God, whose kingdom is everlasting and power infinite; have mercy upon this whole land; and so rule the hearts of thy servants the president of the United States, the acting president of the United States, and all others in authority, that they, knowing whose ministers they are, may in all things seek thy honor and glory; and—*"

Nixon sighed. "A bit old fashioned, do you agree? It sounds like one of my mother's prayers, the Quaker plain speech and so on, the thees and thys."

"It's at six tonight. We thought we'd walk over, you and the first lady and the Eisenhowers. Right up to H St. and across. Four, five minutes."

"Julie's coming over?" Nixon said, his voice brighter.

"She'll walk next to you and David next to Mrs. Nixon so you can talk to each other. Easier to resist being interrupted by questions. The Fords will meet you there, and you'll sit together."

"Any singing?"

"No, sir."

"There better not be any singing. It's a kind of a foolish thing, Ron, but I guess they've got their hearts set on it." Nixon chewed his glasses and studied Ziegler. "They'll be kissing your ass for talking me into it," he said. "That could be useful when the time comes."

Ziegler sighed.

7

Poor Lon Nol

Eight hours later, Frank Szabados, staff secretary of the National Security Council, was culling the evening's wire service reports before heading home. He sat in the NSC's crowded offices in the Old Executive Office Building among a few analysts who were drinking coffee, smoking, and studying overnight cables. He'd been at work for 12 hours, but he never knew when Kissinger would call, at the office or at home, for a news summary. Better be ready just in case.

Kissinger was the first secretary of state to serve as national security adviser at the same time. Having used the NSC to diminish the influence of the prior secretary, Bill Rogers, Henry wouldn't risk letting someone do the same thing to him. Szabados sighed as he tore the long, buff pages off the noisy AP and UPI Teletype machines in a soundproof room in the far corner of the office. He carried a half-inch-thick stack back to his cubicle. He wished Kissinger would call the State press office, which had a lot more resources. But the secretary thought his White House colleagues were more loyal and discreet.

Szabados leafed through his stack. Nixon went to church with Ford? The pool reporter who'd been invited to sit in the congregation (25 worshipers in all; 13 if you didn't count the bodyguards) said they'd shaken hands and sat shoulder to shoulder. Neither said much. They walked out separately with their wives after chatting briefly with a young priest standing in the church doorway.

Talk about cutting the country's throat and applying a Band-Aid. After Nixon's stunt last night, Ford spent his first day in power tiptoeing around the White House, trying to be president without being too much of a president. His only big move was this show-of-unity gimmick.

Frank shook his head. Anything that could lull naïve, credulous observers into thinking the United States still had a coherent executive wasn't a bad thing by any means. But Moscow and Beijing? Hanoi, capital of communist North Vietnam, which had been testing U.S. resolve for months as Nixon's authority and prestige, and therefore his country's, plummeted? Instead of going to church Ford should've visited the press briefing room and warned our enemies not to be tempted to use this distracting episode as an opportunity to take advantage of the United States. But since his aides knew he'd end up talking about Nixon, he'd stayed in the Oval Office, worrying about who would launder Nixon's shirts and organize his appointments with his lawyers.

Almost every article Szabados has reviewed concerned world leaders' reactions to the U.S. crisis, which ranged from bemused to bewildered. Disgusted, he threw the printouts across his desk. As far as he was concerned, during the Cold War the American presidency's one indispensable purpose was reassuring and inspiring friends and deterring enemies. Instead, we were performing comic opera on a global stage.

If Kissinger did call, Frank's recommendation would be to prepare for a busy few months, since the United States had never looked quite so listless and weak. If Frank had been sitting in the Kremlin instead of the White House, he'd be working late thinking of ways to punish America for her fecklessness.

He picked up the day's *New York Times*, which he'd already folded to an inside page, and reread a short article by Malcolm W. Browne that he'd underlined copiously. He'd like to call Kissinger's attention back to this one, too. He was amazed they'd found room for it among all the Nixon news. The headline read, "Pravda Asks Cambodian Rulers To Step Aside for the Insurgents." Szabados swore to himself. The rebels' Paris-educated leader, Khieu Samphan, who was opposing the U.S.-backed president, Lon Nol, was a ruthless communist and Soviet toady. Szabados had read his doctoral dissertation and followed his career since he returned to Cambodia in 1959. Browne made him sound like

Thomas Jefferson. As usual at the *Times*, fascists were fascists, rightists were rightists, and communists were insurgents.

According to Browne, the Soviet news agency Pravda said that Lon Nol remained in power only because of foreign interference in the form of U.S. support.

If that's the case, Frank thought, then Lon Nol's doomed, along with every other leader who depends on the United States. "The hell with it," he said out loud. Taking the *Times*, he walked 20 feet to the deputy NSC director's empty office, closed the door, and picked up the phone on the desk.

He dialed the White House operator. "This is Mr. Szabados at the NSC. May I please speak with the president?"

"Which one?" she said.

"The one who bombed Cambodia," he said.

8

Khartoum Has Fallen

The Golden State Club's driveway, off Hope St. in downtown Los Angeles, was ridiculously narrow, or so it always seemed to Mitch Botstein. On Monday morning, he carefully steered his black, wide-gauge 1965 Bonneville between a high brick wall on the left and the clubhouse on the right, aiming for the parking garage in the rear. Wasn't there something in the New Testament about camels finding it easier to pass through the eye of a needle than it was for a rich man to enter the gates of heaven? If the Christians' messiah was right, this narrow pathway, along bricked-over wheel ruts separated by well-tended grass, must be the road to perdition, because it was for rich men only.

Pulling up to the valet station and leaving the engine running, Mitch got out and shouted a greeting to a short man with black hair and a plaid vest. "*Buenos dias, Pedro. ¿Como estas?*"

"*Muy bien, Señor* Botstein."

"How about putting me right up front next to Howard's Cadillac this time?"

"Not a chance, *Señor* Botstein."

Mitch slapped him on the back, buttoned his blazer, and headed along a carpet made of Astroturf toward the club entrance, which was under a green canopy. The bucolic touches were supposed to mask the gritty sights of downtown. "Hey, Pedro," he said over his shoulder. "*¿Ahora hay cuantos presidentes en los Estados Unidos?*"

Pedro smiled diplomatically as he sank into the bucket seat of Mitch's immaculately maintained convertible and pulled the door shut. He turned down the *gringo* music on Mitch's tape deck – "una mas tequila *sunrise*" – and slipped the gearshift into drive. Actually, he couldn't wait to see what transpired as a consequence of Tricky Dicky's latest scheme. Having overheard numerous white Republicans muttering about their lazy, thieving Mexican housekeepers and gardeners during banquets where he was silently providing table service, he was enjoying the hell out of Watergate. He'd met Nixon and all his buddies often enough, coming by for lunches and fundraisers. As good politicians, Nixon and Mitch both made a point to remember his name. Least they could do. Most they could do, as a matter of fact, since the club didn't allow tips. Most of these rich *Anglo* bastards barely looked at him, except occasionally a sharp glance when they'd left their briefcases or something else valuable in their cars. As if their dirty looks would be a deterrent if he'd turned out to be half as crooked as Nixon's gang. Pedro drove Mitch's big ugly Pontiac past the morning lineup of late-model luxury cars, up a ramp, and out of sight.

Meanwhile, stepping inside the club's wood-paneled entry hall, Mitch greeted the doorman, a smiling black man in a braided uniform standing behind a podium bearing the club seal. "Morning, Bill. I'm joining Howard for breakfast."

"Mr. Morton's in the third floor dining room, sir."

Mitch looked around. He and Bill were alone. He lowered his voice and said, "How's your application for club membership fairing? Probably in the rejection pile with mine and Pedro's."

"I imagine, sir."

"I bet they have separate rejection piles for the women, Jews, wetbacks, and—"

Bill interrupted him. "I wouldn't know, Mr. Botstein. I can tell you that Pedro Gonzalez's no wetback. He was born in Boyle Heights, about three miles from here."

"I know it well, *Guillermo*, but it might as well be Tijuana. I'm from Encino, and I'm only admitted to the Golden State Club when Howard's got a hard-on about something and wants to have breakfast with a mean Jew. So when're you going to start calling me Mitch?"

"When you, Pedro, and my momma and me's upstairs eating breakfast and fighting over who's gonna sign the check with our membership numbers."

"That long, huh?"

Bill leaned forward and lowered his voice. "Or until you finally embrace your fundamental decency and turn Democrat," he said.

"You're killing me here."

"Nixon's burned your playhouse down, Mr. Botstein. You won't carry Beverly Hills in '76."

"Don't worry," Mitch said. "Howard has a secret plan to save the GOP from Richard Nixon."

"You guys take your time on that," Bill said. Mitch grinned and shook his hand and continued along the plush crimson carpet, past California plein air paintings and portraits of past club presidents. In the elevator, which was paneled with mirrors, he adjusted his tie and ran a comb through his curly black hair. He was a handsome guy, or so the girls told him, with an angular, boyish face. He hiked up his khakis and smoothed the front of his jacket. Getting a little snug. Every meeting in politics seemed to occur over a meal. If he kept eating breakfast, lunch, and dinner out, he'd be fat by the time he was thirty.

In the bright, high-ceilinged dining room, well-dressed white men were sitting alone or in groups of two or three. He found Howard working on eggs and tomatoes and reading the *Wall Street Journal*. Mitch pulled out the chair opposite him, sat down, and put his napkin in his lap. A black man in a uniform materialized and offered coffee and orange juice. Mitch thanked him and said to Morton, "Every time I come in here, I want to stand in the doorway of the dining room and say, 'Gentlemen, Khartoum has fallen'."

Morton, a tall, thin man with sparse, painstakingly combed white hair, folded his paper and put it on the empty chair at his right. He took off his reading glasses and tucked them into the chest pocket of his grey suit coat, which hung loosely from his wide, bony shoulders. "Did you incite the masses again on your way upstairs?" Morton said, pushing his plate away, sitting back in his chair, and crossing his spindly legs. "I actually get complaints about you from other members."

A Stanford-trained attorney at a big firm with offices on Spring St., Howard Morton was a member of a quiet group of advisors to the governor of California, Ronald Reagan, who'd be leaving office the following year. Those on the party's conservative wing wanted him to run for president. Reagan wasn't sure yet. He was waiting to see what his fellows suggested. Mitch provided strategic and tactical advice and handled especially delicate projects so Morton and his friends could keep their hands clean.

A couple years before, when word got around that some of Reagan's junior aides were gay, Mitch hired PIs to follow the suspects around during campaign trips, maybe find out when two pair of pointy-toed wing tips were left outside the hotel room door for Mexicans to shine overnight instead of just one. When Reagan's fellows said the fairies had to go, he cheerfully complied, just as he would when they told him it was time to run for president.

Mitch glanced around as he drank his orange juice. Even in a big city like LA, it wasn't crowded on top of the pyramid. The dining room was half empty, and yet it looked as though everybody in town who had power was here. In a few seconds he had spotted the mayor, three city councilmen, two bishops, five judges, and the chairmen or CEOs of two oil companies and three real estate development companies. Morton probably knew them all. He also knew where they'd gone to school, what fraternities they'd pledged, who the lawyers were, where they went to law school, where they went to church. The men slapped each other's backs, mentioned Saturday's game, sent greetings to each other's wives, exchanged drinking and mildly offensive sex jokes, compared boats and vacation homes, bragged decorously about their kids' accomplishments, made tennis dates, winked at and teased each other, bemoaned the media, politicians, minorities, homosexuals (which a few of them secretly were), popular music, and hippies, and wagged their fingers and smiled emptily from across the room when they didn't really want to stop and talk with someone.

When the waiter returned, Mitch ordered an omelet with fried potatoes and onions and sourdough toast. He'd start a diet on a day when he wasn't offered a free Golden State Club breakfast. Stirring cream and sugar into his coffee, he said, "Believe it or not, Howard, the day will come when we're going to need more than white people to elect Republicans."

"Let me know when Pedro and Bill register Republican. Then we'll talk."

"How's the governor doing?"

"Fine. He appreciates all your help."

Howard loved dropping Reagan's name. But Mitch wasn't sure the governor remembered who he was or had any idea what he was doing. He leaned forward. Free breakfast aside, he felt a little uncomfortable eating it at a club that wouldn't have him as a member. "It's important you understand why I'm here," he said, "and it's not to put another Presbyterian in the White House. Nixon, Rockefeller, Ford, all these so-called moderates spend the people's money as if they were Democrats. I think Reagan actually believes what he says about cutting my taxes and getting the government off the back of the economy. A guy like Reagan gets in, and Pedro and Bill might have a chance to get a good job someplace other than here at Gestapo headquarters. And yeah, then we might just get their votes."

Morton smiled thinly. "Calm down, Mitch."

"Plus he's not squishy on the Russians like Nixon and Kissinger."

"Speaking of which," Morton said, "tell me what happened last week."

Mitch slumped back in his chair. "I don't know much more than you do, probably."

"Who's the woman?"

"Nobody."

"How'd she get into Harvard? The White House? How'd she get that close to Nixon?"

"She's smart. I heard her con law professor thought she had a calling to public service, thought she'd enjoy working in the White House. He knew somebody that knows Garment. As far as how she got Nixon's ear, maybe she sent him a memo."

"He's Jewish, too?"

"Who?"

"The professor."

Mitch laughed and took a big bite of his toast. "It's amazing you didn't even have to lower your voice in here when you asked me that question," he said, chewing noisily. "You want to know when I fear big government the most? Coming in here and seeing all you pink-faced ruling-class Gentiles looking like you're about to join arms and sing 'Edelweiss'."

"You started it with the Gestapo crack. I'm just trying to figure out who got us from a nice, clean presidential resignation to this disastrous acting president scenario."

Mitch asked, "What's really your problem, Howard? Because I know it's not that you give a damn about the mad Quaker."

"We're worried about '76. On Thursday morning, it looked like we'd be running against Ford."

"Whereas now? That's probably not going to change."

"Just tell me what happens if Nixon survives the trial."

Mitch shrugged. "From here, I don't see how he gets back to 34 votes in the Senate. But maybe if he slows the thing down, blunts the momentum, maybe turns the tide a little bit, and then they conduct the Senate trial according to the rules of evidence. It's not impossible he could hold on, but it's highly unlikely."

"If Nixon's convicted, how does Ford come out?"

"Depends on how he handles himself as acting president," Mitch said. "He could get lucky and experience a crisis or two to cut his teeth. Something in Vietnam, maybe. At best, it could be a three- or four-month apprenticeship, boosting his credibility for when he becomes president after Nixon's conviction."

"You do see what I'm getting at. Boosting Ford's credibility is not an element of the Reagan game plan."

"Yeah."

"We hear that Haig was pressuring Ford's people about a pardon after the resignation. A pardon was our best hope, because it would've destroyed Ford. And yet even without a pardon, he'd have been so preoccupied with Nixon and his troubles that he wouldn't have been able to establish any momentum for his presidency. Either way…"

"The Gipper would have a leg up in the GOP primaries."

"Which is why Nixon's decision is counterproductive."

"As far as Reagan's concerned."

Morton looked away and said, "Of course none of this is indicative of the governor's thinking."

"Of course it's not," Mitch said sarcastically. "He's—"

"—Confident that the president will be vindicated," Morton said.

"Although if Nixon does happen to be acquitted—" Mitch said.

Morton said, "–then Ford runs as a vice president relatively untarnished by Nixon and Watergate, which also– "

"Totally sucks for Reagan," Mitch said.

Morton brushed the fingertips of his right hand against the white tablecloth. The dining room was almost empty. The black men had cleared the dishes and had even stopped offering more coffee.

Finally, Mitch said, "So Ford getting three or four months to prove himself as acting president and Nixon getting acquitted are both bad. What do you think you can do about it?"

"Nixon needs to change his mind yet again. He needs to quit and leave his mess back at Ford's doorstep where it belongs."

"And what do you want me to do?"

"Find something slimy about Nixon nobody knows yet."

Mitch smiled. "That should take me till lunchtime. Anything else?"

"It would be good to get close to his people. See if you can find out why they stand by the sick fuck. Maybe they know something that will help us. Do you know Ziegler?"

"A little. He's loyal to Nixon unto death."

"So you might start by talking to Emily Weissman." Morton smiled, picked up his newspaper, and stood. "You know, Jew to Jew."

"And tell her what, you disgusting asshole?"

"That in a couple of years, you can get her a lot better job at the White House."

"She's working for Garment and therefore Ford. You think she's still talking to Nixon?"

"How would I know? That's your department."

Mitch smiled. His department indeed. Some more New Testament came back to him. Must've been the Jesuits at Georgetown, where he'd been an undergraduate. As he recalled, it was Jesus, talking about his political enemies. "'This is your hour, and the power of darkness'," he said to Morton.

"Who said that?"

"Some Jew."

9

Too Cold War

Sitting in his mother-in-law's kitchen in Saigon, Frank Szabados used his chopsticks to swirl the flat noodles in his second bowl of *pho tai*. He could smell onion, clove, ginger, and hint of cinnamon. Mai Tji An used three- and four-inch sections of beef bone for her broth, leg pieces that were thick with marrow, which she simmered for hours. An roasted the onions on a grill in her little garden outside the kitchen door.

Back in Georgetown, Anne and Frank's townhouse usually smelled just like An and Ty's Saigon bungalow. Anne, who used her mother's family recipe, usually had a batch of *pho tai* ready. An (which Frank had learned to pronounce *ahn*) and Anne ladled in the noodles and broth while it was still boiling, instantly cooking the raw beef in the bottom of the bowl. Frank considered it the world's most civilized breakfast.

Frank's father-in-law, Ty, sitting across the table, sipped his tea and watched him eat. Ty was eager to learn why Frank had come from Washington with no warning. But he was a good host, and he prized discretion. So he let him eat in peace a little longer.

Just before midnight, Frank had awakened them with his call from the airport. He apologized for the surprise and promised that Anne and everyone else was fine. It took him an hour by taxi to get through the drenching monsoon rain to their house, which was on a quiet street lined with tall, graceful hardwood trees that the colonial French had planted a half-century before.

He appeared on their doorstep in a soggy navy blue blazer and khaki slacks, holding a small duffle and his briefcase. They brushed the rain off his shoulders and hugged him and, seeing how tired he was, made him go straight to bed in Anne's tiny room. He fell almost instantly asleep on top of the bedspread of her twin bed, smelling the sandlewood headboard, the wet, hot summer air coming through the open window, and her shampoo on the pillow.

It was Thursday morning, a week after Nixon's speech. As Frank dabbed at his mouth with his napkin, Ty asked, "So how is President Nixon?"

Frank covered his mouth and coughed. Ty lifted a blue and white teapot from a carved wood trivet on the table and freshened Frank's cup. Frank took a long sip and glanced at Ty, a small, trim man in his early sixties with full, slicked-back black hair and intense brown eyes. He wore slacks and a light brown, open-necked tropical shirt. "He's fine," he said. "Probably a little bored."

"You haven't seen him?"

Was he that transparent? Another reason why he wasn't cut out for the clandestine services. Of course Ty knew of and shared his admiration for Nixon. "I haven't seen him," Frank said truthfully. "Since he moved out of the White House, he doesn't have much privacy. Everyone has to go in the front door, and the media have it staked out day and night. He's been spending a lot of time with his lawyers, obviously. He went to church last Friday with Ford."

"I hadn't thought he was a churchgoer," said Frank's mother-in-law. She and her husband and daughter were Roman Catholic. So was Frank. An was working at the sink wearing pale pink silk pants and a long, embroidered blouse buttoned down the front with slits on the side, the traditional Vietnamese *ao ba ba*. As she dried and put away the breakfast dishes, she hummed and swayed to music on the radio, a mixture of local and U.S. pop songs. Right now they were listening to "Monday Monday" by the Mamas and the Papas.

Frank stood, put his bowl and chopsticks on the counter next to the sink, and thanked An. "It wasn't much of a church service," he said, returning to his chair. "Someone thought it would be a good idea for him and Ford to be seen together."

"We read about that," Ty said. "I assume Ford is keeping his rival close at hand. In Vietnam, we would be wondering about the means the former leader would be employing to get back in."

"They're not exactly rivals," Frank said. "They're not exactly not rivals, either, now that I think about it. Either way, the president stepped aside voluntarily."

Ty shook his head. He didn't understand Watergate. South Vietnam ran on bribes, graft, pilferage, and nepotism. In Saigon a powerful leader couldn't be driven from office for offenses like Nixon's any more than for eating with a fork or putting extra sugar in his coffee. Leaders lost power when someone figured out how to take it from them, when they died, or both at the same time.

Sensing Ty's skepticism, Frank poured him some tea and said, "This conversation is beginning to remind me of the beating I took the first night Anne brought me home." In 1967, he had been stationed at Long Binh post, 25 kilometers northeast of the capital. He was a second lieutenant in the U.S. Army Engineers, commisioned after serving in the ROTC out of Fordham University in the Bronx. He supervised thousands of troops who cleared jungles and built highways. The duty wasn't especially dangerous. One of Frank's buddies joked that since the Viet Cong would end up with the country anyway, they had no interest in blowing up the brand-new American infrastructure.

One night An (she changed the spelling and pronunciation after they were married) came with a friend to a party at the bachelor officers' quarters. They were bright women in miniskirts who worked as switchboard operators at the American embassy. An, who was also going to law school, wondered if Frank had ever met Bob Dylan, Jackie Onassis, or Harper Lee.

Frank got a date because his favorite novel was *To Kill A Mockingbird* and, she claimed later, because he was handsome and had good manners. After he'd taken her to a candlelit dinner at a floating restaurant on the Saigon River, she told him with her delightful smile that if there was to be second date, it would be at the home of her father, deputy vice minister of defense Nguyen Thanh Ty.

As his wife sat down next to him, Ty said, "The first time you were here, I was concerned about my daughter and the American officer with the eastern European accent. Did I seem too inquisitive?"

"It was just short of the bamboo under the fingernails, dad."

"Now I'm worried about you. We have the NSC staff secretary drinking tea in Saigon, nine thousand miles from his paperwork. You're not even staying at the embassy or the Sheraton, both of which, unlike our house, have central air conditioning."

Frank said, "Best noodles in the world?" The couple smiled wanly. They knew Anne's were just as good. His attempt at humor risked offending their delicately nuanced sense of propriety, all the more so because they knew he was still trying to mislead them.

An was now looking down and fingering a spoon on the table. Frank leaned forward to cover her hand with his and said, "Some people are worried about how the instability in Washington could affect South Vietnam. I've been sent to ask around."

"Unofficially," said Ty.

Frank smiled. "Semiofficially," he said.

Ty said, "That's what the State Department is for, military intelligence, the CIA, all those people, and when they fall down on the job, the *New York Times*." He paused. "Does Dr. Kissinger know you're here?" When Frank hesitated just for a moment, Ty pressed. "What did you tell him?"

"I called in sick. I said I had a strep throat."

Ty leaned back with a smile and put his hand on An's shoulder. "My beloved," he said, "our son-in-law is now a secret agent being run by Richard Milhous Nixon."

"Why do you say that?" Frank said.

"Everyone knows that when Kissinger snuck into China from Pakistan to plan Nixon's visit to Beijing, they told the press he had a stomachache."

Frank looked at the table and shook his head. "That's just a conicidence." Actually, Nixon had made the same comparison on the phone a few days before. "It'll serve Henry right," he'd said.

Since it was so obvious to Ty, Kissinger would probably figure it out, too. Frank knew this trip was a terrible idea, but what had he been supposed to say to Nixon? The elected commander-in-chief of the United States, although temporarily out of the chain of command, was still curious about the likelihood of a North Vietnamese operation being mounted to test American resolve. Where would it be? How effectively would the south be able to respond? Did it expect that the U.S. would help? What if we didn't?

While Frank didn't know Nixon well, they'd spoken at the White House holiday reception in 1973, six months after he'd received his doctorate from Johns Hopkins in national security studies and landed the NSC job. After introducing Anne to him and Mrs. Nixon, who stood at his side in the East Room, Frank told the president that their first meeting had been in November of 1956 near a refugee camp in Austria, a few kilometers from the Hungarian border.

He had been 16. His parents, sister, and he were among 200,000 Hungarians who fled after Soviet troops occupied Budapest to put down an anti-communist uprising which began on college campuses and which his father, an English professor at Eötvös Loránd University, had helped organize. The U.S. and other western nations had urged the freedom fighters to rise up but had done nothing when the Soviet tanks rolled, fearing a direct clash with the Soviet Union.

As a consolation prize, President Eisenhower sent his young vice president to express sympathy for the refugees while preparing Americans for an influx of Hungarian immigrants. An Austrian army security patrol was driving Nixon and his party along a snow-covered road through thick, dark woods when they passed a truck filled with weary Hungarians on their way to the army and Red Cross camp at Graz.

Nixon asked the guards to stop the truck. Frank hadn't recognized the evidently important man, but he reached down and shook his hand anyway.

"It was exciting when someone told me who you were," Frank had told the president, "though at that precise moment, I recall being profoundly disappointed that you hadn't handed up a loaf of bread and a roast chicken."

Frank was trim and, at five-eleven, about Nixon's height. He was nearly engulfed by his rented tuxedo. He had thinning blond hair, blue eyes, and a prominent nose. The Marine Band was playing "God Rest Ye, Merry Gentlemen." Nixon's eyes gleamed when he looked at Anne, whose black hair flowed down the back of her fitted red *ao dai*. Those waiting in the receiving line noticed that Nixon held Frank's hand for a long moment and then reached for Anne's hand, put it in Frank's, and held them both between his. It was an oddly intimate gesture for a man who so often appeared reticent.

"I wasn't sure at the time, but Eisenhower did the right thing, both in Budapest and at Dien Bien Phu," he told them. He had mentioned the two most important moments in the 1950s when the U.S. had chosen to stay out of other people's wars. In the second, in Vietnam in 1954, the U.S. wouldn't intervene to help the French against the Viet Minh, precursor to the Viet Cong. He said, "Above all, a president can't risk nuclear war."

"And yet I'd rather we had spent the last twelve years killing Russians instead of Vietnamese," Frank said. Under Nixon's hand, he squeezed Anne's.

Nixon smiled and tilted his head slightly toward the first lady, who was distracting the chairman of the Federal Reserve and his wife in the hope that they wouldn't notice how long they had waited for the president to finish with Frank. "Mrs. Nixon joins me in wishing a Merry Christmas to the last anti-communist," he said.

"The last two," said Anne with a smile.

Nixon told Frank, "I understand why Henry has you shuffling paper instead of writing policy briefs. You're too Cold War and not enough balance of power."

Being too Cold War was also why Frank called Nixon impulsively from the White House basement on Friday night. He was afraid that America's political convulsions were putting its friends at risk. If so, Moscow would end up the winner and Anne's parents and fellow countrymen the losers.

Nixon had picked up the phone immediately. As Frank identified himself, he wondered if the president would remember him from the Christmas party. "And how is your beautiful wife?" Nixon said. "You're a lucky man."

"She's fine, sir. She sends her best. We both have you in our prayers."

"Does she work?"

"She has a Vietnamese law degree and is trying to sort all that out so she can practice here someday. In the meantime, she's working at the World Bank as a macroeconomic trend analyst."

"Her given name wasn't Anne," Nixon said, "and yours wasn't Frank."

"Frank and Anne are actually Ferenc and An. Most people think I'm either Spanish or South American."

"They miss the 'z' in 'Szabados'. Means 'liberated'."

"Yes, sir."

"It'll happen."

"Hungary tomorrow, Mr. President. South Vietnam and Cambodia today. As you may have deduced, that's why I'm calling."

"I know you served. Plus your wife and so on and so forth. You think it's still possible? I think I may have screwed it up already."

Frank told Nixon the truth. Saigon was worse off than in January 1973, when the U.S., South Vietnam, and North Vietnam had initialed the Paris Peace Accords. Nixon had promised to punish communist treaty violations by bombing the north, as he had done twice in 1972, but he'd already passed up several opportunities to do so in response to the north's mischief. By the end of April 1973, it was too late. Watergate had destroyed his ability to rally congressional support behind South Vietnam.

Still, it wasn't over yet. Hanoi hadn't mounted a significant offensive for over a year. They'd been positioning more and more troops and materiel in the south; Saigon had countered their moves. After two generations of war, the chess pieces were in place for the final confrontation. Frank had assumed that Nixon's incapacity spelled the end for the south, that the invisible hand of political fortune had already laid our king on its side.

But Nixon said, "If you'd really like to help, I wonder if Anne, and of course Henry, might spare you for some fact-finding."

"I suppose so," Frank said, surprised. "Where?"

"Tell me more about her father," Nixon said.

10

Hit By A Pitch

Breakfast time Thursday in Saigon was the cocktail hour Wednesday in Washington. At dusk, after a long afternoon of presidential handholding, a desperately thirsty Ron Ziegler trotted down the white steps of Jackson Place, waved at the reporters across the street with his best approximation of a friendly smile, and turned north, whispering a prayer.

Good Lord, deliver me.

He walked briskly but not too briskly, trying to look nonchalant. When Ziegler had left to go home on Monday and Tuesday, the reporters and photographers broke camp and massed around him while he hailed a cab on H St. He hadn't said a word to them either time except "excuse me" and "good night."

This time, he thought he could read their scheming little minds. It had been five days since anyone besides the Nixon family, him, and Rose Woods had seen the ghost of Jackson Place. Maybe tonight, Ziegler was serving as a decoy. Maybe the old man finally wanted a meal that hadn't been schlepped over from the White House mess. The reporters knew that the Secret Service could have his limo and a trail car at the curb in ninety seconds, ready to load Searchlight and Starlight for a quick run to the Eisenhowers' apartment for dinner. Nixon's reemergence would be a better story than another stroll with stonewalling old Ron Ziegler.

Sure enough, the reporters shouted their questions while holding their position across from the townhouse. As he left them behind, and their voices were lost in the noise of rush-hour traffic, he was glad they couldn't see his exuberant grin. *Free at last!* Free of Nixon, and free of the fucking free press.

He walked along H and up 16ᵗʰ St., past the Hay Adams. It was still hot and muggy, but he thought he might take flight. He jogged across I St. with the green light. In ten minutes he was sitting at the cozy little bar in the Carlton, watching the Orioles and White Sox. It was the top of the first with no score. He hadn't missed anything. He was by himself, and no one recognized him. It was the happiest he'd felt in months.

Baltimore's All-Star lefthander, Dave McNally, had just hit Chicago's third baseman on his left thigh with a fastball when a woman slid onto the stool next to him.

"Not your game," she said. "You played football, right?"

Ziegler glanced at her. Blonde, blue eyes, mid-thirties, black skirt and white blouse, thin and pretty. Just like Nancy. He'd promised to be home by nine. Just a couple of drinks, four or five innings, then see if the taxi driver would put the game on the radio on the way to Alexandria. *Good Lord, deliver me.* "In college," he said, looking back at the TV. "But that was then. Now, I'm married."

She smiled and motioned to the bartender, pointing to Ziegler's drink. "Me, too," she said.

Ziegler said, "You too you want a drink or you too you're married? Who are you?"

She cocked an eyebrow and grinned. "Who's on first?"

He glanced at her wedding ring, looked back at the screen, and said, "Bill Melton, the kid from Gulfport, Mississippi. Lousy fielder, good bat. The pitcher just gave him a big pain in the ass. Which actually reminds me of you."

The bartender brought her drink. "You two should put your show on the road," he said, adding pointedly if discreetly, "Anything I can help you with, Mr. Z?"

Ziegler said, "Nick Giordano, meet– " He looked at the woman.

"Bridgette Matheson," she said, shaking Nick's hand.

"Nick's a good friend of my wife and me," Ziegler said. "We've been coming here for five years. I actually have a reasonably good reputation– " He paused for a moment and grinned at Nick. "—here."

Bridgette said, "Stand down, Nick. Just making conversation."

Nick drifted away. Ziegler said, "How'd you know I played football?"

She picked up her glass by putting her thumb and forefinger on the rim. She turned it toward her mouth and sipped gingerly. It was obviously her first scotch on the rocks. "Because I work for the *Washington Post* and spent the day in the morgue reading your clips," she said, wincing at the bite of the liquor.

He planted his elbows on the bar and took a long drink. "Leave me alone. No comment. I'm watching the game. I'm having a drink. I have the night off. There's no news of any kind. I'll pay for your drink if you please go away. I'll give you $500 if you go away." Then he turned on his stool to face her and stared for a moment. "I know every reporter in Washington," he said, "and I've never seen you in my life."

"I just got here," she said. She rattled her drink, starting to get the feel of it, making the ice clink and her bracelets jangle. "The *Post* brought me down from Boston for a special project."

"What's that?"

"You." She put a hand on his arm. "Give me five minutes. I'm not a journalist. I'm a presidential historian at Boston University. You have nothing to fear from me, at least right at the moment. I've never written for a publication that sells more than five thousand copies, and I won't write a word in the *Post* for months. Just hear me out."

He shook his head and muttered under his breath. But a moment later, giving in to sheer curiosity, he stood and picked up his drink and escorted her to a booth along the wall. As soon as they sat down, she reached into a soft leather briefcase, pulled out a bound manuscript, and put it in front of him.

He squinted at the title page in the light of the flickering candle on the table. She said, "You're too young to have trouble reading that. It says, 'The Criminalization Of Political Differences: The Impeachment And Trial of Andrew Johnson'. It's my dissertation, soon to be a major motion picture."

"Why does every scholarly title have a colon in it?" Ziegler said, leafing through the first few pages.

"Because it makes it sound smart."

"Let me guess. Your argument is that Andrew Johnson was impeached not because he was a crook but because the radical Republicans after the Civil War didn't like his moderate policies toward the South. We even figured that much out in the White House. How does it help Nixon?"

Bridgette took another sip and ran it around on her tongue before swallowing. "Impeachment is always political, that's all," she said.

Ziegler leaned back in the booth. "Too bad it isn't 1868," he said. "And to be fair, I don't think Andrew Johnson's boys ever broke into Thaddeus Stevens's house and started reading his mail. Anyway, honey, what's your deal?"

Bridgette said she'd gotten a call on Monday from Ben Bradlee, the *Post*'s executive editor. With Nixon planning to go through impeachment and a Senate trial, he and his editors had decided that the story had exceeded the expertise of their political writers. Because of the presidential disability angle, Nixon's impeachment was unprecedented. They wanted to know everything about how Nixon defended himself – both the legal maneuvers and political moves – and they wanted it set in historical context, which Bradlee thought required an historian.

Ziegler nodded. "A laudable notion," he said. "Only one little problem."

"You won't talk to me in a million years."

He smiled. "It's not just that we hate you. Don't get me wrong. We definitely do. But Jim St. Clair, Nixon's attorney, is the main player, and he won't talk to the media because he thinks lawyers shouldn't. He thinks that if you're going to win, you win on the substance."

"Whereas you know that in a fight like this, politics always trumps substance."

"You sound like Nixon."

She smiled. "I know Barry Goldwater told Nixon last Wednesday night, even as he was urging him to vacate the premises, that he thought you could beat two of the three impeachment articles in House, which means you'd only have to defend against one in the Senate."

Ziegler sat up. "Who told you that?"

"I also know you now have 22 senators instead of fifteen. You won't read this in the paper anytime soon. But Nixon deciding to stay broke the fever. His friends are rallying. You have to get twelve more. We don't think you will. But you've made progress just sitting on your asses in Jackson Place."

Ziegler was stunned. They had no one working for them on Capitol Hill anymore, so they were blind and deaf. He said quietly, "And you know all this because?"

"The *Post* has set up a war room. You should see it. Blackboards and TVs and long sheets of newsprint glued to the wall. They're calling congressmen and senators every day. Maybe five reporters working on it full time."

"Does Bradlee know you're telling me this?"

"Why shouldn't I tell you? It's the truth. I told you I'm not a reporter, so I don't have to play by a reporter's rules. I'm not trying to trick you. I just want to know what happened. The deal is that you keep me informed about your legal and political moves on the condition that we don't write about it until after the trial, and even then, everything I write, you get to see first."

"Plus you'll keep telling me things?"

"When I know something, yes."

"You'll put this in writing? You realize that it's got to be completely secret. Only you and I and whoever I choose to introduce you to can know about it."

She took a legal-sized folder out of the briefcase and handed it to him. Ziegler put it under his drink. He was quiet for a moment and then said, "You know and I know that the *Post* wants Nixon to lose."

"No question about it," she said. "And they think he will. Can you also accept that Bradlee's enough of a professional and patriot that he wants to make sure we get the whole story?"

"Not a chance. He must've been three sheets to the wind when he called you. If we really have seven senators back, give me their names."

"Sure," she said. "You have something to write on besides a cocktail napkin?"

"Well fuck me," he said. "Want another drink?"

"I guess. What was that?"

"Single malt. You should've had a blended scotch your first time."

She smiled. "Teach me," she said.

11

The Ballad Of Cecil O'Brien

After their Thursday morning breakfast, Nguyen Thanh Ty said there was someone he wanted his son-in-law to meet. He said he needed a day to make the arrangements. Frank didn't ask any questions. He was still being coy about the precise details of his mission – Ty had guessed Nixon had sent him, but Frank hadn't confirmed it – so the vice deputy defense minister was also entitled to be mysterious. He went to his study and made some phone calls. Frank heard him talking quietly in Vietnamese.

The next morning, they got into Ty's brown Mercedes and headed north through the morning traffic, toward Saigon center. It was the same sprawling, rambunctious mess Frank remembered – French colonial architecture, long, leafy side streets and wide swathes of appalling poverty, cathedrals, temples, and bars, sidewalk food vendors, men on scooters and bicycles, longhaired Saigon hippies and beggars who'd lost limbs in the war, girls in tight skirts, women in traditional dress carrying parasols against the August sun, Eagles and Rolling Stones songs blaring from taxi radios.

There were more cars than he remembered, more billboards, bustle, and business. He still thought that with some decent leaders and without war, it could be a great city. His fellow GIs, especially the white guys, complained that it was dirty, it smelled bad, and the merchants and bargirls were swindlers. Frank didn't think most of them would have liked New York or Chicago, either. They were comparing Saigon to the civility and homogeneity of their neighborhoods in Charleston, Raleigh, and Waco. He would tell his buddies that their appreciation for Saigon would deepen considerably if they'd ever sampled the shopping or nightlife in Moscow, Pyongyang, or Hanoi.

"Not many Americans anymore," Frank said, gesturing toward the busy sidewalks. Nixon had finished bringing U.S. troops home in early 1973, leaving it all up to the South Vietnamese army.

Ty steered east, toward the coast. He said they were headed to a fishing village called Ham Tan. Frank remembered it. He'd supervised a couple of construction projects in the same district.

They drove with the windows down, their faces buffeted by cords of thick air. Once they'd left Saigon, and the countryside spread out beyond the horizon, Ty saw Frank scanning left to right, as though he were on guard duty back at Long Binh post. He'd only pulled it once in a year, but it had been eventful. A round of rocket attacks hit within 50 feet of the perimeter fence.

"Not many Viet Cong anymore, either," Ty said. Frank smiled but kept watching. The insurgent personnel inside South Vietnam were terrorists who conducted military attacks but specialized in murdering civilians – village heads, doctors and nurses, women and children, at least 3,000 alone at the town of Hue, some buried alive. Eventually the U.S. and South Vietnam sent its own teams to kill thousands of Viet Cong and their sympathizers. It was called Operation Phoenix. The CIA theorists who dreamed it up argued that even democracies, great nations that stood for due process and just war, had to fight terror with terror.

Phoenix hadn't been popular when the news got out. And yet as Frank knew from the cable traffic at the NSC, Israel has begun using the same measures against the Palestinian Liberation Organization. It all made his father's doomed revolution in Budapest look hopelessly innocent. Who knew that they should have been liberating their homeland by lying in wait for the young Soviet-trained bureaucrats who populated Hungary's ministries and slaughtering them along with their wives and children while they ate their dinner?

At Johns Hopkins, Frank had written his dissertation about the U.S. war in Vietnam and its implications for the continuing struggles with and Soviets in the Cold War. By the time he finished his doctorate, he was more optimistic than when he finished army service and started researching and writing. In January 1968, the Viet Cong had launched the Tet Offensive, which turned out to be their high water mark. While many in the U.S. who saw the chaos on TV thought it meant the communists were winning, they actually lost every engagement. The following year, Nixon's B-52s began to destroy their sanctuaries in Cambodia, making it harder to sneak into South Vietnam for their attacks.

By 1972, Saigon wasn't fighting a revolution anymore, if it ever had been. It was fighting North Vietnam, which for years had been the source of most of the Viet Cong's personnel and weapons. What was brewing now, Frank knew, was perhaps the war's final clash of surrogate armies, North Vietnam's supplied by the Soviet Union and China and Saigon's by the United States.

Because of Nixon's troubles, Frank feared the domestic politics would dictate the geopolitics. Besides, no matter how clear the experts found the tactical picture, the American people, once all the troops were finally home, had lost whatever interest they once may have had in investing in South Vietnam's political freedom. Even a strong Nixon would have had trouble keeping the punishing B-52s in the air against Hanoi and the guns and ammo flowing to Saigon.

The Watergate Nixon had hesitated to try, and the Nixon of Jackson Place could do less than nothing. And yet here was Frank Szabados, Nixon's only eyes and ears on the ground in Indochina, hurtling at 65 kph toward Ham Tan along a smooth stretch of highway paid for by U.S. taxpayers. They'd be there in time for a late lunch, Ty had said. Did Frank like escargot?

Frank began to relax. In South Vietnam, speed meant safety. In 1967, Lt. Szabados had spent his 12 months in-country building roads like this one, to keep people and troops moving around South Vietnam, and clearing jungle, to deny the Viet Cong places to hide.

One afternoon he went to inspect a bridge his soldiers were repairing outside a village called Lai Khe, a ninety-minute drive north of Saigon. Lying between the Cambodian border and Saigon, it was garrisoned with the South Vietnam's 5th infantry division and the famed U.S. 1st, which together added up to a 40,000-man safety patrol along Cambodia's porous border. This was years before Nixon had taken office and started pulverizing the Viet Cong's Cambodian hideouts.

At dusk, after the inspection, Frank was in the rear of a thirty-truck convoy heading back to the village. There was almost no other traffic. One of the war's indignities was that host country civilians weren't allowed on the main road, since it was hard to distinguish them from members of VC cadres living in Lai Khe.

The Americans were moving at 20 mph. Frank and his engineers hadn't worked on the Lai Khe road yet, and probably never would. It was just one unpaved lane, full of potholes, and as it approached the village from the north, it passed through a rubber plantation. The army liked to clear vegetation 1,000 meters back from both sides of the road, but too many Lai Khe livelihoods depended on the plantation, so it remained, hugging the road on either side.

Slow speeds, darkness, and a good place for killers to wait. Based on his training, Frank should've been ready. But over the roar of the diesel engines and the truck tires slamming into potholes, only more experienced ears picked out the enfilading small-arms fire. He had been thinking about An's long legs and bottles of cold beer when Cecil O'Brien, a friendly draftee from Pittsburgh, hit the brakes and started to shout.

Just a few months later, the army began teaching truck drivers caught in ambushes to speed up and try to get out of the kill zone. This time they stopped bumper-to-bumper in the middle of the road, since they had to assume that the shoulders had been booby-trapped. Frank and everyone else got out and crouched behind the line of vehicles. Feeling an absurd combination of exhilaration and terror, he peered around the back of the truck and fired his M-16 for the first and only time inside Vietnam, aiming at sound and flashes of light and struggling to control the weapon's recoil.

Somebody radioed for support. In five minutes an AC-47 gunship arrived from the U.S. base and poured fire into the trees. It was now almost pitch dark. Frank kept firing, scores of rounds, as soldiers from either end of the long line of trucks crept into the shadows.

The VC fire slowed, then stopped. The order came for the Americans to stop, too, to avoid hitting those who had overtaken the enemy position. Frank saw flashlights being used along the ground on his side of the convoy, so he got out his and looked around.

Cecil was sprawled out next to the right front wheel, lying on his rifle and bleeding out from a horrifying neck wound. His eyes had already gone glassy. Frank called to him, but he didn't respond. He took off his jacket and bunched it under Cecil's head and tried to stop the bleeding with his t-shirt, but by the time a medic got there, he was gone.

It was a typical VC attack, sadistic, masochistic, and pointless. The enemy lost 23 dead, 57 wounded, and 12 captured. Hiding in some rubber trees, they ruined six trucks, wounded 13, and killed Cecil O'Brien. Frank told the story whenever one of his more liberal-minded friends at grad school waxed eloquent about the nobility of the Vietnamese resistance.

Frank was startled when his father-in-law gunned the Mercedes to pass a yellow Honda on the right. As they sped past, he looked into the smaller car, smiling at the young man behind the wheel, who was driving with a woman and two children. The couple was wearing colorful shirts and sunglasses. They looked like they might be on the way to the beach. Speed meant safety.

At about one in the afternoon, they left the main road and drove along a river for a kilometer or so until they came to the village, which was built around a lagoon. The South China Sea spread out in front of them, glittering, blue, and peaceful.

Frank shut his eyes and drank in the invigorating sea smell. Born and raised to his mid-teens in a landlocked, oppressed country, he experienced the sea as a revelation of perfect freedom. His epiphany occurred soon after they settled in New York City in 1957. After just two weeks, his father had found a job as a super in a building on Sterling Place in Park Slope in Brooklyn, which included a basement apartment for the four of them – Frank and his parents and sister. After two months, they had a used Ford station wagon. One Saturday, they drove to Jones Beach on Long Island. It took them two hours. Frank had never driven that far without someone in a uniform asking who he was and what he was doing.

He remembered the hot sand under his feet, the rushing sound in his ears, people shouting and laughing, smells of things rotting and coming alive. He remembered the girls. Frank was always a little surprised to find that the sea was the same everywhere, its beauty and pungency serving as an eternal invitation to return from the scarcity and bondage of earthly life back to the deep and the ultimate.

"When you first came to Vietnam it was through Cam Ranh Bay," Ty said as he steered carefully through the narrow streets at village center.

"The most beautiful beach I've ever seen. It was six miles long, ringed by mountains and palm trees," Frank said. "It looked like a movie. We only had a few hours in the afternoon and evening. Some of the guys who were stationed there were having a barbeque, and they gave us beers and hot dogs and chicken. A few of the Californians were surfing. We were all wondering why nobody wanted to come to Vietnam. The next morning it was into the choppers and on to Long Binh post."

"I take it that's when you found out why nobody wanted to come to Vietnam," Ty said.

Frank said, "You know what I mean, dad. It was paradise. There was no evidence of the war except soldiers, and they were in swimming trunks. They didn't even bring their weapons to the beach."

Ty stopped the car for a moment to let an old woman carrying shopping bags in both hands cross the narrow street. "I suppose if the war ever ends," he said, looking at Frank, "the Americans will want to build one of their resort hotels for rich capitalists, with beautiful Vietnamese women serving cocktails around the pool."

"Is it too early to make a reservation?"

Ty smiled. A minute later he pulled around a corner and parked. They got out and walked along the alley to Ham Tan's bustling fish market. They passed stalls piled high with black tiger shrimp, blue crab, Vietnamese catfish, and pangasius. If the pale, skinny American looked out of place, nobody appeared to notice. By midday the venders were eager to sell the rest of their wares, get home before the afternoon rains, and go to sleep so they could be back at three the next morning.

Ty led the way to a café that had one wall open to the lagoon. An old man met them at the front and nodded at them and gestured toward the back, where a younger man sat at a table with his back to the wall. He was the only other person in the place. Seeing Ty, he stood and shook his hand.

Ty motioned to Frank and said, "This is Frank," adding gratuitously, "the American."

The man shook Frank's hand. "Nguyen," he said. He might as well have said "Smith."

They sat down. The waiter brought three bottles of "33" beer and a big bowl of raw snails, a delicacy Frank had avoided while in the army, which warned soldiers that they'd contract roundworm that would multiply in their brains and drive them insane. This didn't seem to be a time to be cautious. The snails came with bowls of salt and red pepper. He followed the Nguyens' lead in dipping them in the mixture and washing them down with beer. They were delicious.

"We're in considerable danger," Ty said. Frank knew he didn't mean the snails. "We don't have much time. Nguyen has important friends in North Vietnam."

"How important?" said Frank. Nguyen stared at him. He was small and trim with thinning hair, perhaps 35 years old. He wore black slacks and a white dress shirt, open at the neck. "You're Viet Cong," Frank said. Nguyen stared. "You're on our side?"

Ty said quietly, "It doesn't matter. The answer is complex. We don't have time. Just listen."

"Just listen," Nguyen said firmly. He spoke in lightly accented English. Frank guessed that he had been educated in the west. The man leaned forward. "They are planning an attack. Two, maybe three months. They will pick a place close to Saigon. The reason is to see what Ford does."

"We assumed as much. But where? Tell me where."

Nguyen shook his head. "It doesn't matter where, it doesn't matter when. It only matters what Ford does."

"But if you tell me where, we can be ready."

Nguyen looked at Ty, who nodded, encouraging him. He leaned forward and lowered his voice. "In May of 1972, when the North attacked the South, Nixon sent bombers. The Hanoi leaders did not expect it. They thought the congressmen would stop it, that the Americans would stage more marches and protests. Then in December, he did it again."

"The Christmas bombing," Frank said. "When the peace talks stalled."

Nguyen nodded. "This was after he won his second election. He bombed even more, for 12 days. This time—" He hesitated, looking at Ty again. "This time, half the members of the Politburo were frightened. They changed their view."

Frank was stunned. "How do you know this?"

"Half of them," Nguyen said, jabbing at the table top with his finger. "They said that they believed Nixon had decided to do whatever was necessary to save the Saigon regime. They said they would support no more invasions, no more attacks. They said that North Vietnam should make an agreement with the Saigon regime and wait until Nixon was gone."

"You're saying—" Frank looked at Ty.

Ty said, "He's saying you won the Vietnam war."

"There is more," the man said. "Even the Russians told them to negotiate instead of fight."

Frank sat back in his chair and looked back and forth between two men named Smith. One was a member of his family. The other was what – Ty's cousin? A double agent? Someone sent to fool the United States. To fool the Hungarian-American who loved his wife and her country and wanted to find nothing in the world more than evidence that Nixon's policy of offering a hand of friendship to the Soviet Union while raining fire and steel on the heads of their puppets in Hanoi had actually worked.

Frank said, "I don't believe it. It's impossible."

Nguyen actually appeared to smile. "They want a more profitable relationship with you," he said. "Your president asked them to pressure

Hanoi to stop the war, and so they have. It doesn't mean that they won't start again, but for now, you have the advantage."

"What if Hanoi refuses to stop?"

Ty said, "You know the names of the manufacturers of the North's airplanes and weapons as well as I do. Katyusha, Simonov, Kalashnikov, Tokarev, Antonov. Hanoi makes umbrellas and ashtrays. They have weapons stockpiles from the Soviets, enough for another offensive, but if Moscow won't resupply, no more."

Nguyen stared at Frank. "But now Nixon is gone, far earlier than they had expected, and so they are planning an attack," he said. "It doesn't matter where. All that matters is if the Americans send the B-52s to Hanoi. If they don't, South Vietnam is finished. If they do…"

It had begun to rain. Nguyen drained his beer, stood, nodded at Ty, and slipped past the old man into the crowds hurrying home.

12

We Can Share The Women

Waiting his turn at the taxi stand at Washington National Airport, Reagan operative Mitch Botstein was disguised as borderline degenerate scum. It wasn't on purpose; it was just the way he looked. Because he was too lazy to go the barber, he'd gotten a little shaggy. His jeans, t-shirt, and tweed blazer were comfortable choices for a four-hour plane ride. He had his dad's old leather suitcase in one hand and the beat-up case holding his Martin acoustic in the other.

It was a cool, clear Friday afternoon in early September. As the line inched forward, he was humming the song he'd been teaching himself to play. "Jack Straw" was about a rail-riding grifter who kills his partner, or finds him after he'd been hanged, and leaves the body in a shallow grave. Robert Hunter's words evoked a rugged, menacing, still-epic America. Mitch's fingers itched for his pick and the fret board as the song ran in his head. It had been in the Grateful Dead's set list for a couple of summers, a deceptively sweet tune in which Bob Weir and three other singers married their ragged voices like a prairie church choir in tight, soaring harmony.

Leaving Texas, fourth day of July
Sun so hot, the clouds so low, the eagles fill the sky
Catch the Detroit Lightning out of Santa Fe
The Great Northern out of Cheyenne
From sea to shining sea

He'd learned the song in the key of G. He had learned almost every song he knew in G. He wasn't much of a guitarist or singer, but he loved to play. Chicks digged it, too.

We can share the women
We can share the wine
We can share what we got of yours
'cause we done shared all of mine

He wasn't the only right-wing Dead fan, he was sure, although he'd yet to meet another. When he'd mentioned at the end of a Reagan campaign strategy meeting in Century City last spring that he was seeing the Dead at UC Santa Barbara that weekend, veteran operative Lyn Nofziger, who was bellied up to the conference table wearing his Mickey Mouse tie, sneered about catching venereal disease and lice from the hippie girls. Republicans only booked groups you could wrap a flag around, like the Carpenters, the Fifth Dimension, and Tony Orlando and Dawn. They wanted people around them and their candidates who were young, fresh, clean, and good-looking, with full heads of closely-cut hair, straight teeth, dresses and bras and no pants or perms on the women, no fatties, no profanity, and for Christ's sake no music that you wouldn't expect to hear on Sunday afternoon at the Tomorowland snack bar at Disneyland.

The man in front of Mitch in line was a six-term, 67-year-old Republican congressman from the Midwest. As he got into his cab, he gave Mitch the once-over and sneered. Mitch grinned and nodded a greeting. He had no idea who Mitch was, but Mitch knew him. His suburban district was trending marginal, with more blacks moving in and Democratic registration about to overtake the GOP. He'd won by five points in the Nixon landslide in 1972. Now that Nixon had driven the party into the ditch, he would be gutted and filleted in November's midterm elections as long as his Democratic opponent, who ran the local teacher union, wasn't photographed having sex with a barnyard animal.

Mitch sighed as the congressman's cab maneuvered into traffic. For the time being he was doomed to associate with people who claimed they loved freedom but despised anyone who actually took advantage of it.

Mitch's taxi, a dirty white Plymouth, rolled up and stopped. He met the driver at the back and let him stow the suitcase. Mitch preferred to load his guitar, laying it carefully in the trunk so his suitcase cushioned the neck. He climbed into the backseat and looked for the operator's license. "How you doing, Leroy?" he said.

The man glanced at him in the rearview. "Afternoon," he said, sounding indifferent.

"Key Bridge Marriott, please, my friend," he said. He was sick of Marriotts, but the chain was owned by rich Republican Mormons, so that was where everybody stayed if they were on a Republican expense account. One of the J. Willard Marriotts, the older one, who paid for both Nixon inaugurals, had fallen in love with Astroturf. He thought it looked clean and pretty. He ordered his son to install it in every one of their hotels, including on all the narrow little balconies at the Key Bridge, where Mitch thought the concrete would've been just as good. What was it with Republicans and Astroturf? It looks alive, but it's really dead, a questionable metaphor for a political movement. "You live in the District?" Mitch said.

"Southeast," the driver said. Mitch nodded. Almost all black, shit schools, spiking crime, unemployment at 25%, poverty rate at 35%, 80% Democratic, and a congressman who wasn't allowed to vote. No Astroturf. Barely any grass.

"Not going so well there, I guess," Mitch said.

The man shrugged and kept his eyes on the road. He said, "It's tough on the kids." Mitch didn't think he wanted to talk, so he rolled his window down and enjoyed the ten-minute ride past the Pentagon and down along the Potomac. If he was going to run into Emily Weissman by accident, he had a couple of hours to check in and spruce up.

Tracking her down had taken some doing. He couldn't very well call the White House. They wouldn't have put him through without knowing his name, and all the political guys knew he was with Reagan.

Luckily, the national cohort of overeducated young politicos wasn't as large as people might think. Mitch had graduated from Georgetown in 1969, two years ahead of Emily's graduation from the University of Michigan. He called a Georgetown classmate who went to Harvard Law. His buddy knew two or three people who'd been in her class, and he offered to make some calls. One of them was in

Washington, too, working at the Commerce Department while she studied for the bar.

Mitch got that woman's number. He called and mentioned their mutual Georgetown connection. He said he was a journalist who was thinking of moving to Washington. They flirted a little. He said maybe they could get together when he got to town; she could show him around. In the meantime, did she know anything about that woman at the White House who'd been in the papers for helping Nixon? He could place a freelance piece in *Los Angeles* magazine, he said, if he could get an interview with her, but he hadn't been able to get past Ford's Wolverine Guard. She offered to make some calls. Within a week, Mitch knew that Emily Weissman lived in a building on Massachusetts Ave., a block northwest of Dupont Circle.

Mitch put on a blue Oxford cloth shirt and a tie and grey slacks with his jacket and got a cab from the Marriott. It was a 15-minute ride against the traffic over Arlington Memorial Bridge. Emily's neighborhood had a drug store, two delis, a liquor store, and maybe ten restaurants and bars. Mitch took up a position on a park bench facing the circle, peering into the back of taxis, looking for a redhead.

On Friday, a White House aide would probably go home early, around seven. Her taxi would come up Connecticut Ave. and veer to the right around the circle, heading for Massachusetts Ave. He could see her building from where he sat. The idea was that he'd spot the car and see it drop her off. He'd have a one in three chance she'd change clothes and come back down to get a bite in the neighborhood, enabling him to run into her. *Hey, aren't you Emily Weissman?*

Where it went from there depended on what she could tell him, about Nixon's frame of mind and intentions. Maybe Ford's people had decided it would be in their interests to hurry Nixon's demise and had found some weakness that she'd tell him about. He couldn't imagine Weissman being especially loyal, either to Ford or Nixon. She'd only been there for three months. She had to be thinking about her career. Nixon was radioactive, and one way or another, Ford would be, too. She could be buried with them, or she could come aboard with Reagan, a real conservative, the last great hope of the Republican Party.

Mitch diligently conducted his reconnaissance for almost an hour. Even after rush hour had ended, there were still a lot of taxis, and it was starting to get dark. His head and neck were beginning to ache from straining to look into every cab that roared around the traffic circle and plunged onto Massachusetts. He'd noticed an old-fashioned red leather booth steakhouse on Connecticut. He decided he would get a table and try to run into her there while he was eating prime rib and watching the game.

His backup plan had always been to come back and loiter on Saturday morning. Maybe she'd go for bagels. He'd start with some small talk about his momma's Gravlax. He stood up, closed his eyes and yawned, and stretched his arms, fists to shoulders, then out to his sides.

"Hey!" said a woman in high, thin voice. She was standing on the sidewalk, staring at him. He'd nearly smacked her. She had her purse flung over her right shoulder, and in her left hand she held a black rectangular lawyer's briefcase.

It was a mile and a half from the White House. It was a nice evening, and she had walked home. He hadn't thought of that.

Mitch gazed at her. In the dusk, she was luminous. Green eyes and light freckles on pale, smooth skin, red hair swept behind her ears and down around her shoulders. At the end of the day she looked like this.

"I'm looking for somebody," he said. She stood staring. Why would he be telling her? "I'm pretty sure he lives around here, but I don't have his number. I thought I'd catch him driving home." He made half-hearted feigns at looking over her head and around her, still pretending to look at cabs as though he was afraid he'd miss his imaginary friend. He felt ridiculous.

"You *think* he lives around here," she said. "You look like you're casing the joint. What's your so-called friend's name?"

Her voice was insinuating but somehow not unfriendly. He liked hearing it. But he couldn't think of a name fast enough, so he waxed indignant. "I'm not sure that's any of your business," he said. Remembering the line he had practiced, at least, he added, "Hey, aren't you Emily Weissman?"

She shook her head in disgust and turned to walk away. When he rushed to catch up, she stopped and glared. "No!" she said.

"No to what?"

She looked angry and scared. "To whatever you could possibly want from me. You're the person who called my law school friend. You must've thought you were pretty charming. Didn't you think she'd tell me?"

The agony he felt because he had upset her sapped the energy it would have taken to keep pretending. "I'm so sorry," he said, extending his hand. "I'm Mitch Botstein, from California. I admit I've been trying to find you, to meet you, but I promise I'm not a reporter or an axe murderer."

She hesitated. Then she shook his hand. Hers was small and strong. "I can think of a lot of bad things besides reporter and axe murderer," she said.

"If you have dinner with me," he said, smiling uncontrollably, "I'll rule every one of them out." She hesitated. Barely thinking, he reached for her briefcase. He didn't care anymore about the secrets it undoubtedly contained about the president and the acting president of the United States. He had momentarily forgotten his mission of promoting the interests of Ronald Reagan. She'd had a long day and a long walk. He thought the briefcase must be heavy. He motioned toward it with his hand and nodded his head encouragingly, promising it would be okay. She looked at him solemnly and handed it to him, and they began to walk together.

13

Which Mitch?

Mitch paced back and forth on the sidewalk in front of Emily's building. This was nuts. He'd known the woman a half-hour, and he was thinking about introducing her to momma.

They lived in Encino, but north of Sepulveda Blvd., so he had gone to Reseda High, a San Fernando Valley melting pot with cafeteria-style dating. He took out Jewish girls and also those of whom his Polish mother disapproved. *Please, not my Mitcha with a shiksa!* On the other hand, in the Warsaw Ghetto, she'd learned to be practical. If pressed, she would reluctantly compromise. Once he brought a nice girl home for dinner. She was famous for being Reseda High's first black cheerleader. The next day, sitting at the kitchen table in her apron, momma said with a theatrical sigh that she might be able to live with one of his bikini blondes if it really came to that.

Mitch excluded no girl on the basis of religion or race. He considered rules about forbidden flesh to be a vestige of primitive times when the gibbons and great apes hurled banana skins and ape shit at each other and refused to permit their kids to be swung over to the next tree for the purpose of species integration. Only if a girl didn't like talking about politics or music would he neglect to call again.

He smiled to himself as he leaned against the light post in front of her building. Poor momma. He'd finally fallen for a Jew, and she looked like an Irish schoolgirl from the Bronx.

Emily had told him to wait downstairs. She was back in 15 minutes. His breath caught in his throat when he first saw her through the glass lobby door, coming off the elevator. She'd changed from her business suit into exquisitely fitted jeans, high heels, and a red silk blouse. Mitch's mouth was dry. He'd had a few girlfriends, but this time, and for the first time, the switch had definitely flipped. He was all in. He'd always wondered what it felt like. Now he knew: Extreme clarity, like observing the fine grain of the universe. And supreme irony, God laughing at the love-struck political operative.

Mitch didn't practice momma's religion. But he knew God had given him the gift of empathy. He had once thought it was to enable him to plumb the twisted egos of politicians and anticipate the behavior of voters. But it was really so he wouldn't err right now, in this pivotal moment – because Emily looked worried, and he was absolutely sure he could read her mind. Of course she was scared. He was acting irrationally himself, on instinct and impulse, and she obviously realized she was being reckless, too. It was riskier for her, since she still had no idea who he was.

Mitch thought himself a gentleman. Tonight, he would outdo himself. He wanted to drink her all in, her small, promising body, but he kept his eyes politely fixed on her face. As she came through the door, he desperately wanted to kiss her on the cheek, but he offered his hand again, bowed, and said she looked lovely.

It had gotten dark. She said she didn't care where they went. As she stood on the curb while he hailed a taxi, she answered yes when he asked if she liked music.

He said, "I bet your favorite album is 'Tapestry.'"

Shit, Mitch. He looked away for a moment and shook his head. That had sounded patronizing. He didn't even think it was true. His nervous mouth had gotten ahead of his mind-reading. This was no singer-songwriter chick.

She didn't seem to mind the inference. "Carole King's okay," she said. "My brother actually likes her more than I do, so I gave him my copy. I'm still listening to 'Exile on Main Street' and 'Get Yer Ya-Yas Out'."

"Mick Taylor-era Stones," he said, nodding with respect and mounting wonderment.

"Uh-huh," she said. "The Stones at the peak of their powers." He guessed that her lilting little voice had bewitched Nixon, too. Never mind Reagan and his Golden State Club schemers. Ford would be president for real before the weekend was out. Mitch would conduct an illegal break-in at Jackson Place and kill the crooked, filthy-minded bastard himself. She continued, "Also Santana and Hendrix. Definitely the Who. And I love Motown, of course. I'm from Detroit." She paused and said with an edge, "But you know that." Then she continued as before. "When I'm in a certain kind of a mood, usually on Sunday afternoons, I put on 'Led Zeppelin III'."

He turned and stared at her as a taxi slowed and stopped. "You feel sad on Sunday afternoons?" She nodded. He said, "Do you like 'Since I've Been Loving You'?"

"Jimmy Page's guitar solo destroys me," she said. He held the curb-side door, and as she got in, her thigh brushed against his. She left her perfume floating on the chilly air. He said later that he had experienced perfect joy on just one occasion in his whole life: When he ran around the back of the cab, climbed in on the other side, and saw that she was still there.

Barely thinking about it, he knew where to go, an old bar on 18th St. called Madame's Organ. It had good electric blues almost every night, mostly no-name local acts, but always the real deal, guys who got their chops from Buddy Guy and Jimmy Page. Page also got his chops from Buddy Guy, as a matter of fact. Mitch had always considered him derivative, an overrated cliché player. But he had just superseded the Grateful Dead's Jerry Garcia as Mitch's guitar god, for penetrating to the core of Emily Weissman.

The bar also gave redheads their first drink free. On the way, he was afraid someone had taken her there already or that she'd think it was corny. But she had laughed and ordered a beer. He got one, too. The band was at the back, laboring through the Allman Brothers' "Statesboro Blues," so they found a booth for two near the front.

And then the hard moment came, when she asked why he had been looking for her. He told her, more or less. He said Reagan was interested in all the ways the story might unfold, and he got the job. Seeking her out seemed like a logical first step.

He didn't say that Reagan's fellows wanted to turn her against Nixon and Ford by promising her a job in their conjectural administration. He could never tell her that. As he spoke, he realized it he was making it sound like a completely innocent political science project. He was helping the governor of a major state, and a potential candidate for president, assess the political consequences of recent unexpected events. Reagan was naturally interested in what motivated a bright young conservative like Emily.

If he was misleading her, which he was, he could straighten it out later.

She sat back and sipped her beer. "I get it. So now what?" she said.

"Are you hungry?"

She rolled her eyes. "No. You are, of course. Men are so ridiculous."

He really wasn't, but his stomach was jumpy. "Actually, can we get something to soak up the beer?" he said. "They have good French fries."

"That wasn't even what I meant when I said now what," she said. She smiled and studied him. "You're not on my agenda tonight. I have three hours of work to do."

"I knew what you meant." He motioned to the waiter and called out his order and then put his elbows on the table and smiled. "I was stalling," he said. "I really want to see you again."

"How is that supposed to work? Are you moving to Washington?"

"You want me to? I will."

She laughed and shook her head. "No."

"I really will."

"So I can date someone who's helping a potential challenger to Mr. Ford in the Republican primaries? Count me out."

"I wouldn't have it any other way. But just for the sake of asking, you care so much about him and Nixon because?"

She shook her head. "That's an insulting question. I'm there, aren't I? You can take from that whatever you choose about my world view."

"It looks like the House is going to impeach him next week."

"We think he'll beat Article III," she said. "Even the Democrats in the House would feel silly indicting the president of the United States for ignoring congressional subpoenas."

Mitch nodded. "As articles of impeachment go, it does sound a little whiny. But did you say 'we'? I thought you and Garment worked for Ford."

Emily sat back in her chair, slid her hands into the pockets of her jeans, crossed her legs, and arched her back. "Do you think this interrogation is going to make me hot?" she said.

"So if it weren't for our probably irreconcilable political differences, you'd date me?"

"Maybe." She reached for her beer, drained it, and asked politely for another when the waiter brought Mitch's fries.

"So you like me."

"Not especially." She smiled. God, when she smiled! She said, "Why do you like Reagan? Nixon says he's thin as piss on a rock."

"Nixon said that to you?" She nodded. He was impressed and jealous at the same time. He wondered how often they'd spoken. "Because unlike Nixon, he's a conservative."

"Nixon's not? Ford's not? That's not what my liberal friends say."

This speech Mitch had on autopilot, having given it a dozen times to Young Republicans and county Republican central committees. As he talked and gestured he tried to focus on her amused eyes instead of her alabaster neck or the swell of her breasts. What she needed to understand was that it was all about taxes, federal spending, and the need for more private sector growth. Under Lyndon Johnson, Nixon's big-spending Democratic predecessor, the federal budget had increased 11% a year, under Kennedy 7.1%. She looked like she had pretty shoulders. He wondered about the ring with blue stones on her right hand. Birthstones? What was her birthday? He said, "And do you know what it is under Nixon, with all these job-killing new programs?"

Making her voice breathy, she said, "Tell me, Mitch Botstein."

It was the first time she had ever spoken his name. He wanted to look at his watch and make a note. "Thirteen and a half."

"Wow. That's so big," she said, leaning forward and putting her hands on the table.

He leaned forward, too. He said, "Don't make fun of me. This is important." He put his hands over hers to emphasize his point. She took them and entwined his fingers with hers and pulled him in and turned her head and kissed him. It was deep and unmistakable. He wanted to put his hands around her head, all in her hair, but she wouldn't let go of his hands.

She broke off the kiss. "Take me home," she said.

Oh God. "Now?" he said. "Why?"

He could feel her warm breath. "Because I have to call Len Garment and tell him all about Mitch Botstein," she said sweetly. "He'll probably alert General Haig and Mr. Ziegler. These are definitely the guys you've read about in the papers. They will track you like a dog and kill you."

"Okay." He pulled her in for another kiss. "You're really going to tell them about me?" They kissed again.

She detached and said, "My guess is that it won't be news to my senior colleagues that certain politicians are wondering how they can profit from Mr. Nixon's misery." They kissed. "You taste like beer and catsup," she said.

He loved looking at her. "Your earrings match your ring. They're pretty."

"Thank you," she said. She squeezed his hands.

"Are they birthstones?"

"Sapphires for September. The 24th. Will you remember?"

He met her eyes and nodded. "I'll remember."

"They're from my mom and dad, when I graduated from law school."

"They're Republicans?"

She laughed with delight and shook her head. "Anything but. I'm girding my loins for Thanksgiving. I still have a lot of explaining to do."

"Speaking of your loins, do you want to come to my hotel instead? You can activate the assassins from there. I want to play my guitar for you."

"Didn't you mean to say that you want to make love to me for an hour and then play your guitar?"

"Yes, I did. I definitely did."

She finally let go of his hands, sat back, and smiled. "That's enough for tonight," she said. "Please take me home."

He said, "I'm going to sit on the curb all night and protect your building. I won't let anyone get you."

"That's sweet," she said. She stood up and put her purse over her shoulder. "But I'm still trying to figure this out. You should probably go get a good night's sleep. And don't get your hopes up."

Mitch's heart fell. His eyes started to burn. "You don't mean that." He stood and reached for her hand. She let him take it, but it felt different.

She said, "I can't seem to be able to help liking you. But I'm not sure it's going to be possible to reconcile puppy love Mitch with lying bastard Mitch."

He looked pathetic and hung his head. "So I'm in the doghouse for calling your law school friend."

She kissed him on the cheek. "We're Jews. You're in the wilderness."

"The doghouse is overnight. The wilderness was 40 years."

She tugged him toward the door. "Hadn't you heard? We're a pessimistic people."

14

Strike That, Rose

On Friday, September 12, a week after Mitch's date with Emily, Rose Mary Woods was typing a memo in Richard Nixon's command center on the second floor of Jackson Place. It was 9:15 a.m., and this was his second of the day. He had dictated it the night before using a Dictabelt machine in his little study one floor up. Like the first memo, in which he warned of the likelihood of Soviet mischief in the Middle East, it was addressed to Acting President Ford. This one concerned extremists in the Environmental Protection Agency who put their affection for bugs and birds ahead of economic growth.

Like most of Nixon's memos to those in power, especially when they had more power than he, it began with ingratiating and completely inauthentic self-deprecation. "I hesitate to impose my views on you," Rose had just typed, "when you are receiving so much good advice from the so-called experts." She would have it delivered across the street to the White House by noon. If Ford didn't have someone call by dinnertime and thank him, Nixon would call in Ron Ziegler and order an investigation.

Rose stopped typing for a moment and lifted the earphone off her right ear. She called over her shoulder to the woman at the next desk. "Joan, please turn off the sound on those darn TV sets," she said.

Like Nixon, Rose didn't want to be distracted by events she couldn't control. They had a big Zenith for each network. All three showed the floor of the House of Representatives. The first proposed article of impeachment, devoted to the Watergate break-in and cover-up, had passed by a wide margin on Wednesday. This afternoon, the House would resoundingly pass Article II. It accused Richard Nixon and his operatives of violating citizens' constitutional rights and using federal agencies to harass his political enemies. Article III was expected to be defeated.

That was all a done deal. It had been for a week, just as Ziegler's mysterious blonde historian friend at the *Washington Post* had told them. She had provided surprisingly accurate tally sheets showing how House members would vote. In return, Ziegler had arranged for her to spend a week watching Rose and her team handle Nixon's correspondence. She also wanted face time with Nixon and Jim St. Clair. Ziegler hadn't ruled that out, but first he wanted to see what additional information he could pry out of Bridgette Matheson.

Everybody in the building was already working on Nixon's trial, which was scheduled to begin on December 3, when the Senate returned from its Thanksgiving recess. When Nixon wasn't giving Ford advice, he was shoring up his gradually solidifying support among Senate Republicans, remembering their birthdays with notes or calls, inquiring about their grandchildren, and sometimes delicately arguing one point or another about Watergate.

It probably didn't help much, but as Rose knew from long experience, Nixon always had to be doing something. When her fiancé died during World War II, Rose had left Ohio for Washington, become a classic office wife, and landed the ultimate overachieving high office husband. When he hired her in 1951 as his personal senatorial secretary, it impressed her that he didn't ask about religion or politics. He thought he had good instincts about people, and in Rose's case, at least, he was right. She became closer to him than anyone outside his family.

She resigned from the White House staff the day after he moved out. She would work in Jackson Place as a volunteer as long as she could, paying out of her savings for her apartment in the Watergate. The other four women working at little desks shoehorned into the crowded room were also volunteers. Discreet, competent, and cheerful, they'd all been with Nixon since his congressional days, too.

She took off her headphones and stood and stretched. "Would anybody mind," she said mischievously, "if I opened a window?" The other women groaned their approval. A couple clapped. While Washington was still hot that time of year, the room had been comfortable when they got in at 7 a.m. By mid-morning they all wanted to get some air circulating, but nobody wanted to risk being photographed by the media camped out in Lafayette Square – nobody, that is, but Rose, who always gave the press a big smile when she flung the windows open every morning around this time. The other women watched her closely, because one day, they just knew, she'd give them the finger.

Rose settled back into her swivel chair, put on her headphones, and touched the pedal with her right foot. There was the low, growly voice that had been whispering in her ear for 23 years. *I can certainly understand the passions of those who say that saving an endangered species is worth running the risk of an endangered industry. But in my opinion, their views are fatuous nonsense.*

Rose sighed as she typed. It would be another long day and a quiet, solitary evening. In the early days, after spending twelve hours typing Nixon's letters, speeches, schedules, and memos, Rose and the girls would strap on their high heels and head for the Mayflower or one of the other hotels in 1950s Washington with a dance floor. There'd be a little orchestra or band and sometimes a vocalist. They'd play "Cry Me A River," "That Old Black Magic," and "April in Paris." The other girls usually had dates. Rose would take a turn with the boss's military and political aides.

By the late fifties, the music changed, and almost all her friends had gotten married. She wasn't exactly lonely. She was always over at her friends' houses or they at hers, or back home with her family in Ohio. The Nixon girls grew up calling her Aunt Rose and were always delighted when she came over for dinner. And always, of course, she had his voice. *I did not create the EPA to make a holy idol out of the god-damned environment. Rose, strike "goddamned," please.*

Strike that, Rose. Last September, at the end of another awful month of Watergate, working late in her White House office, she had been transcribing some of the Nixon tapes that Congress had subpoenaed. She was a using a big reel-to-reel machine the Secret Service had delivered just that morning.

It was the worst work she'd ever done, perfect and interminable torture. The voices were sometimes almost impossible to make out, with muttering and interruptions and sentence fragments and coffee cups hitting the tables where microphones were embedded, which hurt her ears.

It was also hard because she loved Nixon and knew that when people heard how he sounded behind closed doors, they'd hate him.

She was working on a conversation that had taken place on the late morning of June 20, 1972, three days after the break-in. Nixon was talking to Bob Haldeman, whom Rose had come to despise, especially after hearing him on the tapes, sitting alone with Nixon. She'd run Nixon for nearly 20 years. When they finally made it to the White House, Haldeman had banished her to a far corner of the West Wing. She spent her days typing his speeches and letters and returning calls to people around the country Nixon didn't want to talk to. Getting a call back from Rose Woods wasn't as good as hearing from Nixon, but it was close, since she'd usually send Nixon a summary of the conversation, if Haldeman didn't intercept it.

Nixon had approved her reduced role, but she still blamed Haldeman, for sidelining her and for cheerfully amplifying the boss's worst instincts. Whatever Nixon had wanted – dirty tricks, using the FBI against journalists, espionage, tax audits of political enemies, or counting Jews at the Labor Department – Haldeman and the frat boys had done.

Nixon had also given Rose some outrageous orders over the years. But she had been man enough to tell him no.

As she'd learned from the tapes, Haldeman grasped the extent of his vulnerability the moment the Watergate burglary occurred. The criminals' funding and lines of authority would be traced back to him. So in those June 1972 conversations, he wanted it all covered up.

At first, Nixon sounded less ashamed than angry. The opposition had been harassing him for years, and now it was their turn. He was going to play it like they played it and kick them right in the ass. *Don't you think? Do you agree?*

But then, in that June 20 conversation, Rose heard him say words that made her feel sick to her stomach. She actually reached for the wastebasket and put it on the floor between her knees, just in case.

She was alone in her office. No one else could possibly have overhead what was coming through her headphones. But she turned the volume down and listened again to be sure. Nixon was revealing secrets that even Haldeman hadn't known. The consequences of anyone else in the government hearing the tape would be mortal, a death sentence. She even thought of calling Haldeman, telling him that he was in danger, too, but she realized she couldn't risk it. Were their phones bugged? Nixon was famous for spying on his enemies. She wondered who was spying on Nixon.

So she did what she had to do, what only she would be willing to do. She closed and locked her door and sat down in front of the tape machine. She rewound the tape to the beginning of the conversation, took a deep breath, said a silent prayer, and pressed the big grey "record" button in the middle of the front panel.

In her panic, she hadn't thought to time the segment she was destroying, so she had to keep stopping to listen to see if it was over. She pressed "record" five times all together. Five separate erasures. She could have no idea that the stops and starts would deepen forensic experts' suspicion that the erasure was intentional. At that moment, all she wanted was to hear was the sound of silence.

It took her a little over eighteen and a half minutes to obliterate words that Nixon should never have spoken, words that no one could ever hear, words that could destroy them all.

Then she went to find him. He was in his hideaway office in the Old Executive Office Building, sitting in an easy chair in the corner with his feet up, yellow pad on his lap, chewing on his glasses. He didn't ask her to sit. Their meetings usually weren't that long.

She told him that something terrible had happened when she'd gotten a phone call. The tape machine she was using was unfamiliar. Somehow she'd erased some of a conversation with Bob. When the phone rang, she must've hit "record" instead of "stop" and then caused the erasure by keeping her foot on the pedal.

He looked at her, swirling his glasses, tugging on his lower lip with one of the temples. He inquired about the date and time of the tape. She told him. He stared at her and then looked away. "Did you hear the conversation?" he said, looking at her again.

She hesitated. "No, sir." He stared at her. She stared back.

"Are you sure, Rose?" he said. She nodded. He told her not to worry. Besides, he said, the conversation wasn't even one of the tapes Congress had demanded.

As it turned out, he was wrong. The tape was on the subpoena list after all. When the erasure became public in late November, yet another Watergate firestorm engulfed the White House. Rose instantly realized what she had to do. She went to mass and asked God to forgive her for the lies she was about to tell. Then she transformed herself into a Johnny Carson punch line. The photo even appeared on the cover of *Time* magazine. It showed her with her right foot on the pedal while she reached for the phone, reenacting what she claimed was the position that had resulted in an accidental erasure. "Like a lamb that is led to slaughter," the prophet Isaiah wrote, "and like a sheep that is silent before its shearers, so the servant did not open her mouth." No one outside of Washington had ever heard of her before. Now there she was, splayed out grotesquely in a yellow and green jumper, exposed and humiliated.

She did it willingly. She did it to save him.

"I need a drink," a voice said. She turned and saw Ron Ziegler slumped in the chair next to her desk, rubbing his eyes.

She took off her headphones and laid them on her desk and then turned and patted his hand. "How's he today?" she asked.

"Reenergized," he said. "We have a new enemy, and he's one of us."

She nodded and sighed. She'd read the memo from Len Garment disclosing that the White House had learned that Reagan's people were sniffing around, which meant he was considering a run in 1976. Garment didn't disclose his source, but Rose knew. "I bet it's the girl in Len's office," she said.

"Emily?" he said, sounding surprised.

"The boss has been calling her."

"How often?"

"At least once a day."

"Len must not know the old man's talking to her so much," Ron said, grinning, "or he wouldn't have bothered to write. I guess she's his newest crush. We could do worse. She's a good kid. Plus she's a redhead."

Rose waved her hand playfully at Ziegler. She said, "If I understand this correctly, the Reagan people want Ford to be president by '76. They think that however it turns out, he'll be easy to beat in the primaries. But what if the boss's acquitted?"

Ziegler shrugged. "Ford's in a better position to run, and Reagan's out of luck. Which is why we have to assume that they're working the Hill themselves to turn senators back against us. Maybe they're even trying to dig up some dirt of their own."

"Bastards," Rose said.

"Politics," Ziegler said.

"What do we do?"

He stood up slowly, put his hand on her shoulder, and smiled wanly. "We win," he said, and headed for the stairs back to the third floor, where Nixon was waiting for him with more questions and projects.

Rose watched him go. He was still a young man. He looked so weary. Just for a moment, as she turned back to her work and picked up the headphones, she wondered if this was all too much for any of them to bear, the fighting, the struggles, the need to win no matter what. They were using themselves up, expending all their years and energy, all their beauty and love, battling day by day so they could lay themselves down, wounded and weary, just to arise and battle again. She felt she'd been fighting forever, and she hadn't gone dancing in years.

15

Tuna Fish Summit

Two or three times a week during his Jackson Place exile, usually just before noon, Richard Nixon would step through the front door and strike a pose on the top step. He inhaled the fresh autumn air while exhibiting indifference to the press corps across the street in Lafayette Park. He kept his chin up and, like a commanding general, surveyed the whole vista that was spread before him, taking care to look over the heads of the journalists. Finally, pretending to notice them for the first time, he smiled tensely, offered a nod that was almost a bow, and walked down the steps toward the bulletproof Lincoln limousine that was purring by the curb.

Sometimes Pat Nixon was with him. Today, a Friday in mid-September, he was alone. He dismissed the reporters' shouted questions with a wave over the roof of the car, smiled brilliantly – Nixon always liked to have the last smile – and let a Secret Service agent load him for the quick drive to his lunch date.

It only took five minutes to reach Julie and David Eisenhower's place on I St. near 22nd. The classroom buildings, offices, and dorms of George Washington University, where his son-in-law was going to law school, spread out for blocks all around their building. Neighbors and students had grown used to seeing the limo and trail car roar up and stop.

A few photographers, alerted by their colleagues in Lafayette Park that Searchlight was probably on the way, staked out the arrival. Sometimes Nixon stopped and talked a little about weather, sports, or what the Eisenhowers were up to. If anyone mentioned politics or

Watergate, he held up a hand in warning, smiled, and followed his agents into the building.

On this particular Friday morning, reporters had overlooked Frank Szabados, a relatively unknown member of Henry Kissinger's national security staff, who had arrived fifteen minutes earlier after walking from the White House. He slipped past the advance agent standing outside the door and took the elevator to the Eisenhowers' apartment on the fifth floor.

Julie had set out tuna fish sandwiches, chips, and milk on TV trays in the living room. She offered Frank some coffee while he waited. Glancing around, he saw evidence of a couple in transition out of their college years, just like him and Anne a few years before – heavy, hand-me-down furniture, a guitar propped in the corner, David's law books stacked on the dining room table.

When Nixon arrived exactly at noon, Frank stood. The president wore a blue suit, pale blue shirt, and crimson tie with an understated pattern. His brown hair was combed straight back and looked fuller on the sides than usual. He looked fit and in command, oddly enough.

The first couple of times, they'd shaken hands, but Frank got the feeling that Nixon didn't welcome it. He wasn't exactly rude, but he wasn't much for pleasantries and small talk. Nixon walked straight to his chair in a corner opposite the living room window, pulled his TV tray closer, and tucked his napkin under the knot of his tie.

"Churchill used to do this, what we're doing," he said, crunching on a chip. "Before the war and all the rest, when Neville Chamberlain, the British prime minister, wanted to appease the Nazis. Churchill's sources in the foreign office gave him top secret information about Hitler's military buildup, and he used it in his speeches in the House of Commons."

Julie had set Frank's chair opposite Nixon's. He took a bite of his sandwich. In the analogy, Nixon had given himself the starring role as Winston Churchill, Great Britain's savior during World War II. "You're comparing Mr. Ford and Dr. Kissinger to Neville Chamberlain," Frank said.

Nixon smiled as if to say "you said it, I didn't" and quickly devoured half his sandwich. Frank was still astonished that he was sitting with

Richard Nixon and at how quickly they'd developed a rapport. This was their fourth meeting since he'd returned from Saigon. Nobody, including Kissinger, had figured out that he'd been out of the country. Everyone who worked in the White House was used to hearing that someone had gotten sick and collapsed in sheer exhaustion. He didn't have the kind of colleagues who dropped off covered dishes. He'd had Anne keep in touch with his assistant and tell her that he was sleeping all the time. He was back in the office by Saturday morning.

Driving back to Saigon, his father-in-law, Ty, had told him about the mysterious Nguyen, whom they'd met over raw snails in Ham Tan village. When Vietnam was partitioned in 1954, Ty was among two million people who fled south. He left behind a brother in Ho Chi Minh's revolutionary movement against the French. Nguyen was his brother's Paris-educated son. Indochina watchers' favorite barroom argument was whether the Viet Minh were communists as well as nationalists. Their apologists said no, and in young Nguyen's case, they were right. He wanted an independent, united, and free Vietnam.

He kept his democratic impulses to himself. After his father helped him get a job in Hanoi's foreign ministry, his gifts as an analyst won him a series of promotions. He now saw everything on the foreign minister's desk, hence his insights about debates in the North Vietnamese Politburo after Nixon's Christmas bombing in 1972. Now that the U.S. troops had left, he didn't want the north to conquer the south, which was corrupt but relatively free and prosperous. He wanted one Vietnam, but not if it was going to be communist.

"How's the nephew?" Nixon said. He's finished his lunch quickly and set the tray to the side, continuing to work on his milk.

"We think he's okay. Anne's folks have a code if they hear something's happened."

"Which is?"

"'Snail's pace'."

"'If they say that, he's in trouble or dead? Easy enough to work into a conversation, I guess. Do you believe him?"

"That the north was intimidated by the bombing? I don't see why not. Why wouldn't they be? I've been meaning to ask you about the

Russians. Is it actually possible that Nguyen's right, that they told Hanoi to stop attacking the south and negotiate a peace settlement?"

Nixon had taken his reading glasses out of his jacket pocket and was chewing one of the earpieces. "Brezhnev promised me he'd try," Nixon said, referring to the Soviet leader. "Henry thought I was a little naïve to expect him to follow through."

"It took guts to bomb the north, especially when you were also trying to improve relations with their allies in Moscow."

Nixon's eyes drifted for a moment. Frank was a fighter, a refugee from totalitarianism who would never take his freedom for granted and would probably be willing to kill for it. And now he had the beautiful wife from Saigon. Good for him. Good for them.

But Nixon didn't like being congratulated for dropping bombs. The civilian casualties, members of Congress saying he was acted like an outraged tyrant, all the death and destruction and waste. He hated thinking about what his mother would have said. When he was growing up in Yorba Linda during World War I, Hannah would go into the sewing room in their little house a few times a day for her prayers. He'd hear her soft voice murmuring thee, thine, and thy will be done. She was praying for peace in Europe. She hated the war. She hated all war. Her son had dropped 20,000 tons of explosives on North Vietnam in two weeks.

Because of his campaign style, everybody thought he was a brawler, but he had never been as tough as he acted. The trick was to bob and weave, bluster and threaten, but avoid striking a blow until you had no other choice. Kennedy and Johnson, who started the Vietnam war, had better shots than he at Mt. Rushmore. But Nixon never would've been reckless enough to put U.S. troops in Indochina. Getting out had been a son of a bitch, a thousand times harder than getting in. The right said he was too soft on the communists, the left too hard. His policy was to be both, giving the Soviets a stake in reining in Hanoi while he did whatever was necessary to help the south survive in the meantime, even if it meant he had to be the first Quaker carpet bomber.

He was proud of making tough decisions. He complained that his aides weren't doing enough to make sure the world knew how much he agonized about invading Cambodia or bombing Vietnam. But he believed that having to resort to such savagery meant that the United States had been unforgivably inept.

Nixon stared at Frank, swirling and chewing his glasses. The young man was right about one thing. He'd been worried as hell that the bombing would derail U.S.-Soviet relations, which was the main event in foreign policy, no question. Even Kissinger had been a little nervous. "What you should understand about your friend Henry is the Holocaust," he said. "He and his family barely got out in '38. Everybody says what the Nazis did was horrible. Henry says it's also terrible what the rest of the world did to humiliate Germany after World War I and create the conditions for it."

Frank knew the story well. "So it would've been natural to resist bombing Hanoi," he said, "for fear of disrupting your dialog with the Russians, which was creating a more stable world."

"As it turned out, the Soviets don't really give a damn about Vietnam, except they'd love to have the harbor at Cam Ranh Bay. I thought they'd sell Hanoi out for a deal with us, and I still do. So yes, I believe Anne's nephew."

"Cousin. Yes, sir."

"Last spring Kissinger even told me that if the Soviets put Jews in gas chambers, it wasn't an American concern. Maybe a humanitarian problem, he said."

Frank smiled. "A pretty narrow definition of national interest," he said.

"You see what he was driving at. You create a balance among nations and otherwise leave them alone, unless they pose a threat."

"Works on paper," Frank said.

"Speaking of paper," Nixon said, sitting up in his chair, "did you bring me any?"

Frank suppressed a sigh. He'd been dreading the question. In their last two meetings, Nixon had pressured him to steal documents from the White House, especially anything about Kissinger's advice to Acting President Ford in the event Hanoi attacked South Vietnam. So far, Frank hadn't complied. He was afraid of getting caught. The compound was full of workaholics who grabbed lunch in the White House mess or ate at their desks. Frank already looked suspicious leaving the grounds for an hour and a half. If he'd been carrying a thick folder filled with Eyes Only documents? A briefcase? What was he supposed to do, slip them under his jacket or in his pants?

Nixon sensed his hesitation. "I have a security clearance," he said testily. "I'm the president."

"I'm not worried about you, obviously," Frank said. "But they do brief you, right? Henry says during staff meetings that he's talking to you."

Nixon batted the air. "I get a bland intelligence and tactical summary every morning," he said. "There's better information in *Newsweek.* Henry calls with generalities and reassurances. I know when he's bullshitting me." He stared at Frank. "You're worried about Kissinger finding out?"

"Shouldn't I be?"

Nixon grinned. "He wouldn't like it, but he could live with it." He paused. "Haig's the one you have to watch out for." Frank looked surprised as Nixon continued. "His office may be in the White House, but his heart's at the Pentagon. You maybe read about the yeoman."

"The kid who was spying on the White House?" Which was exactly what Nixon wanted him to do now.

"Worse than Watergate," Nixon said, "but we couldn't do anything about it except reassign the assholes that did it. The public finds out that the military doesn't trust the president, and you've got a problem, especially when you're clinking glasses with the communist Chinese."

"Did Haig know about the yeoman? He was still working for Kissinger then."

Nixon paused and then said, "Probably."

"You don't seem especially upset about the military undermining civilian authority."

"You're from communist Hungary. Are you really surprised?"

"America's different."

Nixon laughed cynically and twirled his glasses. "Governments are different," he said. "People are the same. Nobody trusts anybody. Just watch out for Al Haig. I don't think he'd mind me trying to put some lead in Jerry's pencil as far as Vietnam's concerned. He served, and he probably still wants to win the son of a bitch. But he and the brass wouldn't care for the idea of us meeting, and your bringing me the Vietnam files would send them completely around the bend."

Frank hadn't said that he would. "Mr. President, do you really think you can influence war policy from Jackson Place?"

Nixon stood. He called out to Julie to tell the Secret Service he was leaving. "Just get me the documents," he said. "And give Anne my best. You're a lucky man."

16

Breakfast and Dinner

Mitch Botstein returned to Los Angeles the day after his and Emily's first evening together. They'd talked three times since – long, get-acquainted conversations they didn't want to end, the kind that teenagers have. His heart leapt when she said she'd meet him for dinner on her birthday, her day of days, when she probably had her pick of invitations.

As soon as she said yes, he made a reservation at Gadsby's Tavern in Old Town Alexandria. It was a favorite with highly-educated young people who worked in the government. Some had actually fallen in love there while discussing the interstate commerce clause and the Continental Army's second encampment at Morristown, New Jersey. Mitch wasn't sure if George Washington had eaten at Gadsby's, but it had a reliable 18th century pedigree and candlelit dining, an historic setting for an historic date.

He asked them to put a dozen roses on the table with a note saying, "Love, Mitch." No. "Yours, Mitch." Maybe "fondly"? No: Love. His mother took him to Neiman Marcus and helped him pick out a sapphire and silver necklace to match her earrings and ring. He worried that she and her parents, once they heard about it, might consider it presumptuous, but momma, with her old-world instincts, promised that they would reckon it as a gesture of respect.

He didn't want to dwell on how much he wanted to sleep with her. That seemed a little disrespectful, too. But he couldn't help it. Emily had been so comfortable with him on the phone, so inviting. Her little voice made him crazy. He remembered how she'd looked at him, the feel of her hands pulling him in, her mouth, her smell. He yearned for her day of days to end with a night of nights. He hoped she wouldn't keep him languishing in the wilderness. He wanted to plunge through the surging water and enter the promised land and be engulfed by its fecundity and abundance. Go down, Moses and Mitch!

He also needed to get word to his bosses that there wouldn't be any milk and honey for them, at least from Emily Weissman. He invited himself back to the Golden State Club so he could tell Howard Morton, Ronald Reagan's fellow, that against all reason, she had turned out to be a true-blue Nixonite, unreachable and unmovable.

Morton was at his usual table in the sunny, half-empty dining room. This time he was having a soft-boiled egg in a silver eggcup. A black man in the kitchen had tapped carefully around the crown, breaking the shell but leaving it in place to keep the egg hot. As Mitch watched, Howard lifted the top off with his spoon, pried out and ate the little sliver of egg white, and then dipped strips of buttered toast in the yoke.

"You look like Prince Charles having breakfast," Mitch said. "When he was eight."

Howard waved at Mitch's meal with his spoon. He was having oatmeal with skim milk and no sugar, black coffee, and half a grapefruit. "Can we get you some berries and sprouts?" Howard said. "You're either running for office, which I guarantee I would've heard about, or you're getting laid. What's her name?"

Mitch had also been jogging and going to the Y near his apartment in Westwood to work out. When he was bench-pressing, he daydreamed about how Emily's strong little hands would feel pressing urgently up against his chest.

He said to Howard, "How do you keep so fit?" Mitch's gift of empathy made him a genius at redirection. He knew that flattery was a surefire way to deflect an unwelcome inquiry from a vain, powerful man.

"I play squash and tennis with other rich people," Morton said. "Why did you change the subject?"

Mitch shrugged. "I noticed I was putting on a little weight."

"You told her we'd bring her aboard, that she could write her own ticket?"

"She wasn't interested, Howard. What did you want me to do, throw her in the trunk and drive her to Sacramento?"

Mitch spoke with total confidence, because she really wouldn't have been interested, and after their phone conversations, he had a better idea why. Emily was one of those non-Republican Republicans who trusted the federal government more than the free market. She liked Nixon's funding for the arts and humanities and public television, the EPA, indexing Social Security payments to inflation, methadone clinics instead of more prisons for inner-city junkies, pretty much everything conservatives hated. Plus she favored détente with the Russians, making nice with the Chinese, and getting out of Vietnam, the full Nixon-Kissinger appeasement package.

She claimed that Nixon had a heart and said that she wasn't so sure about Goldwater and Reagan. Yes, she was hopeless. And yet she was so confident about who she was and what she believed. Mitch wanted her so much that he was at least theoretically open to the idea that he was wrong and she was right.

"You've been at this over a month," Howard said, dabbing at his bloodless lips with his white cloth napkin. "Nixon's been impeached. He's locked himself in the attic like— What's his name?"

"Boo Radley? Quasimodo? Lyndon Johnson's drunk brother?"

"And every once in a while I see some asshole on TV say that he might be acquitted. What the hell are you doing with yourself, Mitch?"

"It took me a while to get to her. Besides, it's not my only lead."

Howard sat back and sipped his coffee. "And please don't think you're the only asset we have in the field," he said.

Mitch grinned and said, "You think I'm surprised, knowing and loving you as I do?"

"Tell me how she seemed to you."

Christ, would the bastard just let it go? "She seemed liberal," Mitch said sharply. "She seemed inclined to think that Reagan's a right-wing lightweight who wants to throw everybody off welfare except oil companies and agribusiness."

Howard said, "And she says that's bad?" He motioned at a waiter and pointed to his empty coffee cup. Then he looked at Mitch. "You state her point of view with your usual passion," he said, "although it's not what you're usually passionate about. This misguided girl appears to have made quite an impression."

Mitch leaned back in his chair, shrugged, and waved his hand. "You asked me for a report, and I've given it to you," he said. "She's not interested in Governor Reagan."

Mitch didn't want to talk about Emily in this place anymore. He didn't want Morton to speak of her again. He felt rage rising in his throat as he stared at his supercilious tablemate. Morton was sometimes mentioned as a President Reagan's attorney general. Putting this twisted, scheming old bigot in charge of civil rights? Fuck Watergate. Even entertaining the notion of Howard Morton in the cabinet should be an impeachable offense.

Mitch caught himself. Morton was studying him closely. He hoped his face hadn't betrayed him. Now Mitch looked around impatiently for the waiter. He needed to drink some more coffee and suck it up. When his cup was full, he leaned forward. "Are you ready for some good news, counselor?" he said mischievously. Mitch was back, still in the game, not completely pixilated by his pecker. The future of the republic first, the love of his life second.

Howard seemed relieved. "By all means."

It wasn't anything definite yet. Mitch had been working the phones ever since he'd gotten the assignment, calling around to political friends in LA and Washington, asking if anybody knew about any shoes that hadn't fallen at the Watergate. The Nixon and Reagan people, with their principals occupying opposite spectrums of the party, were cagey rivals. Everybody knew everybody. A few opportunists managed to stay on the fence, with a toe in each camp and the numb nuts and consciences that went along with maintaining the posture. They either didn't understand or care about the substance of issues, or they cared more about the campaign and government jobs they'd get depending on who was in and who was out.

With his phone calls, Mitch had been letting the greater community of vicious backstabbers know he was in town and open for business. Sure enough, somebody with apparent Nixon ties was offering him information that they said would be fatal. If it got out, Mitch was told, Nixon would have no path to acquittal in the Senate. His fifteen votes would turn into five, maybe none.

Morton was hooked. "He ordered the break-in? Erased the tape?"

"It has something to do with the dirty tricks," Mitch said. "I don't know yet."

"When will you?"

"Soon. And whether I get the goods depends on what you're offering."

"Do they want money? A job? An autographed photo of Ronnie and Nancy?"

"I don't know that, either. Some guy calls me at night at my apartment. He won't tell me his name. I've got a meeting set next Friday. It's all cloak and dagger. He's going to call the night before or morning of and tell me where to go. He says he wants to play me a tape."

He could tell Howard was impressed. "Why that long?" Howard said.

He wasn't about to tell Howard, but he'd actually picked the date, since next Tuesday was Emily's birthday, and he planned to be back in Washington. Mitch just said, "He says it's worth waiting for."

"If it's money, he's got it. Within reason."

Mitch nodded at Howard and tipped his coffee cup. "Fiscal conservatism is the watchword of every Reagan foot soldier," he said.

Howard said grimly, "Stop fucking around, and close the deal."

Mitch got into Washington National airport Tuesday afternoon and checked into a room close to Gadsby's, in a romantic old hotel with a Tudor theme. It would be a quick ride after dinner. He called the restaurant from his room and asked them to reserve a taxi for them in advance. He'd pay for the waiting time. But what would Emily do with the flowers? Maybe they'd better go to her apartment.

He put on his blue blazer and grey slacks with cuffs and shiny cordovan loafers and got a cab. Humming the Rolling Stones' "Wild Horses," he floated into the restaurant a few minutes early, cheerfully greeted the maitre d', who was dressed as a Revolutionary War officer, and gave his name.

"Yes sir," the man said. "Party of four." Before Mitch could correct him, he looked up from his book and nodded at someone over Mitch's shoulder. "Are these perhaps your guests?"

Before he could turn around, he smelled Emily's perfume and felt her hand in his. He turned and saw her with a middle-aged couple who were looking at him uncertainly. She had on pearls and a black cocktail dress that grazed her knees. Her hair was up. She stood on her toes and kissed him on the cheek and said, "Mitch, I'd like you to meet my parents, Sidney and Marian."

Mitch felt a stab of disappointment. But then he had a startling surge of contrary feeling, a sense of peace and rootedness, as if unseen arms embraced him. This sensation of wellbeing preceded, just by an instant, his grasping exactly what she meant to say to him by bringing them.

It was an intoxicating moment, a revelation. He smiled at Sidney and Marian as though he'd always known them and reached for their hands. He said that Emily spoke of them with pride and devotion.

Then he turned to her and frowned. "But somebody tampered with my reservation," he said. "Call Nixon and get the Plumbers out here."

Her father watched as she laughed and poked Mitch in the side. Sidney understood the urge to be alone with a woman. Then she shows up with her folks? He was impressed that Mitch hadn't shown even a glimmer of irritation. As they turned to follow the hostess into the dining room, Sidney put his hand on Mitch's shoulder, urging him go ahead, behind his wife and daughter, who were walking arm in arm and whispering to one another.

They had a table by a window with a pane of old-fashioned rippled glass. It captured the flickering candles and the light in their faces like reflections in water. They ordered Cornish game hens, prime rib with Yorkshire pudding, and brook trout. The evening was festive from the first. Emily had worried all afternoon, since her folks disliked Reagan even more than Nixon. She relaxed before they'd finished their first bottle of wine. Mitch defended his man matter-of-factly but kept turning the conversation back to Sidney and Marian.

Where had they grown up? How had they met? He wondered how they reconciled their religious backgrounds, not that they had any explaining to do after producing such children as Emily and, he was sure, Bennie.

They asked about his parents. His father had a Chevrolet dealership in the San Fernando Valley. His mother had stayed home with Mitch and his three sisters. After the Warsaw Ghetto uprising in 1943, the Germans sent his mother, her parents, and her two brothers and two sisters to Auschwitz. Before the war was over, they had murdered everyone except momma. She'd ended up in Chicago after the war, where she'd met Mitch's father. He told Emily's folks that his passion for individual freedom and vigilance against tyranny, which he felt Republicans represented better than Democrats these days, was rooted in his family's near-annihilation.

Emily could tell by the way her parents talked to him and looked at each other that they liked him, though she had already figured out that establishing rapport with skeptics was an integral part of his skill set. Before the meal was over, in any event, their attention shifted to her, since over lunch, she'd told them about President Nixon's phone calls, and they'd discussed the matter all afternoon.

"It seems strange to your father and me," Marian said. She wore oval glasses and had her light brown hair in a bun. Marian's father, Emily had already disclosed to Mitch, was the redhead. "It's not appropriate, and not especially safe for you, I might add."

"I told your irresistible if hopelessly naive daughter the same thing," Mitch said, smiling at Emily and crossing his arms across his chest. He already knew the details, but he relished her being on the spot.

Emily was sitting back in her chair with her legs crossed, swirling her wine. "It's innocent enough," she said. Glancing at the people at the next table, she edged her chair closer, leaned forward, and lowered her voice. "He calls with little projects. He always says, 'I just wanted to check a few things'. I send him memos and reports in the afternoon pouch to Jackson Place, usually some issue about the evidence for one of the impeachment articles. Sometimes he reads something out of the paper that he says I might find amusing. It's usually only a minute or two." She turned to her father and said, "Every time he calls, I make a note of the time and the content."

"Does Garment know?" Sidney said. "What does he say?"

He says that it's happened before." She elbowed Mitch, who was sitting at her right. "In case anyone thinks I'm an idiot," she said, "I know he's a little sweet on me. But he never says anything to me that doesn't have to do with work. And I haven't even seen him since August 8th."

While they were having coffee, Marian went to the ladies room. Sidney got up, too. Mitch assumed he was going to make an end run for the check and was about to stop him, but Emily touched his arm.

"Let him," she whispered as Sidney walked off. "They're giving us a second." She edged her chair closer and kissed him. "You were wonderful," she said. "And thank you for the roses."

"So you forgive me for being a scheming bastard."

"No," she said, stroking his hand. "But you're so cute. Plus my dad likes you, and I want to meet your mother."

She was wearing her parents' earrings. Mitch reached into his jacket pocket and took out her gift. She opened the box, nodded at him with a smile, and reached behind her neck to unclasp her pearls, a timeless expression of femininity that seemed to make Mitch's heart skip a beat.

She leaned close so he could put the necklace around her neck. The candlelight played in her green eyes and the blue stones and silver that lay against her skin. "Happy birthday," he said. "Many more, just like tonight."

"I owe you an explanation," she said.

"You do not," he said.

"They called Monday and insisted on coming down for my birthday," she said. "I couldn't say no. They got here this morning, in time for a late lunch, which is all we had planned. I had already told them I had a date tonight. I gave them a quick tour of the White House and took them to the mess."

"So I guess I already missed the 'why did our daughter destroy America?' conversation you were planning for Thanksgiving," he said.

"When I told them about you, they were understandably curious."

"You went to work for Nixon and then showed up with a Reagan guy," he said. "They weren't curious, they were panic-stricken."

"You were already in the air from LA, so I figured— Well, I just figured. I wanted you to meet them so much."

"I assume they're staying with you. May I entertain them tomorrow while you're seducing Nixon?"

Emily smiled at him. "I have a tiny studio apartment," she said. "No extra room, or hardly any. They're at a motel near the airport. They both have to be back at work Thursday, so they're leaving first thing in the morning."

"Oh," Mitch said. He looked at his watch and then took her hand. "I happen to have a cab laid on."

"Do you now," she said. "I guess you were expecting we'd be going somewhere."

"Would they like to use it? I'll take care of it."

"I would like them to use it. Did you bring your guitar?"

"You bet," he said. "It's in my room."

She kissed him again and whispered, "Let's send them home and go to my house."

17

The Full Milhous

The next morning, Bridgette Matheson earned the off-the-record interview with Richard Nixon that she had coveted for weeks. The breakthrough came as she sat at the dining room table on the first floor of Jackson Place with Ron Ziegler and Rose Woods, Nixon's aides.

When Nixon set the house aside for former presidents, there had only been one, Lyndon Johnson, and he never used it. Nixon had been the only living president since Johnson's death in 1973. Even when there were formers again, most preferred suites at the Mayflower. Jackson Place's old floorboards were battered and creaky. The stale-smelling rooms were unwelcoming, with no overhead lights, just old table and floor lamps. The Smithsonian had sent over castoffs from its collections – lumpy sofas and beds, uncomfortable straight chairs, and coffee tables scuffed by ancient heels. This morning Bridgette, Ron, and Rose sat around a Duncan Fyfe dining room table that curators had earmarked for Jackson Place once they realized it was a late 19th century knockoff rather than a Federalist-era original.

Amid the smudgy and undistinguished portraits of Jackson, Washington, Jefferson, Pierce, and Lincoln that hung on the walls, Rose and her fellow volunteers had put up color photos of Dick and Pat on the Great Wall of China, Nixon with Leonid Brezhnev in San Clemente, and the Nixon family posed in the White House solarium during happier times. Finding the cupboards bare, without even a tea-kettle or toaster, the women had stocked the kitchen, enabling them to serve coffee and snacks and manage a light lunch or dinner for the Nixons if they were staying in.

Rose had put out cookies and brought flowers for the center of the table. She sat on the edge of her seat with her back straight and ankles crossed under the chair, taking shorthand notes in her steno pad. Ziegler slumped back with his cup in one hand and his other hand in his pants pocket. He desperately wished there were something in the coffee besides Coffeemate.

Bridgette kept her notes in an old-fashioned marble book with a black spine. She had already filled four. After Nixon's Senate trial, she planned to write a series of articles about how he and Congress had prepared for the confrontation. Beginning with her first meeting with Ziegler at the Carlton bar a week after Nixon's speech, she'd been generous with what she'd learned from the *Post's* congressional reporters. She helped Ziegler maintain a running list of the names of the senators who were back in their column or tending in that direction. She provided tips about the tactics the House's impeachment managers would use when making their case against Nixon on the Senate floor. In return, she'd spent hours with Ziegler and Rose and had even gotten a brief interview with Nixon's dour attorney, Jim St. Clair.

She looked at the glowering Ziegler with a worried smile. They had grown to trust each other, by and large. Ziegler liked her because every tip she'd given them so far was golden. She admired Ziegler's stubborn faith in Nixon, a difficult, deeply conflicted if substantial man. She had seen enough of his correspondence to know that most of it contained pragmatic policy advice for Ford and other members of his administration about arms control, relations with the Chinese, and various domestic and electoral questions. This was the work he obviously relished.

When it came to lobbying the senators who would decide his fate in a little over two months, he did nothing beyond dutifully making calls and writing notes his staff suggested. Playing defense bored him. More accurately, it shamed him. Bridgette had come to the conclusion that Nixon was fixated on being taken seriously as an intellectual. He wanted everyone to know how hard he worked, how many books he'd read, and how he agonized over tough decisions. She'd read two hundred presidential biographies herself. Until now she had never imagined that the most powerful person in the world could harbor all the insecurity of a boy at a softball game who was afraid he'd be picked last. Being misunderstood or despised by tens of millions must have been an unimaginable agony.

"What's our magic number this morning?" Ziegler asked Bridgette.

"Still nine or ten needed to acquit," she said.

Ziegler sat up and put his coffee cup on the table. "You said eight or nine last week," he said.

She shrugged. "What's the difference?"

"Between zero and two," Rose said brightly.

"Maybe between acquittal and conviction," Ziegler said.

"I admit there's some movement," Bridgette said.

"In the wrong direction," Ziegler said. "What the fuck. Sorry, Rose."

Bridgette took a deep breath. "How much do you really know about Emmett Walsh?" she said.

Notwithstanding the value of the intelligence she brought them from Capitol Hill, they had both decided that they didn't much care what Bridgette wrote about them after the Senate trial. Their public standing as Nixon's diehard loyalists was already so pitiable that they assumed it couldn't get much worse. Rose looked at Ziegler. "Emmett's what the boss calls a dull tool," she said.

Ziegler also found it liberating to be honest to a journalist. Looking at Rose and nodding, he said, "I find him unbearably pompous."

"The boss can't stand him," Rose said. "He managed to sneak in for meetings maybe twice. I was supposed to interrupt after ten minutes. The second time he actually left the Oval Office and hid in my office and told me to go in and tell Emmett that he had been called away for reasons of national security."

"These are revealing and helpful observations," Bridgette said. "He sounds like the kind of guy I wouldn't want around, either. So you'll excuse me for asking why you made him the secretary of the Treasury. I learned in graduate school that it's a pretty important job."

Ziegler sighed. "He's one of Reagan's San Francisco lieutenants, which is to say he's somewhere to the right of Attila the Hun," he said. "He was for Nixon, too, but lukewarm. He runs a big bank, but I think more as a front man, since he doesn't know how to add or subtract. His father was chief justice of the state Supreme Court or some damn thing."

Rose said, "Governor Reagan called himself to lobby for the appointment. It was after Watergate started to get bad. The boss resisted but finally decided it would help lash down that faction of the party to put a Reagan conservative at Treasury."

"It didn't work," Bridgette said. "And maybe he's not as dumb as you think, because he's why you're starting to lose ground. Walsh is calling senators and making the case against Nixon, and when he's speaking as a member of Nixon's cabinet– ."

Ziegler interrupted. "We got that."

Bridgette's pen was poised over her notebook. "So what were you thinking, naming a guy the president doesn't like, who isn't loyal, and who you thought was an idiot?" she said.

"You just don't get Dick Nixon," Rose said to Bridgette. "Imagine waking up every day thinking that while you were sleeping, your enemies were awake and gaining ground. He thinks you only win by anticipating events, by dodging the waves crashing on the beach. That's why he works all the time, and why we do."

She paused and looked at Ziegler. "That's why he gets scared when he feels happy," she said. "He thinks God created joy to make him lose focus and fail."

As Bridgette listened and wrote, Ziegler said, "Last spring was the tipping point. It was the day he fired Haldeman. He realized that he'd lost control completely."

"How do you know?" Bridgette said.

"He told me. He said, 'You realize, Ron, that it's all over, don't you?'" He rolled the bottom of his empty coffee cup on the table. "Richard Nixon as a captive of other people's agendas is the most pathetic creature imaginable," he said. "He makes decisions he never would've made in his right mind. Emmett Walsh was one of them."

"Whereas Watergate was a good decision?" Bridgette said, looking back and forth between them. "The cover-up? Hiring Haldeman to run the White House to begin with?"

Ziegler glanced at Rose, whom Haldeman had isolated from Nixon, and then stared at Bridgette. "Sore subject," he said.

She stared back. Too bad," she said. "Sore country."

Rose said, "When it came to politics, he wanted young men who would shut up and do what he said. On policy, especially foreign policy, he was at least willing to have a conversation, to test his instincts. As a matter of fact, he insisted on it. But he decided after losing his elections in 1960 and 1962 that he couldn't stay ahead of the curve unless he was in complete control of the politics."

"So Haldeman did whatever Nixon wanted."

"Pretty much," Ziegler said.

"The break-in, organizing dirty tricks against Nixon's political opponents, everything," she said.

Ziegler smiled. "Nice try," he said. "There's no evidence Nixon ordered those personally."

"He didn't have to. Just a nod and wink at Haldeman."

Ziegler shrugged and said, "The only thing he's got going for him in the Senate, as your own investigation has shown, is that there's no smoking gun either on the break-in or dirty tricks."

"What's he going to say when you tell him he's got a mole in the Cabinet?" Bridgette said.

Ziegler looked at her with a grim smile and stood up. "He's going to be pissed," he said. "Come upstairs and tell him yourself. But hold onto your pantyhose. Under normal circumstances, for your first interview, he would have done his best Woodrow Wilson. But you're about to get the full Milhous."

18

Bare Country

Mitch smiled when the phone rang at 5:30 in the morning in his apartment in Los Angeles. Because of the jet lag, he'd been awake for half an hour, thinking about the dimple in the small of Emily Weissman's back and the smooth skin on the insides of her thighs. She had freckles on her shoulders and chest, but not there. He was wondering about all the whys and wherefores of freckles, their serendipity and fickleness. Mitch just loved freckles.

When he picked up, she whispered, "Are you alone?"

"No," he said, "and she has the sweetest, roundest little bottom you ever saw."

"Don't ever say round."

"Even with sweet and little?"

"Even."

"Are you at work?"

"I was just remembering that the last time I had my office door closed," she said, "the president of the United States didn't resign."

He put his free hand behind his head and grinned at the ceiling. "Why did you close your door?"

"Because I'm talking to my boyfriend, and I might say something I shouldn't."

"About what?"

"Are you trying to get me to talk dirty in the White House? About making love to you."

"So you liked it."

"You're fishing for a compliment about your performance. That's cute."

He glanced down toward the foot of the bed. "It's only fair," he said with a groan. "You're getting rave reviews here. There's something about the sound of your voice."

"Oh, boy. Save it for me."

"I make no promises. Is Garment in yet?"

"Probably. What made you think about him?"

"I'm thinking about him on purpose. It helps. Does he know about us?"

"He knows about you, and when he saw how tired I looked yesterday morning, I think he figured out about us."

"What did he say?"

"He didn't say anything. He looked at me in a fond, sad way."

"Does he want you, too? You're knocking over all the president's men like bowling pins."

"You'll understand when you're middle-aged and powerful, and you're around attractive, intelligent, attentive young women all the time. Powerful men are all the same. The gentlemen just keep their hands to themselves."

He sat up on one elbow and stared at the Grateful Dead poster on his bedroom wall. "When I'm middle-aged and powerful," he said, "the only woman I'll be looking at fondly is you."

"Superlative answer," she said. "Gotta go."

Mitch rolled out of bed and pulled on his pajama bottoms. He got the *Los Angeles Times* from outside his front door and started a pot of coffee and spread the paper open on the kitchen table.

Bill Boyarsky, the veteran political correspondent, had a news analysis about the ambivalence of Ronald Reagan's supporters toward Nixon's improved prospects for acquittal in the U.S. Senate. As Republicans, they claimed they wanted Nixon to win, but as conservatives, they were deeply frustrated because he had never met a communist or a big-government program he didn't like. A few of the authorities Boyarsky consulted were honest enough to admit that Nixon's demise would discredit his moderate philosophy and help conservatives seize control of the party once and for all. While Howard Morton wasn't quoted, Mitch could smell him and his minions lurking behind references to "veteran observers" and "Reagan insiders."

Mitch had just put on the Rolling Stones' "Sticky Fingers," thrown open the curtains and patio doors, and started to make the bed when the phone rang again. He picked it up in the kitchen. "Well, hello," he said brightly.

A male voice said, "I'm calling about our meeting. Are you still interested?"

Mitch grabbed a pen and paper. "Just tell me where." He listened for a moment. The man mentioned the name of a southern California bar, about an hour's drive from his apartment. Staring at the phone hanging on the wall, Mitch said, "You're kidding me."

Mitch's contact wasn't kidding. He got to the front gate a little before 5 p.m., as instructed. In exchange for directions to his ultimate destination, he offered the book of ride coupons that came with his admission ticket to the first teenager he saw.

He made his way down Main Street and around the Sleeping Beauty Castle toward Bear Country. He remembered reading that Ron Ziegler had worked here once, as a Jungle Boat pilot. What was it with Republicans and Disneyland? Mitch thought it must've been the way the place appealed to their fetishes for attractive young people, slavishly cheerful customer service, and excellent sanitation. Half the employees were picking up candy wrappers.

His instructions were to order something at the Mile-Long Bar, which had mirrors at either end. Mitch, who had never been there, thought it should be the Forever Bar, since the reflections were at least theoretically infinite. Mitch nursed a root beer and thought about telling whomever he was meeting that they should either grow up or see a shrink.

Then a tall, gangly, tan young man with curly blond hair appeared at his right elbow. He looked about 18. He was wearing khaki slacks, a white polo shirt, and boat shoes. "Follow me," he whispered.

They left the bar and walked past the Wilderness Outpost to a bench that was about as secluded as a bench could be in a theme park on a Friday evening. The kid sat down and put the briefcase he was carrying on his lap. Mitch said, "So did Howard put you up to this?"

The man looked around and then opened the briefcase and motioned to the seat next to him. After Mitch sat, he saw that the briefcase contained a portable cassette player. It had a single earplug. The man handed it to Mitch, who hesitated for a moment and then put it in his right ear.

The man pushed the play button. Mitch heard a voice he didn't recognize. He glared at the young man. "That's not even Nixon," he said, starting to hand back the earplug. "I don't have time for this."

"Just keep listening," the kid said.

Mitch did. The voice, now vaguely familiar, continued. *One day the buzzer goes off, and I go into the president's office, and he's sitting there with Haldeman.* After a few more seconds, Mitch swore quietly. He was listening to the end of the Nixon presidency.

19

Talk About the Weather

It had been chilly in Washington, and on Sunday morning, September 20, it was raining hard. A few dozen congregants, most wearing their raincoats for the first time in months, had hurried up the front steps of Holy Trinity in Georgetown for the early service. With its classical pediment and four massive Ionic columns, the building seemed mythic, more like the Parthenon than a parish church. Some members still remembered when Jack and Jackie Kennedy had come to mass when they were in town, beautiful, tragic young divines submitting to the humility of worship and prayer.

Frank and Anne Szabados usually enjoyed walking to church from their brownstone near Washington Square. Frank had broached the idea of staying home because of the weather, but Anne, who had otherwise been quiet all morning, had insisted. They got a cab to the church, ran up the steps, and found a pew near the back.

The air in the monumental nave was warm and damp and, once mass began, thick with incense. As they sat, Anne slid a few inches further away from him than she otherwise would have. She was wearing plaid wool slacks and a black turtleneck sweater. Her black hair was pinned up and covered with a silk scarf, as her mother had taught her when they went to church in Saigon. She sat with her legs crossed, self-contained and separate, busy marking the scripture readings and songs in her missal and hymn book.

Frank sighed to himself. Their short weekend wasn't starting well. They'd both worked all day Saturday. He was routinely at the White House six days a week. Anne was working horrendous hours as a member of a task force at the World Bank that was conducting an emergency study of the impact on global financial markets of the dizzying spike in oil prices that had followed the Arabs' 1973 embargo.

Since they didn't have pets or children, their small talk was about energy policy and Soviet adventurism. On Saturdays they usually went to dinner and sometimes a movie. But last night, Frank had gotten home too late. They'd hardly spoken. She said she was tired, but it was more than that. He was sure he understood why she was angry. But there was nothing more to say. He'd finally left her with her book in the living room and gone to bed.

As they watched from their pew, a young British Jesuit, standing behind the broad marble altar wearing a white cassock alb and a green stole around his neck, pronounced absolution. With his accent, he sounded like a Canterbury Anglican. The couple were still getting used to hearing church services conducted in English. In Hungary and Brooklyn, Frank had grown up with the Latin mass. Anne was a teenager in Saigon at the time of Vatican II, when the church first permitted the use of the local vernacular. So she had at least known what the ancient incantations sounded like in her own language.

At the moment the priest made a flamboyant sign of the cross with his right hand, Anne nudged Frank with his elbow. "You should go to confession," she whispered without looking at him.

Frank felt his cheeks color. He was surprised she was still so upset. It's true that she'd told him she was scared that he'd end up in jail or worse. Anyone in Saigon or Budapest who did what he was doing stood a good chance of getting himself shot. He'd done his best to reassure her that such things didn't happen in the United States. But now, she was upping the stakes. Frank assumed she wanted to make sure he realized that even though he'd ignored her warnings, he couldn't hide his reckless behavior from God.

She'd made a point to call him out at the climax of the penitential rite, which occurred at the beginning of the mass. Protestants read their confessions out of a book and got a handy blanket absolution that at least theoretically accounted for every transgression, from masturbation to murder. The cops might still have something to say, or your mother when she did the laundry, but at least you were off the hook with God Almighty. But for Catholics, the general absolution during mass didn't cover mortal sins. For actions you planned and carried out knowing full well that they would offend against heaven and your neighbor, you had to go to confession.

As far as his wife was concerned, one example of a mortal sin was if you were stealing top-secret documents and smuggling them out of the White House so that the disgraced, constitutionally incapacitated president could interfere with the lawful conduct of U.S. foreign policy. Anne wanted him to come back that afternoon or before work on Monday and sit in a booth and tell a stranger behind a mesh screen a story the church could sell to the *New York Times* for 50 years' worth of altar wine and wafers.

When they stood to say the Our Father, Frank reached for her hand. She let him, but her grip was tepid. She kept her eyes on the altar.

Frank thought the situation was far more ambiguous. Wasn't the defense of Anne's country a higher good than slavishly observing rules and regulations about the handling of paperwork? Besides, he doubted that when it came to the Vietnam war, the left-wing Jesuits who ran Holy Spirit parish could be counted on to respect the confidentiality of the confessional. He'd also heard enough homilies excoriating the Nixon administration to know that he would get more than ten Hail Marys for his penance. Just for starters, they'd tell him to cease his secret meetings with Satan.

Anne let go of his hand when they passed the peace. They smiled at the strangers around them and shook their hands. "The peace of Christ," everyone said. After they sat down again, Ann took hold of her missal with both hands and crossed her legs again. Frank kept his hands to himself for the rest of the service.

He hadn't even given Nixon that much information yet. Yesterday he'd photocopied about 20 pages of Henry Kissinger's memos and reports to Ford, using both sides of the page. Folded in half, the packet was just thin enough that he could put it in the inside breast pocket of his suit jacket without causing a perceptible bulge as he sauntered through the gate just before lunchtime. He had met Nixon again at the Eisenhowers' apartment and sat opposite him in his usual chair while the president put on his reading glasses and scanned his haul of purloined records.

"More treaty violations by the north," Nixon said, flipping the pages.

"Also by the south," Frank said.

Nixon didn't respond. He kept reading. He marked a few passages with his fountain pen. When he was finished, he dropped the documents on top of the legal pad on his lap, took off his glasses, and began to chew on one of the earpieces. He stared into space for a moment and then looked at Frank. "I can see what Henry's doing," he said. "When Hanoi attacks, he won't want us to respond, but he's not telling Ford that in so many words. He's preparing the ground, the way he does. Do you agree?"

Frank said, "He stresses growing congressional opposition to any U.S. aid to Saigon, especially because of– " He hesitated.

"Say it," Nixon said sharply. "Because of Watergate." He flicked his glasses in Frank's direction, a gesture of absolution of his own. "Henry tried to get me to bomb again last March and April, when the communists tested us," he said. "They knew I'd squandered my advantage, that I couldn't make it stick in Congress." He paused and looked away. "Besides, I was spending all my time trying to save my own skin," he said.

"'It's even worse now," Frank said. "Except for a few diehard Republicans, there's almost no support in Congress for helping Saigon."

Nixon closed his eyes. He knew how bad it was, whose fault it was, why the country had a non-president president. In his two months in the White House, if something didn't absolutely have to be done, Gerald Ford hadn't done it. His major initiatives had been to sign the Forest and Rangeland Renewable Resources Act and declare August 26 as Women's Equity Day.

He'd been especially reticent when it came to foreign policy. He'd sent word to the King of Jordan suggesting he put off a state visit to Washington in August, declined an invitation to address the UN General Assembly in September, and postponed visits to Japan and the Soviet Union scheduled for November that Nixon and Kissinger had been planning for months.

Nixon, who would probably have been outraged if Ford had been more assertive, was now irritated that Ford was being so passive. Pundits and academic experts by and large didn't like Nixon but urged Ford to act like a caretaker. Nixon despised pundits and academics and anyone who listened to them.

"The hell with the Congress," Nixon said. "Leaders lead."

"Not without the authority conferred by voters," Frank said.

"Ford's authority is conferred by the Constitution," Nixon said.

Frank shook his head. "It's temporary, and it's almost totally constrained."

"So you don't think he'll act when Hanoi makes its move?"

Frank said, "Politically, he can't. But he has to anyway, for the sake of 60,000 dead Americans and 20 million Vietnamese."

"Why can't he?" Nixon said, twirling his glasses. "You can't impeach an acting president. Do you agree?"

"But I wonder if the Pentagon would even follow Ford's order to mount a counterstrike."

Nixon stared at him. "Because?" he said.

"He'd be acting without either congressional or electoral support. The brass would be afraid that if the operation failed, they'd get all the blame."

Nixon scowled. "I had Congress and public opinion with me when I went to China," he said, "but the Pentagon didn't like it, so they planted spies in the White House." He sucked on his glasses. "You know who's sicced spies on me this time?" Frank shook his head. Nixon said, "Son-of-a-bitching Ronald Reagan."

"How do you know?"

Grinning without a glimmer of joy, Nixon said, "The *Washington Post* told me."

By the time church was over, the rain had stopped. Frank and Anne could see blue sky poking through the clouds, so they decided to walk home. The first fallen leaves of autumn, soaked and flattened into daubs of yellow, brown, and red, spotted the old, uneven concrete. The sun glinted in the windows of Georgetown's historic townhouses as they walked along. A few people had opened their flues and lit fires, sweetening the brisk air.

After they'd gone half a block, Anne reached for his hand. A block later, he put his arm around her. She leaned her head against his shoulder. When he looked down, he saw that she was crying.

He stopped and put his hands on the sides of her face and wiped the tears from her cheeks with his thumbs. "Tell me what's wrong," he said.

"My father called last night," she said quietly. "Before you came home. I wanted to tell you, but I couldn't. I was too angry."

He had a horrible premonition that her bad mood hadn't really been the result of his stolen documents, that he would have something more to confess. He said, "What did he say?"

"He asked me about the weather," she said, laying her head against his chest. "I said it was cold and that it was supposed to rain all night. He said, 'I envy you. In Saigon this year, autumn has come at a snail's pace'."

She stared up at Frank, who didn't grasp what had happened at first. Then he remembered the signal they'd agreed on about the man from Hanoi who had risked his life to send a message to Richard Nixon.

She said bitterly, "They can't say that nobody died at Watergate anymore," because Nguyen, her cousin, was probably gone.

20

Who's Howard?

Mitch sat at his kitchen table, staring at his Radio Shack cassette recorder. He'd played the five-minute recording a half-dozen times since Friday evening. It still astonished him. He was the custodian of evidence that had eluded congressional and federal prosecutors for months. The tape proved that Nixon was personally responsible for Watergate's most notorious abuses of the electoral process.

All he had to do was get it to the right reporter at the right paper, and Nixon would be finished. The public wouldn't tolerate his refusal to resign. His support in the Senate would disappear. He'd scurry back to California, leaving the wreckage of his presidency for the hapless Gerald Ford to clean up. It would be just the outcome Reagan's fellows wanted.

The phone rang again. Mitch didn't answer. It was Howard Morton. He'd called every 15 minutes since leaving his second message on Mitch's answering machine, demanding to know what had happened in the meeting. This was Sunday evening, two days after the meeting at Disneyland. Morton liked his reports as soon as they were available. Mitch had decided to make him wait.

He went to the refrigerator and got a bottle of Miller High Life and wandered into the living room. It was dark and quiet. He wondered what Emily would think of his décor, a prosperous young bachelor's juxtaposition of a few expensive pieces with dorm room leftovers like his bricks-and-boards bookshelves and rock star posters. He had just one lamp, which sat on a table next to the big black leather easy chair he used for reading and watching TV. On the wall over the matching couch was a framed print of a highly impressionistic Peter Max painting showing Jimi Hendrix with fire shooting out of the headstock of his guitar.

His second-floor apartment had patio doors that opened onto a little balcony looking out over Tiverton Ave. He stepped outside into the cool evening.

As he stood drinking, the phone stopped ringing. He should just call Howard back and tell him. He'd be the hero of the hour and on the fast track for a top job in Reagan's '76 campaign and probably the White House.

But all that could wait. He was entitled to savor the moment. All weekend, he'd enjoyed the privileged status of being the only person in the world who knew what the next couple of weeks held for the United States. He looked down on the street. No pedestrians. Just a few cars glided by. It felt as peaceful as a battlefield at dawn. While the armies were converging, all you could hear were the songs of crickets and birds.

Besides, at their last meeting Howard had actually wondered if Mitch would complete his assignment. Let him stew a little longer.

When he finally heard it, Howard would love the back story. Mitch's mysterious source, the author of Nixon's final destruction, was a pathetic 18-year-old kid from San Diego, Biff Michaels. Biff was short for Bradford. He lived in the ULA dorms with a Georgian named Parker. They were rushing the same fraternity, Delta Phuc Phace or some goddamned thing. Mitch could never keep all the houses straight, whether at Georgetown or in LA. Besides, he couldn't stand the frats' Jim Crow segregation, bogus secret rituals, binge drinking, and caveman disrespect for women.

Yet Greek life persisted as one of the ways the ruling class sifted and sorted young elites. For their own distinct reasons, Biff and Parker had desperately wanted to pledge Delta Psi Cho. Because only one of them had impressed the pledge committee, Mitch was in possession of the ultimate secret about Richard Nixon.

As Biff told the story, Parker was an infant politico, a prodigy who'd caught the bug when he was five. He'd first volunteered for Nixon when he ran for president in 1968, riding his bike around his Atlanta neighborhood and leaving literature and bumper stickers under people's windshield wipers. He hung around Nixon-Agnew headquarters, cheerfully making himself useful to overworked paid staffers who were only about ten years older than he. He joined the Teenage Republicans in high school and signed up for the Young Republicans his first day on campus at ULA.

Mitch thought Parker sounded enough like the younger Mitch that he could understand how Parker's contacts and temperament had helped him work the system at the fraternity. They wanted members who were going to matter on campus, and Parker had looked like a better bet than Biff, a surfer with a C average who smoked a lot of pot, listened to Steve Miller records, and probably got into ULA because his father was a notable alumnus and big contributor.

On the Saturday night in pledge week, Biff and Parker went to a beer-drenched reception at Delta Dip Pshit's stately house that featured some of its most distinguished alumni members. These happened to include Garrett McCann, Nixon's personal aide and coordinator of dirty tricks for the 1972 campaign. A federal jury had convicted him of perjury in the spring. On his way to spending 18 months on Terminal Island, he had decided to let his Brylcreemed hair down at the old frat.

Sitting with Mitch on the bench at Disneyland, Biff said, "McCann's exactly what Parker wants to be."

"He's doing federal time," Mitch said. "Parker might set his sights a teeny-weeny bit higher."

"Just the opposite, man," Biff said, shaking his head. "At the party, he went right up and introduced himself and talked about working on both Nixon campaigns. You could tell the guys from the fraternity were impressed. McCann kind of pretended he knew him and said that they must have been at the same events during the campaign, all this crap you wouldn't believe."

Biff squirmed in his seat. His knees bobbed up and down nervously. "You should've seen the way Parker looked at him, like he was some kind of a god," he said. "The guy already looks like my fucking dad. He's super clean cut and had on a suit and tie on Saturday night at this stinking dump of a fraternity."

"It was probably a sport coat and slacks," Mitch said.

"Everybody's staring at them with their mouths hanging open," Biff said, looking at Mitch and blinking his eyes. "I figure that if they're comparing Parker with me, now I'm totally hosed. My dad didn't pledge a fraternity. He didn't have to. He was always smart, and he got into his first choice medical school." Biff rubbed his eyes and looked away. "He said I was a terminal screwup and that only a frat could straighten me out."

Mitch felt bad for the kid, but jeez. "Tell me about the tape," he said.

"McCann was going to give a little speech and answer questions about Nixon, so we go into the living room," Biff said. "Parker and I are in chairs right in front of the stereo. He sees they've got the same tape deck he has. One side plays, the other records. There're some blank tapes right on top of the machine, and the microphone's plugged in. Maybe they record their secret meetings. So he slips a tape in and records everything Garrett McCann says. He says he wants a souvenir of his brush with greatness. Nobody's paying any attention. Everybody's either drunk or crushing on McCann."

Wanting to speed the story along, Mitch said, "So you stole it, and now you're giving it to me, because you hate his guts. I don't blame you. How did you find me?"

"Parker's got all these political contacts, and somebody told him to be careful, that there was somebody around town looking for dirt on Nixon. He wrote your name down. I think he was going to save it in case he ever wanted to ask for a job. I got your number from the phone book. I'm not even sure what McCann's saying. But Parker said Nixon's enemies would love it. Because of the dirty tricks, he said."

"So you're getting even with Parker by screwing Nixon," Mitch said.

Biff stared at the sidewalk in front of him, where Mitch noticed an empty Milk Duds box. Somebody should tell Walt and have the teenager responsible hurled off the pinnacle of the Matterhorn. "I hope I'm getting even with Garrett McCann," Biff muttered, "the son my father didn't have."

"Nicely played," Mitch had said, patting the kid on his knee. "You're actually better at this than your former roommate."

Mitch finished his beer, closed the patio door, and went back to the kitchen. The phone was ringing again, right on schedule. He got another beer, sat down at the kitchen table again, and pressed play on the tape machine.

Once more he heard McCann's voice, now unmistakable above the sounds of guys talking and laughing in the other room: "One day the buzzer goes off, and I go into the president's office, and he's sitting there with Haldeman. And they say, 'Do you know—' – by they, Bob says it, the president's sitting there – 'Do you know anyone who can do Dick Tuck-type stuff? We should have someone like that'."

The president's sitting there. That was the killer. Nixon was obsessed with Dick Tuck, the Democratic trickster who'd dogged his early campaigns. His most famous prank was when Nixon campaigned in LA's Chinatown in 1962. Some kids were holding signs purportedly saying "welcome" in Chinese. Thanks to Tuck, one sign read, "What about the Hughes loan?", a reference to a controversial payment that industrialist Howard Hughes had made to Nixon's brother Donald.

But Nixon had denied playing a direct role in setting up a dirty tricks apparatus in the White House. He claimed that Haldeman, McCann, and others who had undertaken these and Nixon's even more notorious operations had been overzealous. His error, Nixon said, was not setting a high enough moral standard.

But there he was, McCann now claimed, sitting in the Oval Office listening to Haldeman give the order and applying the commander-in-chief's imprimatur by his presence.

The first smoking gun, about Nixon's role in the Watergate cover-up, had driven Nixon from the White House. Mitch was pretty sure this one would create an immediate vacancy at Jackson Place.

Mitch shook his head, sat back, and drained his second beer. Dick Tuck hadn't caused Nixon to lose the 1962 election, and dirty tricks didn't help him win in 1972. Too bad there hadn't been anyone around with the guts to tell Nixon to leave the politics to the grownups and confine himself to kissing communists on all four cheeks and spending the taxpayers' money.

The phone rang again. "Fuck it," Mitch said. He stood and picked it up and said, "I'm here. For Christ's sake, Howard."

"Who's Howard?" Emily said.

21

The Other One

Nguyen's death blew Frank's cover. Anne Szabados saw to it.

As soon as he returned from Saigon, Frank had wanted to tell Henry Kissinger about his father-in-law and their meeting with Nguyen. He thought he and Gerald Ford were entitled to know that the bombing campaigns in 1972 had rattled Hanoi and convinced the Soviets that the U.S. would refuse to let Saigon go down the tubes.

But Nixon had resisted. He said it wouldn't make any difference, because when it came to Vietnam, domestic politics always prevailed. Besides, they'd have to reveal their own secret meetings, to which Nixon had become considerably attached. He had told Frank somewhat mysteriously that the right time to tell Ford would come.

It wasn't what Nixon had meant, but the moment came when Anne said that they were going to Saigon to see her parents. She told Frank that she's bought the tickets already. He should be packed by Monday afternoon. He couldn't very well call in sick again, and she forbade him to manufacture another rationale for his absence. So on Sunday afternoon and evening, he wrote a long memo to Kissinger revealing his work for Nixon, his and Ty's conversation in the village of Ham Tan, and Nguyen's death.

Then he called Nixon and asked if they could meet at the Eisenhowers' on Monday at lunchtime. When Nixon asked why, Frank decided he should use the same code words as Ty and Anne. "For me, Sundays always seem to move at a snail's pace," he said, feeling vaguely ridiculous.

Nixon's response was impatient. "What?" Then he was silent. "I see," he said, pausing again. "I'm sorry. I'll see you tomorrow." He hung up without waiting for a response. Nixon hadn't mentioned Nguyen, either. Did he really think someone was listening to his calls? Frank remembered Nixon's warning about Al Haig and his friends at the Pentagon and felt a chill.

"I suppose you're going to tell Kissinger," Nixon said the next day as they sat behind their TV trays. Their egg salad sandwiches, chips, and milk remained untouched while they talked.

"Anne wants to be with her parents," Frank said. "I can't let her go alone." He stood up and handed Nixon the memo.

Nixon put on his glasses and read it quickly. "I see you mention bringing me the documents," he said, flipping the pages. "Henry won't care. They didn't tell me anything I hadn't already guessed, anyway. I know him so well." He finished reading, tucked the memo under the plate on his TV table, and began to worry his bottom lip with the earpiece of his glasses. After a moment, he said, "Your report won't make any difference. Do you agree?"

Frank nodded. "I'm sure Mr. Ford and Dr. Kissinger won't care that we still have the military advantage. Congress and the media have the political advantage, and for them, the war's over."

Nixon smiled mirthlessly and said, "Congress wants the communists to win."

"Some members think they deserve to."

"Even though we have the means to prevent it," Nixon said, clenching a fist. "Even though hitting the sons of bitches hard one more time will stop them."

Frank paused and said, "It's been a long war, Mr. President."

Nixon stared at him. "Now you're sounding discouraged," he said. He paused and said, "It's got to be rough with your wife."

"She hadn't seen him since she was a little girl, just before the partition in 1954. But she feels responsible for what happened."

"Because she married you," Nixon said quietly. "Because you helped me."

"She looks at the situation in Vietnam pretty much the way we do," he said. "But she says I engaged in an unauthorized intelligence operation that I wasn't remotely qualified for. We had no security or backup. It obviously got Nguyen killed. Now she's afraid her father's in danger."

"And maybe you as well," Nixon said. Frank didn't answer. "Do you know what happened?"

"No."

"When do you leave?"

"Tonight."

Nixon fidgeted in his chair. He fumbled with his reading glasses. "Do you need any money?" he said. "For the plane and so on and so forth. We don't have much, with the legal fees and all the rest. But we can help if you want."

The intimacy of Nixon's awkward gesture took Frank by surprise. He was usually relentlessly unsentimental. He thanked him and declined. Leaving the apartment, he stopped by the White House and left his memo for Kissinger with a cover note saying he'd be gone for a week on personal business in connection with a death in his wife's family. The details, he said, were in the memo. He was tempted to clean out his desk before he left but decided not to give in completely to pessimism about Kissinger's reaction to his disloyalty.

Late that afternoon, they flew from Washington Dulles to Charles de Gaulle airport in Paris, where they got a flight to Saigon. They arrived at dinnertime Tuesday and took a cab to Anne's parents' bungalow. By the time they got to the front door with their luggage, Ty and An were framed in the open doorway, waiting.

An had laid out a light supper on the kitchen table. They took their plates into the living room and sat with them on their laps. They talked about the flight and the food, Anne's work at the World Bank, An's views on Saigon traffic, when Frank and Anne planned to give them grandchildren, everything but the tragedy that had brought them together. Ty and An's sense of proportion, their always waiting for the fitting time, struck Frank as being very old European. From his first evening in their home on his second date with their daughter, he had made a point to try to reciprocate their poise and delicacy. For all he knew, they thought he was very Vietnamese.

While the women cleared the table and did the dishes, Ty led the way to his study, which opened off the living room. He collected books about the U.S. Civil War. Frank had given him a copy of Abraham Lincoln's collected works. These shared space with crosses and icons and stacks of Vietnamese manuscripts and Defense ministry documents.

Ty paused to let Frank enter and then closed the door behind them. A long window overlooked the street. Ty closed it and lowered a blind made of bamboo. His reading chair and lamp were in front of the window, but he motioned toward his small desk, which faced into the room from an inside wall. Ty took the chair behind the desk, Frank a small chair facing it.

"Are you and mom in danger?" Frank said.

Ty wore a patterned silk shirt and khaki slacks. With his slender, well-manicured hands, he was fussing on his crowded but orderly desktop with books, papers, notepads, pens, and an antique letter opener that looked like a samurai sword. Without looking at Frank, he shrugged. "The Viet Cong are not very strong in Saigon anymore," he said.

"Still." Ty didn't respond. Frank said, "Can you tell me what happened?"

"I got a message from his sister," Ty said. "My brother's other child. She called someone, and they called me, the way families do between north and south. Nguyen's minister sent him on a mission outside of Hanoi, to visit Russian engineers who were working on a dam project. It must have seemed odd, since he was an analyst who spent most of his time reading and writing. He never got there. They found him two days later, buried in a ditch."

He paused and stared at his son-in-law and said, "They bound him head to toe and buried him alive." Frank closed his eyes and shook his head. "Please don't tell Anne," Ty said. "I told her mother that he was shot, that it was fast."

"So someone saw us in the restaurant," Frank said.

"It could be they learned he was an anti-communist, or always knew," Ty said with a shrug. "Perhaps he was noticed reading some documents he shouldn't have. The timing suggests a connection with our meeting."

Frank leaned forward. "It wasn't for nothing," he said. "I've told Dr. Kissinger what Nguyen told us. He'll tell Ford."

Ty shook his head. "It won't make any difference," he said.

Frank said, "That's just what Nixon says."

Ty picked up the letter opener and stood it on its point, putting two fingers on the handle to hold it in place. "Even when Nixon was strong, few of us in the government believed that the United States would continue to take risks for us once your troops were gone," he said. "When he bombed Hanoi he was trying to impress his friends, not his enemies. He was telling us that he was willing to withstand savage attacks by his political opponents to continue to support us."

"And now it appears, at least to you, that they defeated him," Frank said. "I know you appreciate that Watergate is more complicated than that."

Ty set down the letter opener and laid it along the edge of the desk. "Be that as it may," he said, "who else would have done what your Mr. Nixon did? Who else will?"

Frank said, "You're discouraged, too."

"It's not complicated, my son," Ty said, just a little curtly. "The Russians are increasing their military aid to Hanoi. Year by year, your Congress is cutting aid to Saigon. When the next offensive comes, the one my nephew promised, your ally will run out of bullets after six months."

"I'm sorry," Frank said.

"I'm glad you met Nguyen," Ty said in a softer voice. "It helps you understand that every Vietnamese wants one Vietnam, free of foreign interference. More and more, people assume it will and even should be a communist Vietnam. It's partly Mr. Nixon's fault. A leader's disgrace discredits his friends and his causes. Besides, we're not a model democracy."

"You sound almost resigned to the fall of South Vietnam."

"Not resigned, but prepared." Ty glanced away for a moment, as though he was embarrassed. "We would have to leave," he said. "As Catholics associated with the regime, we'd be marked first."

A sudden mental image of his in-laws bound and buried in a ditch terrified Frank. 'Then you'd come live with us," he said, extending his hand across the desk. Ty took it. They were surprised to find that they both had tears in their eyes.

Frank was struck by the miraculous irony of a Hungarian refugee promising sanctuary to a Vietnamese in-law. It was doubly ironic since it appeared that America was on the brink of an epic failure. Somehow it had squandered the high ground in Indochina. Maybe it had failed to appreciate Vietnam's hunger for unity. Maybe it had fought too ruthlessly or, as Frank believed, not ruthlessly enough. When Nixon had taken the war up Hanoi's front steps in 1972, victory was in reach. But then the politics of Watergate had rendered him impotent.

Frank was an honest cold warrior. He had yearned to stop Hanoi in order to thwart and embarrass Moscow. He wanted freedom for South Vietnam, too, especially now, because of Anne and her family. But he knew how he'd feel if the great powers had fought over Hungary. Most Vietnamese noticed that the superpowers hadn't chosen European countries for their proxy wars. So millions of them had come to hate foreigners, whether French, Russian, or American, more than they hated communism or capitalism.

Ty stared back at Frank and tightened his grip for a moment. He knew his people would miss the Americans after enduring the vengeance of Hanoi's war-hardened Stalinists. He feared for friends in government and the military whose daughters hadn't married as well as his had.

Frank and Ty had just released each other's hands when the telephone on the desk rang. Ty answered it. His eyes widened and fixed on Frank. "Yes, sir," he said, standing up. "One moment, please." He handed the receiver across the desk. "It's the president," he said in a whisper.

"How did Nixon get your number?" Frank said, standing and reaching for the phone.

"Your country's government is very confusing," he said with a smile. "It's the other one."

22

The Same Chair

Mitch Botstein hadn't worn his three-piece charcoal grey suit since he graduated from Georgetown. He'd been exercising to impress Emily, so it felt loose. Soaked through with sweat, sticking to his back and thighs, but loose.

To impress Emily. His heart seemed to clench like a fist when he thought of her.

A Filipino in a white uniform had poured him a cup of coffee. He drank without tasting it. He hadn't had any breakfast, and it made his stomach sour.

According to the antique clock on the wall, it was 8:15 a.m. Nobody had said a word for thirty seconds or so. In the silence, the clock ticked louder than Charlie Watts.

Mitch sat back in his chair, with his legs crossed. He hoped he looked calmer than he felt. He had promised himself that he wouldn't let the White House intimidate him. The buildings and offices, though power-saturated, did not. But he hadn't been prepared for how it would feel to have the undivided attention of Len Garment, the White House counsel, and Richard Nixon's aide Ron Ziegler.

He didn't know it, but he was using the chair Emily Weissman had on the night of August 8, after Nixon's speech. She'd sat there many times since. If she'd left a hint of her perfume on the polished maple arms, he wasn't consciously aware of it. He was thinking about her all the time anyway. She hadn't returned his calls since Sunday night. Was she in her office, which had to be just a couple of doors away? So near and suddenly so impossibly far.

Ziegler was again at the left, and Garment was behind his desk. They had been listening to Biff Michaels' tape from the fraternity party. Len had his elbows planted on either side of a portable cassette deck, looming over it like a basset hound with his supper dish. Exhaustion and anxiety had sharpened the wrinkles in his long face. He was on his third cigarette.

Mitch glanced at the giant Duke Ellington photo behind Garment's desk. On a better day, he'd have asked about Garment's days as a clarinet and sax player in a big band. But it appeared that the days were only going to get worse.

Ziegler was slumped in his chair. With his fingertips he casually dangled and twirled a bone china coffee cup bearing the presidential seal. The stewards had left a full pot of coffee on a side table, but Ziegler hadn't had any. Mitch studied the circles under his eyes. He didn't look like drinking coffee was his problem.

Garment said, "We should listen again."

"Why, for chrissakes?" Ziegler said. "Unless you're going to erase it, in which case let me get Rose or Al Haig over here. They're the experts on destroying evidence." He looked with disgust at Mitch. "I assume you've made copies," he said. Mitch didn't answer. He'd made three. Before he left for Washington, he'd given one to momma and asked her to put it somewhere safe. The other two were in his briefcase.

Garment pushed the button. Mitch had heard it a dozen times now. McCann talked about how he could understand why people thought Nixon ought to be working on world peace instead of setting up dirty tricks. But no: *The president's sitting there.*

"He's lying," Ziegler said.

"Why would he lie?" Garment said.

"He can say he was just following Nixon's orders," he said.

"It's not what he told the special prosecutor or the Senate committee," Garment said. "He didn't say it at his trial. He said that the order came from Haldeman. He could've avoided jail by giving them Nixon."

"Maybe he was trying to impress the trust fund babies at ULA," Ziegler said, "Garrett says the conversation occurred in the president's office. Did the taping system pick it up?"

"Apparently not," Garment said, "but maybe the meeting happened sometime before the system was installed."

Mitch felt overlooked. Looking back and forth between the two men, he said, "Do you think anyone hearing this tape will believe that Nixon didn't order the dirty tricks?"

They stared at him. "I didn't hear anyone address the sniveling little scumbag," Ziegler said.

Mitch turned to Ziegler. "I'm not responsible for your latest scandal," he said, "and if it weren't for me, you wouldn't even know about it."

Garment took a long drag on his cigarette and looked at Mitch with an expression that made Ziegler's seem friendly. He looked with the narrowed eyes of a blood enemy. "If it weren't for Emily," he said. "So fuck you."

Mitch knew why Garment enjoyed insulting him. Mitch didn't think Garment would ever try to sleep with her, and she'd never sleep with him, because he was married and a hundred years old. But Mitch knew how men were. Garment hated that he had her. Now, it appears, he didn't, which is why Mitch thought he could see a glint of triumph in Garment's eyes.

Who's Howard?" That's what she had asked Sunday night.

She already knew. She had just wanted to see what he said.

"Nobody," he'd said. "Just a friend."

She was silent for a moment. "Nobody," she said in her quiet, small voice. He instantly knew that he'd broken her heart. Before he could speak, she did, in a cold, distant manner he hadn't experienced before. Someday it would be her courtroom voice. "We found out last week that Governor Reagan's people have secretly recruited Emmett Walsh to persuade senators to vote to convict," she said.

Mitch misjudged again. "I swear to God I don't know anything about that," he said.

"But Howard Morton does," she said, "because he's the one who's yanking Walsh's chain. That took us about an hour and a half to figure out."

Mitch didn't answer. He couldn't think of what to say.

"Then we heard that Morton has another operative in the field, trying to find dirt on President Nixon," she said. "They say this one's a real piece of work. We didn't have the name yet, but we were on the verge. But the way this person was described, I never imagined, even for a moment..." Her voice broke.

"Emily—"

"You made it sound like you were taking polls and writing memos," she said. "You're a disgusting spy and saboteur. That's why you were lurking outside my house. I should've listened to my first instinct when I found out you lied to my friend. What's your assignment? To see what the gullible woman said while you were fucking her?"

"Please, just—"

But she had hung up. When the phone rang yet again ten minutes later, he was sitting in the living room with the lamp turned off, staring into space. He walked back to the kitchen and picked it up and said the only word he would ever use from that night forward when answering the telephone.

"Hello?" he said while sitting down at the kitchen table. He rested his head in his hands.

This time it was Leonard Garment. "I'm calling on behalf of the acting president of the United States," he said, "who asks personally if you are enough of a patriot to consult with us before taking any further action that would be detrimental to the interests of this administration or Richard Nixon."

Mitch closed his eyes and said yes. Garment told him to be in his office by Tuesday morning and hung up.

23

Boneheads

While Mitch was meeting with Garment and Ziegler, Emily Weissman worked behind her desk just two doors away. She'd been in since seven, because yet again, thanks to Richard Nixon, it was panic time in the White House counsel's office.

She'd closed her office door. She didn't want to see Mitch. Wiping her eyes with a tissue and drinking black coffee, she surveyed the surrealistic wreckage spread across her desk.

Her priorities yesterday had been the usual stack of presidential pardon requests and a bulging file containing Richard Nixon's miscellaneous research projects. This morning, before she'd even taken off her raincoat, she'd gathered these and every other nonessential file and document in her arms and slammed them down again on the credenza behind her desk. All that remained before her were an expanding file containing all the information she'd been able to scrape together on Nixon's dirty tricks operation, a transcript of Garrett McCann's speech at the fraternity, a sterling silver tray from the White House mess with a pot of coffee and china cup and saucer, and a box of Kleenex.

For an hour and a half she'd been studying, speaking briefly to colleagues via intercom, muttering to herself, and crying.

They were all such ridiculous boneheads.

For example, Emily's first serious boyfriend was Sean McKenzie, the Cass Tech quarterback their senior year, a tall, lean, blond god of high school. Cass was a prestigious and highly competitive public prep school on Detroit's east side. In that era, it was more famous for

University of Michigan- and Ivy League-bound scholars than for its ath-
letes. In the fall of 1966, Cass went 3-3-1 in football, finishing seventh
out of twelve in its league.

But on a magical Friday night at the end of September, as the
accustomed acrid stink from Ford's River Rouge plant hung over the
stadium, Sean pierced the sky with four towering touchdown passes,
leading the Cass Tech Technicians to a 32-7 victory over last-place
Mumford High.

It was the most exciting game of the season. Emily was in the stands
with her parents and little brother. When she saw Sean Monday afternoon on the way into their pre-calculus class, she poked him in the
side, smiled up at his handsome, surprised face, and said in her high
little voice, "Good game, you big meatball."

To the astonishment of a half-dozen cheerleaders who'd assumed
that one of them would be Sean's first-round pick, he asked her to
dinner and a movie. For two or three months, they went out every
weekend. They had a great time talking about sports and politics. On
Saturday night, they'd get in his silver Pontiac and drive over the bridge
onto Belle Isle, in the middle of the Detroit River. They made out and
talked for hours while listening to the Four Tops and Supremes on the
radio and watching the stately red sign of the Roostertail Club glitter
in the night sky and shimmer atop the coursing black water.

When Sean invited Emily to the winter formal, her mother used
her employee discount at Hudson's to help her buy a sleeveless white
gown. It was fitted and sleek. In high heels, she'd be able to rest the
side of her face against his heart as they slow-danced to "When A Man
Loves A Woman." He was going to borrow his father's black tux and
plaid bow tie. After the dance, he was anticipating going the final six
yards in a cloud of dust. While she hoped to hold the line, she was
also a pragmatist. She really liked Sean, so she knew it was going to be
close.

But then he blew it. On the Sunday afternoon of the weekend
before the formal, they had planned to study together for their world
history final. Her parents would let them use her room in the apartment as long as the door was open. Sidney and Marian trusted her,

146

so they stayed in the living room and kitchen. During their diligent review of the English Reformation, while making sure they didn't confuse Bloody Mary and the Virgin Queen, Emily was looking forward to a squeeze and a kiss or two.

On the morning of their study date, he called and said that he didn't feel well and wanted to stay home. When she heard on Monday from her best friend that he'd spent the afternoon at a bowling alley with his teammates, celebrating the end of the season, she dumped him.

All her friends said she was crazy. He'd made an innocent mistake. He just wasn't quite grown up enough to tell her what he wanted.

But she couldn't stand a liar. And now she was working for Richard Nixon and in love with Mitch Botstein. Emily grinned hopelessly at the contents of her desktop, shook her head, and blew her nose. *I'm calling them boneheads?*

Her phone rang. As she picked it up, she knew who it would be. He always started talking without saying hello. "So the trial starts today," Nixon said. "I feel bad for John and Bob and the rest."

"Yes, sir," she said with studied reserve. It was Tuesday, October 1. Former attorney general John Mitchell, chief of staff Bob Haldeman, and five other Nixon operatives were being tried in federal court for their roles in the Watergate cover-up.

Nixon went right to work trying to figure out why Emily had a certain tone in her voice. "People must be feeling pretty down over there," he said.

"We are," she said, "but not because of the trial."

"Ah," he said. "You mean the McCann matter. Does Len think it's very much of a problem?"

"He looked in on me for a second a half-hour or so ago," she said, "and mentioned that his first thought was that he was in possession of evidence that should be handed over to the special prosecutor."

Nixon now had two reasons to be alarmed. The second was that Emily's tone obviously had to do with more than passing discouragement. But the first reason was more urgent. "I, of course, would not, as it were, advise or recommend that course," he said.

"No, sir."

"It's, ah, just what St. Clair said about the, uh—"

"The smoking gun tape last summer," she said. When Nixon's attorney, Jim St. Clair, had first heard Nixon and Haldeman on the June 23 tape talking about ordering a cover-up, he told his colleagues that if the White House didn't release it to the public, he would. Otherwise, St. Clair said, he could be indicted for concealing evidence.

"You think this is basically the same situation," Nixon said. His comment was meant to elicit Emily's legal opinion as well as discover if her view of him had changed.

She said, "McCann's case was over when he pled guilty. To get leniency from the prosecutors or the court, all he had to do was mention your name. We do feel the tape impinges on your situation."

"I see," Nixon said. Now disliking her tone as well as what she was saying, he continued emotionlessly. "You're thinking it should be given to the prosecutors and the House," he said, "so the impeachment managers can use it in the Senate trial in December."

Emily paused. She knew she was torturing him. "Actually, no," she said.

Nixon's voice brightened. "Really?"

"It was recorded illegally and surreptitiously at a college boozer, and it's a statement by a man who's already been convicted of perjury. If it were true, he presumably would've said it when it really could have helped him and not just while trying to impress drunk, horny teenagers."

"You're goddamned right," Nixon said. "Good thinking." He quickly added, "Of course McCann's lying. It never happened. I have no recollection of being present when Bob gave Garrett the order."

"I understand that is your recollection, sir."

That tone of voice again. Nixon continued, "Although it's reflective, of course, uh, of my, ah, understandable desire at the time, in the view of the savage tactics that had been used against us in the past, to have some, uh—"

Bonehead-in-chief. Emily said, "To have the White House conduct a campaign of candy-ass seventh-grade foolishness because somebody put up fake signs at a Nixon rally 20 years ago." He was silent, and she plunged on. "Mr. President, it doesn't really matter what we do now, anyway. It's all up to Reagan's people." She stopped and waited, but Nixon, stung as he so rarely had been by his obsequious young aides, still said nothing. She said, "If they give it to the press, we're done in a day."

The "we" was what he'd been waiting to hear. Emily hadn't abandoned him, at least not yet. He perked up a little. "The young man that found the tape is a good friend of yours, I understand," he said.

Her answer was indirect. "He came in this morning to see Len and Mr. Ziegler," she said.

Nixon understood. "It's got to be a little tough. Thank you." He hung up.

The tension of the morning, plus speaking truth to Nixon and drinking half a pot of coffee, had gotten to Emily. She had to make a run to the ladies' room. She looked at her watch. It was almost eleven. The meeting had to be over by now. Besides, why should she be a hostage in her own office? She picked up her purse and flung the door open.

Mitch was walking by. He'd just left Garment's office. Ziegler had stayed behind and was still talking quietly to Len. Mitch stopped and stood with his hands in his pockets, looking at her with his soft brown eyes and ingratiating, hangdog smile. She stared at him. She'd imagined this terrible moment and was trying to remember what she had planned to say when a rangy man with thinning blond hair who'd just entered their suite of offices spoke while looking back and forth between Mitch and Emily.

"Excuse me," he said, "but I'm looking for Len Garment."

Emily was relieved to have an alternative to talking to Mitch. Turning to face him, she said, "And you are?" He looked a little familiar. Had she seen him in the White House mess?

Extending his hand, he said, "Frank Szabados from the NSC. Dr. Kissinger wants me to talk to Mr. Garment immediately."

24

One More Thing

Nixon and Ziegler met that afternoon on the third floor of Jackson Place. Washington had gotten hot again. But Nixon hadn't taken off his jacket, so Ziegler didn't, either. Rose Woods and her crew had scared up a small round floor fan and wedged it in one of the windows overlooking Lafayette Square, on the opposite side of the little room where Nixon had his big brown chair and ottoman.

"Rose says you took the little punk to lunch," Nixon said, fiddling anxiously with his reading glasses and adjusting the yellow legal pad in his lap. "Do we know what he's going to do?"

Ziegler had has back to the fan. The air was hot and humid, but it still felt good against his damp neck. If they ever got back to the White House, Ziegler would recommend installing air conditioning in the townhouse. He was unaware that Nixon, who until Sunday night had been reasonably optimistic about his chances of surviving Watergate and returning back across Pennsylvania Ave., had already dictated a memo to Rose telling her to remind him to give the order "when the time comes."

But then they had learned about Mitch's smoking gun, implicating Nixon in personally ordering White House dirty tricks. Ziegler and Garment had spent three hours with Mitch that morning, bullying, threatening, and cajoling. It had all added up to abject begging. Mitch was motivated by ideology rather than any abhorrence of Nixon's ethics, which weren't that much worse than Mitch's. But did he really want to destroy a presidency? Was what they had done in foreign and domestic affairs so abominable that he was willing to put the country through even more agony? What were Reagan's men offering him? What could they offer him instead?

"Nothing," Ziegler said, completing his thought aloud. "We couldn't offer him anything except appeals to his decency."

Nixon looked startled for a moment, wondering how decency could possibly be a factor. Watergate had reignited the civil war that had been simmering inside the Republican Party since the end of World War II. The far right distrusted Nixon even more than the antiwar left did. He was a moderate, a pragmatist, and a traitor to conservatism. Nixon's 1972 landslide had momentarily quieted them, but Watergate provided a promising new opening. They were determined to raise the party of Goldwater and Reagan on his and Gerald Ford's graves. The stakes were so high, and the prize so close at hand, that Nixon knew there was nothing Mitch's handlers wouldn't do to destroy him. "Rotten luck that we got the only conservative Jew in the country," he said. "For the love of Christ, doesn't he realize that the far right hates the Jews even more than I do?"

Zeigler winced. He disliked that kind of talk, and Nixon knew it. In the White House, he had grown used to its going unchallenged. He sometimes took pleasure at his aides' discomfort.

Ziegler once again reminded himself that the rules were a little different in Jackson Place. Nixon could always fire him, but then he'd be talking either to the wall or to Rose, and she wouldn't tolerate him at his worst. Ziegler looked fixedly at Nixon and said, "Botstein told me his mother was the only member of her family to survive the Nazis."

Nixon swatted the air with his reading glasses. "The Holocaust is their excuse for everything," he said.

"This time, we are," Ziegler said. "When I asked him how he could justify his gutter tactics, he asked how we could justify having your advance men use off-duty cops and firefighters to rough up demonstrators at campaign rallies. Just so you follow the analogy, that makes us the brown shirts." Nixon was silent. Ziegler said, "The kid just doesn't like big government. He says it always breeds abuses of power."

Nixon closed his eyes for a moment. Ziegler was so naïve. No statesman ever proclaimed peace and justice at a summit meeting, wearing a $2000 suit and clinking champagne glasses, unless he'd waded up to his chin in a river of shit to get there. "So that's the end," he said. "He's going to leak the McCann tape. He's going to screw us and save the party for the meathead from California."

Ziegler said, "Not necessarily."

Nixon's eyes crinkled at the corner as he tugged at his lip with his eyeglasses. He was smiling as though he'd known all along. "The girl," he said.

"Don't get me wrong," Ziegler said. "He's a determined little bastard. He definitely wants Reagan to take on Ford and win. The effect of the Emily factor may be that he will decide he doesn't want to win this way, entirely irrespective of the fact that she'll never speak to him again if he does."

"Ain't love grand," Nixon said, his eyes drifting off. "The kid does some fornicating and falls in love with America all over again. Let's have a vigorous, honest debate on the issues and some apple pie."

Nixon had just gotten the good news that Mitch Botstein would probably not leak the dirty tricks tape to the newspapers. His reaction seemed ambiguous. He was never one to jump for joy. But Ziegler thought there was something else lurking behind his narrow, cunning eyes. He hesitated and said, "Mr. President, Botstein knows you've been calling her quite a bit. We don't want to risk anyone else finding out about that."

Nixon squirmed in his chair. He looked embarrassed, like a boy caught with a dirty magazine. "On occasion, I have asked her to, ah, check some facts and figures. Research and so forth and so on," he said.

Ziegler said gently, "You might have Rose or me call her instead. Just tell us what you need."

Nixon looked away. "Fine," he said.

"One more thing," Ziegler said. Nixon glared at him. "Are you ready to tell me about Frank Szabados?"

Nixon sank back into the cushions. He looked deflated. Would he lose both his protégés on the same day? "What do you want to know?" he said sullenly.

Jackson Place

"He came to Len's office this morning. He said the acting president and Kissinger had asked him to inquire of the White House counsel about whether he was in trouble for stealing top-secret national security documents and smuggling them to Julie and David's apartment."

Nixon stared at Ziegler. "Is he?" he said.

"Len says not especially, though he wouldn't encourage it in the future."

Nixon said, "You're saying Ford actually saw Frank and listened to what we'd learned about Vietnam?"

"Evidently."

"Score one for the Prince of Darkness," Nixon said. Ziegler thought the old man, behind his thin, tense smile, still looked a little disappointed.

153

PART TWO

November and December 1974

25

Tea in Saigon

The men sitting side by side in big easy chairs with crocheted white armrest covers could have been brothers. Both 63, in the thirty-year saga of the Vietnamese war they were fraternal twins, sometimes friends, other times rivals, linked forever by destiny and a familial sense of purpose.

They were still trim and fit, moving with the assurance of powerful men who enjoyed dominating weaker ones. Vietnam's French colonial rulers, now long gone, had jailed them both for their revolutionary activities. This afternoon, they were caged in a small meeting room on the first floor of Hanoi's old Presidential Palace.

Their quiet meeting space was as plush and pampering as they were lean and hard. Soon after the turn of the 20th century, the French built the palace in the ornate French style to house their colonial governors. When North Vietnam got its independence from France in 1954, Ho Chi Minh, its first president and the revolution's godfather, spurned the building as a monstrosity of colonialism. Until his death in 1969, Ho lived in a traditional Vietnamese stilt house that he built nearby, though he and his ministers and aides used the palace for their meetings and to receive foreign visitors.

Filtered through drawn white floor-to-ceiling curtains, the gentle afternoon light suffusing the room was out of keeping with the intensity of the men's conversation. A servant had brought tea on a tray and left it on a table between their easy chairs. It was lightly scented with lotus. They ignored it.

Over the last few years, defeat had divided Le Duc Tho and Vo Nguyen Giap, diplomat and general. Each had cause to suspect and resent the other. And yet at long last, as they met this afternoon, they believed they were finally planning the beginning of the end of Vietnam's war of national liberation. Even among scarred, cynical warriors, hope has a tendency to mitigate rivalry, at least for the moment. And so they had greeted one another as old friends, with smiles and, after a moment's hesitation, a cautious embrace.

General Giap's face was round and ruddy. He smiled easily, although often insincerely. His handsomer, more polished and emotionally restrained comrade, in a black Mao suit, had let his hair go grey. Giap's, though thin, was slate black. Still Hanoi's minister of defense, he wore a military uniform even though he had lost his battlefield command two years before thanks to the pathetic weaklings on the Politburo, a stinging rebuke in which his unsentimental comrade Le Duc Tho had played a significant role.

Now it looked as though the war criminal Nixon's shame would rescue Giap from his.

The general was internationally famous for organizing North Vietnam's Tet Offensive in January 1968. It was an historic turning point in the battle of wills between a hapless superpower and an artificially divided nation of determined peasants. America's most privileged young people had always understood the folly of Washington's imperialist adventure. They had been protesting for years on their college campuses, proclaiming that they had nothing against the Vietnamese people and refusing to go fight and kill them.

Then Tet awakened the masses in America to Vietnam's righteous anger. The day the attacks began, tens of millions of contented petit bourgeois switched on their Sears and Roebuck color television sets, settled in front of their TV dinners, and were stunned to see the devastation that Giap's fanatical, self-sacrificial guerrillas were able to wreak in and around the enemy capital of Saigon.

Slowly but surely, thanks to Tet, the masses began to turn against their masters' illegal war of aggression. Giap liked to remind the other man what a lasting gift Tet had proved to be, how Le Duc Tho had used it as an instrument of torture in the epic diplomatic ruse he had put on for the Americans.

Beginning in 1969, Tho held secret negotiations in Paris with Nixon's toady, Henry Kissinger. Facilitated by the French, the meetings first took place in a drab little house in a factory neighborhood, the last place anyone would have expected to find an imperialist lackey such as Kissinger, who liked his private planes, five-star hotels, and large-breasted motion picture actresses.

Each time, the little professor or one of his subordinates arrived with carefully prepared talking points and elaborate proposals for phased withdrawals and interim political coalitions. Tho and his colleagues spent four years shitting on Kissinger's papers and driving him mad with frustration.

Hanoi's strategy was simply to wait for the yeast of Tet to rise. Tho never had any intention of negotiating or permitting any of Saigon's puppet leaders to stay in power for a moment after the U.S. left. As opposition to the war intensified, Nixon would have to bring his troops home, Congress would cut the funds for Saigon, and the puppets would crumble. Tho especially enjoyed the infuriated expression on Kissinger's face whenever someone on the Vietnamese side mentioned the findings of public opinion polls in the United States or the latest member of Congress to denounce the war, especially when it was a Republican.

But General Giap's colleagues had noticed that while Tet had been a mighty propaganda, it was a military failure, leaving the Viet Cong desperately weak and virtually irrelevant in the south. So in the spring of 1972, Giap turned from guerilla war to conquering the south by more conventional means. By then, most U.S. troops were gone. The war was more unpopular than ever, and Richard Nixon was running for reelection. In May, he was planning to fly to Moscow for a summit meeting and come home with color photographs showing him signing arms control treaties with the Soviets that he would use for his campaign commercials.

Tho didn't think Nixon would risk sending his bombers against North Vietnam. If Moscow, Hanoi's friend and sponsor, canceled the summit, he could lose the election. Besides, Tho knew from studying the deepening lines on Henry Kissinger's soft, sullen face that he had grown desperately weary of the very idea of Vietnam. He wanted to get back on his private plane and go looking for communists in Moscow and Beijing who would actually talk back to him and sign agreements. Surely Kissinger would tell Nixon to keep his infernal B-52s in their hangers.

This time, Le Duc Tho got it wrong. Hanoi invaded the south with 200,000 regular soldiers armed with the most modern weaponry Moscow could provide. Aided by a few remaining U.S. troops, the puppet army held the line. Then Nixon unleashed his bombers, wave after wave against targets in the north. When it was over in October, Giap had lost again. At the cost of half its army, Hanoi had gained control of Quang Tri province. Within months, the south had won it back. The north lost the stomach for another such offensive anytime soon.

Giap had gravely underestimated the puppet soldier and imperialist president. That's when they took away his command. When Nixon bombed again in December and the peace treaty was signed in January, some of the sniveling cowards on the Politburo and in Moscow actually took the position that North Vietnam couldn't win the war on the ground as long as the madman Nixon, the unpredictable, savage traitor to his pacifist Quaker religion, was in the White House.

And now, he wasn't. Now he was locked up across the street, fighting for his political life. The United States, having battled North Vietnam to a draw in 1972, was committing an epic and unprecedented act of political self-immolation. The puppets were losing their puppeteers. Hanoi estimated that Saigon's firepower and the mobility of its forces were down by at least half because Congress had cut its supplies of weapons, fuel, vehicles, and aircraft. Meanwhile new Soviet aid was flooding into North Vietnam.

The Politburo's military committee had met in October, considered all the gifts that Watergate had bestowed on them, and decided that the time had come to strike.

Giap said, "So it will be Phuoc Long province in December."

"It seems to be the ideal choice," Tho said. "It's just over 100 kilometers from Saigon, so it will startle and discourage the enemy. There also are many other tactical advantages, as you know. The puppet regime has used its strong position there to disrupt our efforts to supply our forces further to the east."

Giap grinned his joyless grin as he asked a question which was designed to torture his old friend, who had gotten the answer to the same question wrong when they were planning the 1972 invasion of South Vietnam. "Will the Americans use their air power?" he said.

Tho didn't alter his expression or take his eyes from Giap's even for a second. "There is nothing Ford can do," he said in the same tone of voice as before. "Kissinger tried to get Nixon to bomb last spring, but was afraid because of Watergate. Ford's situation is even worse. He's completely paralyzed by his ambiguous position, especially in foreign relations. He won't even take a meeting with an ambassador. Congress and the American press wouldn't stand for any aggressive military moves."

"So by not resigning, Nixon actually fucked his friends in Saigon," Giap said with a laugh, slapping the armrest of his chair with his palm. "If Ford were president in his own right, he'd have more latitude."

Tho nodded. "In that event, it would be somewhat riskier for us," he said. "Our offensive would be more of a test of how much effort Ford was willing to make with Congress to get funds to oppose our invasion."

Giap smiled at Tho, whose unwavering composure he and others sometimes found annoying. His politically minded colleagues in Hanoi, the diplomats and Marxist-Leninist purists, were always so sure they could predict what the capitalists would do. Giap had learned to think like a general, and winning generals always respected their adversaries. After 1972, he would never underestimate the Americans again.

Giap had deeply personal reasons to fear that Tho was actually right this time. He had been suffering and fighting for over a half-century, since he was ten and the French bastards began to murder his family. His father fought all his life for Vietnam's freedom and died in a French prison after World War I. They even arrested one of his older sisters. She got sick in her dark, pestilent cell and died a few weeks after she was freed.

He had longed for this moment ever since, for the footprint of the foreigner to be swept from the soil of his united homeland. He'd repaid the French by humiliating them at the battle of Dien Bien Phu, and he now endured the humiliation of his own losses. After all that, he couldn't fully accept these tidings of good fortune, that after all he'd done and endured, victory would finally come not because of anything he or his people had done but thanks to the political antics of a bizarre American who spent his time as president either bombing or bugging his enemies.

Giap cocked an eyebrow at Tho and smiled wider to mask his irritation. "What about the boy from the foreign ministry?" he said, probing for a weakness in Tho's certitude, for a reason not to trust this impossible gift of impending victory. "He must've told the Americans something."

"The café manager was Viet Cong," Tho said. "The traitor met with his uncle, a Saigon official we know well, and an American the manager of course didn't recognize. We think it was probably his son-in-law."

"From the White House," Giap said, nodding impatiently. "I knew that much when I concurred in the order to have him killed. But what did he learn?"

"It's more a matter of what young Nguyen knew and could therefore repeat," Tho said, "and we can only guess what that is based on what the foreign minister was doing and reading. He could've been warning that there would be an offensive soon."

Giap chuckled without joy. "Your friend Kissinger would have deduced that on his own," he said. "Did he want to defect?"

"He had already gone to the trouble of sneaking into South Vietnam."

"Then maybe it was family business," Giap said, not entirely sure if he was kidding. He hoped they'd made a careful enough study of the foreign minister's files.

For the first time, Le Duc Tho's face broke into a wide, genuine smile. He had big, shining eyes, so the effect was unnerving. He leaned forward and patted the air reassuringly in the direction of Giap's hand on the armrest, as though he wanted to touch it but didn't want to risk giving offense. "You worry too much, my friend," he said. "The Americans' corruption will destroy them and everything they touch. By January you will be the king of Phuoc Long province, and in the spring we'll have tea in Saigon."

For the first time, Giap could see that Tho wanted that outcome as desperately as he did. He'd spent over ten years in prison compared to Giap's one. He too had never known a day's peace. If they weren't fighting, what would they do with themselves? Giap was sometimes afraid to find out. Was Tho as conflicted as he was about winning by virtue of Nixon's incompetence? Or was he so eager for the victory that his judgment about the Americans was clouded? Another unsuccessful invasion could destroy them both, not to mention any chance of a unified Vietnam.

And now Le Duc Tho, already celebrated as the most canny, Machiavellian negotiator in modern history, had planted the image in his head of their sitting together on the sidewalk patio of the Hotel Continental in Saigon.

Giap smiled back. The image wasn't as tantalizing as Tho had perhaps hoped. To taunt him, the French had served Giap lotus tea every day in prison. He'd hated it ever since.

26

Phase Two

Next week was going to be Rear Admiral Skip Wiggins' first Thanksgiving since his divorce. Bill Sanchez, his school buddy from back in Texas and former aide in the Pentagon, called him up to see what he'd be doing for the holiday. Skip said he wouldn't be doing jack shit. His ex-wife, son and daughter, and half his net worth had moved to Tampa. He sure as hell wasn't going to drive all the way down there for the privilege of sitting in a goddamned Waffle House on the Friday morning after Thanksgiving with a couple of sullen teenagers who wouldn't say ten words between them.

So Bill suggested that one night after work they get together and have some dinner at their old spot in the underground mall in Crystal City, near the Pentagon. They hadn't been there since the night of August 8, when Richard Nixon had announced that he wouldn't be resigning after all. Just a few minutes before, Skip had implied that the good guys at the Defense Department, the only ones left in the government who gave a damn about national security, had figured out how to maneuver the Quaker commie kisser out of office.

Skip hadn't been embarrassed about being proved wrong about Nixon's plans, since Skip was never embarrassed.

"The corrupt son of a bitch must have something he's using for leverage against Congress," Skip said, drinking half his first beer in one swallow. Bill didn't think his friend looked well. He'd gained even more weight. The buttons on his khaki shirt were straining, and his t-shirt was showing through. His complexion was sallow and pale. "Maybe J. Edgar Hoover gave him some of his FBI files before he died, the ones on the senators and congressmen and all the little boys and girls they were screwing. Maybe Nixon had his plumbers steal them. Who knows?" He finished his beer.

Both men would retire from their obscure desk jobs the following year. They would receive no more promotions or raises. Being involved in Joint Chiefs chairman Thomas Moorer's program to steal White House secrets had ruined their careers.

By now, Bill was more or less at peace with it. He was planning to return to Brownsville with his wife and their three sons, coach high school football, go hunting with his buddies, and enjoy his pension and veterans benefits.

But Bill was just a captain. Skip had fallen from far higher. He'd once expected that his next assignment would find him in the U.S. Pacific Fleet's commander's mansion at Pearl, running massive battle drills across the whole south Pacific, sending carrier groups into the Taiwan Strait and up the Suez Canal to demonstrate American might, not to mention having about 15,000 men and women kissing his ass 24 hours a day. Instead, he was living in a one-bedroom apartment in Alexandria, eating Swanson's frozen potpies and drinking Budweiser, all because he'd followed orders and helped Admiral Moorer and his cabal of national security hawks keep tabs on a president who seemed determined to sacrifice America's hard-won advantage to Moscow, Beijing, and Hanoi.

The waitress brought their blue cheese and bacon cheeseburgers and onion rings. Skip glanced at her and jerked the hand holding his half-empty glass up and down a few times, signifying a reorder. She looked at Bill, who shook his head and smiled that he was fine. She shot an angry glance at Skip and went to get his beer. "You don't think Milhous will win in the Senate, I hope," Bill asked. "The Democrats picked up three seats in the mid-term elections. That can't be good for Nixon."

Skip shook his head, chuckled, and drained his beer. "Billy, I love you," he said, slamming the glass down on the table, "but you're a dickwad when it comes to politics. Nixon's trial is next month. Same Congress is in office till January. The outgoing Republicans are going to be more likely to vote for Nixon because they've got nothing to lose. George Aiken from Vermont, who's retiring—"

Bill said, "– to be replaced by a Democrat, I saw, some big liberal Catholic named Leahy."

Skip shrugged. "Anyway, Aiken's got a Richard Nixon wall of honor and glory in his office, framed pictures and letters, the whole nine yards," he said. "There was an article about it in the *Washington Post*. Crazy old bastard said he's using his remaining weeks in office to wage a personal campaign to get six more votes for Milhous in the Senate trial. He goes by their offices. They sit there gassing about the good old days. Then he presents a free can of Vermont maple syrup and says wouldn't it be great if they stuck together behind the old man one more time."

"So the newspapers are where you're getting your inside information now," Bill said. He regarded his friend with affection but also a considerable amount of resentment. Skip always wanted to be in the know, or wanted you to think he was. If there was a hidden agenda, a system running within the system, Skip would take you aside and whisper in your ear about it. Who the coach's real favorites were on the football team. The secret to getting promoted faster in the Navy. What usually malevolent interests held the real power in American society and politics. He even presented himself as an expert on women's secret, most wanton desires and how they needed to be mastered and dominated by strong men.

Bill went along with most of it, except the stuff about women. His wife would kill him if tried any of that. They'd been buddies since third grade. Besides, Skip's stories and theories were usually pretty entertaining. When they were with their fellow officers, he used Bill as a foil, telling him he was a naïve babe in the woods and pounding him on the back. He'd tell Bill to stay close, that he'd look after him and make sure he got ahead in this mean old world in spite of his failure to be enough of a realist to understand how it really worked.

One morning Skip called him down in Charleston, where he was in command of a guided missile destroyer, and said that new orders were on the way. Soon they'd be working side by side with the chairman of the Joint Chiefs. The Pentagon was deeply concerned about the course of U.S. foreign policy under Nixon. The president's rhetoric about a "generation of peace" with the communists and "peace with honor" in Vietnam amounted to a capitulation to America's most ruthless enemies. Skip managed to throw in something about the Jews and the banks being behind it all. This was a leitmotif of Skip's worldview. Bill wanted to ask why the banks, whoever was in charge, would want Moscow to take over everything, but there was usually no point in calling Skip on the inconsistency of his arguments, so Bill had stopped trying years before.

Phase one of the program was to gather intelligence about Nixon-Kissinger policies that would put vital national interests at risk. A Navy yeoman assigned to the White House would steal national security documents and send them to the Pentagon for analysis.

Skip said phase two would begin if their colleagues decided that Nixon had gone too far.

"What's phase two?" Bill had said on the phone while sitting in the captain's quarters on board the USS Semmes, in port in Charleston harbor.

Skip had laughed. "That's need-to-know basis information only, Billy boy."

"So I don't need to know?"

"You don't need to 'cause you got me to. You know I always got your back, you dumb fuck. Look out for your orders."

Back at the restaurant, Bill said, "So what happened to phase two?"

"Say what?" Skip had finished his second beer and waved the glass at the waitress, who had glanced over from the other side of the room. Bill had never seen Skip drink so much so quickly. It looked like he'd be driving him home.

"Stopping Nixon and the Jews and the banks and the Russians."

Skip picked up something in his friend's tone of voice. He looked at him for a moment and then looked down at his lap. "You always thought I was full of shit," he said, glancing up with a smile that Bill realized he hadn't seen in years, in more innocent times back in Texas.

Bill smiled back. "Just sometimes," he said.

Skip sighed. "All I can tell you," he said, "is that something about Nixon scared the stripes off the boys in military intelligence. I don't know what it was or what they thought they could do about it."

"Something he was going to do?"

Skip shook his head. "It was more like what he knew, something he had on them, maybe something he could hurt them with."

"And they were willing to drive him out of office because of it?"

Skip said, "I actually felt like they were willing to kill him."

Bill felt goose bumps rise on his forearms. He looked at Skip's face, seeking reassurance. This had to be more of the same. Another conspiracy, another cabal within a cabal, more grassy knolls sparkling in Skip's glassy, beery eyes. This time, Bill yearned to see Skip's best sly grin and that "if you only knew what I know" wink. But Skip just looked down again and reached for his cheeseburger.

27

Howard Who?

Emmett Walsh was sitting in his graciously appointed office at the Treasury on the Monday afternoon before Thanksgiving. He was in the midst of finalizing his complicated evening schedule with his chief of staff, who sat in an armchair opposite his desk, when he looked down at his desk phone and saw the light start to blink on and off on the direct line to his secretary.

He instantly knew it was Howard Morton. He felt a moment of panic. He would rather hear from an angry Gerald Ford after an 80-point drop in the Dow.

And Morton knew it. Not long after arriving in Washington, Walsh had figured out that Morton always waited until late in the day Eastern time to place his calls – usually just a few minutes before five. He'd laboriously question Morton about Richard Nixon's prospects in his Senate trial, making Walsh describe his conversations with Republican senators in minute detail, sometimes keeping him on the phone for an hour when they could've covered the same ground in five or ten minutes. When he wanted to enhance and extend the torture, he would elongate his words or pick apart Walsh's, asking whether he meant to say "committed" when he really meant "absolutely committed" or "committed for now."

Walsh looked helplessly at his aide, Ben Claussen. A call from Morton usually wreaked havoc with his late afternoon and evening. He was a member of the Cabinet, for goodness sake, with commitments and responsibilities beyond the understanding of a provincial lawyer out in California.

And yet Morton acted as though he owned him.

Janice knocked on the door. After a moment, she poked her head in. "It's Mr. Morton," she said.

Emmett nodded at her and then rolled his eyes at Ben as he leaned forward to reach for the phone.

"Do you want me to stay?" Ben said.

Emmett shook his head and then called to Janice, who was about to close the door. "I'll call Mrs. Walsh after this," he said.

"Good luck," Ben said with a smile as he turned to follow Janice.

Morton picked up the phone. "Howard!" he said in his most resonate, confident voice, the one he used when greeting Morton and their friends at the Golden State Club in Los Angeles or his buddies at the Bohemian Club in San Francisco. The men would slap each other on the back, grasp and hold each other's hands, and stare into each other's calculating eyes, probing for weakness or fear.

Emmett often used such moments to make a comment about football or baseball. Tall and handsome, with broad shoulders and thick white hair, Emmett looked like he must've played sports in college. But he hadn't. He wasn't even much of a fan. Every Monday morning Ben, who had also been his executive assistant when he was chairman of California Empire Bank in San Francisco, prepared a memo summarizing the weekend's key college and pro games. He just needed enough information to fake his way through a business lunch or dinner's opening rounds of small talk.

"Good afternoon, Mr. Secretary," Morton said. "I hope I haven't caught you at an inconvenient time."

"We were just going over a troubling new report that just came in from the Fed on exchange rates," Walsh said. Actually, he'd been briefed on it earlier in the day. But Emmett couldn't help the little lie. Howard always acted as though he didn't have anything better to do than talk to him about his secret plots for Ronald Reagan.

With lower-level operatives such as Mitch Botstein, who had also proved to be a grave disappointment, Howard Morton could afford to be blunt. But ever since he had figured out how to maneuver Walsh into Nixon's cabinet, he had spoken to him with elaborate respect, always using his title instead of his first name. When it was called for, he did his damage as with a flick of the surgeon's knife. "I imagine you have some good people to help you understand all that," Morton said in an ingratiating tone. "All the nuances, I mean, since you're so busy."

Being subtle, Morton risked that Emmett would miss the point. In his same hail-fellow voice, Emmett said, "Never too busy to talk to you, my friend."

Howard's voice turned icy. "How gracious of you," he said.

Emmett got the point this time. "Did you get our report?" he said.

"Has there been another one since Friday that I missed? I certainly hope so, Mr. Secretary, because that one read a lot like last Monday's, which sounded like the one the week before."

"That's because the situation has been the same for a couple of weeks."

"It's been the same for a month," Morton said.

"Whatever you say, Howard. We still have a seven-vote margin for conviction."

"To be precise, you have five who seem committed for now and two who are still on the fence but leaning against Nixon. Do you have your copy with you? Let's go over the list again, one by one."

Frustration welled in Emmett's throat. "I'm not sure that's necessary," he said. "Ben and I told you everything we know as of now."

Morton was silent for a moment. Emmett immediately regretted his impertinence. "I'm afraid you misunderstand the purpose of your adventure in Washington," he said in a quiet, smooth voice. "My job is to ensure that everyone on Governor Reagan's team feels personally accountable for a good result in the 1976 election. And you have more to lose than money and power, Mr. Secretary."

Emmett closed his eyes. He knew just what Morton meant. It had happened years before. But he'd evidently never be able to escape his sordid little sin.

Morton repeated his earlier question, using precisely the same tone of voice. It was another of his ways of saying that he wouldn't be deterred or defied. He said, "Do you have your copy with you?"

Emmett wedged the receiver between his ear and shoulder, rolled his big leather chair closer to his desk, and reached for his copy of Ben's memo. "Right here," he said.

"Let's go over the list again, one by one," he said. "We'll start with that one-armed bastard Bob Dole." Morton reserved special venom for potential rivals to Ronald Reagan in presidential politics, especially when they were moderates. "When's the last time you talked to him, and what exactly did he say?"

It was ten minutes to six before Emmett hung up and pressed the intercom button. He knew Ben had left already, but Janice would still be there. He asked her to get Mrs. Walsh on the phone and sat with his head in his hands until the buzzer went off again.

He picked up. "Hi, darling," he said.

"Howard Morton called again," Eleanor Walsh said. "I can hear it in your voice."

He rubbed his eyes. He didn't want her to be upset or to worry. "He's just a stickler," he said.

"He's a prick," she said. "Can you come home soon? I'll make you feel better, beginning by pouring you a bourbon and water."

He looked at his watch. Emmett could picture Ellie sitting on the couch in their quiet, meticulously decorated living room in Bethesda. From watching her affectionately for many years, he knew that when she was talking on the phone to someone she loved, she liked to look at the family pictures arrayed on the coffee table. He was sure that was what she was doing now. She'd told him at breakfast that she planned to get her hair done. She was probably wearing the blouse he'd bought her three weeks ago in Paris, where he and Ben had gone to attend a meeting of NATO finance ministers. She'd said it would look pretty with a black skirt she'd just found at Woodward & Lothrop. She worked hard to keep her figure. She loved it that after 30 years of marriage, he was still proud to be seen with her.

He hated to disappoint Ellie, but tonight, it couldn't be helped. "Thanks to Howard, I had to move my late afternoon meetings to early evening," he said. "I'll get some dinner here. I have to make some calls, too. The Tokyo markets and all that. Maybe ten or eleven. I'm sorry."

"I'll be fine," she said, though she sounded disappointed. "I have a lot to do still, getting ready for Thanksgiving dinner."

"When do the kids get in?"

"Sarah Wednesday morning so she can help me, Jimmy and his family Wednesday night. They worry about you, too."

"They shouldn't," he said. "I'll be home as soon as I can."

His car was waiting on Old Executive Way, between the White House and Treasury. The driver headed up 15th St. to K, across to 21st, then back south toward Pennsylvania. They turned left into an alley and stopped a half-block in. Murmuring about a meeting with some nervous Wall Street bankers who didn't want to be seen at his office, Emmett told his driver he'd get a cab home. He said goodnight and darted into the service entrance and down a hallway to the main stairs.

The Hotel Excelsior was a sleepy old place with apartment-style suites and a sizeable number of semi-permanent residents. If someone recognized him, they'd assume he was coming for drinks or dinner with a member of Congress or the diplomatic corps. If they speculated he was meeting his mistress, so be it. It wouldn't have been big news in Washington, though he'd regret it if someone thought ill of Ellie. But it couldn't be helped. He bounded up two flights of stairs to the third floor. He knocked quietly on the door of the suite at the end of the hall.

Ben Claussen greeted him in bare feet. He'd changed from his business suit into jeans and a white t-shirt. He was shorter than Emmett and just as solidly built. His grey hair was cut short. He smiled as the secretary edged past him into the living room of the suite. He put the "Do Not Disturb" sign on the outside knob before he closed the door.

Howard's call had given Ben some extra time to make everything perfect. A room service table draped with a white cloth was set for two. Their salads were already in place, and steaks cooked medium rare were waiting for them in the food warmer hidden underneath the table. Ben had lit candles on the table and, Emmett could see, in the bedroom. He had poured them each a glass of wine.

Emmett surveyed the scene and smiled at Ben. "You're a sight for sore ears," he said.

"How was Howard?" Ben said.

"Who?" Emmett took his face between his hands, smiled, and kissed him.

28

Thanksgiving in Detroit

In Los Angeles, Mitch Botstein sat in his apartment in the dark, playing his guitar and singing. It was a nice evening. A cool breeze came through the screen off his little patio. He was having a beer and thinking about making himself some dinner, though he'd pretty much decided that it would be easier just to have another beer.

Mitch had a 1962 Martin D-28, which was, he would readily have admitted, far more guitar than he deserved. It was made of Brazilian rosewood, with exquisite if understated ivory highlights in the neck. It was the acoustic instrument you'd see Eric Clapton or Neil Young playing.

He'd scored it off a friend back in high school who was desperate to put together a down payment on a 1960 Rambler. The kid's parents had given it to him for Christmas, an inlaid pearl before swine scenario. Mitch wasn't about to tell him that the guitar was worth at least as much as the car. He asked for $200. Mitch would've paid $1000. He gave him $75.

Mitch used to joke to his parents that he wanted to be buried with it. He never got a chance to tell Emily. Mitch suppressed his self-pitying thought by pounding on the strings a little harder. He had been learning a Rolling Stones song, "Angie," which was either about Mick Jagger leaving a girl or Keith Richards trying to kick heroin. The point is that it wasn't Angie doing the dumping. The song had complicated arpeggios that Mitch was still struggling with.

Emily loved "Angie." He never got a chance to play it for her.

"For chrissakes," Mitch said out loud. He started at the beginning again with the A minor chord and sang the song through in his squeaky tenor:

Oh, Angie don't you weep, all your kisses still taste sweet; I hate that sadness in your eyes; But Angie, Angie, ain't it time we said goodbye?

Emily Weissman and Howard Morton had said goodbye to Mitch the same week. Emily found out that he was spying for Howard. Howard had found out that he was a lousy spy. He could've turned Garrett McCann's fraternity tape over to the newspapers, finished Nixon, hobbled Ford, and won a job in the Reagan administration in January 1977.

Instead, he had momma send her copy of the incriminating cassette to Washington by express mail. He gave it and the two in his briefcase to Len Garment, who finally got a chance to burn some White House tapes. Garrett McCann's momentary indiscretion was now lost to history.

Mitch was conscious of all his motives. He definitely wanted to get Emily back. That hadn't worked. She still wouldn't return his calls. He also wanted to regard himself as she had when they first met, committed to a cause without being willing to do whatever it took to win. And maybe he didn't want to spend his career in the shadows of great events, ruining the careers of gay campaign aides and destroying presidents in the name of freedom and democracy.

Being summoned to the White House had made its impression, the Marine guards and hushed hallways and all that, as had the appeal to his patriotism. Garment and Ziegler had seemed like good guys. He'd even hoped he'd get a chance to meet Nixon. But it never came up. When they were all done, after Mitch had sworn in the name of all that was holy to keep his mouth shut about what had happened, Garment thanked him for his cooperation and showed him the door.

But Angie, Angie, ain't it good to be alive?

From Garment's office in the White House, as Len and Ziegler listened, he had called Howard Morton and told him that the lead just hadn't panned out. He said you could hear McCann on the tape talking about dirty tricks, but he didn't reveal anything the public didn't already know. How would a drug-addled freshman have known any better? But Howard was skeptical. He questioned Mitch obsessively about what McCann had said, making him recite it word for word, over and over. Since he was making up the benign version as he went along, he said something a little different each time.

Howard noticed. He said he was gravely disappointed that Mitch hadn't acquired the tape anyway, just so they could be sure. He had already insisted that Mitch give him Biff Michaels' name. Now he asked for his number. When Mitch resisted, he could tell that Howard was done with him. He said he'd be in touch if Governor Reagan ever needed anything more.

Mitch's month-to-month retainer, paid through Morton's law firm, had run out at the end of October. He'd spent the last month making calls to try to get work, but the last weeks before a midterm election was not the time for a political consultant to scare up business. Everybody who had a chance of winning had his team in place. Besides, the Reagan people had probably blackballed him, and maybe the Nixonites, too. Nobody told him they had. Everyone just thanked him for calling and wished him well.

His savings would be gone in a couple of months. Then it would be back to momma's in Encino.

Angie, Angie, they can't say we never tried

The phone rang. He got up and laid his guitar on the couch. He had finally stopped worrying it was Howard and wishing it was Emily. Maybe it was a job offer. Maybe the secretary general of the United Nations wanted to get his views on the crisis in Cyprus. He went to the dark kitchen, sighed, and picked up.

It was Sidney Weissman. "Marian and I were disappointed by what we learned from Emily," he said in his quiet voice.

So now he was going to be dumped by her father, too? He closed his eyes and said, "I understand."

"But it sounds like you did the right thing in the end."

"I thought you despised Nixon," Mitch said.

"We support our daughter."

He hesitated. "How is Emily?" he said. He liked saying her name out loud.

"She's miserable. She misses you."

Mitch's heart beat faster. "She does?"

"Of course," Sidney said. "But she has a tendency to be unforgiving. She doesn't think she can trust you. I'm not sure she can, either, but her mother and I have discussed it, and we think she should give you another chance."

Mitch smiled. "I appreciate the thought, Mr. Weissman. I only wish mom and dad got a vote in these situations."

"We'll see," Sidney said. "We surprised you at dinner that time. Have you ever spent Thanksgiving in Detroit?"

29

One Plus One

Frank Szabados was typing so furiously and concentrating so hard on what he was writing that he didn't realize someone had been sitting at the chair next to his desk, watching him. He only noticed her when he stopped for a moment and turned to reach for his Styrofoam coffee cup.

"How long have you been there?" Frank said, startled but also relieved at the interruption. He'd gotten to work at six in the morning, and it was almost noon.

"Approximately since the Johnson administration," she said with a smile. "I'm really impressed. You type almost as fast as a girl."

Emily Weissman had her legs crossed and her hands folded in her lap. She twisted around in her chair to scan the cluttered office, which was quiet for a Wednesday morning. Just a few of Frank's colleagues were still studying cables, writing reports, and talking on the phone. "It looks like a considerable element of our national security apparatus has gone home to mother," she said. "I guess it hasn't occurred to you that the Soviets might attack when everyone's fallen asleep watching the Redskins game."

"We only excuse personnel responsible for assessing threats from little countries," he said.

"Like Moldova?" she said.

"And Mauritius."

"Don't forget Mauritania."

"I hope you're getting some time off," Frank said. He paused, sat back in his chair, and gave Emily a skeptical glance. "Tell me now, or

178

I'll call everyone back. If the legendary Emily Weissman is staying in town for the weekend, we're probably in for a constitutional crisis."

"Very funny," Emily said. She nodded her head at his typewriter. "You're working pretty hard," she said.

"I bet you wonder what on."

"I bet I know," she said.

He grinned. "Jackson Place has been clamoring for it," he said. "I've already heard from Rose Woods twice and Ziegler once today."

"How about the acting president and Dr. Kissinger? Any clamoring from that quarter?"

Frank shrugged, glancing back at his typewriter. "They're pretty busy," he said.

"I doubt they're eager to get the NSC's comprehensive policy review and recommendations on Vietnam," she said, "especially when they've been drawn up by someone who hates all communists everywhere and will probably recommend that we use the most primitive methods imaginable against Hanoi."

Frank frowned. "Hate is such an ugly word," he said. "Speaking of which, have you called him back yet?"

Emily looked at her hands. "I don't hate him," she said in her quiet, small voice.

"So have you?"

"No," she said.

"Life's too short, Emily," Frank said. "Take it from a fatalistic Hungarian."

"He's a lying dirt bag," she said.

"Where I come from, at least in the government and in politics, everyone's a lying dirt bag. My people have learned to make allowances."

Emily nodded at the binders, memos, and newspaper clippings piled on Frank's desk. "How's it going?"

As Nixon had predicted, Henry Kissinger hadn't been surprised that the incapacitated president had tried to meddle in Vietnam policy. Kissinger and Ford made sure that Frank was appropriately chastised by Len Garment, the White House counsel, for stealing documents for Nixon. On the same day, they gave Frank the plum assignment of overseeing an exhaustive interagency review of U.S. Vietnam policy. He oversaw a team of analysts who had access at all levels at the Pentagon, State Department, and CIA.

Ford had also decided to put Nixon back in the loop on Vietnam. He was getting the same morning tactical briefing as Ford and copies of all Kissinger's memos and reports. One factor in Ford's calculations, besides the likelihood that Nixon would figure out how to get them anyway, was Nixon's steadily improving political standing. Thanks to the midterm election and the relentless lobbying of Senator George Aiken and a few other Nixon loyalists, it now appeared from press accounts that he was within four votes of being acquitted on each of the two articles of impeachment the Senate would take up in December.

Most important, Ford had been impressed by the intelligence that Nixon and Szabados had developed on the effect of the Nixon administration's 1972 bombings on the Hanoi government's morale. He had told Kissinger he wanted to know what all his options were in the event of a new communist offensive against South Vietnam.

"I'm almost done," Frank said. "It'll be ready by dinnertime. Who's asking?"

"Rose called me once," she said. "Ziegler has actually called three times since eight."

"Which one told you to come check on my progress?"

"Both," she said. "Miss Woods said Nixon's been asking about it every 20 minutes. Mr. Ziegler mentioned that if would help, I should have sex with you."

Frank stared at her longingly for a moment and then hopped to his feet, turned off his typewriter, grabbed his suit coat from the back of his chair, and extended his hand.

Emily looked shocked. "Anne wouldn't think that was very funny," she said.

Frank grinned and pointed at a wall clock. "It's lunchtime," he said. They walked out of the NSC offices, down the steps on the west side of the Old Executive Office Building, and across to the White House. It was cold, and they didn't have their overcoats, but they were only outside for a minute. The mess, operated by the Navy, was in the mansion's basement, near the situation room. Though they normally would've needed a reservation, today the dining room was half empty. A steward in a navy blue uniform showed them a table for four, set with a white tablecloth and heavy silver bearing the presidential seal. They sat side-by-side as he took away the extra place settings. Emily ordered a tuna fish salad, Frank a BLT. They both asked for iced tea.

They'd become friends after meeting in Len Garment's office on the day the Watergate trials began. Frank and Anne had had Emily over to dinner a couple of times. They were hoping for a double date if she ever patched things up with Mitch, whom she obviously adored.

They had spent hours comparing notes about Nixon's perverse magnetism. He wasn't what they had expected from seeing him on television, where he always looked like he was trying too hard. In private, he was droll, even playful, smiling more authentically than the joyless, toothsome grin he used for the cameras. Most of all, he'd won over his newest young acolytes by the intensity of his focus on them and what they most cared about. With aides, Nixon had no patience for the rhythm of a normal, relaxed conversation that swirls around the edges like water in a vortex, certainly but gracefully approaching the heart of a matter. Nixon bored in relentlessly, beginning to talk before you'd even sat down, extracting what you knew and believed and making it part of his perpetual deliberativeness. He wouldn't necessarily shake your hand or ask about your ailing mother, but you could tell you were important to him, and especially when he was the most important person in the world, it was heady.

In early October, he had stopped calling Emily. She didn't know that Ron Ziegler had become aware of Nixon's little crush. She assumed it was because she had insulted him with her sarcastic comments about Garrett McCann's dirty tricks operation. Either way, it was probably for the best. But she missed the jolt she got when she heard his deep and notorious voice on the phone. She even missed his inept flirtation.

Instead she got occasional requests on his behalf from Rose and Ron Ziegler and, just today, from Len Garment, an assignment that could only have come from Nixon, though Len didn't say so.

Frank was still seeing him, but now openly, at Jackson Place, usually along with another aide who provided the daily tactical briefing. The reporters across the street in Lafayette Square had demanded to know about the change of procedure. Gerald terHorst, Ford's press secretary, had finally gotten across the White House's rationale for keeping Nixon up to date on national security issues, especially because the city rang with speculation that he might actually be acquitted and make it back to the Oval Office.

The steward brought their tea. They each had a long silver spoon tucked handle first into a folded cloth napkin nestled next to the glass. These rested on bone china saucers with blue and gold trim. It was Mrs. Nixon's china. Emily and Frank added lemon and sugar and clinked their glasses in a Thanksgiving toast. "To the president and first lady," he said.

"Where will they be tomorrow?" Emily said after taking a sip.

"I actually don't know," Frank said. "Mrs. Nixon can't stand Jackson Place. She wants to stand by him, but she spends at least two nights a week with the Eisenhowers or in New York with the other daughter."

"They've been locked up for over three months," she said. "The Fords are playing it smart and getting out of town the day after Thanksgiving. Mr. Nixon should take her to California for the long weekend."

Frank smiled. "And risk being seen climbing down from his cross?"

"People wouldn't begrudge him Thanksgiving. He could nail himself back up on Monday."

Frank tipped his glass at Emily for aptly embellishing the metaphor. "Whatever he's doing seems to be working," Frank said, lowering his voice and looking around the dining room, where just a few other parties were huddled in conversation. "He assumes he'll be back by the first of the year."

Emily looked away as their meals arrived, smiling a thank you to the steward and then watching as Frank murmured a grace. Emily used the opportunity to give thanks silently and also ask God for strength and courage. She picked up her knife and fork and cut off a piece of lettuce and tomato and took a bite. "So about Vietnam," she said.

Frank crunched his sandwich and shook his head. "Every indication we have is that the communists will stage a substantial offensive soon, fairly close to Saigon," he said.

"How can we tell?"

"Reconnaissance photos showing the deployment of Hanoi's 4th Army Corps, some human intelligence, plus common sense. They read the newspapers, too. They know the impeachment trial starts next week. We'll be even more distracted than we have been lately. Besides, Hanoi won't risk waiting for Nixon to come back."

Emily nibbled at her salad. "You're sure he would respond the way you want him to?"

"He didn't last spring, but all because of Watergate. He devoted his first term to doing everything right in Vietnam and scaring the communists into living with a stalemate. It would've been like Korea, divided indefinitely between north and south, slave and free. But as soon as he got into trouble, he seemed to lose interest. Dr. Kissinger couldn't get him to focus on Vietnam. Hanoi couldn't believe it was so lucky."

"So Nixon would be getting a second chance to win the war," she said.

"But it can't happen that way," Frank said. "January would be too late. We've got to persuade Ford to act now. That's the main benefit of bringing Nixon back in. If Ford is willing to respond to the offensive with air strikes against the north, Nixon should lend his support. I'm already talking to Ziegler about having him issue a statement."

Emily's green eyes drifted. That was actually one aspect of the secret project she was working on for Garment. When it came to presidents, did one and one make one? Did an acting president and an incapacitated one add up to a unitary executive when they agreed on the use of military power? Would the joint chiefs follow Ford's order or balk? Would Congress stand for it, or would they try to cut off the funding or impede Ford in some other way? A whole new class of Democrats would take office in January after basing their campaigns on opposition to Richard Nixon and any more U.S. involvement in Vietnam.

A dramatic escalation of the war in the middle of Nixon's Senate trial could tear the country in half.

Emily gazed at Frank as he finished his sandwich and drained his tea. This soft-spoken and gracious if perhaps fanatical young man was helping the United States decide what to do in the most pivotal moment of military challenge and opportunity since World War II. As for Emily, she was trying to determine what the U.S. could actually accomplish of Frank's vision in the light of political circumstances unlike any in American history. She leaned forward and put her elbows on the table and stared at him. "How did this even happen?" she said. "I feel like I just graduated from high school."

"You obeyed your rabbi," he said, "and Anne and I went to the White House Christmas party and met Richard Nixon."

"So now you're blaming God."

"Seriously, are you going home? If not, come to our house. We're having some friends over that you'd like. We'll probably be talking about Watergate and war powers all day. It would be a nice break for you."

She patted his hand. "I have a flight to Detroit tonight," she said. "We're planning an old-fashioned Thanksgiving – my mother's dry turkey, my beautiful little brother Ben, and my dad reading us Lawrence Ferlinghetti poems after dinner and promising to fix the fireplace in time for next year."

Across the street in Jackson Place, Nixon was sitting in his little study on the third floor, staring at the wall and chewing on his glasses. His valet was packing his suitcase in his bedroom next door. The president had decided to take Mrs. Nixon home to San Clemente for Thanksgiving after all. Their daughters and sons-in-law would fly with them that evening, and they'd have dinner together Thursday afternoon at La Casa Pacifica, their home in San Clemente, just like old times.

Nixon hadn't traveled by air since August. Whether he was incapacitated or not, the Secret Service insisted on the full presidential security package when he was outside the District of Columbia, and that meant the use of Air Force One for the flight to California.

As Frank and Emily had realized, traveling so ostentatiously interfered with the aspect of the monkish suffering servant that went along with his Napoleonic exile. Up until now, he'd refused to consider it. His family was surprised and delighted that the holiday spirit had somehow gotten a hold of him.

For the sixth time in two hours, he looked at his watch and reached for the phone to ask Rose Woods if Frank's memo had arrived yet.

30

Ty Cobb's House

Late on Thanksgiving afternoon, with the day's sharply etched sunshine nearly gone, Mitch and Emily stood in front of a dilapidated house on a side street in Highland Park, Michigan, where Emily had grown up. They'd walked six blocks from her parents' apartment building. She said that if he wanted to see what there was to see in her hometown, this and the abandoned Ford plant were pretty much it.

It felt twenty degrees colder than when they'd started out. They were bundled up against a cold front that was making its way across the Midwest, Emily in a dark blue pea coat and red muffler, Mitch his battered old leather bomber jacket. They kept their hands in their pockets. They hadn't touched since Emily gave him a halfhearted hug when he surprised her at their apartment that afternoon, having been invited to dinner by her father.

When her mother suggested after the meal and another half-hour of stilted conversation in the Weissmans' small living room that she show him around town, Emily offered a walking tour of the neighborhood. She wasn't about to get into a warm car with Mitch Botstein and his big brown eyes and soft, knowledgeable hands. She planned to tell him to get a cab back to his hotel after their walk.

"You're sure Ty Cobb lived here?" Mitch said, shifting his weight from one foot to the other. The red brick house had two and a half stories and a big front porch on the left-hand side. The lawn, which sported a sign reading "For Rent," looked dead. The little city, where Henry Ford had built his first assembly line, was in steep decline. Ford had closed its last factory in town the year before. Even its famous elm

186

trees, which once stood forest thick along the city's residential streets, were dying.

"He moved downtown later," she said, "but everybody insists that he rented this place for a year or so." Avoiding Mitch's eyes, she looked down at the sidewalk. Each section of concrete bore the name of the city and the year it was poured. "My friends and I rode our bikes down this street almost every weekend," she said. She pointed west. "There's a spot down there where the roots of a tree pushed the sidewalk up. They patched the gap with asphalt. If you ride over it fast enough, you're airborne for a second."

"Who taught you to ride?"

"My well-meaning, problem-solving father." She said this sullenly.

In the ensuing silence, which Mitch dreaded more than her anger, he said, "You'd think the city would make the effort to be sure." He paused. "About Ty Cobb, I mean."

Emily was twisting her upper body back and forth, trying to keep warm. "Bill Haley was born in Highland Park," she said in a disinterested voice, as though she couldn't help telling him, knowing he'd be interested.

"'Rock Around the Clock'? That's pretty cool."

"The Ty Cobb thing is best left alone as far as I'm concerned."

Mitch started running in place. He wasn't trying to keep warm. He was impossibly anxious and trying as hard as he could not to say or do the wrong thing. "Isn't he considered the greatest baseball player in history?" he said. "That's something to be proud of."

She glared at him. "He was a bigot and a vicious thug," she said. "One time he leapt into the stands and beat up a handicapped heckler."

"He was in a wheelchair?"

"He didn't have any hands. Plus Cobb always slid into second with his sharpened cleats up, aiming for the knees."

Mitch shivered. His teeth rattled. "One of those guys who will do whatever it takes," he said. He saw that her eyes were damp. He stepped toward her.

She stepped back and said, "Tell me exactly what they sent you to do. If you don't tell me the truth right now, I'll never speak to you again, Mitch, I swear to God."

He looked in her eyes and said, "Howard Morton was looking for people we could turn to Reagan and help us get Nixon out of the presidency. He told me to find you and see if you would betray him and Ford."

"Which you dutifully did, using any means necessary." She wiped tears away with the back of her hand. "I was nuts to go out with you that night," she said.

"So was I."

"Why? You were getting just what you wanted."

"What I wanted changed when I met you."

"I don't believe you."

"I admit I lied at first. But did I offer you anything that night?"

"You never got the chance. You questioned me about my loyalty, which I made abundantly clean wasn't up for grabs."

"I'm actually not so easily deterred," he said. "But I was asking you political questions that night because I was interested in who you were and what you thought. I wanted to know everything about you."

She said, "Because you had somehow decided you loved me. But what if you hadn't?"

He said, "I did. I do. And I'll give anything to prove that you can trust me."

She shook her head. "It's not that easy."

"Only because you're making it hard."

"You have no idea how hard I can make it," she said. "If it weren't for my father, even this conversation would never have occurred."

"He wants what's best for you."

"You can't be what's best for me if you're responsible for the two worst months of my life. I wish my father had minded his own business. I should've told you to leave, but I didn't want to ruin everyone's day by making a scene."

They fell silent. It was dark now. Ty Cobb's house was empty, but some of its neighbors glowed from within. A few had wood fires burning. They caught faint hints of music, TV, and happy voices.

Without speaking they began to walk back toward her apartment. It got colder by the minute. They reached Woodward Ave. and stood waiting for the walk signal. They could see her big brick building looming in the darkness, almost every window aglow. Cars rushed by them.

Mitch felt flakes of snow against his face. He shivered again and looked at Emily. "I'm moving to Washington," he said.

Emily stared up at him. "Why?"

"Why do you think? I lost my job with Howard. I still have friends around town from my Georgetown days. I should be able to get some political work, maybe a staff job on Capitol Hill."

"When did you decide?"

When your father called," he said. The light turned green. As they stepped into the street, he told her to be careful, and she slid her hand into the crook of his arm.

31

Meeting Madame Manet

At noon on the day after Thanksgiving, Gerald Ford's motorcade was hurtling at 70 miles an hour along Interstate 5 toward Palm Springs. He and Betty and the rest of their traveling party had arrived at LAX just after eleven in the morning aboard SAM 26000, one of the twin blue, white, and silver Boeing 707s that were designated as Air Force One only when the president was aboard.

The Fords were heading to Rancho Mirage, a little green patch in California's vast, scruffy low desert. For the rest of the long weekend, they would be guests of billionaire Walter Annenberg, owner of the *Philadelphia Inquirer, TV Guide* and *Seventeen,* who had just finished his term as Nixon's ambassador to Great Britain. He and his wife, Lee, were notoriously undemanding hosts. Ford looked forward to a restful couple of days playing golf, swimming, and, tonight, watching Alabama play Auburn at Birmingham.

He also hoped he'd get a better night's sleep than as an itinerant in the White House and, in the last two months, a worried husband.

It didn't help that Ford wasn't getting enough exercise. He was annoyed at Richard Nixon about a lot of things but none more than that he'd turned Kennedy's indoor swimming pool into the press briefing room. As vice president, Ford had used the pool at their house in Alexandria twice a day. But they hadn't been home for weeks.

In September, Annenberg had visited Ford at the White House to talk about the last few weeks of his work in London. He thought that Ford, who'd been athletic all his life, seemed tense and antsy. Annenberg suggested that they install a new pool on the White House lawn. He even offered to help pay for it. But Ford said they'd just be digging up another White House scandal.

So Annenberg invited him and Betty to come to California over Thanksgiving weekend and enjoy their 400-acre estate, which was called Sunnylands, and, incidentally, to go for a dip.

History's first acting president was riding in California's first acting presidential motorcade. The 15 cars had the San Bernardino Freeway to themselves. Squads of motorcycle cops from the cities and towns Ford sped through took turns blocking the eastbound onramps for a mile ahead of and behind them. Black and white California Highway Patrol cars used their lights, sirens, and speakers to nudge drivers who were already on the road over onto the shoulder. They wondered why an officer had stopped them only to sit there in his cruiser, watching his rearview mirror. Then they saw it – twenty outriders thundering down the left-hand lane with their gleaming bikes in precise formation, leading a decoy limo and then the big black Lincoln with the Fords.

Since Nixon was still using the presidential limousine, this was the car Kennedy had used in Dallas, though completely rebuilt, its Brougham roof permanently fused in place ever since that morning in 1963. Gold-fringed American flags atop each fender flapped in the wind. The Secret Service had masked the presidential seals on the doors. Right behind were vehicles with Ford's aides, agents, and doctors and a pool of reporters and photographers.

In the back seat, the acting president was reading Frank Szabados's report. The binder with thick black covers was marked "EYES ONLY," which meant that only its addressees, Ford, Nixon, and Henry Kissinger, the secretary of state, were allowed to read it.

Betty Ford was nestled in the corner between the edge of the seat and door. She was finishing a mystery she'd started when they left Washington early in the morning. She wore a colorful print dress and black pumps and had pulled a grey cardigan sweater around her shoulders.

Ford put a finger at his place, closed the binder, and reached over and touched her arm. A former model and dancer, Betty Ford had always been slim. She'd lost weight in the last few weeks. Her eyes were tired, and her face looked chalky beneath her wavy auburn hair. Looking up, she reached across her chest and smiled and patted his hand to say that she was fine.

When the Nixons moved to Jackson Place in August, Betty Ford didn't think it would look right for them to live in the White House. Ford agreed at first. But the Secret Service and his staff offered a barrage of security, logistical, and finally symbolic arguments about why it would be better for everybody if he gave in and lived above the store. They used a guest bedroom in the family quarters so the Nixons wouldn't have to move their things.

It was sometimes hard for a first lady to find her niche and even harder for an acting first lady. For the first few weeks, journalists looked for evidence that they were exceeding their roles as caretakers or that they enjoyed the White House too much. Neither provided critics with any ammunition. Ford did the minimum necessary to keep the executive branch running. He delegated everything he could to Nixon's cabinet. Betty had been virtually invisible. The public only saw her leaving the White House with her husband or returning. Almost no one outside of Washington or Grand Rapids would even have recognized the sound of her voice.

Then in late September, she learned she had breast cancer. Most families didn't talk about the disease. Victims still felt ashamed, as though it were their fault. But Betty Ford had no such impulses. She asked the White House press office to issue a matter-of-fact statement saying that she would undergo a mastectomy. She thought it would help women get diagnosed more quickly. She was also enough of a politician to appreciate that candor from the White House would be a novelty.

Soon she was getting more mail than the Nixons and her husband combined. She wasn't a first lady, but she'd found her niche.

Ford turned back to his reading. The report's ultra-classified designation didn't mean he couldn't talk to his wife and most trusted adviser about it. The two agents in the front seat were prized for their discretion. "Listen to what he wants," he said, shifting in his seat so he was facing Betty as he read. "Three weeks of B-52 sorties against strategic, industrial, and governmental targets around Hanoi, including the defense ministry and intelligence directorate.'" Glancing at her, he paused and then continued. "'Massive bombing of the Ho Chi Minh Trail and its associated oil pipeline operations aimed at radically diminishing the communists' capacity to resupply their forces for the indefinite future'." He flipped a few more pages. "He wants me to give an address to the nation," he said. "He's even written it." He sighed and looked at his wife.

She had laid the paperback on her knee. "This is just if the north attacks?" she said.

"They will," Ford said. "It's one thing for me to cancel a trip to Japan or put off appointing ambassadors until Nixon's trial is over. But we're about to be challenged by a regime we fought for ten years and that killed 60,000 of our people."

Ford watched his wife and waited. His square Midwestern visage had begun to make everybody feel better. His thinning blond hair was combed back from his broad forehead, which seemed to deepen the effect of his friendly blue eyes. The public's periodic glimpses of him puttering around the White House, playing with his dog, and walking hand-in-hand with Betty in the Rose Garden had been deeply reassuring after the chaos of Nixon's last year.

But Ford realized that people were also reassured by his determination to do as little as possible. Millions were appalled because Nixon had exceeded his authority. No one was in the mood for Ford to do so as well.

Betty said, "It's wasn't your war."

"I voted for appropriations for it when I was in the House," he said. "I gave speeches in support of it. Thousands of Michigan boys died over there."

"People are so tired of Vietnam," she said. "I think they'd just as soon worry about something else."

Ford smiled. She was teasing him. This had been their process for nearly 26 years. She was voicing all the rationalizations she knew were tempting him. She wanted him to hear how unimpressive they sounded aloud. He said, "Nobody in the White House thinks I have the authority. There's no funding for a renewed air war. I'd trigger the War Powers Act and God knows what else, and that's assuming I could get the Pentagon to do it."

She nodded. "All true," she said.

"You think it's the right thing to do?"

"I can't say," she said. "Just don't be persuaded by the wrong excuses."

"You mean there are right excuses?" he said. "Maybe I can get you to send me a memo."

She smiled and leaned forward a few inches, offering her cheek. He kissed her, and she returned to her book. Ford looked out the window on his side, where Mount San Jacinto loomed along the highway to the south. He loved the mountains of California and Colorado. Where he grew up in southern Michigan, the tallest peak was the pitcher's mound at Grand Rapids South High School. This mountain filled the window. Ford leaned forward and lowered his head so he could see all the way up to the tree and snow lines, which shone in the midday sun. He thought it was the biggest thing he'd ever seen. "We could retire out here," he said.

"When will that be, Jerry?" she said gently.

Ford drank in the mountain for another moment and slumped back in his seat. He still held Frank's report, a dead weight resting on his lap.

Just a year ago, he'd been the Republican leader in the House of Representatives. The prospects for a GOP majority were so remote that he assumed he'd never be the speaker of the House, and that was fine with Ford. He enjoyed his post so much that he'd turned down offers to run for governor and the Senate.

Then Nixon called and said he wanted to make him vice president. Nixon's first, Spiro Agnew, had resigned after being caught taking bribes from contractors in Maryland, where he'd been governor. Ford knew Nixon had picked him because he was noncontroversial and nonthreatening and almost certain to be approved by the Senate. He'd spent the next six months defending and supporting the president.

Then the smoking gun tape came out, proving that Nixon had been involved in the Watergate cover-up from the beginning. After that, his advisers told him to stop making public statements about the scandal. He would need every bit of his legitimacy as an unelected president. He couldn't afford to waste it defending the indefensible.

Nixon had called him in for a photo and brief chat in on the morning of August 8, the day chosen for his resignation speech. In retrospect, Ford had realized that Nixon hadn't actually told him that he'd resign. He was relying on Ford's and everyone else's confidence that he had made an irrevocable decision. "Jerry, whatever happens," Nixon had said, "I know you'll do an outstanding job. I picked you because I knew that you had the temperament and experience for this office." Ford had thought "whatever happens" had referred to the challenges Nixon assumed he'd face as president. And while Ford was indeed serving in the Oval Office, for all the executive authority he was wielding, he might as well have spent his time dusting the furniture and vacuuming.

Three and a half months of the acting presidency had left Ford feeling claustrophobic, a captive of Nixon's troubles and Nixon himself. They didn't talk much. Gerry terHorst, Ford's press secretary, and his other advisers said it would create the impression that Nixon was still in charge. But each week, he got at least a half-dozen policy memos from Jackson Place. Nixon always expected to hear back. After all, it was still his administration. So Ford had to read page after page of his earnest prose and then drop Nixon a line saying that he'd referred his excellent suggestions to the appropriate official or department.

Meanwhile, Ford's political team kept bringing up the 1976 election. They wanted him to run, and they said it would be better if he began to assert himself more as acting president, to show he was up to the presidency. He'd even gotten a memo suggesting that it was better that Nixon hadn't resigned, since Ford would have been tempted to offer him a pardon that would've shielded him from criminal prosecution and ended the otherwise endless nightmare of Watergate. Such a move, his aides said, would have been politically devastating, virtually guaranteeing that other Republican candidates, especially

Ronald Reagan, would challenge him in the 1976 primaries. The best outcome, they concluded, was for Nixon to be acquitted so Ford could run as a vice president in an administration that had been vindicated by the constitutional process. It would be even better if in the meantime Ford could show his mettle in a crisis or two.

Ford clutched the black binder and stared out the window at the dry scrub and dirt on the desert floor as it washed by in a silent brown blur. Constitutional prudence constrained him, while his political interests required decisive action. His heart said that Hanoi shouldn't be allowed to get away with aggression against South Vietnam. But how much more fighting should the American people be expected to endure? Besides, Kissinger insisted that the loss of Saigon wouldn't materially affect the larger issues of improved relations with the Soviets and Chinese.

In the midst of it all, Ford was supposed to discern the one right thing to do. He opened the binder again, turned to the beginning, and reread Frank's summary and recommendations.

A little before one, the motorcade left the freeway and headed south on Bob Hope Drive. Sunnylands lay behind a low stucco wall and a vast ring of oleander trees. The outriders, decoy limo, and press cars peeled off as Ford's driver turned into the gate. The public wouldn't see Ford again until a photo op on the golf course that afternoon.

The estate was verdant and lush, Eden in the midst of wilderness. According to local lore, a famous caddy at the nearby Tamarisk Country Club, Scorpy Doyle, had kept Annenberg waiting too long to tee off one day. When he complained, Doyle said, "Why don't you build your own fucking golf course?" Annenberg decided that Scorpy Doyle had a great idea. His luxurious par 73 course, nine meticulously tended greens and 18 overlapping fairways, was the most elegant in the desert. Annenberg also owned *The Daily Racing Form,* and the names he gave the holes sounded like racehorses. Number two was "The Soft Touch," number ten ""Elegantissima." Somewhere along the epically long driveway, amid the trees and water and swatches of emerald green, Ford realized how much he'd been looking forward to the weekend.

He set the binder down on the seat and reached for his wife's hand. Vietnam would keep for two more days.

Their car slowed and veered right, following the edge of a planter filled with blooming succulents at the front of the house. They glided beneath a massive porte-cochere, where Walter and Lee Annenberg were waiting. He was wearing a red blazer, white shirt, and grey slacks. Lee, who was thin and regal-looking, had on a yellow dress with white piping.

"Mr. Acting President, we bid you welcome," Annenberg said in his deep voice as Ford got out and extended his hand.

"The way you say that, Walter, it almost sounds like it means something," Ford said with a smile.

Lee greeted Jerry, then Betty, who said, "I love your yellow."

"I'll bet you can guess what house you'll be in," Lee said. They had three guest bungalows, each with a different color scheme. Pat Nixon preferred the yellow one, and Lee Annenberg had guessed Betty would, too.

They escorted the Fords inside. They had hired legendary architect A. Quincy Jones to design their house, an airy, light-drenched, modernist showpiece for their collection of impressionist and post-impressionist paintings. They stood out brilliantly against the interior walls of cream-colored Mexican cantera stone.

Betty stopped in front of a portrait of a middle-aged woman sitting in profile in a garden, her hat drawn over the eyes and a veil covering the rest of her stern-looking face.

"Suzanne Manet, nee Leenhoff, painted in 1880 by her husband, Edouard," Annenberg said. He loved to tell friends about his paintings. He called them his children. "His father hired her as his kids' piano teacher when the painter was a teenager. She may have been the father's lover first. In any event, she and Manet didn't marry until his father died."

Betty and Lee, both 56 and married before, exchanged mischievous glances. "How old was she when it was painted?" Betty asked.

"Fifty," Annenberg said. "It was the last time she sat for him."

"She's gaining on us, Lee," Betty said.

"She has nothing on either of you," Annenberg said.

"Except that she looks considerably more expensive," Ford said.

"I bought her two years ago," Annenberg said. "She used to belong to Vladimir Horowitz. He kept the painting in his practice studio in New York City. He treasured her because she had taught piano." Ford hadn't expected him to disclose the price, and he didn't.

"She looks as though she's concentrating pretty hard," Betty said. "Maybe she can still hear Horowitz playing Chopin and Liszt from here."

"We hope you'll both be as comfortable with us as Madame Manet," Annenberg said. Ford wasn't sure, but he thought his friend had spoken equivocally. Besides, she didn't look very comfortable. After a few minutes, Lee asked if Betty would like to get settled. As the ambassador led him toward his study, Ford had a funny feeling. Annenberg stepped aside as he entered.

Richard Nixon was waiting for him, sitting in Annenberg's easy chair, tugging at his lower lip with the temple of his reading glasses.

32

A National Security Can't

"**S**o fancy that," Bridgette Matheson said. "They're both in California."

"Fancy that," Ron Ziegler said. He took a sip of his scotch and stared at himself between the liquor bottles lining the mirror behind the Carlton Hotel bar in Washington. He was trying not to look directly at Bridgette. But he could see her face in the mirror, too. She was smiling.

"I thought we had a deal," she said.

"I didn't promise to tell you every time he left the house."

"Technically true. So I shouldn't be upset if he shows up in Moscow next week, or maybe on the moon."

"We shut down the Apollo program."

"That's just what you wanted us to think."

She sipped her white wine. They met for drinks periodically under the watchful eye of Nick Giordano, the bartender. Ziegler wasn't surprised that she'd called and suggested tonight. The Friday morning papers had the first Nixon family photo the public had seen since August 8. Ziegler had persuaded Nixon to permit a press pool on the plane, a wire service reporter and photographer who would give the rest of the press corps access to their notes and photos. The three couples were shown smiling a little stiffly in the narrow dining room in the San Clemente house.

Then the Friday edition of the *Washington Star*, the evening paper, published a photo of Ford on the golf course at the Annenberg estate. Bridgette had naturally put one and one together and called Ziegler.

"Are they going to meet?" she said.

"They live across the street from each other and haven't met in three months."

"So they're due."

Ziegler motioned to Nick for another drink. "It's a two-hour drive from the desert to San Clemente," he said. "You wouldn't be suspicious if one of them was in New York and the other in Philadelphia."

Bridgette closed her eyes and leaned her head to one side and brushed his shoulder and then opened her eyes and looked right at the mirror, finally catching Ziegler's. "What reason in the world," she said, "would anyone have to be suspicious of Richard Nixon and Ron Ziegler?"

He smiled back. Then he saw Nick arching his eyebrow at him from the end of the bar. "You want to get a table and have something to eat?" Ziegler said, nudging her gently so she'd raise her head from his shoulder.

"Nope."

"Me, neither." He shook his head at Nick and gave him a thumb's up to say all was well.

"Why didn't you go with him?"

"It would've looked suspicious," he said. She smiled. He said, "Seriously, Rose and I both couldn't go. It's a lot more fun for the family to have her along, and someone had to stay in Washington to oversee our massive apparatus. To keep his finger on the throbbing pulse of Capitol Hill."

"Mr. Ziegler, please," she said, waving her hand in front of her face.

Nick brought his drink. He paused to take a sip. Then he said, "Rose and I planned the movement before they left."

Bridgette put her wine down and reached into her purse for her black marble notebook. "The main issue would be fooling the press," she said.

"There're just two in the pool, and they're staying down the street at the San Clemente Inn. We put the old man in a sedan with two agents, and they left at five this morning. He was slumped in the back seat in case anyone was watching that early, but no one was. They got to Annenberg's six hours before Ford. Nobody was staking out the gate yet. The Fords had barely left Washington."

"I'm surprised you didn't want to be there to make sure everything went well."

"Rose is there. Rose could run the Pentagon."

She said, "You coordinated all this with the White House?" Ziegler shook his head. She sat up straight on her barstool. "This was a surprise party? Jesus, Ron, the poor bastard finally gets out of Dodge for a few rounds of golf, and there's Nixon in his face. You guys really are assholes."

"It wasn't my idea, Bridgette."

"What does he want to talk to Ford about so badly?"

He turned to look at her. "That I can't tell you."

"You won't tell me."

"I can't."

"That sounds like a national security can't."

"I can't say."

"Okay. You'll tell me later?"

"You called me an asshole," Ziegler said.

She poked his arm with he elbow. "You know I love you," she said.

"My wife loves me," he said. "You and Ben Bradlee are just using me."

"Nancy and I have actually talked about it. We love you for the same reasons, I, of course, from a discreet and proper remove."

"And that is?"

"Because you're one of the most loyal men we've ever met."

He shook his head. "I hate that sappy crap," he said.

"And, on the other hand, so like Mr. Nixon," she said. "Have I told you lately that you're within three votes of acquittal in the Senate? The last stand of the Nixon loyalists has put steel back in the Republican backbone."

Nixon's trial in the Senate would begin in four days, on Tuesday, December 3. "What about the Emmett Walsh factor?" Ziegler said.

"Negligible and shrinking," she said. "He may even have helped you. Some senators resent him using his position in Nixon's cabinet, especially when he's obviously promoting Reagan against both Nixon and Ford."

Ziegler drained his second drink. "Then I hope Emmett keeps calling senators, and good old George Aiken keeps dousing them with maple syrup," he said, putting his empty glass on a cocktail napkin and pushing it away. "But we're going to win by a straight party-line vote."

She stared at him. "I promised you the Rose Garden back if you were extremely lucky, but not by that margin. There're 40 Republicans in the Senate. You won't get them all."

He turned on his stool and put his hand on hers and stared into her eyes. "Yes, we will," he said.

33

Henry's *Penthouse*

Al Haig, the White House chief of staff, was at his desk a few blocks away when his intercom went off. He had on a blue blazer with brass buttons and a white shirt, grey slacks, and a red tie with thin navy stripes. He looked as fresh and alert as he had when he got to the office that morning. He pushed the flashing button on his phone and listened.

"It's the admiral," his secretary said.

He pushed the other blinking button and picked up the receiver. "Happy Thanksgiving, Sam," Haig said. He didn't look up from his paperwork.

"Are you aware that as we speak, Searchlight is meeting secretly with Passkey in California?"

"The last time I made an independent determination," Haig said, "this was still regarded as a free country."

"I can't believe you're so blasé about this. Why aren't you there?"

"The acting president doesn't need a babysitter. You wouldn't worry so much if you were cognizant as to the subject matter of their discussions."

"You think we don't know? That's why I'm calling. We know exactly what the tactical folks have recommended when the north attacks. What we don't know is if the Joint Chiefs would follow the order if Ford gives it. Have you taken a look at the Congress that takes office in January? It looks like the Socialist Workers Party. If we make a wrong move, the House and Senate appropriations committees will squeeze us dry."

"I'll be sure to tell the acting president that you would defy his lawful order because Congress might cut your pension."

"I'm the least of your problems. First you've got Nixon stealing documents from under your nose. Next he's riding around southern California in the trunk of a Mercury Grand Marquis like a goddamned wetback. Now Ford's tempted by grandiose visions of saving democracy for the gooks. Who's in control at the White House, anyway?"

Haig sat back and stared at the American flag opposite his desk. "I admit I gave serious consideration to squashing the Hungarian youngster that the president of the United States had befriended," he said. "But then I remembered what side I was on in the Cold War."

Sam's voice turned cold. "You watch your mouth, general."

"If you're so worried about the White House, admiral, maybe you should send someone over to keep an eye on us," Haig said. "You have another yeoman available? Maybe you could recall Skip Wiggins and Bill Sanchez from the pit of humiliation and ruin into which you cast them as a consequence of your last bumptuous escapade of counter-constitutional espionage."

"You knew just what we were doing. It was a legitimate operation."

Haig had been Kissinger's aide then. He'd known about the spying but didn't tell Nixon or Kissinger, fearing a scandal that would damage the military's legitimacy. "I told Tom Moorer and all of you geniuses in military intelligence that you had nothing to fear from the Nixon administration," he said. "But you were convinced that the biggest red baiter since Joe McCarthy was selling us out to Chairman Mao."

"But you didn't try to stop us, did you, Al?"

"And now we've got at least a slim chance to turn it around again in Vietnam. But you sound more concerned about having enough money to get your office painted every year."

Sam was silent for a moment. "It was never entirely about Nixon and Kissinger's policies," he said. "That's just all we told Wiggins and Sanchez."

"I count at least three military careers that were destroyed because you wanted to read the contents of Henry's briefcase," Haig said, raising his voice and waving a hand in the air. "You say it wasn't just because we were talking to the communists. Fine. I assume you weren't looking for his *Penthouse* magazine. Why the hell are you big tough spooks so scared of Dick Nixon?"

"Al," Sam said, "you absolutely, positively, definitely do not want to know. Just get the presidential playpen back in line, would you, please? Happy Thanksgiving to you, too." He hung up.

34

Ambushed

Walter Annenberg closed his study door behind Gerald Ford and left him alone with Richard Nixon. For an awkward moment, the acting president stood staring at him. Then Ford glanced over Nixon's shoulder. He could see a large framed photo of the Annenbergs with the queen and Prince Philip. Walter was wearing a morning coat and a medal denoting him as a member of the Order of the British Empire.

Ford looked calm, but he was seething. Nixon, who had the only comfortable chair in the room, didn't move. Then he caught himself and struggled to his feet. After hesitating again, he stepped toward Ford and offered his hand. "Did you have a good trip?" he said. "How's Betty?"

Ford shook Nixon's hand and stared at him. "Better every day. Pat?"

"Enjoying the weekend, at least. That townhouse is a downer."

"I assume she's not here with you," Ford said. "Betty would have liked to say hello."

Ford stared at Nixon, waiting. It was his show. Nixon's eyes darted around the room. The only other chair was behind Annenberg's desk. That wouldn't do. He wished he'd thought about the seating before. He should've asked the household staff to set it up properly. He wasn't good at improvising and now found himself completely overcome by the moment. He turned back to Ford and looked at him desperately.

"Here," Ford said. He walked to the patio door and opened it. Outside were two cushioned white chairs, shaded by trees and a long white trellis. They overlooked Lee's rose garden. It was a cool, clear desert afternoon. They would be comfortable in their lightweight sport coats.

A moment after they sat down, a middle-aged man in a uniform materialized with two glasses of lemonade on a tray and set them on the glass-topped table between their chairs.

"You haven't had any lunch," Nixon said as the man slipped away.

"I'm not hungry," Ford said. He sounded as angry as he ever did. He was famous for speaking in slow, even cadences. Some people, including Nixon, underestimated his intelligence as a result. Measured wasn't the same as plodding. At moments like this, his diction helped him keep his cool. He said, "I would have appreciated knowing about this in advance."

"Ah," Nixon said. He sat with his legs crossed. "Of course, with more people being made aware– "He gestured with his right hand as he spoke, rolling it over the wrist in Ford's direction over and over. "You have the danger of leaks and so forth and so on."

"Sometimes you have to trust people," Ford said.

"I've tried," Nixon said with a terse chuckle. He lowered his hand and grabbed the armrest. "It achieves mixed results."

Ford nodded and offered a weak smile. "But we keep trying," he said, "if for no other reason that they find out anyway."

"They don't find out everything," Nixon said, adding quickly, "I always told our people that it's the cover-up that gets you."

"You were right about that."

"Sometimes I'm right," Nixon said. "Usually not. Of course you know that. We've known each other a long time." Ford had come to Congress two years after Nixon, in 1949. "You could've played pro football," he said, "and I almost got into the FBI. But we opted for politics, so here we are."

"Here we are," Ford said.

Nixon paused, and Ford waited. It still wasn't his meeting. He resisted the temptation to mention the weather. Finally, he said, "You came into El Toro."

Nixon nodded. "LA for you," he said.

"We rode in Jack Kennedy's plane and car the same day," Ford said. "I hope it's not an omen."

Ford hadn't meant to allude to Nixon's ambush, but Nixon assumed he had. "As you know, I was in Dallas that day," Nixon said. "You and the rest on the Warren Commission got it right. I can't stand these conspiracy nuts, blaming it on Johnson and Hoover and so forth and so on. They just can't stand the idea that a pathetic little home-grown communist killed Saint Jack."

"Johnson thought Castro was involved or at least had known what was going to happen," Ford said. "We didn't dare reveal his suspicions. It would've led to World War III, since people would've demanded that we destroy the Russians' allies in Cuba." Ford decided to move things along, since he'd guessed the purpose of the meeting. "Which brings us to Vietnam," he said.

Nixon squirmed in his chair. "It's going to be tough, Jerry," he said, making a fist and looking at Ford with his sternest expression, his thick brows nearly hooding his eyes. "But you're going to have to kick 'em hard."

"Are you telling me what to do, Dick? Because that's not the way this is supposed to work."

"I'm only telling you what you know to be true," Nixon said. "There's nothing magical about communism or the glorious Vietnam revolution or the thugs in Hanoi. If you strike them, they break and bleed and whimper just like the rest of us. That's the insight that was won for us by the poor fellow who got killed in Vietnam, young Frank's in-law. The decisive factor in Vietnam continues to be our willingness to counter their support from the Soviets with the power we have, as I showed in 1972."

"And as you failed to do last spring."

"That was because of Watergate. I knew I'd lost the edge."

Ford stared at Nixon. "This is all because of Watergate," he said, taking in their meeting and Sunnylands and the whole creation with a broad sweep of his hand.

Nixon glared at Ford. "I beat Congress on Vietnam," he said. "They wanted to bug out, and I wouldn't. So now they beat me with this penny ante shit."

Ford said in his low, even voice, "You handed them the club." Nixon looked away. Ford went on. "Let's at least be honest with one another," he said. "Your policies in Vietnam worked where Johnson's had failed. You turned the war around and gave our allies in Saigon a fighting chance. But the advantage we won required the United States to continue to be strong, and that required an undiminished presidency. That, you failed to deliver."

"My Vietnam critics became my Watergate critics, right down the line. As a matter of fact, the whole thing goes back to the Hiss case."

"So what? You're supposed to be the political genius. An adversary uses every weapon he's got. You fought the war brilliantly, made inroads with the Soviets and Chinese, and won an historic reelection. But you also gave them the burglaries, cover-up, and dirty tricks, plus everything Haldeman's crew was doing with the IRS and FBI. You might as well have stood on the South Lawn and taken your pants off."

"Don't just blame them," Nixon said. "I take full responsibility."

"But they're going to jail, and so far, you're not," Ford said. "And now you want a shot at redemption. For the sake of your legacy, you want me to fix Vietnam."

Nixon closed his eyes. He hadn't bargained on being psychoanalyzed. He had never relied on anyone for redemption and wasn't going to start now. But he had to see the conversation through. He'd promised Garment and Ziegler that he'd at least try. He opened his eyes and looked at Ford and said quietly, "If you hit them once more, Jerry, I guarantee they'll fold, and 20 million people will have a chance for a better life."

""Watergate also devastated us in Congress," Ford said. "If I act as the NSC recommends, the Democrats will take it out on the military, and we'll be diminished even further in the eyes of our own strategic adversaries."

Nixon stared at him with his dark, grey eyes. "So you won't bomb."

"I didn't say that. I'll consider your advice, Henry's, and the Chiefs'. If and when the communists attack, I'll threaten and bluster. But if you insist on asking me today, I'm 50-50 or less when it comes to the kind of massive response the NSC staff has recommended."

"What does Henry say?"

"You know what Henry says. He says it would be a grave tactical and political risk for scant geopolitical gain."

"So letting Vietnam go down the tubes clears the way for making deals with the Russians and Chinese, and too bad for the poor bastards in South Vietnam."

Ford said, "Saving Saigon was your play last year. Don't blame me if we decide we can't afford to clean up the mess you left behind. You can't go back and alter the course of history."

Nixon looked out over Lee Annenberg's roses. He could see the rough brown mountains in the distance, towering above the lush green of Walter Annenberg's artificial paradise. He couldn't change history? He already had.

35

Have Him Bring Biff

It hadn't taken Howard Morton long to find Biff Michaels. He just called up a Golden State Club buddy who served on the ULA board. Bradford Michaels II, the father, was a top alumni donor. Based on what he'd already learned from Mitch, Morton understood the motives behind Michaels' philanthropy. Some men gave to their colleges to get their name above the door of a new biology lab. Michaels had done it to get his damaged spawn through the door despite his drug habit and 2.2 high school GPA.

In ten minutes, his friend called him back with the name of Biff's dormitory and his room and Social Security numbers. The trick was making contact. A prominent corporate attorney couldn't just knock on some little mediocrity's door one night and announce, while peering through the billowing marijuana smoke, that Ronald Reagan's operatives were wondering about the missing Nixon tape.

It would've been a perfect job for Mitch. Too bad. But Morton could tell that the arrogant little Jew wasn't on board anymore.

Something had obviously happened with the redhead. He'd get to the bottom of her, too. Reagan had been working with the FBI for years, informing on his left-wing Hollywood friends and using the agency to help keep his son Michael out of trouble and get him information about his daughter Maureen's married lover. The agency had no business helping Reagan with his personal problems, but he was pro-FBI, and he was on a White House trajectory. Morton would reach out to the Detroit field office. Mitch had said Emily Weissman's father was quite the radical. Maybe they kept records on his antiwar activities.

Then he'd use his business contacts to see if there happened to be one of those simple-minded flag-waving patriots on the board of the hospital where Sidney worked. They'd be upset to learn that one of their employees was an agitator. Morton could also use it against Emily if she planned to stay in government.

But first things first. Bradford II was a heart surgeon in San Diego and, as luck and marginal tax rates would have it, a Republican. Reagan's fellows had organized fat cat cocktail parties all over the state so he could amass a war chest for 1976. Morton called the staffer who was planning a reception at the City Club in San Diego and gave him Michaels' name. "Tell him you've heard that his son is making quite an impression on campus," he said, in his careful, knowing voice. "It's horseshit, but I want them both there. Do you understand? So tell him you hope he'll bring, um, *Biff* along. Comp them both. Tell them to be on time so they don't miss the governor. Call me back the moment they're confirmed."

Howard arrived just as the reception began and a half-hour ahead of Reagan and his party. He gave his name to one of three women seated at a table by the entrance. She smiled and tried to hand him his nametag. He ignored her. He got a soda water with lime from the bar and began to circulate, scanning the names. He found father and son in a corner, looking uncomfortable and out of place. Bradford was tall and handsome, with thick, slicked-back hair, black with streaks of grey. Biff had curly blond hair and needed a haircut. He was wearing wrinkled khakis, a sport coat, and boat shoes, and he smelled like cigarettes. Morton assumed his father had tied his tie for him.

"Are you the famous heart surgeon?" he said, extending his hand and introducing himself. "And his son, the big man on campus. The governor's looking forward to meeting you."

"We were surprised to be included," Dr. Michaels said. "I'm a big supporter, but I've never been involved before."

"Then you've got some catching up to do," Morton said. "Would you excuse us for a moment, son? There's someone I want your father to meet." He led Bradford to the other side of the room and introduced him to the county Republican chairman as the prominent surgeon Morton had told him about. He quickly made his way back to Biff.

"Your dad looks familiar," Morton said.

"He looks like Garrett McCann," the kid said sullenly. "Everybody says so. When he was young, I mean."

"This is something of a coincidence. I'm remembering a conversation I had with a colleague of mine regarding Mr. McCann. Something about a speech at a fraternity party."

"You know Mitch?" Biff said. "Man, I thought he was going to stroke out when he heard that tape. He said Nixon was done. He said it proved he had been involved in something really bad from the very beginning. I keep waiting to see something on TV."

"You still have the tape?"

Biff stared at him. "I gave it to Mitch."

Howard looked down into his cocktail glass for a moment. He fought off an urge to smash the kid's face with it. He looked up with a tense smile. "I don't suppose you thought to make a copy," Morton said.

"Nope. That was the only one."

"Do you remember what it said?"

Biff screwed up his face. He was trying hard. But he'd been smoking a lot of pot. "He was talking about being someplace with Nixon," he said. "It was something they were going to do. Didn't Mitch tell you?"

Morton briefly considered getting the names of everyone who had been at the fraternity party and heard McCann implicate the president in dirty tricks. He could have them swear out affidavits. But he couldn't be sure what they'd actually say, especially if they were as impaired as Biff Michaels. Besides, he couldn't use his own law firm. People would quickly figure out that Reagan's fellows were investigating Nixon, and that would be fatal.

By the time Bradford came back, Biff was alone. The county chairman had quickly ended their conversation when he saw Morton turn and leave the room. "Where's Mr. Morton?" he said to his son in a harsh voice, as though it were his fault that their new friend had gone. "What were you talking about?"

"That time I met Garrett McCann at the fraternity," Biff said. Just then there was swell of excited voices. Ronald Reagan had arrived and was standing behind a row of stanchions, smiling and waiting for his aides to organize a receiving line. The crowd surged toward him. People pushed past Bradford and Biff. Unfamiliar with the protocol, they waited for someone to tell them what to do. They stood and stared as Reagan began to greet the other guests with smiles and handshakes and pose for pictures in front of a row of flags. They were so angry at each other. They always had been and always would be.

36

Talking U.S. Grant

The headquarters of North Vietnam's 4th Army Corps was on a windswept plateau in the northern reaches of Phuoc Long province, in the Central Highlands. The commanders of Hanoi's People's Army had formed the corps just that summer. It was yet another consequences of Watergate and the neglect by the distracted Americans of their ally in Saigon. In early 1973, the north had decided it would have to live with the puppet regime indefinitely. Now it had built a hammer to destroy it once and for all.

Although they were deep inside South Vietnam, just 120 kilometers north of Saigon, Hanoi's troops moved with impunity in the province's remote and most lightly inhabited regions. The terms of the Paris Peace Accords in 1973 had permitted them to stay. Their supplies came over the border from Cambodia, the terminus of the Ho Chi Minh Trail. But they were hemmed in by Saigon's control of the provincial capital, Phuoc Binh, and of Route 14, which ran southwest to northeast through the province. With the puppet astride the road, Hanoi couldn't resupply and coordinate with its troops to the south and east.

It had been a stalemate for two years. The stalemate was about to end.

In the green canvas command tent, manufactured in the Soviet Union, General Giap sat smoking Panda cigarettes from China with his field commander, Major General Hoang Cam. It was Monday, December 2. They had two card tables pushed together, and they sat in folding metal chairs. A few junior officers worked quietly around them. Cam had spread a map over the tables. He was briefing Giap on his plan for the battle, the first major offensive against South Vietnam since 1972.

"The puppet has gotten lazy," he said. "He has a little over a thousand soldiers in the area, maybe 1,500 at most. Four battalions, artillery, plus some Popular Force platoons."

Giap chuckled. "The so-called Popular Forces are children armed with slingshots and spitballs," he said.

"That's what they give the boys," Cam said. "The girls fight with hairbrushes and chopsticks." He pointed to a spot along Route 14. "We'll hit them here. We think there's just one enemy company, relatively lightly equipped. The puppet has to bring in 500 tons of rice every month to feed the local population and their troops. We harass them each time, which has given us a good idea of their defenses."

"That's why the Politburo chose Phuoc Long," Giap said, standing and pointing to the map himself. "It's surrounded by mountains and almost completely isolated. It will be hard for the puppet to get reinforcements in quickly, especially once you control the road. After you seize Phuoc Binh and Route 14, we should be able to hold the province indefinitely."

Cam stood up, too, and looked at Giap with an expression of deep respect. He was short and trim like his senior colleague, with black hair and lively black eyes. "If we're successful, it will be the first capital we've seized since your historic victory in Quang Tri," he said.

"Ancient history," Giap said with his joyless smile. "We won and soon lost Quang Tri over two years ago."

"You would've achieved far more in the 1972 offensive if it weren't for the imperialist's bombers."

Giap's smile faded. "And the sun would stay up if the earth weren't spinning," he said.

Cam turned to face his colleague, his arms at his sides, a stance of vulnerability and humility. "I didn't mean to offend you, Minister Giap," he said. "You are the hero of Dien Bien Phu, the greatest general since U.S. Grant."

"You didn't offend me, general," Giap said, putting his hand on Cam's shoulder for a moment. "But when we're on the battlefield, we talk like soldiers. Le Duc Tho, Le Duan, and all the idealists in Hanoi think our victory is written in the stars. They've convinced themselves that the puppet troops are undersupplied and demoralized and that the Americans and their bombs are gone for good."

"You don't think they are?" Now Cam looked concerned. At 54, he was nearly ten years younger than Giap. He was smart, but he wasn't hard. Born in Hanoi and trained in China, he was too young to have been persecuted by the French colonists before World War II as Giap and his family had been. He'd spent his whole career in the army, starting as a squad leader and working his way up.

Phuoc Long would be his biggest campaign. The future of Vietnam depended on his success. So did Giap's career and reputation. He shouldn't make his battlefield general worry about factors behind his control. But it was important that he learn to be a realist. Only realists won battles.

Cam had put his cigarette on an ashtray on the table, and it had gone out while they talked. Giap took his pack from the chest pocket of his fatigues, shook a cigarette out, and offered to Cam and lit it for him. Then he lit one for himself, took a deep drag, and gestured with his head, inviting the younger man to follow him outside.

They came through the flaps of the tent into a drizzly, windy afternoon. The 3rd Infantry Division of the 4th Corps bustled around them, 6,000 dedicated young soldiers who had been galvanized for the fight to come. The encampment was ringed with mountains and the deep green of the highlands terrain. To the south, mist-covered hills hid the object of the massive assault they were mounting. If it weren't for the preparations for war, the view would've been beautiful.

Giap directed Cam's attention to the north, toward Cambodia and Laos. "You mentioned General Grant," he said. "I wonder if he could have defeated the slave states while simultaneously preventing Canada from smuggling them arms and reinforcements."

"You refer, comrade, to the puppet's border with Cambodia and Laos."

"All 1,700 kilometers of it. Imagine if that were our problem and not Saigon's."

"But in this instance, the puppet regime is the slave state. We and our revolutionary brothers in Laos and Cambodia are the liberators."

Giap grinned mirthlessly. "Remember, comrade, that we're soldiers first," he said. "Forget about the politics and who's right and wrong. Tyrants win wars all the time, maybe more often than not. When Nixon bombed our sanctuaries in Cambodia, it set us back two years."

"But Nixon's gone," General Cam said.

Giap threw away his cigarette and took a deep breath. The air smelled rich and clean, thick with the wet earth and plants and, as always outside in nature, the scent of things that had died and were rotting. He loved the Central Highlands. It felt as alive and peaceful as anyplace in Vietnam.

But he had to return to Hanoi soon and brief his comrades. Le Duc Tho would be curious about how the preparations were going. So would Le Duan, the functional leader of North Vietnam since Ho Chi Minh's death. Comrade Ho had wanted to negotiate with the south. He had an almost mystical faith that Vietnam would be unified one day and believed that waiting for the inevitable was better than war. But Le Duan always wanted to attack and fight. He'd been pushing for an invasion for two years. He thought victory was his destiny. Now he'd get his wish.

Giap looked at Hoang Cam, who now watched proudly as a squad returning from a patrol marched through the mud past the command tent. The soldiers turned and saluted the two generals, one of them a living legend. They stood side by side, straightened their backs, and returned the salute.

After they had passed by, General Giap sniffed the fragrant air again. There was something sour on the wind now, from a fire burning nearby. He suddenly thought of the smokestacks of the U.S.S. Enterprise's strike group, which was just 1,400 kilometers away in the Philippines. At flank speed, she could be off the Vietnamese coast in less than a day. She would outrun her escorts and probably rendezvous with other allied ships already in the neighborhood. She would

218

be formidable. As far as anything Hanoi could do was concerned, she would be invincible. During his 1972 invasion, the Enterprise had seeded mines in Haiphong Harbor while her air wing destroyed army barracks, petroleum depots, railroad stations, and other targets in North Vietnam.

U.S. B-52s based in Guam and at U Tapao airfield in Thailand could reach Hanoi in an hour. If they were deployed, only the humanity or political prudence of the imperialist commanders as they selected their targets would save the capital of North Vietnam from annihilation.

General Giap lit another cigarette and looked back to the south as the smoke billowed around his head. General Cam was right. Only Richard Nixon was crazy enough to unleash such horror, and for the time being, he was wounded and powerless. It was all the time they would need to win the victory they'd awaited all their lives. He turned and walked back inside the tent.

37

It's Begun

For a week, Pat Nixon and Rose Woods had huddled in the cluttered bullpen on the second floor of Jackson Place, watching the live coverage of Richard Nixon's Senate trial. Rose's platoon of loyal, tight-lipped ladies hadn't had much to do lately. When the trial began the previous Tuesday, she had sent them home so she and Pat could watch alone. They had shouted at Nixon's tormenters and applauded and whooped in support of his defenders. Sometimes they held hands, hugged, and wept. It had all been awful. They hadn't missed a second of it.

It was Thursday, December 12. The whole country was transfixed by history's first televised impeachment trial. Only Richard Nixon didn't seem to care.

Most observers, including Ron Ziegler's friend Bridgette Matheson, believed that his most loyal Republican friends in the Senate, a few of whom, such as George Aiken, would retire in a few weeks, had brought Nixon to within a vote or two of the 34 he needed to be acquitted. From past experience, Rose had assumed that with his fate being decided in front of a global audience, he'd be buzzing with anxiety.

But since returning from California after Thanksgiving, he'd been as serene as she'd ever seen him. He'd only dictated a handful of letters and memos. He hadn't even been especially stir-crazy. He had visited Julie and David's a couple of times, and the week before he'd asked the Secret Service to take him and Pat for a drive along the Blue Ridge Mountains to see what was left of the fall foliage.

He had spent most of the time closeted with Ron Ziegler in his study one floor up. That's where he was this afternoon. Since 7:30

in the morning, he'd placed a half-dozen calls to Len Garment, the White House counsel. Rose had wondered what all that was about. She knew enough not to ask. If it amounted to anything, she knew she'd find out soon.

On the screen of one of the three big Zeniths in Rose's office, the cameras showed James St. Clair, Nixon's attorney, as he wrapped up his daylong argument against the first article of impeachment, which accused Nixon of organizing a cover-up of the Watergate burglary. The trial was taking place in the chamber of the House of Representatives, presided over by the chief justice of the Supreme Court, Warren Burger.

This afternoon, as she had for the last week, Pat sat at one of the volunteers' desks. Rose had rolled across the creaky floorboards on her stenographer's chair so they could sit side by side, as they often had many years before. When things had gotten busy in Nixon's senatorial office, Pat came in and answered mail and the phone along with Rose and the other staffers and volunteers, identifying herself to callers as Miss Ryan, her maiden name.

The women were small, thin, and always meticulously dressed and coifed. Along with sisterly commiseration, they had had been swapping outfits for 20 years. This morning, they had independently decided to put on something resolutely cheerful. As of that evening, the trial would be half over. Article II, alleging that Nixon improperly used his power to punish his enemies, was up next. Pat wore a silk print dress with a floral design in green and persimmon red, Rose a Santa-red wool suit with white piping. They had both been thinking about Christmas and the gift of their impending release from Watergate and, one way or the other, from Jackson Place.

Born to Irish Catholic fathers, Pat and Rose had the same rosy complexion and lively eyes. Pat was a strawberry blonde, with finer, more porcelain features. Rose still went to mass. Pat, with her Christian Scientist mother and Quaker husband, had fallen away. After her mother died, she had helped her father raise her two younger brothers on a hardscrabble farm thirty miles south of Los Angeles. During the loneliest days of her girlhood and adolescence, she had longed for a sister as a helpmate and friend. As a political wife, she had thanked God and her husband for sending her Rose.

This afternoon, she didn't like what she was hearing from her husband's attorney. She glanced at Rose and waved at the TV screen, where St. Clair was shown standing motionless in the well of the House, his hands grasping the sides of a podium. She hadn't seen him smile yet.

"I don't think he's really for Dick," she said. Her family had moved from Nevada when she was little. Pat had the flat, indeterminate accent of a southern Californian. She remembered that St. Clair had nearly bolted from Nixon's team when the smoking gun tape became public in August. Pat knew that her husband wasn't to everyone's taste and had learned to spot the skeptics quickly. She had an equally keen eye for infatuated newcomers. "Haven't you seen through him yet?" she'd say to his most star-struck assistants.

Outside their close circles of family and friends, no one really knew her or Rose or how easy it was to get their Irish up. The public Pat was dutiful and cheerful. No president's wife had traveled as much and as widely. She'd spearheaded a massive mercy mission to Peru after a killer earthquake in 1970 and, at her insistence, became the first first lady in history to visit a war zone. She wanted to visit wounded soldiers in a field hospital and get an idea of what combat conditions were like. After the pilot of the Huey she was riding in had plunged into the landing zone as quickly as he could to evade Viet Cong fire, a photographer captured an image of her smiling and wearing a dress and pumps, framed in the open doorway between soldiers draped in bandoliers.

People had never heard of Rose Woods until she became famous for what she claimed was her accidental erasure of eighteen and a half minutes of one of the White House tapes. In a generation or two, women with their gifts would lead corporations and run for the Senate and president. In their time, devotion to Richard Nixon and absolute discretion were their most celebrated virtues.

"I admit Jim isn't exactly one of us," Rose said, "but I've never seen anyone work harder than he has on this case. He absolutely wants to win for the boss."

"He may want it for himself," Pat said. "But Dick says that to win in the courtroom, you have to be a true believer. People can tell St. Clair doesn't have his heart in it."

"No one's arguments will change any votes at this point," Rose said.

Pat raised her chin and shook her head. "I know all about what Ron's special friend at the *Post* says. I'm talking about the country, not the Senate," she said. "Nobody will have any respect for Dick after this."

They'd been through a lot with him, crisis after crisis, including devastating campaign defeats in 1960 and 1962. They'd both been in his motorcade in Caracas in 1958 when an angry mob attacked them. They all could've been killed, and Rose was cut on the face by flying glass.

With all that, these seven days of televised Watergate testimony had been the worst of all. Pat especially hated hearing Nixon's taped mutterings echoing in the House chamber with the obscenities bleeped over, each mechanical tone inviting the listener's imagination to insert the worst possible vulgarity.

Nixon's language and bigotry were just salt in the deeper wounds of Watergate. Members of the House, serving as prosecutors, played tapes in which the president appeared to condone pressuring the FBI to limit its investigation, paying hush money, and encouraging his aides to lie. St. Clair and Nixon's other advocates replied with arguments about Nixon's national security concerns and his Socratic conversational style, in which, they said, he stated outrageous propositions to see how others would react. Saying he could get a million dollars from his buddy Bebe Rebozo as hush money for Watergate defendants, St. Clair argued, wasn't the same as doing it, especially because Rebozo's million dollars never materialized.

Whether Nixon was guilty or not, he had damaged himself mortally by discussing such things and recording the conversations. More than anything, Pat and Rose felt terrible for him. They loved him despite his insecurity, desperate hunger to be admired, and relentless preoccupation with what was best for him. They also knew his softer, considerate and solicitous side and his devotion to his family and the few people he trusted.

Besides, the women despised his critics' unctuousness and opportunism. In politics, someone was always out to get you, and Pat and Rose believed that the Democrats were using Watergate to get back at Nixon for Vietnam, for beating them in 1972, for Alger Hiss, and above all to get more power for themselves.

All those things, they could talk about, and they did. It was harder to admit, even to one another, that they felt imprisoned and ashamed because of Nixon's atrocious choices. Rose knew the working Nixon far better than Pat. She'd listened to conversations that were far worse than the ones the House prosecutors used for their case. She worried that the tapes Pat had heard already had introduced her to a Richard Nixon she hadn't met yet despite 34 years of marriage. Above all, Pat Nixon and Rose Woods knew that if he and Bob Haldeman hadn't muffled and marginalized them, Watergate would never have happened.

In some mythical, collegial Nixon White House, Pat and Rose would've been superstars. They were tough, plainspoken people who loved to laugh if the jokes weren't too raw and hear gossip if it wasn't too mean. They took practical, humane positions on politics and policy. Everyone knew Pat had tried to get Nixon to put a woman on the Supreme Court. She favored women's and reproductive rights as well as amnesty for Vietnam draft dodgers. For her part, Rose did everything she could to keep members of the Nixon family in communication with one another despite the boss's incessant secret keeping and triangulation. He hated confrontations, especially with his family. He also wanted everything exactly his way. Aunt Rose served as an honest broker, softening the blow when he made a decision his family didn't like and gently taking him to task when he had failed to take their opinions and feelings into account.

On the issues, Nixon was usually wise enough to heed good advice, especially Pat's, even if it went against his instincts. He knew himself well enough to understand that when he'd already decided what to do, people who disagreed shouldn't be permitted to get close enough to try to change his mind. When tempted by dirty tricks and other unavailing plots against his enemies, Nixon should've kept his women close at hand. Instead, he and Haldeman warded off the better angels of his nature, unleashing the darkness that found its inevitable expression in the scandal that had now engulfed them all.

Pat and Rose watched with considerable relief as St. Clair finished his statement. It was 5:30. Before long, the chief justice adjourned the trial until the following morning. Pat lit a cigarette and took a deep draw. "I wish I could be as confident as Dick," she said, leaning back in her chair and crossing her legs. "He keeps telling me I don't have to worry, everything's going to be fine."

"We're feeling pretty good," Rose said. "His friends have rallied around."

Pat blinked at her friend through the cigarette smoke. "If it were really a matter of one or two senators," she said, "he'd be frantic. He's got something else up his sleeve. He always does."

"Me, too," Rose said. "Namely a cold bottle of Chablis in the fridge."

"Go forth," Pat said. "I'll man the fort."

"Nobody ever calls this late," Rose said. "I'll be right back." She ducked down the stairs to the kitchen on the first floor. A moment later, the phone rang. Pat got up, walked to Rose's desk, and picked up. "Miss Ryan," she said.

A man said, "I beg your pardon?"

"May I ask who's calling?"

"Frank Szabados at the NSC," he said. "Excuse me, but is this the first lady?"

"Guilty as charged."

"I'm so sorry, ma'am. Good evening, Mrs. Nixon."

She laughed. "Don't worry, young man. How can we help you?"

"May I speak with your— May I please speak with the president?"

Pat peered at the row of buttons along the bottom of the receiver. "I don't know how to transfer you," she said. "I'm sure the operator would have put you straight through to him."

"He told me to reach him through Miss Woods, ma'am."

"Rose will be back in a minute. May she call you back? Or perhaps you'd like to leave a message."

"Please tell him that it's begun."

"What's begun?"

"The invasion of South Vietnam. The communists have attacked Route 14 in Phuoc Long province. He said I should let him know right away."

Mrs. Nixon stared at the phone and said, "What do you expect him to do about it, for goodness sake?"

38

The Second Ford Administration

Emily Weissman and Frank Szabados agreed to meet for a quick bite before dawn the next morning at a place on 13th St. N.W., four blocks from the White House. When he called her the night before to make arrangements, she had questioned his choice of a restaurant. But Frank said there wasn't anything else open early enough. Emily hadn't been eating breakfast, anyway, so she said she'd come along for coffee.

Frank was smiling and holding the door when Emily walked up at six. It was dark and frigid outside and bright and warm inside. She found a yellow table with red plastic chairs by the window and sat watching bundled-up men and women hurry past on the sidewalk. They were Washington's blue-collar wage earners, on their way home from working graveyard or heading in for early shifts. They were almost all black. It occurred to Emily that they occupied the same socio-economic cohort as her parents. Many seemed to be Sidney and Marian's age. She wondered if their children would ever have a chance to work as professionals in the White House.

Frank sat down and put a tray in the center of their table. Emily stared at it. "So you're really having hamburgers for breakfast," she said. "You'll be dead before you're forty."

"I'm having an Egg McMuffin," Frank said, "and so are you." He put hers on the table in front of her along with orange juice, coffee, and a napkin.

"Is it kosher?"

"No less than you are. It's made with Canadian bacon and American cheese."

"So it's fine international cuisine," she said.

Frank sat down and put his napkin in his lap. "It's all the rage among you capitalists," he said. "They introduced it last year. Where have you been?"

"At law school in Boston, eating Philly cheesesteaks. A place in Harvard Square delivered 24 hours a day."

"That sounds like the munchies to me."

"Torts, contracts, and con law," she said, "and sometimes munchies." She unwrapped her sandwich carefully with her fingertips and held it up so she could see what was in the middle. "How do they make the egg round?" she said.

"I don't know."

"If they went to the trouble of making the egg round, why is the cheese square? I assume it would be easier to create a round cheese slice than a round portion of scrambled eggs. Plus it's on a round muffin. This thing's a mess. It won't last."

"I hope you never have the opportunity to interrogate me in court," Frank looked at her over the rim of his coffee cup as he washed down a bite of his sandwich. "Eat your breakfast," he said. "It's going to be a long day."

"I imagine so," she said, nibbling on a corner of the cheese. "How goes the war?"

"Is President Nixon making a statement?" Frank said. "He said he would."

She shot him a tense look. "What do you mean by a statement?"

"An endorsement of Ford using any and all means to enforce the terms of the Paris Peace Accords, which the communists have now flagrantly violated."

"I wouldn't necessarily know. Nobody's said anything in Len's shop."

"He told me he would," Frank said, sounding perturbed.

"Then I suppose he will," she said. She ate a little more of her sandwich and washed it down with orange juice. "What's the latest?"

"It began about 12 hours ago, Friday morning their time," he said. "An infantry battalion of regular troops attacked a South Vietnamese position along a road that the south absolutely has to hold to keep from losing the war for good."

"Maybe it's just a feign."

"It's an invasion," Frank said. "We just got word two hours ago that the Viet Cong have attacked nearby, at a place called Bu Dop."

"Do you ever sleep?"

"Not last night. The only good news is that it's been raining torrentially for the last few hours, so we may get an extra day to reinforce the position. Even with that, it doesn't look good. They picked an isolated spot where they have an overwhelming advantage." Emily had finished her sandwich. "Would you like another?" Frank said with a grin.

She glared at him. "What about Ford?" she said.

Frank looked at his watch. "Dr. Kissinger is taking me along when he briefs him at 7:30," he said.

"When you'll advocate the greatest conventional air strike since the firebombing of Dresden in World War II. Nobody would think it of you, sitting here so beatifically with your Egg McMuffin. You probably have to go."

"Ten minutes," he said, sitting back with his coffee and smiling. "Anne tells me the enemy is also moving on your works."

She sighed. "He's coming next week to look for a job," she said.

"Where's he going to live?"

"Certainly not with me."

"But you've lifted the anathema."

"I've agreed to a series of meetings, with precise times, locations, and agendas agreed on in advance," she said.

"I believe that in your country, those are called dates," he said.

"Ours may require chaperones."

"Should Anne and I wear sidearms?"

Emily sat forward and brushed her hair behind her ears. "When did you know you loved her?" she said in a quiet voice.

"We were at dinner in Saigon. It was our very first time. She smiled at me in a certain way she has."

Emily arched an eyebrow and said, "Sometimes a smile is just a smile." Frank shrugged. She said, "Anyway, that's not how it was with our parents, or at least with mine. The whole love at first sight phenomenon, I mean."

"My mother was a teaching assistant for my father at the university in Budapest," he said. "They detested each other at first. Their affection grew slowly out of shared interests, work, politics, all that. Yours?"

"It grew out of me," she said. "They dated in high school and got careless one night in the backseat of an Oldsmobile."

"Lucky for us," he said. "I'm sure they had no regrets the second they saw you. Are you second-guessing your feelings for Mitch?"

She fiddled with her empty coffee cup, suspending it in the air with her fingertips. "I'm stuck with those," she said. "It's the only time I've been in love in my life. But there isn't going to be any more monkey business until the second Ford administration." She looked at Frank's usually pale face. "You're blushing," she said.

He looked at his watch again. "The fever of war is rising in my blood," he said. "Let's get to the office."

They buttoned their coats, left the restaurant, and hurried along F Street into the teeth of a bitter wind toward the southeast gate of the White House. Once inside the Old Executive Office Building, they parted ways. Frank had to collect his exhibits for the meeting in the Oval Office with the acting president. When Emily arrived in the counsel's office, she found Len Garment and Ron Ziegler waiting for her.

"Take off your coat and come on in," Garment said through the open door.

"You gentlemen are early," she said. She put her coat on the hook on the back of her office door and reached across her desk for a blue folder. Her usual chair was available in Garment's office. Len was smoking and drinking coffee. Someone had poured Ziegler a cup, but it was sitting untouched on a corner of Garment's desk. He was slumped low in his chair, holding onto the armrests and dangling his right foot on the opposite knee.

Emily sat down, put the folder in her lap, and put her hands on top of it. "So you guys are sure about this," she said.

"We're not," Garment said.

"He is," Ziegler said.

She opened the folder, which contained two letters. One was addressed to the speaker of the House, the other to the president pro tem of the Senate. She handed one to each man.

"This is it?" Ziegler said.

"I'm not sure I care for the tone of your voice," Emily said. "I worked through lunch yesterday."

The letter had a space at the bottom for Richard Nixon's signature. Ziegler read the complete text aloud. It said, "My temporary inability to discharge the powers and duties of the Office of President of the United States no longer exists."

39

Emmett Wept

On most Sundays, Emmett and Ellie Walsh sat reading the newspapers in their breakfast nook in Bethesda and went to the 11 a.m. service at the Methodist church in Chevy Chase. Its parishioners were used to seeing politicians and high-ranking officials at church and tried to respect their privacy. During coffee hour, they usually kept the conversation light and inconsequential. When he and Ben Claussen had returned from China after meetings with the finance minister, people just asked if he'd gone to the Great Wall or seen a panda bear.

Today would be different. The whole world was astonished at Richard Nixon and terrified at the thought of what he might do next. In both papers, the whole front section was dedicated to the latest crisis. They'd both read almost every word. Emmett was working on the *Washington Post* now. It had a two-deck banner headline: "Massive Nixon Bombing Continues As Resignation Demands Escalate." Another story detailed the House Judiciary Committee's plans to convene on Monday morning for emergency consideration of another article of impeachment alleging that Nixon had committed war crimes. Ellie and Emmett hadn't watched the three networks' Sunday morning public affairs programs. If they had been, they would've heard Nixon's media critics yelling themselves hoarse.

Emmett was one of the top four members of Nixon's cabinet and fifth in the line of succession. People at church would naturally hold him accountable. The pastor, who tried to be balanced but tended to be liberal, would undoubtedly denounce Nixon's actions while looking at

Emmett, as though there were something he could do about it. There would probably be reporters. So they'd decided to stay home.

By lunchtime Friday, the U.S. had recommenced the air war over Vietnam. Within an hour of the communist attack at dinnertime Thursday Washington time, Acting President Ford had issued a statement denouncing Hanoi and had ordered the U.S.S. Enterprise from the Philippines to the South China Sea. Before he could take any further action, Nixon reclaimed the presidency. He had delivered both his letters by 9 a.m. Friday. By ten, following Frank Sabados's recommendations almost to the letter, Nixon had ordered tactical strikes by the Enterprise's Air Force and Marine aircraft against North Vietnam's ground forces in Phuoc Long province plus B-52 sorties out of Thailand against a dozen positions along the Ho Chi Minh trail, the communists' resupply route through Laos and Cambodia.

According to news accounts, the Pentagon had at first resisted Nixon's orders on the grounds that Congress hadn't appropriated any funds for the operations. The White House replied that as long as the planes and ordnance existed and the flight crews were in place, as commander-in-chief he had the right to order their use in a national security emergency. Whether Congress would pay for replacements was a problem for another day.

In the darkest days of Watergate, Jim Schlesinger, the Defense secretary, had asked military commanders to let him know if Nixon gave any strange orders. He evidently had visions of the president encircling the White House with tanks to hold onto power. When Schlesinger told the Joint Chiefs that he and the attorney general agreed that Nixon's Vietnam orders was lawful, they followed them scrupulously.

On Saturday, Nixon set his face for Hanoi. Many of the military and industrial sites that the U.S. had destroyed or crippled in December 1972, such as railroad yards, petroleum depots, power plants, and airfields, had been rebuilt. The U.S. attacked these first. In his report, Frank wrote that the message was "if you fix it, we break it, as day follows night." Applying lessons learned in 1972, when Hanoi had shot down 15 B-52s, F-111s based in Thailand were deployed against Hanoi's air defenses, both fighters and missile sites, before the bombers arrived.

The stormy weather and low clouds gave the Americans an additional advantage. By the end of the second full day of air operations on Sunday, the U.S. had only lost four aircraft.

In the second wave, Nixon ordered the re-mining of Haiphong Harbor and bombing raids against Hanoi's defense, intelligence, and foreign ministries. In a decade of full-scale war, the U.S. had never taken such a step. North Vietnam said that over 2,000 people, most of them bureaucrats, secretaries, and cleaning people, had died in three hours, including the deputy foreign minister. Hanoi's fabled Citadel, once the home of Vietnam's emperors and now the location of key government offices, was a smoking ruin.

On the CBS Evening News on Saturday night, Walter Cronkite had devoted the first 20 minutes to what critics called Nixon's Advent bombing, interviews with constitutional experts who said he'd shredded what was left of the Constitution, and coverage of massive demonstrations on college campuses and in Lafayette Square across the street from the White House.

Almost every nation in the world had expressed shock or disgust at the United States' savagery. No one from the Nixon administration defended the president. Some analysts speculated that his staff and cabinet were on the verge of open revolt.

Nixon hadn't been seen in public since he and Pat had walked from Jackson Place to the White House on Friday. Ron Ziegler, back in his old position of press secretary, sent word to the press corps that the next briefing would be Monday morning.

On Saturday afternoon, the White House issued a written statement. Nixon had drafted it himself in longhand a few days before, while still living and working in Jackson Place. "In January 1973, after a ten-year war in which nearly 60,000 brave young Americans died," he wrote, "North Vietnam promised to cease hostilities against allies of the United States in South Vietnam. The actions I have ordered are the ones I vowed to undertake if Hanoi violated the Paris Peace Accords. Our air operations will continue, and will continue to escalate in severity, until the enemy ceases its aggression and withdraws all its regular army forces from Phuoc Long province." The *Post* quoted unnamed administration sources saying that direct strikes against Le Duan and other top leaders, including the use of Green Berets and other special forces units, would be next.

"I think he's gone completely insane," Ellie said.

The winter sunlight angled through her big kitchen window and fell across the newspapers on the table. The house smelled like bacon and pancakes. It was quiet, warm, and peaceful, the furthest things from falling bombs. Emmett looked up from his paper, gave his wife a weak smile, and gazed out the window at the leafless, ash-colored river birches in their back yard. "I don't know him very well, as much as I've tried," he said. "I always got the feeling he was avoiding me. He certainly seems determined now." Though he preferred the fiscal conservatism of Ronald Reagan, Emmett never had anything particularly against Nixon. He was surprised to be offered the job at Treasury. Only after the Senate confirmed his nomination did he learn that Howard Morton had been behind it from the beginning.

Ellie waved at the papers. "Nobody wants all this," she said.

"Not quite nobody," he said. He folded the *Post* in half and passed it across the table to Emily, pointing to a passage on an inside page that he thought she must have missed. She had her reading glasses on a necklace. She put them on and read aloud. "'I fully support President Nixon's efforts to bring an end to the illegal aggression against our allies and the cause of freedom in Indochina,' Reagan said." She took her glasses off and stared at her husband. "I thought Howard's whole idea was to maneuver Nixon and Ford out and Reagan in," she said.

"Ron's a simple man," he said. "He sometimes lets his principles get in the way of his political interests. Howard's job is to ameliorate Reagan's better instincts."

"Howard's job is to get Howard into power. Does Reagan even know what he's up to?"

"I sometimes wonder."

She put the paper down and stood, collecting his coffee cup. "I'll bet Nancy wishes he'd kept his mouth shut," she said, pouring him a refill from a percolator on the counter. "Nobody else is defending it."

She put the cup on the table and stood behind Emmett, massaging his shoulders.

"There are actually some other supportive quotes," Emmett said. "A few Republican members of Congress spoke up, along with the veterans groups. Even a southern Democrat or two are in favor. They've been drowned out in the general hysteria." Emmett closed his eyes and leaned his head against her stomach. "I can't imagine what tomorrow will be like," he said.

When the phone rang, Ellie moved to answer it, but Emmett stopped her by holding onto her hands. "I'll get it in my study," he said, standing and kissing her on the cheek.

Walsh closed the door and glanced around the room, which was lined with books he hadn't read and filled with furniture he didn't like, all chosen by an interior decorator. He missed their penthouse in San Francisco and farm in Napa. He settled behind his desk, sighed deeply, and picked up.

"I'm surprised to find you at home," Howard Morton said. Walsh noticed that he'd dropped the pretence of "Mr. Secretary." "Aren't you on the NSC?"

"He hasn't called a meeting," he said.

"But you will."

"Of the National Security Council?"

"Have you even bothered to read the 25th Amendment?"

"Please get to the point."

"If the vice president and a majority of the cabinet agree that the president's still incapacitated, they can notify Congress within four days, whereupon Congress decides who the president really is."

"But it's been two days, and that hasn't happened."

"It will when one of you calls the vice president and demands that the cabinet be convened for a vote. Ford can't very well refuse."

"Nixon's obviously not incapacitated. He's conducting the most ruthless air campaign since World War II."

"I didn't call to get your historical insights. Your instructions are to call the meeting and say you think Nixon's nuts."

Emmett clutched the phone. "We're at war," he said. "Even the governor is supporting the president. What you're suggesting will incite total chaos. It might even get people killed. I understand that you think it would cause more problems for Nixon and Ford. But I won't do it."

Howard was silent. Emmett closed his eyes. He knew what was coming next. Howard would invoke his ancient sin. It was the leverage he'd used to force him to try to turn senators against Nixon. In the early 1960s, Morton had been working in the mergers and acquisitions department of California Empire Bank. One of his clients was a publicly traded pharmaceutical company that was getting its ducks in a row to acquire a competitor. Over drinks at the Bohemian Club, he'd shared the details with a friend who went out and bought stock in the smaller company, made a killing, and sent Ellie a mink coat at Christmas as a thank-you present. They kept it. Emmett didn't realize he'd committed a felony. Howard Morton, his friend's attorney, did.

"Don't bother," Emmett said. "I'll make the call." He hung up, put his face in his hands, and wept.

40

Stinky and Stinkier

On Monday morning, Ron Ziegler stuck his head through Emily Weissman's office door. "How're we doing, gorgeous?" he said. "I expected to see you chin deep in those big-ass law books like on the Perry Mason Show."

Emily looked up from her yellow legal pad and glared at him. She wasn't in the mood for his Rat Pack shtick. "We have no precedents, no legislation, no opinions, no case law, no regulations, no nothing," she said, waving at a small stack of folders on her desk. "I would settle for an article in *Reader's Digest*. I even called to get advice from my constitutional law professor at Harvard, who incidentally is a major Nixon-hater."

"I assume you said we'd kill him if he told anybody."

"Of course."

What'd he say?"

"He said he trusted my judgment. Imagine that. And if you make a crack about my tender years, I quit."

Ziegler grinned. "I was just going to say that it's fitting and proper—"

"For the one who dug the hole to dig us out of it," she said. "Len beat you to that observation last night." She turned back to her work, hoping Ziegler would leave. Len Garment had called Emily at home and described his phone call from Vice President Ford. The secretary of the Treasury had lodged a formal request for a cabinet meeting to decide whether it agreed that the president's incapacity had come to an end. As White House counsel, Len had asked Emily to plan the meeting, which was scheduled for four that afternoon.

Emily was improvising, since no such event had ever occurred before. She had quickly realized that it came down to the atmospherics and the agenda, including the precise words that Ford would use to introduce the subject and conduct the meeting.

In August, Nixon claimed that the distractions of his Watergate defense had kept him from spending enough time on the public's business. Would Walsh try to convince the cabinet that it was still true? With his defense in the trial well underway and almost entirely in the hands of others, Nixon now had plenty of time to fulfill his constitutional obligations.

So Walsh needed another play. Emily's greatest fear was that he would allege that Nixon's actions in Vietnam were evidence that he was emotionally imbalanced. If just one or two others agreed, they'd be in deep trouble. Nixon would never submit to a psychiatric exam. Even if he would, they wouldn't have time. He had taken back the presidency Friday morning. The constitution gave the cabinet until Tuesday morning to notify Congress that it believed he was still incapacitated. Once the idea was introduced and actively considered that the president was a head case, the cabinet might punt to Congress just to cover its rear.

Without putting down her pen, Emily refreshed her coffee. Ziegler was still standing there. There was a second teacup on the sterling silver tray on her desk. Without looking at him, she tilted the bone china carafe in his direction.

He made a face. "No, thanks," he said. "I have a press briefing in a half hour, and I'd prefer not being awake."

"Do they know about the cabinet meeting?" she said.

"Not yet," he said. He wandered into her small office and gazed at the items on her wall. She displayed her University of Michigan and Harvard diplomas, side-by-side color portraits of the Nixons, a Janis Joplin poster, and a small framed photograph of one of a bridge's spires against a brilliant blue sky. "Where's this?' he said, gesturing at it.

"The might Mac," she said. "It's the longest suspension bridge in the world, connecting the upper and lower peninsulas across the

Straits of Mackinaw. Every summer we'd drive up from Detroit to visit my mother's parents in St. Ignace. We used to have to take the ferry, but then they built the bridge in the late fifties. It was my favorite thing in the world. Every June I couldn't wait to get my first glimpse of it."

"You were a short teenaged girl," he said, "and it was a pointy object thrusting upward." Emily didn't answer. She kept making notes on her legal pad. He sat down in the chair next to her desk and watched her work for a moment. "What's the matter?" he said.

She looked up and shook her head. "How's the president?" she said.

"Al Haig and I just talked him out of calling Liddy and putting a contract out on Emmett," he said.

Emily was about to offer a pallid smile when she saw the look on Ziegler's face. G. Gordon Liddy, one of the Watergate burglars, was famous for devising a plan to kill an obstreperous newspaper columnist by putting LSD on his steering wheel. Maybe Ron wasn't kidding.

Ziegler rolled his eyes. "Liddy's in jail," he said.

She said, "The president can't think the cabinet will vote against him."

"It's just another wild card in an impossibly volatile situation," Ziegler said. "We've already got massive anti-war demonstrations, an impeachment trial, and the House Judiciary Committee meeting this morning to accuse him of crimes against humanity."

Emily nodded her head in the direction of a stack of newspapers on the corner of her desk. "The guy at the *Post* says that since the bombing started, the Republicans are lining up behind the president in the Senate," she said. "If the vote were held today, he'd be acquitted with a few votes to spare. He might even get a Democrat or two."

"But it won't be held today," Ziegler said. "Instead we'll have Emmett Walsh's little drama. Everybody around here's worn out. Hell, I know I am. Ford will be puffing his pipe and looking like a president in a Norman Rockwell painting, the essence of steadiness and sanity. They may be tempted to hand the country over to him just so everybody can get a good night's sleep."

240

"Even if the cabinet turns against him," she said, "it then goes to Congress, which has three weeks to decide whether he's in or out. Imagine that chaos, with bombs still falling in Indochina."

"So we'd have the impeachment trial and some kind of incapacity inquiry running simultaneously."

Emily nodded. "My nightmare scenario for this afternoon's meeting is that the cabinet decides it wants to have a debate instead of a quick vote," she said. "That could get out of control quickly, especially if people start talking openly about the president's state of mind."

"Which is weird on a good day."

"I've written a talking point for Ford where he says that it would be redundant to trigger a second congressional process with the impeachment trial underway."

"That won't work," Ziegler said, shaking his head. "At least one self-righteous asshole will say that they don't have the right to make that decision for Congress. After all, theoretically maybe Nixon deserves to be both convicted and declared incapacitated."

"Or one or the other," she said. She put her pen down and leaned back with a sigh.

Ziegler ran his fingers along the edges of the folders on Emily's desk. "I guess Walsh is still carrying water for Reagan," he said.

"It's hard to imagine Reagan taking the risk that it would get out."

"Unless he can say he had no idea what his people were doing on his behalf."

Emily looked at Ziegler. "Do you think Howard Morton might have something on Walsh? Could they be blackmailing him?"

"Why do you ask?"

She looked away. "You've never met my father," she said. "He's the finest man I know – decent, principled, the soul of intelligent patriotism. This conservative guy on the board of the hospital where he works got an anonymous call claiming that he was some kind of a dangerous radical. The caller said he had FBI pictures of dad attending an antiwar demonstration at Wayne State University."

Ziegler waved a hand dismissively. "That's a badge of honor at this point," he said.

"I'll destroy anyone who tries to hurt my father," she said quietly.

Ziegler let an affectionate expression soften his features for a brief moment. "Nothing will come of it, Emily," he said. "We'll have the president call the chairman of the hospital board if you want."

"I know," she said. "He actually laughed it off. But my mom's upset. It feels like something clutching at us from the pit of hell."

"You put it that way," Ziegler said, "and it sounds positively Nixonian."

"Even worse in this case."

"You think it's Howard Morton. That's what prompts you to say he may be behind Emmett's request for a cabinet meeting."

"And why Walsh was lobbying against Nixon in the Senate."

"The more controversy for Nixon and Ford," Ziegler said, "the better for Reagan, even if the country falls apart in the meantime. But why would Morton go after your family?"

"To get back at Mitch. Maybe he figured something out about us."

He cocked his head and looked at Emily. "Then you know who to ask," he said.

"I already have," she said. "He called this morning. He's in town, looking for a job on Capitol Hill."

"So you've forgiven the shifty little weasel."

"Provisionally," she said. "Not that the weasel and I are any of your business."

"Maybe he was behind Emmett's latest move." She shot him a warning glance, and he shrugged an apology. "Does he think Morton was?" he said.

"He didn't say," she said. "Don't forget that he's still for Reagan. He just said that if Howard's got something stinky on Emmett Walsh, the natural thing for us to do would be to see if there's something stinkier."

Ziegler looked at his watch and stood up. "In seven hours," he said. "Fat chance." He patted Emily on the shoulder and headed back to his office in the West Wing.

Then Emily's intercom went off. "Get in here," said Len Garment.

41

Laying Pipe

Mitch Botstein had called Emily from his hotel right around the corner on Pennsylvania Ave. As an unemployed person, he actually couldn't afford his room at the Willard, one of Washington's most elegant hotels. But he couldn't afford the Holiday Inn, either. He was only going to be in town for a few days, his BankAmericard still worked, and he wanted to be as close to Emily as he could in case she could get away for a quick lunch or dinner or two.

He just wanted to be close to Emily, period. He had a couple of interviews on Capitol Hill that afternoon, but in the meantime he'd go see what was going on right outside her office. He would valiantly protect her from the angry mob. He put his bomber jacket on over his khakis and open-necked dress shirt, slid his room key in the coat pocket, left the room, and headed for the elevator.

His heart sank when she told him about the ridiculous smear against her father. It was yet another blow she had absorbed because of him. He knew instantly that Howard Morton was behind it. It was the kind of thing he loved to do, even if it wouldn't add up to anything. Attending an antiwar demonstration was something that could be used against someone ten or 15 years ago, but not now.

Howard knew that. But something had gotten under his skin. Maybe he had tracked Biff Michaels down and found out that Mitch had lied about the dirty tricks tape. It was just like Howard to lash out in sheer hatred.

Mitch punched the "down" button. He knew exactly how Howard felt about him, because as of 15 minutes ago, when he heard about

Sidney from Emily, it was exactly how he had begun to feel about Howard.

Mitch got out on the first floor and walked through the lobby, which was lavishly decorated for Christmas. A quartet in Victorian dress stood in front of the fireplace singing carols. As a non-observant Jew, he was supposed to be offended. But he couldn't help enjoying the holiday's festiveness, especially since it powered about a third of the consumer economy every year. He loved to tell his Gentile friends that Jews wrote "White Christmas" and "Rudolf the Red-Nosed Reindeer." On the other hand, he wouldn't want to hear "Silent Night" while waiting in line for the sullen bureaucrats at the DMV or post office, especially if it was sung in German.

Mitch stepped into the revolving door. The music, color, and inviting warmth gave way to a grey, cold, windy day. Standing in front of the hotel, he could hear the demonstrators across the street from the White House in Lafayette Square. He turned toward the sound and in five minutes was standing in the midst of them – students from Georgetown and George Washington universities, some older folks, and a few Vietnam vets in their combat fatigues, four or five hundred people in all. A young man with a megaphone was standing on Andrew Jackson's statue and leading a call and response of "No more war, no more bombs, no more Nixon." The crowd would've been even bigger just three years before, when there were troops on the ground, and hundreds of thousands of high school seniors and college students were mulling the choice of going to Indochina or fleeing to Canada to avoid the draft.

Mitch stood watching as a vet regaled a couple of college kids with his Vietnam stories. He was about Mitch's age. He had big black glasses, long hair held back with a bandana, and a roach clip hanging from the flap on the chest pocket of his jacket. The name above the pocket was "MULLIGAN." It was a war, he was saying, where you couldn't tell who the enemy was, where even the people we were fighting to defend didn't seem to want us there. Besides, how could a little country like Vietnam ever threaten America?

Mitch was briefly tempted to join the conversation. He would have mentioned how many people around the world depended on the

United States for their security and, someday, a quality of life as good as ours. He would've thanked the man for his service but asked if he had ever visited China or East Germany and gotten an glimpse of what was in store for the people of South Vietnam.

But Mitch kept quiet. He felt a little ashamed of himself around veterans. Like most of his highly achieving buddies, he'd gotten draft deferments while he was in college during the Johnson administration and had been out of the reach of the draft by the time Nixon was elected and changed the Selective Service rules. He hadn't been afraid to fight, nor had he opposed the war. But he hadn't considered it an overwhelming personal or national imperative, either. He just had other things he wanted to do. He supposed it would've been different, for him and a lot of guys, if Hanoi had ever figured out how to attack the U.S.

Somebody bumped against him. Mitch turned toward a well-dressed man who had just walked up. He lifted a sign over his head, pointed toward the White House. It said, "PEACE, PLEASE."

Mitch asked the man where he worked.

"The Justice Department," he said, glancing at Mitch, lowering the sign to chest level. "Are you a reporter? I took an early lunch."

"I'm a desperately out of work political consultant," Mitch said. "But isn't that the boss in there?"

"For the time being," the man said. "We lost the war fair and square. Now he's firebombing Hanoi to distract attention from Watergate and his own impeachment trial. I think he and the country have gone insane."

Mitch shrugged. "Hanoi assumed we were all distracted by Watergate, which is why they jumpstarted the damn thing," he said. "You think they should get away with violating the peace treaty they signed?"

The man turned and stared at Mitch. Before he could speak, Mitch offered his hand and said his name. "Brian Wilkins," his companion said, taking his hand. "Did you go?"

Mitch said, "I probably should have."

"I didn't, either. My big brother Sam was killed six years ago at Khe Sanh. He was born the day after Christmas. It's called St. Stephen's

Day, which appropriately enough was named for a martyr. I remember it as the day he taught me to throw the football I got for Christmas when I was five."

"I'm sorry."

"My brother's death was one too many. He never even should've been a soldier. And now Nixon's targeting civilians. We're bombing government offices on purpose. For God's sake, Mitch."

"The communists murdered three thousand civilians at Hue, just a few months before they killed your brother."

"We're not them," Brian said.

Mitch looked toward the Old Executive Office Building, a hulking grey wedding cake that lay to the west of the mansion. Emily's office was on the second floor. He wondered what Brian would think if he knew he was in love with the woman who had made it all possible. By keeping him in play for the last four months, his pint-sized girlfriend was enabling Richard Nixon to test the proposition, long asserted by critics of prevailing Indochina war doctrine, that the only thing that had kept the U.S. from winning the war and assuring South Vietnam's freedom was its refusal to match Hanoi's systematic brutality.

The U.S. had committed plenty of atrocities, at My Lai and elsewhere, but never as a matter of policy. "Isn't that what war is?" Mitch said, half to himself, half to Brian. "You kill their people to make them stop killing yours. You kill so you can stop killing as soon as possible."

"So you could justify using nuclear weapons," Brian said. "You justify murdering cleaning women and the children they brought to work with them last night because they don't have babysitters."

"I can't justify anything anybody does during war," Mitch said. "That's why I don't think anybody should ever start one."

"But when we're in one, you have to draw the line somewhere, or you stop being human. How monstrous are you willing to be in defense of our high ideals?"

Mitch didn't answer. He and Emily had broken up over exactly the same question. And he'd never even told her how he made a name for himself in politics.

A few summers back, rumors began to circulate among journalists covering Ronald Reagan in Sacramento that some of his aides were gay. Howard Morton hired Mitch to investigate. He'd had the guys followed, tried to bug their hotel rooms, and even attempted a break-in at one of their apartments.

It had been a stinking little Watergate all its own, and he'd been a Ronald Reagan plumber, hired to catch private citizens who were laying pipe on their personal time. He didn't have anything against gay people. But Morton believed that in the Republican Party of the late sixties and early seventies, the so-called homosexual ring was a liability for Reagan. Mitch put together enough information that Morton was able to convince Reagan to fire the poor bastards.

He turned to his companion and repeated, "I'm sorry about Sam." Brian nodded. They shook hands again, and Brian raised his peace sign over his head.

As he headed back to the hotel, Mitch realized he had a dilemma, namely whether to tell Emily how he'd gotten his start with Reagan. She was bound to ask one day. He'd promised her total honesty, and he had meant to keep the promise.

What now complicated the question was that Mitch hadn't put everything in his first report to Howard Morton. He'd heard a lot of names during his gay-busting investigation. Not all were staffers and operatives who could be quickly and easily replaced. A few were top money men whom Reagan would need in his drive for the White House.

Two of their names had come up in conversation just that morning. Was Emily entitled to know this, too? After speaking to her from his hotel room, Mitch had hung up the phone and cursed Howard Morton out loud. Then he called the White House operator and asked for Len Garment. When he came on the line, Mitch told him everything he'd learned back in his Reagan days about Secretary of the Treasury Emmett Walsh and his longtime aide, Ben Claussen.

42

The Bones of Hannah Milhous

By its very nature, the Oval Office wasn't appealing to Richard Nixon, at least as a private workspace. It didn't have any corners, which meant there was no place for his easy chair and ottoman. Nobody would have wanted to see an easy chair in the Oval Office, anyway. So right after his inauguration, he had commandeered room 180 in the old EOB as what reporters took to calling his hideaway office.

It also had a conference table and a desk that had been made for Theodore Roosevelt. Nixon rarely used these. The Secret Service had used one of the desk drawers for the reel-to-reel machine that recorded all his phone calls.

The tape recorder was gone, but Nixon was back. He was meeting on Tuesday morning with his chief of staff, Al Haig, and press secretary, Ron Ziegler. The two men used antique chairs facing Nixon. He had a yellow legal pad in his lap and his stocking feet on the edge of the ottoman and was tugging at his lower lip with the earpiece of his reading glasses.

"I'll say one thing," he said. "It's never dull."

"I would readily propose," Haig said with a thin smile, "that we accept your proposition as being axiomatic."

Nixon looked at Ziegler and said, "Ford called me last night, of course, but I don't think he had the whole story."

"I don't either," Ziegler said. "Len says he got some information about Emmett. He called Emmett, and Emmett called the vice president and withdrew his request for an emergency cabinet meeting."

Nixon stared at him. "What was it?"

Ziegler shrugged. "He burbled to Len about some old insider trading deal that Howard Morton has got against him."

"Who the hell is Howard Morton?" Nixon said.

"That silk stocking attorney in LA," Ziegler said. "Reagan's guy, the one with the comb-over."

"Oh, yeah. So that's why Emmett canceled the meeting."

Ziegler shook his head. "That's why he called the meeting, and why he had been trying to screw us in the Senate," he said. "Morton was blackmailing him."

Nixon said, "So why did he cancel the meeting?"

"We were blackmailing him."

Haig looked startled and said, "Mr. President, I would strongly demur as to the selection of verbiage Ron has employed in this particular connection."

Nixon waved his glasses to reassure Haig. "We took the tapes out, Al," he said. "Don't get your bowels in an uproar." He turned back to Ron. "What was it, sex or money?"

"Len won't say."

"Who told him?"

"Len won't say."

Haig looked indignant." Ron, with all due respect to Leonard's secret sources," he said, "I believe the president has a right to know."

Nixon looked at his watch and said, "As a matter of fact, as of an hour ago, my interest in the matter became strictly prurient. There's nothing the big dumb bastard can do to us now."

"The four days are up," Zeigler said. "But there's something we had better do for Emmett."

Nixon looked at Haig. "Will you please have the attorney general call the U.S. attorney in San Francisco?" he said. "Tell him someone may try to sell us a phony stock rap against the secretary of the Treasury. Say it's just Reagan's boys, playing politics with the people's business."

Haig made a note. "Yes, sir."

To Ziegler, Nixon said, "Why didn't this leak?"

"It did. Both wire service guys came to my office yesterday afternoon at two and said they heard there was a meeting involving Ford at four. They didn't know the subject, but they'd guessed a couple of possibilities, and one of them was the right answer. They had stories written and ready to file, all except my quote."

"So we dodged a bullet," Nixon said. "What'd you say?"

"I'd talked to Garment not five minutes before, so I said, 'I swear on the bones of Hannah Milhous that there's no meeting of the cabinet'. I even promised to take them into the cabinet room and have them wait all afternoon to see if anyone showed up. That did it. They didn't file."

"When you absolutely have to drag the president's dead mother in," Nixon said with a tense look at Ziegler, "that's the way we do it."

There was a knock at the door. The men turned and saw Henry Kissinger stride in. Nixon began to look around the room for another chair. Kissinger stopped him.

"I can't possibly sit down," Kissinger said. He stood between Haig and Ziegler's chairs, facing the president.

"Hemorrhoids?" Ziegler said.

"Sheer exhilaration," Kissinger said. He was a small, compact man with curly brown hair and black glasses. While he was immaculately tailored, his waistline showed evidence of too many 12-course Chinese banquets and rich meals on 14-hour flights. "I just got a phone call from Le Duc Tho in Hanoi."

Nixon fidgeted in his chair. "He called personally?"

"He proposed an immediate meeting."

Nixon looked at Haig and Ziegler. He had hoped for a reaction from North Vietnam, but not necessarily this soon. "So you're going back to Paris for peace talks," he said.

"No, sir," Kissinger said. "He was calling to request an invitation to Washington for Le Duan, their top leader. If you issue it, they will immediately accede to our terms for the cessation of air operations by withdrawing their 4th Army Corps from Phuoc Long province. Mr. President, the North Vietnamese are suing for peace."

Nixon looked stunned. Haig and Ziegler stood up. They each shook Kissinger's hand, then one another's. The three men stood staring at Nixon. He was gazing past them into the center of the room, chewing on one of the stems of his glasses. Perhaps it was because of what Ziegler had said. But for just an instant, he had thought he'd heard the voice of his mother, talking to God in her sewing room in their little house in Yorba Linda. *Thy will be done.*

43

The Saturday Night Massacre

Frank and Anne Szabados lived in a townhouse that, in the colorful tradition of Georgetown's homeowners, had been painted bright blue. The houses next door were yellow and grey. When they bought it the year before, Frank had wanted to add red and white stripes to make a patriotic statement, but Anne convinced him that the local preservationists wouldn't tolerate their going that far. Frank said he didn't know what preservationists were. He agreed to stick with the blue after Anne told him they were a lot like investigators in the Hungarian internal security services.

It was a chilly, snowy Saturday night, three days after the White House had announced a ceasefire in Vietnam. Mitch and Emily were sitting next to each other on a second-hand sofa in the living room on the second floor. On their scuffed maple coffee table, Anne had put out spring rolls made of shrimp and pork along with dipping sauce and bowls with spicy nuts and raisins and slices of cucumber and cheese. They could smell their dinner of curry beef simmering in the kitchen.

Frank was serving drinks and hovering. He had Ella Fitzgerald's Christmas album on the stereo. Anne was curled up in an old easy chair facing the couch. The rest of the room was a cheerful mélange – throw rugs on the hardwood floors, heavy old bookcases bulging with books and journals, a big spruce Christmas tree filled with miniature white lights, and, on the wall above the couch, a large ink-on-paper rendering of a seaside scene in the Vietnamese style that had been a wedding gift from Anne's parents.

"It's great you have a house," Mitch Botstein said, sipping his beer. "Jews like apartments, in case political conditions shift and we have to leave quickly."

"Both sets of parents wanted us to own something," Anne said.

"They even helped with the down payment," Frank said. He was standing next to Anne's chair, his left hand resting lightly on her shoulder. He wore jeans and a blue dress shirt. "But as you can see, they believe in real estate instead of comfortable furniture. The mortgage payments are a bit out of our reach, so we save in other areas."

Like Anne, Emily was drinking white wine. Her thick red hair grazed the shoulders of her emerald-green cocktail dress. She said, "How often have your parents met?"

"Just at our wedding in Baltimore," Anne said. "Frank was in his second year of graduate school."

"Enough time to form a friendship and an impervious alliance," Frank said. "They take turns asking us about grandchildren. Mine get the odd-numbered months."

Anne poked him in the leg with his elbow and smiled up at him. She was wearing a blue *ao ba ba* and black slacks. Emily and Mitch shot a glance at one another. She was smiling, too. Her green eyes glittered. Since he'd gotten to Washington, they'd had lunch once and talked every day. This evening, he'd picked her up outside her apartment. When they'd met at the front door, she'd kissed him on the cheek, and they held hands in the cab on the way to Frank and Anne's. It felt like they were going to the eighth grade dance.

With a nudge, Emily said, "Tell your news."

"A congressman from the California central valley needed a legislative assistant," Mitch said. "Since they don't have telephones or daily mail delivery, he didn't get the word that nobody in politics is supposed to hire me. He's a good man, a former high school principal from Lindsay."

Where's that?" Frank said.

"North of Porterville," Mitch said, pretending to sound offended that Frank didn't know.

"So you'll be working on—" Frank said.

"Agricultural policy, especially the congressman's visionary initiative to reduce salinity levels in irrigation water," Mitch said. "It's good, honest work, where a man can get back to the earth and feel the moist soil between his fingers." Emily rolled her eyes.

"Where are you going to live?" Anne said, with a glance at Emily. "We assume not Porterville or Lindsay."

"There's a Georgetown mafia of congressional aides," Mitch said. "I found a room in an apartment with one of them. We'll split the expenses, liquor, and women."

"Already we're pushing our luck," Emily said.

Frank and Anne had invited them to celebrate the end of the war, but it was also so they could finally get a good look at Mitch. When it came to work, there wasn't much they could talk about. Frank assumed that Emily had been intimately involved in Nixon's secret plan to take back the presidency, but that was still too sensitive for casual conversation. Mitch thought that Frank probably had something to do with the short, brutal, and wildly successful Vietnam air war, but he wasn't going to bring that up over drinks and hors d'oeuvres. Frank probably couldn't talk about it, anyway. While Anne knew from Frank that Mitch's prior job with Ronald Reagan had caused the breach with Emily, she didn't want to risk reopening that wound.

Based on her week at the World Bank, Anne could have filled them in on what the Organization of Petroleum Exporting Countries was expected to do at its upcoming meeting in London insofar as the benchmark price of crude oil was concerned, but that didn't seem to be the ticket, either.

Mitch ventured an observation based on what he'd read in the paper. "So this historic peace conference," he said to Frank. "That's going to be quite a deal. Anything the congressman and I can do for you from the water salinity perspective?"

Frank smiled. The White House had invited North Vietnam's Le Duan and President Nguyen Van Thieu of South Vietnam to Washington on New Year's Eve to sign a comprehensive peace treaty declaring an end to hostilities in Vietnam and including Hanoi's historic concession that South Vietnam had the right to exist. The

U.S. was working with its allies on a multi-billion-dollar reconstruction package for both nations. Administration sources said that the U.S. was prepared to restore full diplomatic relations with communist North Vietnam.

The only thing that brought politicians together more reliably than dropping bombs was making peace. Every indication was that Richard Nixon would still be in office to preside at the peace conference. Final arguments in his impeachment trial had ended two days before, on Thursday afternoon. The Senate would vote in two days, on Monday, December 23. It now appeared that all 40 Republican senators and two conservative Democrats would vote to acquit Nixon. He only needed 34.

"This has probably been a difficult time for your parents," Frank said to Emily.

She sipped her wine. "They hated the bombing," she said, "and they can't help blaming me." She saw that Anne's eyes were glistening. "You probably have family in the north," she said, leaning forward and looking at her with concern.

Anne nodded and wiped away tears. "It's also a little complicated for us," she said. Frank squeezed her shoulder. She reached up and touched his hand for a moment, then put her hand back in her lap.

The couples fell silent. Ella was singing "White Christmas." It would be a long time before Frank and Anne could talk to anyone about Nguyen, Anne's late cousin, who had persuaded Frank and ultimately the U.S. government to take such ruthless measures against North Vietnam. Their reticence wasn't just because the information was top secret. The U.S. had saved an ally and its imperfect democracy. Anne's parents and friends were safe. But she considered Hanoi's people to be errant friends instead of foreigners. In the last week they had suffered horribly at the hands of the United States, and Frank had helped bring it all about. She had talked to her parents in Saigon almost every evening for a week. They still hadn't yet heard whether her uncle, a senior official in the Hanoi government and Nguyen's father, had survived the attacks on Hanoi.

"My mother hardly ever talked to me about her war," Mitch said. "But when I was about to go to college, she said I should be sure to find out why the allies never bombed the concentration camps."

"She and her family were sent to Auschwitz," Emily said to Frank and Anne.

"Tell her that it wouldn't have helped to stop the slaughter of Jews by killing even more," Frank said.

Anne looked up at her husband. "We killed hundreds of thousands of Vietnamese to save Vietnam," she said.

"That's an imperfect analogy," Frank said. "We were holding a repressive regime accountable for its aggression against our allies."

"I imagine the inadequacy of the analogy is lost on the families that are having funerals in Hanoi this week," Anne said, staring into space. Frank didn't reply.

"We could've bombed the train lines leading to the camps," Mitch said. "We could've targeted the gas chambers."

"Would your mother have wanted that, even if she'd been killed?" Emily said.

"She didn't exactly say," Mitch said, "but she probably would have considered it a form of deliverance. Anyway, she never asked me about it again. I think she would have been afraid to learn that we had been indifferent to her suffering, or maybe that it was for some bogus PR reason, like our not wanting to give the Germans a chance to say that we were as bad as they were."

"Would the Americans' making the wrong choice have been easier for her to accept if their hearts had just been in the right place?" Frank said.

Mitch said, "It would have made it that much easier to her to consider herself an American."

"It makes you wonder if Nixon was saving Vietnam or himself," Emily said to Frank.

"Good question," Anne said, looking at Emily, then her husband. "So which was it?" Frank looked at Mitch and shrugged.

"I don't know him like they do, but I know the answer," Mitch said. "Both." He finished his beer. "That might be what momma was getting at, knowing I was going into a line of work where nobody ever does anything for strictly the right reason."

Three miles away, Ron Ziegler, Rose Woods, and Bridgette Matheson were having a wrap party at Jackson Place. Rose and her cheerfully efficient volunteers had spent the day packing the records of Nixon's four-month exile and sending them across the street to the White House. The volunteers had gone home. Rose had put out cheese and crackers on the dining room table on the first floor and poured a glass of wine for Bridgette and herself. Ron was drinking scotch.

"I'm going to miss this place," Ziegler said.

"Hooey," Rose said. "It's a dump, and you know it."

"It's been a highlight of my whole life," Bridgette said, raising her glass, "working with the two of you."

"An episode that soon comes to an end," Ron said with a smile. "Under our agreement, your privileged access ends the second he's acquitted."

"Don't go all mushy on me," Bridgette said.

"If he's acquitted," Rose said.

"He will be," Bridgette said. "At which point I finally get to start writing."

"But only by eight votes," Ziegler said.

Rose looked startled. "I was perfectly content with the 34 we needed," she said. "Forty-two is an embarrassment of riches."

Ziegler had finished his first drink and was rolling the bottom of the glass around on the tabletop. "You're here to write history," he said to Bridgette, "and he's just made it. Four months ago he couldn't get a United States senator to return his phone call. Now he's about to beat two articles of impeachment. He's gotten back 27 senators while winning the war that has been a thorn in the side of three presidents."

"Three and a half, counting Jerry," Rose said.

"So what more do you want?" Bridgette said. "You've won."

"I don't want it to be a party line vote," he said. "I want more Democrats."

"You'll get a couple from the south because of Vietnam," she said. "You won't get a majority in the Senate."

The women exchanged glances as Ziegler got up and went to the kitchen counter and poured another drink. He showed the strain of the last two years more than anyone else in Nixon's circle. He looked pale, and he'd gained weight. His dark hair was getting long and stringy.

Bridgette would later write that he had borne Nixon's burdens as his own, like a son who has to defend his miscreant father every day against the other kids' taunts in the schoolyard, because that's what loyal sons did. Ron couldn't deny Nixon's idiosyncrasies and pettiness. He had actually been the victim of one of Nixon's most famous public tantrums. During a visit to New Orleans in the humid Watergate summer of 1973, Nixon was trying to keep the White House press corps away as he prepared to address a veterans' convention. When Ziegler and the reporters followed him anyway, he grabbed Ron by the shoulders, whirled him around, and gave him a shove.

As miscreant fathers often were, Nixon was genuinely sorry, and he told Ziegler so later that day, in front of the rest of the staff on Air Force One. While he had no illusions about Nixon's character, he thought its shortcomings were far outweighed by his historic opening to China and arms control breakthroughs with the Soviets. Ending the war completed the trifecta in what Nixon called his structure of peace. What was Watergate compared with policies that had made the world safer for hundreds of millions? Assuming he was acquitted, Nixon would have to govern for another two years. Ziegler thought a grudging outcome in the Senate trial would weaken the presidency and make it harder to capitalize on the administration's peacemaking initiatives for the sake of Americans and the whole world.

He brought his drink back to the table and sat down. "What do we need to do to get more Democrats?" he said to Bridgette.

She reached for a piece of cheese and a cracker and took a bite. "Nixon made the progress he did in the Senate because most members applied a reasonable doubt test," she said. "The smoking gun tape was his only unmitigated disaster, and yet even there he was able to recover some ground."

"His cover-up didn't last long," Rose said. "Two weeks later he told the FBI to go ahead with its investigation."

"Plus they never managed to pin the dirty tricks on him," Bridgette said. Ziegler took a long drink and looked at Rose, who met his eyes and stared back. They hadn't told Bridgette about Garrett McCann and the fraternity tape. "Still, there's a residue of suspicion that results from the accumulation of so many abuses and allegations of abuses," Bridgette said. She paused and looked at Rose. "Senators wonder most about what was on that tape gap," she said.

Rose looked away. "The less said about that, the better," she said.

"We never talked about it," Bridgette said. She'd brought it up a few times, but Rose had changed the subject. Bridgette assumed she was embarrassed.

"And we never will," Rose said. She picked up the plate with the cheese and crackers and set it on the kitchen counter.

"The problem is that people assume the worst," Ziegler said. "They think it was when he admitted ordering the Watergate break-in or something like that. If we could remove that element of suspicion, we might scare up a few more votes." There was a loud crash. Ron and Bridgette got up and rushed to the kitchen, where Rose was standing and staring at pieces of broken china in the sink.

"Sorry," she said. "I guess I'm tired." She looked at Ron and Bridgette. "This has been fun," she said, "but I have to get back to work."

A couple of hours later, at about six California time, Len Garment arrived in the bar of the Hilton on Century Blvd. near LAX in Los Angeles. His flight had gotten in an hour before, and he was catching the redeye back to Washington in three hours. He knew his meeting wouldn't take long.

Howard Morton was waiting for him in a booth along the wall. Garment slid in opposite him before he had time to stand. Morton extended his hand across the table, but Garment chose that moment to reach for the appetizer menu and pretend to study it.

"It's good to see you, Len," Morton said, withdrawing his hand. "But I was a little surprised about the venue. I would've been happy to have you to the Golden State Club for dinner."

Garment put the menu back, reached into his jacket pocket for his cigarettes and lighter, and lit up. "I wouldn't be caught dead in the Golden State Club," he said.

"Why not?"

"Because I'm a Jew, you moron."

Howard blinked slowly. "I guess you had a rough flight," he said.

Garment smiled. "Not especially," he said. "I slept like a baby. We've had a busy couple of weeks."

A waiter walked up. "Would you like to order something?" Howard said.

Garment shook his head. The waiter said he'd give them a few moments and left. Garment said, "We know you blackmailed Emmett."

Howard blinked again. "I don't know what you're talking about," he said.

Garment took another drag on his cigarette. "Emmett told me himself, and we've confirmed you represented the guy who gave his wife the mink coat. We actually think we could indict you for insider trading. We also know you organized Reagan's purge of homosexuals. And we know you're behind the illegal use of raw FBI files to intimidate a member of the White House staff."

"I don't intend to listen to any more of this," he said, beginning to slide out of the booth.

"I spoke with the agent you called in the Detroit field office," Len said. "He says you mentioned Reagan's name and his support for the bureau. You alluded to the favors the agency had done for him already, which may also have been illegal. The agent swore out an affidavit. Maybe I should share it with your partners, the bar association, and the U.S. attorney in Los Angeles. Take it from us. In the post-Watergate era, this kind of shit will definitely stick to you."

Morton settled back into the booth and stared at Garment. "You're a miserable stinking son of a bitch," he said. "What do you want?"

Garment leaned forward and blew cigarette smoke in Howard's face. "I'm actually not sure Ronald Reagan has a future in national politics anymore," he said. "But you'd better tell him that 1976 definitely won't be his year. If we see him on the ballot in any state, we'll wrap you around his neck and squeeze until he begs for mercy. We've got enough to destroy you both." Garment put out his cigarette in an ashtray on the table and left Howard Morton sitting in the bar.

44

Promise Me

Ron Ziegler couldn't get the idea out of his head that Richard Nixon was entitled not just to survival but to total vindication. "Most of Nixon's young aides had seen their White House jobs as a means of advancement," Bridgette Matheson would write later in the *Washington Post.* "In the crucible of Watergate, Ziegler's engagement had become more and more emotional, even existential. His conception of his own place in the world, any hope he had for experiencing a life of meaning and value, came to hinge entirely on the condition of Nixon's reputation."

On Sunday afternoon, Ziegler asked to see the president, who invited him to the Lincoln Sitting Room in the family quarters, where Emily and Nixon had met in August. It was a cold day. This time Nixon had a wood fire blazing in the little room. He'd been smoking his pipe after lunch. The wood and tobacco smoke entwined alluringly.

He and his overstuffed easy chair and ottoman were back in their accustomed corner. He was wearing a blue tweed sport coat, slacks, and a tie and sat with his feet up, twirling his reading glasses. The ten-page document on his lap was the news summary the press office prepared each day. Ziegler had assigned a big team to today's edition, since he knew the Sunday papers and the networks' morning shows would be brimming with commentary about the momentous events of the last ten days – Nixon reclaiming the presidency, bombing Vietnam, and now standing on the brink of an historic peace agreement and acquittal in the Senate.

All that, and Nixon was still angry.

"I beat them again," he said to Ziegler, picking up the document and waving it in the air, "and the sons of bitches can't stand it. There hasn't be a shot fired in anger in Vietnam for five days. Every North Vietnamese solider is out of South Vietnam or on his way. And what's the headline on the lead editorial in the *New York Times?*" He put on his reading glasses and read from the report: "'At What Cost, Mr. Nixon, At What Cost?'"

"They were never going to pat us on the back," Ziegler said. "But the American people know better."

Nixon didn't care what Ziegler thought the American people knew. He cared what journalists were telling them and what historians would write. He turned the page and found another entry. Ziegler could see he'd underlined it with his fountain pen. This was from the digest of the Sunday political talk shows that one of Ziegler's staffers had prepared. Nixon read a portion aloud: "'Interviewed on Face the Nation, reporter David Broder said that it was hard to avoid the impression that RN had found it fortuitous to maneuver himself back into the presidency and order the assault to improve his prospects in the Senate'."

"It's a natural enough conclusion for a professional cynic like Broder," Ziegler said.

"He knows damn well that Ford wouldn't have bitten the bullet on Vietnam," Nixon said. "He told me as much when we met at Walter and Lee's."

Ziegler smiled and said, "Did you hope that he would act, or hope that he wouldn't?"

Nixon was chewing on his glasses and gazing into the fire. It wasn't a question an aide would've dared ask him before he'd experienced the abject vulnerability of his Watergate disgrace. Even now, Nixon didn't answer directly. He didn't have to. Ziegler was well aware of Nixon's mixed motives. He was driven both to be the indispensable man and to make tough, necessary decisions. The imperatives couldn't be separated.

"I gave him the opportunity," Nixon said after a moment. "Even if it had been Jerry's instinct to act as I did, he couldn't. We both knew it. That's why Hanoi moved when it did."

"And if you had resigned in August?"

"The bastards smelled victory. They would've tested him anyway."

Ziegler shifted in his chair. "What rankles me," he said, "is this party-line Senate vote. You just finished the war the Democrats started. We deserve acquittal on that basis alone."

Nixon watched Ziegler carefully. He said, "We're going to get acquittal."

"I was talking to our friend at the *Post*," Ziegler said. She thinks we could get some more Dems, maybe even a majority, if we could give them something dramatic. Like on the tape gap, for instance."

Nixon shot him a look. "Forget it," he said.

"Of course if there's something about it we're ashamed of," Ziegler said, "that's different."

Vaguely intrigued, Nixon said, "You're saying it could help us if we could prove it really was an accident, that Rose really did just push the wrong button or some goddamned thing."

"So that's really what happened," Ziegler said, watching Nixon's face carefully.

"You think I erased it?"

"Not necessarily," Ziegler said. He sat looking calm in a chair across from Nixon's, his notebook balanced on his knee. He was inwardly astonished at his boldness. Before Watergate, he never would have ventured such a conversation. But he and Nixon had been through so much together that he knew their bond of trust was for all intents and purposes indissoluble.

Besides, he just wanted to know. He wondered if the erased portion of conversation from June 20, 1972 had revealed that Nixon had ordered the Watergate break-in. That's what most of his critics believed. Or maybe it had to do with dirty tricks or something far worse, a crime that hadn't even been imagined.

They'd battled back from the brink of oblivion and were safely ensconced in the White House with two years left of Nixon's second term. His national security team was at work planning another summit meeting with the Russians and reengaging his relationships with leaders in Europe, China, and Japan. At home, inflation was nearing 11%, because of a startling rise in oil prices and the loose money policies Nixon had urged on the Federal Reserve. Would they finally be able to get to work again, or was more scandal looming?

Ziegler saw a hint of a smile play across Nixon's face. "You're afraid we didn't deserve to win," Nixon said, "or that we survived just to die another day."

"I know the other side didn't deserve to win," Ziegler said, "but I do worry that there's something else."

"There is," Nixon said, hesitating for a moment. "But it's not what you think." Ziegler stared and didn't speak. The president shifted his weight in his chair, struggling to sit up straighter. "As you know," he said, "I, uh, on occasion have drawn parallels between the Watergate matter and the Hiss case."

Ziegler nodded. "It's the cover-up that gets you, not the crime," he said, quoting the maxim that Nixon was fonder of repeating than obeying.

"I knew Hiss was guilty," Nixon said. "There was absolutely no doubt in my mind. So by desperately trying to persuade the committee otherwise, he only managed to dig himself in deeper." As a freshman congressman in 1948, Nixon spearheaded an investigation by the House Committee on Un-American Activities of charges that Roosevelt-era diplomat Alger Hiss had been a spy for the Soviet Union. He'd questioned Hiss relentlessly, opening the way for federal prosecution. Hiss was ultimately convicted of perjury. Dwight Eisenhower was so impressed by Nixon's work that he chose him as his running mate in 1952. Nixon owed his national profile and probably his presidency to the Hiss case.

"Something told you he was guilty," Ziegler said.

"Not exactly," Nixon said quietly. "Someone told me."

"Whittaker Chambers," Ziegler said, nodding. Chambers, a journalist, had been in a communist cell with Hiss and was his principal accuser. While not everyone on HUAC believed Chambers, Nixon always did and later used the Hiss case to construct a narrative about his superior political instincts.

Nixon shook his head. "Someone else," he said. He lowered his voice. "During the war, we broke the Soviets' codes. Military intelligence figured out that Hiss was a spy by decoding the cable traffic. When I started working on the case for the committee, they called me to the Pentagon one day and showed me the cables."

Ziegler looked stunned. "So you didn't break the case?"

"I worked my ass off," Nixon said sharply. "We had to develop evidence against Hiss that was completely independent of the secret intelligence."

"But what does it have to do with Watergate?"

Nixon waved at Ziegler with his glasses. "That's what was in the conversation that got erased," he said. "Haldeman and I were talking about where the Watergate investigation might lead. Bob wanted to get the CIA to tell the FBI to limit its investigation on the grounds of national security. I gave in eventually. But at first I said it was a terrible idea to get the spooks involved in politics. The one exception, I told him, was the role they played in the Hiss case."

His dark eyes shining, Ziegler said, "And so you told him the story. You told him that military intelligence had helped you get Hiss." Nixon nodded, and Ziegler said, "But Mr. President, that's exactly the answer we've been looking for. Number one, the tape gap isn't about Watergate at all. Number two, it'll silence those who've been saying for years that you persecuted Hiss unfairly."

"But the blessed thing's been erased," Nixon said.

"So let's reconstruct the conversation for the press based on your and Bob's recollections, his notes, whatever."

"Forget it," Nixon said again, this time pleadingly. "Forget I ever told you."

"Sir, I understand you feel embarrassed that you had a secret source, but we can deal with that."

Nixon pushed the ottoman away with his stocking feet, planted them on the floor, and leaned forward. "You're missing the point," he said. "The Russians still have no idea that we've broken their codes. The program is still producing vital intelligence. The Pentagon wouldn't tolerate our threatening to make it public. Hell, I wouldn't tolerate it. It could put U.S.-Soviet relations in a tailspin. The military wouldn't want the scandal, either, especially in the wake of Watergate and with this new Congress coming into office. Feeding intelligence files to a congressman? The lunatics who put a spy in the White House are the same ones who have everything to lose if this comes out. It already drives them crazy that I know, especially when they think about my using it as leverage against the Joint Chiefs. That's why the damn thing got erased to begin with."

Ziegler said, "So you did erase it."

"I did not," Nixon said.

Ziegler said quietly, "So Rose did after all. But she did it on purpose."

"She actually told me it was an accident," Nixon said. "And she's never said anything different. But if this comes out, she would probably go down the tubes. You don't want that. Until now, only three people knew about Hiss and the Pentagon – Bob, Rose, and I, and none of us is ever going to speak of it."

Ziegler fidgeted in his chair. "It would effectively end Watergate and get us some more Democrats in the Senate," he said. "Plus it proves once and for all that Hiss was guilty."

Nixon shook his big head at Ziegler. "I never should have told you," he said. "We can't use this. I know these bastards. They play for keeps."

"But you did tell me," Ziegler said. "Mr. President, it's part of history."

"Just promise me," Nixon said. "For God's sake, Ron. Think of the risks."

Ziegler shrugged and smiled but didn't answer. Normally he would give Nixon time to sleep on it, but they didn't have any left. The Senate would vote on the two articles of impeachment the following afternoon. If he could get something about the tape gap into Monday morning's papers, it could make a difference in the vote. The Senate might even decide to wait a day to give senators time to digest the information, which would sanctify Nixon's defining success in the Hiss case and solve Watergate's most notorious mystery.

Their conversation drifted to other subjects. Ziegler permitted Nixon to think he planned to honor his wishes. But he'd never been surer of anything in his life. Nixon would be angry at first, as would the Joint Chiefs and Soviets. But they'd get over it. Meanwhile, the revelation would give Nixon a boost in the history books and lend new energy to his last two years in the White House. Ziegler decided that as soon as their meeting was over, he'd place a call to Bridgette Matheson at the *Washington Post* and tell her he finally had a story she could use right away.

45

Nixon Knew

Looking up from the writing table in her bedroom on the mansion's second floor, Pat Nixon watched as the last light of day faded and the Washington Monument began to glow in its ring of massive spotlights. The White House Christmas tree glittered in the foreground. It was barely five in the afternoon on Sunday.

Though she couldn't see it, she took pleasure at the thought that thanks to her, the White House was now lit just as brilliantly. The first president's mighty obelisk had stood fully erect for nearly a century and been illuminated at night for goodness knows how long before anyone realized that the president's house formed a perfect triangular constellation along with the Washington Monument and Lincoln Memorial. The White House exterior lighting project, from the design to the fundraising, had been left up to a girl from Ely, Nevada, which didn't even have a streetlight the year she was born.

She'd brightened the mansion's gloomy interior as well, installing gold and off-white taffeta drapes along the hallway that ran through the family quarters and doing up Dick's bedroom with white walls and cornflower blue carpet. Her bedroom was next door to his. Nobody could sleep in the same room with a man who dreamed in policy and political memos and got up two or three times a night to make love to his Dictabelt machine.

She turned back to her letter. Dick's sister-in-law, Donald's wife, had written about how upset she was about the vulgarity on the White House tapes. Pat suspected Clara Jane of enjoying some payback after all the years Dick had held Don at arm's length because of his shifty business deals and inept influence peddling. It was Don's own fault. It was in his nature to maximize the advantage of being the vice president and president's brother. But Clara Jane was a proud woman, and she needed to show Pat that Dick wasn't perfect, either.

Pat wrote back soothingly. She understood how Nixon's family and friends felt about the tapes. But they were never supposed to be made public. Besides, Clara Jane had to understand the pressures of the office, what it was like for Dick to feel as though everyone was out to get him. She wrote that they both remembered fondly how Nixon had sometimes used his brother's house in Whittier as his local headquarters when he was in the House and Senate. Clara Jane would handle his phone calls and make lunch. She concluded by saying that someday soon, they'd all be together again in California, getting reacquainted as family and living normal lives.

She'd been concentrating hard on her letter and hadn't heard her husband come in. She turned and saw him sitting with his legs crossed on one of the green sofas that flanked the fireplace. She put down her pen, turned in her chair, and smiled. He still liked to make unexpected entrances. It helped him feel in control of situations, even with her. "Dinner's at six-thirty," she said.

"Just us?" he said.

"Julie called and asked if we wanted them to come. The way she said it, I could tell that they'd just as soon stay home."

"Is that all right with you?" he said.

"It would have been nice," she said, "but David's got so much studying. I told them not to come because you were pretty busy."

"Do you think they wanted to come, or was she relieved?"

"She said she'd come over tomorrow," Pat said. "Maybe we could have lunch together."

"She doesn't have to," he said.

"I could tell that she wanted to tomorrow," Pat said. "She offered, I didn't ask." This was how communication usually went among members of the Nixon family. Nobody ever wanted to impose. Since they wouldn't say what they wanted, you had to guess based on tone of voice or body language. Then you said it was what you wanted, too.

Nixon looked at the stack of mail on Pat's French-style desk. "A lot of family drama, I suppose," he said. "Better you than me." Nixon wouldn't deal with the shirttail relatives. He was always afraid they wanted something. He didn't like to say no, which meant he'd be stuck. He also didn't want to hear their advice about how to run the country or deal with Watergate. So he left most family matters to Pat and Rose.

Pat stood and walked to the other sofa and sat down. "Do you want me to have them build a fire?" she said.

He shook his head. "We'll be going in to dinner," he said, "and I have one going in the other room." He paused and said, "Unless you want one."

""I could've had one if I wanted," she said. "Are you getting back into the swing of things?"

"It feels different," he said. "Like before Watergate, but different from that as well."

"A different normal."

He smirked. "The latest new normal," he said, proud of his allusion to the media's various "new Nixons."

Her eyes drifted. "I didn't think we'd still be here," she said. "I kind of got used to the idea of going home."

"Do you still want to?" he said.

"I'm glad we'll be able to finish," she said. "It feels like a second chance. What about Christmas?"

"I thought we'd fly the day after," he said. "Have the family down for Christmas dinner here and then see who wants to come with us to California for a few days. We have to be back on the 30th, of course, for the Vietnam thing the next day."

"That's fine," she said. He didn't reply or move. She expected him to go back to the Lincoln Sitting Room for the hour and a half before dinner. "Is everything all right?" she said.

"I know this has been tough on everybody in the family," he said. His voice sounded raw.

"They know you're sorry," she said. "They also know it wasn't all your fault."

"Do they? Do you?"

"You don't have to apologize to me," she said, reaching between the two couches and patting him on the knee. "You know I'm for you all the way."

"Haldeman and the rest are gone," he said. "Rose is where she should've been all along."

Pat smiled. "That new normal, I like," she said. "Are you going to keep Al as chief of staff?"

"You think I shouldn't," he said.

"I didn't say that."

"Haig's tough and loyal," he said.

"To you?"

Nixon looked into the empty fireplace. "Mostly," he said. "I know he still talks to his military friends. I understand it. It's actually helpful, since they'll never completely trust us."

She chuckled. "And I don't trust them," she said. "You should've fired Tom Moorer for stealing all those documents from the White House."

"Henry and Al told me I couldn't," he said. "Crisis of confidence among the troops and generals and all that, especially given what we were doing with the Russians and the Chinese."

"That part feels a little like the old normal," she said. "I still think Al was in on it."

Nixon waved his hand and changed the subject. "Ron and I were just talking about the vote tomorrow," he said.

"Are we status quo?" she said.

"He wants a bigger win."

She smiled. "This isn't big enough?"

"That's what I told him."

She stared at him, wondering, as usual, what he may have been getting at, what new development he was trying to prepare her for. Her husband always said things for a reason. The room was dark except for the lamp on her desk. In the shadows, he looked younger, with his long nose and sharp, dark hairline. He sat still and composed, his small hands folded in his lap. He was the president again, the way he'd always wanted. "He loves you, you know," she said.

He tilted his head back and stared up at the ceiling. "Six-thirty?" he said, looking back at her. She nodded. He stood and touched her lightly on the shoulder and left the room and walked back down the hall.

Ron Ziegler was in his office in the West Wing, fingering a photocopy of a page of Bob Haldeman's handwritten notes that his assistant had found in the files. They corresponded to the June 20, 1972 tape containing the erasure. Haldeman had written the words "Hiss," "military," and "codes." It wasn't much. Bob had been canny enough not to go into too much detail. He'd written just enough to jog his own memory if he ever needed to revisit the conversation. But based on what Nixon had told him, Ziegler thought he could convince Bridgette Matheson to file a story.

He'd called her two hours before, as soon as he left his meeting with Nixon. They had plans to meet in the Carlton bar in 20 minutes. He opened his desk drawer and got out a business-size envelope that said "The White House" for a return address. He folded the copy and put it in the envelope, slid it into his jacket pocket, and took his overcoat off the hook on the back of his office door.

He emerged from the West Wing into the bitterly cold evening and walked down the driveway to the northwest gate. He jaywalked across Pennsylvania Ave. and headed along Jackson Place toward the townhouse, now locked and dark. As he walked past the staircase, Ziegler smiled. It would wait a long time for a visit from a former president, since there wouldn't be one until January 1977. Even with that, Ziegler was sure Nixon would never want to set foot in the drafty old place again.

Ziegler remembered the time in August when he'd gone to the Carlton bar and first met Bridgette. He'd been hoping in vain to escape from Nixon and Watergate, if only for an evening. He patted his chest to make sure the envelope was still there and looked along H St. to the west, where the traffic came from. It felt good to be ahead of the story for once. After the trial, maybe he and Nancy could find some time to get away, maybe even just for a week. He felt as though he'd been working all his life.

As he stepped into the street, a blue sedan that had been idling by the curb with its lights off suddenly roared toward him. He turned and saw a man wearing thick black glasses and a hat sitting in the driver's seat and staring. The car hit him in the side, shattering his back and rupturing most of the organs in his body. His skull split when it hit the pavement. As he lay dying, the car sped east on H St. and turned south onto 14th St., toward Virginia.

The crime was never solved. Richard Nixon knew instantly who had done it.

46

Sympathy for the Devil

Emily Weissman was in her office before seven the next morning, reading and rereading the *Washington Post*'s coverage of Ron Ziegler's death. She was almost overwhelmingly tempted to call Ziegler's assistant to find out if he had said anything about what his plans were after leaving the White House the evening before.

It would've been so easy just to pick up the phone and ask her. Emily knew the woman well, and she was sure she'd be in the office. But she hesitated. She had promised Mitch that she wouldn't do anything until Len Garment got in. She wanted to keep the promise. But she couldn't just sit there much longer. Cold, righteous anger had begun to muffle her sadness. She'd done all the crying she intended to do last night. But she had to do something if she was going to hold herself together.

She looked at the clock on her office wall. If Garment wasn't in by 7:15, that meant she should make the call.

Len had called a little before six the night before with the news that a hit-and-run driver had killed Mr. Ziegler. By 6:30 Mitch had heard it on the radio and come to her apartment. She was sobbing when she opened the door. They went for a drink and talked about her dealings with Ziegler during the months he'd been with Nixon at Jackson Place. He'd enjoyed stopping by her office and acting vulgar and obnoxious, but she'd seen through it from the beginning. She'd always liked him, even during their long meeting on August 8, when he and Garment had questioned her about her secret dealings with the old man.

Mitch winced when she told him about Ziegler's offer to help after Howard Morton, Mitch's former handler for Ronald Reagan, had gone after her father. Otherwise Mitch listened and asked a few questions and held her hands across the table. He got a stack of cocktail napkins from the waitress so she could dry her eyes.

After two hours and two glasses of wine, he walked her home. He spent the night on the couch in her studio apartment. By five he was sitting up reading the paper by the light of a small high intensity lamp next to the couch. The window behind him faced Massachusetts Ave., which was still dark and empty. Emily's bed was against the opposite wall, under a framed picture of the Rolling Stones illuminated in eerie orange light while they performed "Sympathy for the Devil" at Altamont Speedway in Alameda County, California. It was the 1969 free concert where a member of the Hells Angels, who'd been hired to provide security for the concert and paid in beer, had stabbed a fan to death.

Emily's kitchenette and the entrance to her little bathroom were on the left, opposite her apartment door. When Mitch heard her stir, he poured some coffee from the pot he'd already made. He sat on the edge of her bed, put her mug on the floor, and watched her awaken. He had the paper on his lap. When she opened her eyes and looked at him, he held up the paper. "Good morning," he said. "This stinks."

She was wearing red flannel pajamas. Her hair was a soft blur around her pale face. She rearranged her pillow so she could sit up and lean against the wall. She folded her legs, pulled the covers over her lap, and took the coffee. "Is there something new?" she said.

"No," he said, "which is the first thing that stinks." He looked back at the paper, which had a news article about the accident and a long, surprisingly positive profile of Ziegler under the bylines of a veteran *Post* political writer and someone named Bridgette Matheson.

He was more interested in the news article. Witnesses said Ziegler was struck by a dirty, light blue mid-sixties Chrysler sedan. Although the bulb over the rear license plate was evidently burned out, a pedestrian standing on H St. saw by the streetlights that the car had blue Maryland plates, with two letters and four digits. She said one of the letters and two of the numbers were caked with mud. She wrote down the rest. By press time, nearly eight hours after the accident, the police hadn't gotten a hit on the partial. Another witness mentioned the driver's hat and glasses. No one knew where Ziegler was headed. The police guessed that he was hailing a cab to go home.

"What else stinks?" Emily said.

"The so-called administration source who said he'd been drinking."

She was silent. "Mr. Ziegler did drink a lot," she said, "but usually not in the office. If he was walking south to north, that's the way to the bar he liked at the Carlton. He usually went after work." She paused. "It says administration sources? Is that the same as White House sources?"

"It could be anybody in the executive branch. If it was White House, they would've said so."

"So it probably didn't come from anyone who really knew him and his habits."

"Probably not."

"Anyway, you'd expect the cops to be the ones who knew he'd been drinking instead of some anonymous somebody somewhere in the government."

"What bothers me the most," he said, "is the apparent lack of curiosity about at least the possibility that he was assassinated."

Emily paused in mid-sip. "You're kidding," she said, looking over the rim of the mug.

He put his hand on her foot under the covers and squeezed. "He's Nixon's most intimate aide, the architect of his comeback," he said. "This is a guy who knows more than anyone about the guy everybody wants to know about. The night before the Senate vote, a mysterious car with obscured plates kills him and doesn't stop. It's actually not that easy to kill a man with a car. You have to know what you're doing." She stiffened and pulled her foot away. Looking offended, he said, "There's a whole chapter about it in the political operative's source book." She glared at him. "Seriously, I don't even know how I know that. I read it somewhere."

She slid her foot back under his hand. "Just for purposes of discussion," she said, why do you assassinate someone?"

"Because of what they've done or what they're about to do."

"Everybody knows what he's done. So we want to find out what his plans were last night. I'll bet I can find out from his office."

According to the *Post*, no one in Ziegler's shop had been available for comment. That also alarmed Mitch. Someone at the White House must've put a lid on the story. He squeezed her foot hard. "No way," he said. "It's too dangerous."

"Because– " She stopped, horrified at what she was about to say.

"Because the smoke screen about his drinking would have come from the people who killed him."

"Which would have to mean that it was somebody in the government," she said. "That actually sounds ridiculous out loud. Why would someone in the government want to kill Ron Ziegler? Somebody in the press corps, I could buy." Mitch smiled grimly and stood up. She watched as he went to the counter to refresh his coffee. "I thought you might come to bed last night," she said.

He sat down and put his hand back on her foot. "I thought about it," he said.

"It would have been a life-affirming act," she said.

"We would have been seizing the moment and laughing in the cruel face of death," he said. "But afterward, I'd have been stuck in your crappy single bed."

"You didn't say anything about my crappy bed the first time."

"It would've been ungallant."

"And unwise."

He leaned toward her, just an inch or two.

"You have coffee breath," she whispered.

"So do you." They kissed. She embraced him. He put his hands in her hair and looked at her face with a smile he couldn't contain, even under the circumstances. Putting his lips close to her ear, he said, "I love you. But you have to go to work."

"I'd love you even more," she said, "if you were working for us."

"Don't do anything without talking to Garment," he said. She nodded. But two hours later, as the second hand on her wall clock approached 7:15, she got out the staff directory and found the extension for Ziegler's assistant. She was reaching for the phone when the intercom buzzer went off.

It was Garment. "The president wants to see us," he said.

They walked together to Nixon's EOB office, where they found him sitting in his chair in the corner, his feet up on the ottoman. He was holding a business-sized White House envelope that appeared to be stained with blood.

"Our deepest condolences on the loss of your friend and devoted colleague," Len said as he and Emily sat in the two chairs opposite Nixon.

Nixon nodded. He looked at Len, his lips twitching. "Ron was—" His voice broke, and he stopped. He fingered the envelope for a moment. Finally, he said, "Tell Emily about the call we got from the president pro tempore."

"They were offering a delay in the Senate vote out of respect for the president and his friend," Len said. "I told him that we didn't want this tragedy to stand in the way of the nation's business."

Nixon gazed at a space between them. Emily could see that his eyes were red. Garment had obviously been crying, too. She didn't think he'd slept. But he'd put on a clean shirt and tightened his tie before coming to see the president.

"I'm told we may pick up a few more votes now," Nixon said. "Ron wanted a majority. He may actually get one." He looked at Emily and gestured at her with the envelope. "They found this in his pocket," he said in a cold voice.

She looked surprised. "The paper said he wasn't carrying anything except his wallet and keys," she said.

Nixon looked at Garment, who again turned to Emily. "Last night the director of the Secret Service and I called on the chief of the Metropolitan Police," he said, "on the basis of needing to determine if there was a threat to the president. He gave it to us."

"Is there anything in it?" she said.

"If there was, somebody took the contents and left the envelope." She said, "I don't understand."

Garment said, "The contents would've been removed at the scene immediately after the accident or, more likely, by someone in the police department who had access to the envelope before it got to the chief."

"Why didn't they take the envelope, too?"

Nixon said, "They're sending me a message."

Emily felt goose bumps. She said, "Who's they?"

Nixon said to Garment, "I guess they don't teach about the mysterious subtleties of the federal government in constitutional law classes at Harvard."

Her eyes flared. "If you gentlemen called me in here to gloat about my naiveté, point taken," she said. "How about we call Mr. Ziegler's office and find out what he was planning to do last night?"

Nixon shot a look at Garment. "You'll do no such thing, young lady," Len said. "That's an order."

"Nobody else is getting killed around here," Nixon said in ragged voice.

Garment said, "You start poking around in Ziegler's shop, you'll just put more people in danger, especially them and you."

Nixon barked at Garment. "Can we find somebody we can actually trust to sweep the phones in the White House?"

"Our phones are bugged?" Emily said.

"Ron was on his way to see his friend at the *Post*," Garment said, with a glance at Nixon, "and there's somebody waiting in a car."

"Goddamned military spooks," Nixon said. Emily thought his face looked ravaged. For a moment, he looked beaten.

Emily looked back and forth between the two men. "Why are you telling me?" she said.

Before they could answer, Nixon's intercom went off. He picked up, listened, and said, "I'll take it, please." Another pause. Nixon closed his eyes. "Nancy, I'm so sorry," he said. Emily made a move to stand up, but Garment gestured at her to stay put. He listened for a while. "Christ Church in Alexandria, Saturday the 28th at 11," he said, motioning to Emily to make a note. "Of course I will, I'd be honored. Thank you." He listened for a few more moments. "I promise we'll find out," he said. "Whatever it takes. I wouldn't— I can't—" He closed his eyes and covered them with his free hand. He took a deep breath and said, "My old man had five sons, but I never had one. I love my kids, but Ron was—"

Emily looked at her lap. Tears welled in her eyes. She was afraid to look at Garment. She made notes just to keep her hands busy.

When the call was over, Nixon said to Len, "Would you please see if you can reach Gordie Partington?" Gordie was the speechwriter who'd resigned on August 8.

Garment nodded. "I'll let Al Haig know," he said.

Nixon shook his head. "Al's not in the building," he said in a neutral voice. "This morning he accepted my appointment as supreme commander of NATO. He needs to be in Brussels right after the first of the year. I told him to take a couple of weeks to get ready."

Garment and Emily exchanged glances. Garment said, "You want me to tell Gordie to start thinking about Ron's eulogy?"

Nixon said, "Just have him call me."

47

On The Holy Mountain

On the Saturday morning after Christmas, Richard and Pat Nixon squeezed into George Washington's pew with Nancy Ziegler, her two school-age daughters, Cindy and Laurie, and her and Ron's parents. The elder Zieglers had raised their son as a Presbyterian. Nancy was Episcopalian. When they'd moved to Alexandria so Ron could serve in the White House, historic Christ Church, built in red brick in sturdy, unpretentious Georgian style, was a logical choice for their home parish.

Nixon asked to be seated on the aisle, next to Nancy. Her open, pleasant face was solemn and composed. Pat was on her left, between her and the girls, holding her hand and Cindy's.

It was the Nixons' first public appearance since his acquittal on Monday afternoon by a 49-51 vote on both articles of impeachment. The church was packed. Everyone from his cabinet and senior staff had come. Betty and Jerry Ford, Rose Woods, and Bridgette Matheson sat in the pew behind the Nixons. Chief of staff Al Haig, just named to the NATO command, sat with the cabinet on the far side of the church.

More Washington bigshots were craning their necks for glimpses of Bridgette than of the Nixons, Fords, or any other familiar faces. The first of her articles about Nixon's final comeback, in which Ziegler played the co-starring role, had appeared in Friday's *Washington Post*. Nobody had heard of her, and nobody could remember Nixon ever giving such access to a journalist.

Given the resemblance between her and Nancy Ziegler, salacious speculation was already rife. Nick Giordano, Ron's bartender and protector at the Carlton, had found a seat near the back and sat with red eyes, clutching his handkerchief. He would have willingly quieted the gossip with his first-hand testimony and, if necessary, both fists and the heavy heel of one of Ron's scotch glasses.

As the organist finished playing a quiet J.S. Bach prelude, the president stole a few glances at his surroundings to get his bearings. He'd never spoken at Christ Church. When it was built in the second half of the 18th century, the Protestants were in the ascendant in Anglicanism, so the nave had few sacramental trappings. The church was still dressed for Christmas. But finding a cross or an image of Christ took energy and enterprise. The little altar where the Episcopal version of the mass was said during Sunday services looked like an afterthought.

Towering over it was a bulbous pulpit that Nixon would reach using a narrow stairway behind the altar on the right. His advance men had briefed him, but he was nervous about tripping. He would feel ridiculous way up there, but it couldn't be helped. He patted his chest for the tenth time, making sure he had his single page of notes in his jacket pocket.

He wouldn't be using a prepared text. He'd spoken to Gordie Partington, however, and put him to work on another project.

The music stopped. A priest in cassock and surplice, the classic choirboy getup, and a white stole around his neck stepped behind the altar. Nixon was the first to stand, and for just a moment, he was alone, his shoulders square in his dark grey suit, a strip of his white dress shirt showing above his jacket collar and under his wavy brown hair. As the rest of the congregation stood, he looked down and helped Nancy to her feet.

In a sonorous voice, the officiant began the liturgy. "I am the resurrection and the life, saith the Lord," he said. "He that believeth in me, though he were dead, yet shall he live." Nancy sobbed quietly at these words and took Nixon's arm to steady herself. He patted her hand and blinked rapidly to try to keep his eyes dry. Anxiety and adrenaline usually saved him from expressions of emotion in public, but this one was going to be rough.

"And though this body be destroyed," the priest said, "yet shall I see God." Nixon distracted himself with a thought about what God and he knew about Ziegler's destruction compared to almost everyone else. In nearly a week, reporters had learned nothing more about Sunday evening's accident. The consensus was that he'd been drunk when he'd stepped into traffic. Nobody mentioned the driver's hat and glasses anymore. It turns out that the witness wasn't so sure about them. It had gotten dark, which is why the other witness might have gotten some of the letters and digits wrong in her partial plate ID. The police now said it might've been a kid or a Christmas-addled suburban shopper who hadn't realized how badly his victim was hurt. Maybe the driver was afraid to confess after learning who it was. The police vowed to keep looking.

The White House quietly encouraged the media to accept this narrative. With the Senate vote looming and all the tension of the last four months coming to a head, poor Ron had so much on his mind. Nixon knew it was unfair to him and cruel to Nancy and the girls, but it couldn't be helped. You couldn't have people thinking the Pentagon was killing people, at least in the streets of Washington three days before Christmas.

Garment had interviewed Ziegler's assistant. She told him about finding the page of Haldeman's June 20, 1972 notes and confirmed that Ron's appointment had been with Bridgette at the Carlton. Garment told her that these were now matters of national and her personal security and that she was to keep them secret. He also promised her that, one way or another, Ziegler's killers would pay.

After the Bible readings, the verger came to the Nixons' pew and opened the little white door. Walking stiffly, the president followed him to the staircase. Once he was safely in the pulpit, Nixon looked out and saw the press pool in the back, two or three TV cameras and still photographers. His expression was blank. It was a relief for once not to have to smile at the sons of bitches. He scanned the congregation quickly and let his eyes fall on Nancy. He smiled and nodded encouragingly.

She had a black veil over her blonde hair. She gazed at him with stricken eyes. Nancy and Ron had been born in the same hospital in Covington, Kentucky and delivered by the same doctor. The first time he kissed her, they were five, and his kindergarten teacher gave him a spanking. She'd been a cheerleader when he played high school football. She married him just before he started working for Nixon in his first presidential campaign in 1960.

For the last six years, he'd worked six and half days and 80 hours a week. They'd had no social life since Watergate, and their daughters rarely saw him. Faithfully, uncomplainingly, running their home and volunteering with the Girl Scouts and the hospital auxiliary, reading her Bible and playing tennis, Nancy Ziegler had hung on until the day when it would all finally be over. And now it was.

Nixon began with his usual self-referential boilerplate. He talked about Ziegler's parents, Dan an Ohio businessman, Ruby a registered nurse, hardworking Midwesterners just like Frank and Hannah Nixon. He talked about the Zieglers' daughters, whose poise in adversity reminded him of Tricia and Julie. He talked about Nancy's beauty and grace, which reminded him of Pat's, and Ron's part in his administration's great initiatives and loyalty to the president in the dark days.

Then he paused and took a deep breath. "The American people are entitled to be proud of their president," he said, staring at the TV cameras, "but because of my actions in connection with the Watergate affair, many of our people are ashamed of their president, and for that, I apologize to every man, woman, and child in the country I love."

He turned back to Nancy and her children. "And I'm sorry," he said, "for using up so much of a husband and father's energy and time. I took advantage of Ron Ziegler's friendship. He should have been at home with you last Sunday instead of spending yet another evening helping me, a night when on a dark street in this lonely capital, he gave his last full measure of devotion." With this Lincolnian flourish, he met Haig's eyes for a moment and then looked back at the vice president's box, where he saw Rose Woods whisper in the ear of Bridgette Matheson.

In a moment, Nixon wrapped up. "The poet Sophocles wrote, 'One must wait until the evening to see how splendid the day has been'," he said. "Ron Ziegler and I had some mountaintop experiences together. This morning he stands at the foot of the holy mountain, where there is no more pain or sorrow, where, as the prophet wrote, God will wipe away the tears from every face and take away the disgrace of his people."

The worldly-wise congregation in Christ Church had not expected such sentiments in a Richard Nixon eulogy. A Ziegler family friend sitting in front of Nick Giordano began to weep. He got an extra handkerchief out of his jacket pocket and reached over her shoulder and handed it to her.

Nixon continued, "I would not occupy the presidency today if it weren't for Ron Ziegler. I don't know what I can possibly do to repay my country and his family for his sacrifice and all the sacrifices that have been made by young Americans in the war that finally comes to an end next Tuesday."

Nixon paused and blinked his eyes and gathered his strength. "After all that has occurred in the last six years," he said, "it is natural to look ahead to the end of my public service. Ron deserved to enjoy the same luxury. So while the day has by and large been splendid, I worry about tomorrow. I have never feared history's judgment more than in this moment, as I stand humbly before Ron's wife and daughters, their eyes full of sorrow but empty of judgment. May God be as forgiving as they."

Heeding Rose Woods' whispered invitation during the service, Bridgette Matheson arrived at the Carlton at ten that evening. Nick Giordano came from behind the bar to give her a hug and show her to a table in the corner, where Rose was waiting with two glasses of white wine and three thick expanding files stuffed with top-secret documents.

Bridgette sat down and picked up her glass. "To Ron Ziegler," she said. They clinked glasses and sipped. She said, "I was surprised when you called last Sunday. I would've naturally told my colleagues that

Ron and I had an appointment, but as you asked, I've kept it to myself for the time being, for the sake of the good times with you and Ron."

"In the spirit of Jackson Place," Rose said.

Bridgette smiled weakly. "But now I really need to know what's going on," she said.

"It could have been disastrous for the country and maybe even for you if it got out why Ron was going to meet with you," Rose said.

Her eyes flaring, Bridgette said, "So I guess it wasn't an accident." Rose shook her head. "Then in the name of everything that's still decent in the world, give me the names of the filthy bastards who did it, and tell me why," she said. Rose shook her head again.

Bridgette put her wine down and sat back in her chair. "So the cover-up continues," she said with a sneer.

"It's better if people don't think such things happen in the United States," Rose said.

"Even though they just did."

Rose pushed the files across the little table. "This is everything we have on the Pentagon spy ring in the White House," she said. "Everything we know. There were a couple of sketchy stories in the *Post* early this year. We downplayed it at the time, to protect the military and to keep the boss's policies on track. It goes deeper than anyone knew. The intelligence community is acting like a shadow government. You write about that. It's a better story for an historian. The other one's just police reporting."

Bridgette didn't look at the file. "Did they kill Ron?"

Rose nodded at the file and said, "You just write about that. And be careful. Nick's going to drive you home tonight, just in case. I'm pretty sure they wouldn't bother following me, but you never know."

Bridgette leaned forward and pulled the files a little closer. "It's like getting Al Capone on a tax rap," she said.

"It's what Ron would want," Rose said.

"You're sure about that?" Rose nodded. "That was quite a speech the boss gave," Bridgette said. "Did he mean any of it?"

Rose looked sad and sipped her wine. "You ain't seen nothing yet," she said.

48

The Calm Before the Peace

Late on Tuesday morning, New Year's Eve, Vice President Ford was stationed in the Oval Office, doing his good-natured best to keep things civil between the South and North Vietnamese officials who had gathered for the noontime treaty ceremony. The mix and mingle had begun at 11:15. President Thieu and his aides, in their immaculately tailored suits, stood behind Nixon's desk, muttering among themselves and looking at the pictures on the tables and walls. The members of the North Vietnamese delegation, all in Mao suits, were huddled the other end of the room, near the door to the cabinet room. Henry Kissinger, the secretary of state, shuttled between the groups with his translator.

Ford was pleasantly surprised he had such a prominent role, not only during the preliminaries but also in front of the cameras in the East Room. His aides said President Nixon wanted him to stay close, especially when the three leaders sat down at the green felt table to sign the treaty instruments. Ford was to stand directly behind Nixon.

Ford looked at his watch. There was a half-hour to go. The tension was so thick that he was afraid that war would break out again over Nixon's coffee table. He approached Thieu and said, "Mr. President, it's time to make the first move. Remember, we won."

Thieu, short and compact, glanced toward the men from Hanoi who had been his bitter adversaries since he seized power in Saigon in 1963. "I suppose I should count my blessings," he said. "Two months ago, when it looked as though the communists would win, I was deciding between exile in Paris or Garden Grove, California."

"We would've been happy to welcome you in Detroit or Ann Arbor," Ford said, stepping aside and opening the way of reconciliation across Nixon's blue and gold carpet.

Thieu smiled, walked over to Le Duan, and extended his hand. "We will find ways to work together," Thieu said.

"At least the foreigner is gone," Le said, offering his hand. The White House photographer snapped a photo in which Ford stood between the two leaders with a broad smile on his face. A pundit called Ford's moment of détente the calm before the peace.

A moment later Len Garment came in and whispered that Nixon, still in his hideaway office, wanted a few minutes with Ford before the ceremony. Trailed by two of Ford's Secret Service agents, the men walked through the cold sunshine across Executive Way and up the steps to the old EOB. Len stepped aside as Ford entered room 180 and closed the door behind him. Alone for a moment, Garment took out his cigarettes, lit one, and leaned against the wall with a sigh.

Ford found Nixon in his accustomed corner, with his stocking feet on his ottoman. He was twirling his reading glasses. "Are they behaving themselves?" he said.

Ford saw a large envelope on the chair opposite Nixon's. It was addressed to him. He picked it up, sat down, and put the envelope on his lap. "I left Henry in charge," he said.

"Then all is lost," Nixon said. He nodded toward the envelope in Ford's hand. "That's my speech to the nation tonight," he said.

"Of all the speeches you've given about Vietnam, it will be the one history will remember most," Ford said, patting the envelope. "We'll begin the new year at peace."

Nixon gazed over Ford's shoulder. "When Ron Ziegler left the White House on December 22ⁿᵈ," he said, "he had a meeting with that woman from the *Post*. He was peddling a story about the tape gap that he thought would help me. Somebody killed him for it."

Stunned, Ford said, "He was murdered?"

Nixon told Ford about the military breaking Soviet codes, its role in the Hiss case, and Rose erasing the tape. He said that the White House had purposely minimized the significance of the Pentagon spy ring. But the military and intelligence establishment's suspicions about Nixon and Kissinger's policies, especially toward the Soviet Union, were deep and profound. The phones in the White House were probably bugged, enabling Ziegler's killers to learn of his plans.

"How would they have known that's what Ron was going to talk to the reporter about?" Ford said.

"He probably mentioned the tape gap when he called her."

"How would they have known the Hiss story was on the tape?"

Nixon paused and said, "When the erasure became public, you'll recall that Al Haig looked into it. That's when he made the crack about the tape being erased by a sinister force. He showed me Haldeman's notes from the meeting. He didn't understand them, but I did. I remembered what Bob and I had been talking about and realized why Rose erased it."

"You told Haig?"

Nixon shook his head. "Not about the Russian codes and so forth and so on," he said. "I told him it was nothing, just another of my old stories. He must've been gossiping with his buddies across the river and told them what I'd said about the erasure, that it was something about the Hiss case. When they heard Ziegler had a story about it that was big enough for the *Post* on the eve of the impeachment vote, they obviously put it all together."

Nixon stopped. Ford waited, still holding the yellow envelope with the speech, turning it over and over in his hands without thinking about it, wondering why Nixon was going down this road. "Ron told me what he was going to do," Nixon said. "He thought it might swing some more votes our way in the Senate. I told him not to do it, but I didn't order him not to, if you get the distinction."

"It wasn't your fault, Dick," Ford said.

"I could have stopped him," Nixon said in a dull voice.

"It wasn't your fault."

Nixon twirled his glasses. His eyes looked distant and watery. "When you're sitting here," he said, "everything's your fault. I could barely look Nancy in the face on Saturday." He collected himself and gestured toward the envelope in Ford's hand again. "Thanks to your skillful handling of the acting presidency," he said, "your approval rating is 65%. Hell, even mine's 45% and inching up. As you may have noticed, Reagan's scaled back his schedule and fundraising. We're pretty sure he's not going to take you on in '76."

"Mr. President—" Ford said.

Nixon shook his head. "Jerry, that's not a Vietnam speech," he said. "It's a resignation speech. You'll be sworn in on New Year's Day at noon."

PART III

April 5, 1975

49

Up and In

It was Friday afternoon, and so far Mitch Botstein had one reason to be proud of himself. Getting three relentless overachievers, Emily Weissman and Frank and Anne Szabados, into his big black Bonneville convertible and 40 miles up I-95 to Memorial Stadium in Baltimore for a baseball game may have been his greatest triumph. A buddy on the Hill had helped Mitch get four seats in the tenth row, along the first base line.

Emily was relatively easy to persuade, since it was the Orioles' home opener against her beloved Detroit Tigers. Besides, her boss, Len Garment, still couldn't tell her no. Anne hadn't had too much trouble getting the day off at the World Bank, either.

Frank was the toughest. He'd never been busier. Bridgette Matheson's articles on the Pentagon's spy ring had raised urgent concerns about unreconstructed cold warriors in the government, especially in the military and intelligence services, who were resisting or actively undermining the dramatic improvement of relations with the communist world that Richard Nixon had unleashed. Dozens of federal agencies and departments had international portfolios. After firing Tom Moorer, chairman of the Joint Chiefs of Staff, and ordering courts martial for him and all the officers involved, President Ford had directed Frank to organize a study of how the massive federal bureaucracy could be brought into alignment so it would speak with one voice on foreign and national security policy.

Frank's report would reveal some unpleasant presidential secrets as well, such as Nixon's successful attempt to destabilize Chile's elected

left-wing president and Kennedy's unsuccessful efforts to assassinate
Cuba's Fidel Castro. While Congress was planning to hold hearings
of its own, Ford had gotten the jump on the Democrats by announc-
ing his comprehensive reforms the day Bridgette's first article had
appeared. His move was so precisely calibrated that cynics speculated
that the White House was now bugging the *Post's* newsroom.

On opening day in Baltimore, the bright afternoon sun crept across
the red dirt of the infield and PA announcer Rex Barney called out the
lineups. The travails of weary Washington seemed a thousand miles
away. Mitch finished filling in his scorecard as the Orioles took the
field and the Tigers' leadoff batter, shortstop Ed Brinkman, stepped
to the plate.

Emily sat between Mitch and Anne. Frank was on Anne's other
side. Emily had on jeans and a Willie Horton jersey. She'd threaded
her thick red ponytail through the back of her Tigers cap. Since it was
Frank and Anne's first major league game, she was giving them some
pointers. "Baltimore's starter's going to be tough for us," she said. "Jim
Palmer won at least 20 games every season since '69, and he got the Cy
Young last year. I love Mickey Lolich, who's going for us, but Palmer's
the best pitcher in baseball. He won't want Ed on base in the top of the
first in the first game of the season. Look for him to come up and in."

Anne nodded thoughtfully and surveyed the field. "Which one's a
pitcher?" she said.

Mitch smiled, proud again. He had the coolest girlfriend ever. She
loved the Stones, baseball, and him. She also had a framed letter from
Richard Nixon on her office wall. He had written it with a fountain
pen in his boyish hand on a small piece of stationery.

THE WHITE HOUSE
12-31-'74

Dear Emily,

I write from the Lincoln Sitting Room on my last night in the White House. I vividly recall our conversation here on the evening of August the 5th. I shall always be grateful to you for having had the courage to share the unfashionable views of your rabbi in Cambridge. To a considerable extent, the people of Vietnam also have you to thank for peace, and the South for its freedom.

I hope our paths cross again someday. Mrs. Nixon joins me in sending our warmest regards to you and Mitch.

Fondly,

Richard Nixon

Nixon's resignation had been a considerable shock to the nation. After his brilliant victories in Vietnam and in the Senate, why had he done it? With his blessing, Garment spoke on background to the capital's most influential reporters and columnists. He told them that Nixon had been devastated by Ziegler's death. In his anguish, he'd faced up to the realization that the nation would be better served by a president who shared his principles but wasn't carrying so much baggage.

Garment didn't deny Nixon's political motives. He thought that as incumbent president, Ford would have a better shot at the nomination and a general election win in 1976. Nixon was proud of his legacy as a peacemaking global statesman and a domestic policy moderate and feared it would be tarnished if he tried to hold onto power. Sure enough, the possibility of a challenge from the right to his and Ford's pragmatic conservatism receded with Ronald Reagan's announcement in January that he wouldn't be a candidate.

Nixon and Ford ameliorated the trauma of Nixon's decision by carefully coordinating their moves and statements. In his brief resignation speech on New Year's Eve, which Gordie Partington had helped him write, Nixon said he had informed Ford that he would not accept a presidential pardon because of Watergate. He knew a pardon would cripple Ford. Besides, he bargained that since the Senate had acquitted him, the special prosecutor would be open to a deal. Sure enough, in January Nixon agreed to a two-year suspension of his law licenses in California and New York. He spent a month or so in silent exile at his and Pat's seaside home in San Clemente. In mid-February, Ford sent them to Hanoi to participate in opening ceremonies for the new U.S. interests office, precursor to the opening of full diplomatic relations with North Vietnam.

Ford agreed to both of Nixon's personal requests. He kept Garment as White House counsel and promised to appoint Emily as his deputy once she passed the bar exam. Among her assignments was assisting military prosecutors in building their case against the officers involved in the spy ring.

As she had predicted, Jim Palmer came up and in to Ed Brinkman and walked him. He scored on a fielder's choice, leaving Detroit up by a run. Frank and Anne celebrated boisterously. They settled down when Mitch told them there were at least 17 rounds of play to go. "Why don't you explore?" he said. "There's nothing like a major league baseball stadium. Get the feel of the place and drink in the sights and smells. Take your time. Maybe bring me back a hot dog with mustard and a beer."

Frank stood and smiled, winking at Mitch as he stepped into the aisle, and let Anne walk up the steps ahead of him.

Emily kissed Mitch on the cheek. "This is fun," she said. He reached down and picked up a big bag of peanuts. "Where'd you get that?" she said.

"I bought it on the way in. Remember? I sent you guys ahead to the seats."

"Oh, yeah," she said. ""So have you decided yet about the campaign job?"

He shrugged. "I just don't know how I feel about working for a socialist," he said.

"President Ford is not a socialist."

"Have you seen the figures on inflation, unemployment, and the growth in government spending under Nixon?" he said. "I left some articles at your apartment."

She rolled her eyes. "We actually get the *National Review* at the White House," she said.

"But I'm giving it serious consideration," he said. "If you and Frank are working there, it can't be all bad."

She turned and looked at him. "What are you up to?" she said.

"Nothing," he said. "Have some peanuts."

"I don't like peanuts."

He looked stricken. "How can you be a baseball fan and not like peanuts?"

"I stopped eating them after I had braces. Bits of the shells got wedged in my teeth."

He gestured at her with the bag. "Grab some," he said. "Dig down deep."

"What's going on?" she said. "Isn't there a movie line that goes with this?"

He nodded. "'This one's eating my popcorn'," he said. "It was in 'The Sting'."

She reached in. "There's definitely something hard," she said.

"I love when you talk dirty," he said.

She withdrew her hand. She held a small red box that said *Cartier*. "Why, Mitch Botstein," she said. She looked at him and smiled, and started to cry, and threw her arms around him, and knocked the peanuts out of his hand. And he felt proud again.

Author's Note

Students of the Nixon administration will quickly notice that in *Jackson Place*, Len Garment is still serving as White House counsel in August 1974. In the timeline that does not include Emily Weissman and her rabbi, he left Nixon's staff that June. The real Ron Ziegler flew to San Clemente with Nixon in August, served as chief of two non-profit commercial associations, and died in 2003.

An entirely fictional character, White House aide Garrett McCann's only spoken words, about Richard Nixon's alleged involvement in the instigation of campaign dirty tricks, are borrowed from an oral history interview with real-life Nixon appointments secretary Dwight Chapin that Nixon library director Tim Naftali conducted on April 2, 2007.

During the Cold War, millions of Americans concluded that Nixon had clawed his way to national prominence by unjustly persecuting diplomat Alger Hiss. To my knowledge, no one ever told him that the United States had decoded Soviet cables that clearly implicated Hiss in espionage against the U.S. In what I assume was a perverse coincidence, the VENONA decoding project, run by U.S. Army intelligence and later the National Security Agency, wasn't made public until 1995, the year after Nixon's death.

Unrelated to the Hiss case except in this story, the Pentagon's espionage against the Nixon White House remains one of the era's most intriguing mysteries. Nixon and Kissinger downplayed it in their memoirs. Journalist and novelist Jim Hougan presents a detailed account in *Secret Agenda: Watergate, Deep Throat, and the CIA* (Random House, 1984) and suggests that the purloined documents may have ended up at the CIA.

In his book *No Peace, No Honor: Nixon, Kissinger, and Betrayal in Vietnam* (Free Press, 2001), Larry Berman contends that Nixon always assumed that North Vietnam would violate the Paris Peace Accords and intended to use U.S. airpower to punish Hanoi and preserve South Vietnam at least until the end of his second term in 1977. Berman argues that Watergate thwarted him. For the effects on elite morale in Hanoi of Nixon's bombing campaigns in May and December 1972 and for changing Soviet attitudes toward the Vietnam war during the Nixon years, I relied on a presentation by Stephen J. Morris of Johns Hopkins' School of Advanced International Studies at a Nixon Center conference in Washington in 1998, the 25th anniversary of the Paris accords.

I am grateful to the late Nick Thimmesch for his profile of Ron Ziegler in the February 24, 1974 *Washington Post* and to Francis Wilkinson for his essay on Rose Woods, "Nixon's Real Enforcer," in the December 25, 2005 *New York Times*. A monograph by Richmond, California City Council member and Vietnam veteran Thomas K. Butt, "Before and After Vietnam 1969-70," provided insights about the life of a U.S. Army engineer in and around Saigon.

Seth Rosenfeld describes Ronald Reagan's cozy relationship with the FBI in his book *Subversives: The FBI's War on Student Radicals, and Reagan's Rise to Power* (Farrar, Straus and Giroux, 2012). Operative Lyn Nofziger, who died in 2008, proudly detailed his foul purge of two of Reagan's gay aides in his memoir, *Nofziger* (Regnery Gateway, 1992).

I discussed Nixon and his men with each of my story's trinity of real-life heroes, Garment, Woods, and Ziegler. I offered eulogies at Rose's and Ron's memorial services at the Nixon library in Yorba Linda and Christ Church Alexandria, respectively.

My friend of nearly 30 years, legendary publishing maven Bill Thompson, cheerfully offered his usual keen advice. I am grateful to Judge Andy Guilford for his careful reading as well as to my wife and colleague, Kathy O'Connor. Before her distinguished service at the Nixon library from 1995 to 2009, Kathy was former President Nixon's confidential secretary and last chief of staff. All told, she cared for Nixon and his family for 29 years. No one outside his family knew him better, and he never had a more loyal friend. She was holding his hand when he died on April 22, 1994. She made many helpful suggestions. I'm especially grateful for her idea that Nixon and Ford's surprise meeting should take place at Sunnylands.

John H. Taylor
January 16, 2014

About the Author

John H. Taylor served as chief of staff to former President Richard Nixon and director of the Nixon library in Yorba Linda, California. An Episcopal priest, he lives in California with his wife, Kathy. This is his second novel.

CPSIA information c
Printed in the USA
LVOW11s19322711
415835LV00